THE DRAGON WITH A GIRL TATTOO

A DRAGON HUNTER NOVEL

KATIE MACALISTER

ALSO BY KATIE MACALISTER

DARK ONES SERIES
A Girl's Guide to Vampires
Sex and the Single Vampire
Sex, Lies, and Vampires
Even Vampires Get the Blues

OTHERWORLD DARK ONES SERIES
Bring Out Your Dead (Novella)
The Last of the Red-Hot Vampires
The Undead in My Bed (Novella)
Fistful of Vampires Anthology
Shades of Gray (Novella)

ZORYA DARK ONES SERIES
Zen and the Art of Vampires
Crouching Vampire, Hidden Fang
Much Ado About Vampires
Unleashed (Novella)

GOTH FAIRE DARK ONES SERIES
In the Company of Vampires
Confessions of a Vampire's Girlfriend
A Tale of Two Vampires

REVELATION DARK ONES SERIES
The Vampire Always Rises
Enthralled
Desperately Seeking Vampire

RAVENFALL DARK ONES SERIES
Axegate Walk

DRAGON SEPTS
GREEN DRAGON SERIES
You Slay Me
Fire Me Up
Light My Fire
Holy Smokes
Death's Excellent Vacation
(short story)

SILVER DRAGON SERIES
Playing With Fire
Up In Smoke
Me and My Shadow

LIGHT DRAGON SERIES
Love in the Time of Dragons
The Unbearable Lightness of Dragons
Something Dragon This Way Comes
(Formerly titled Sparks Fly)

DRAGON FALL SERIES
Dragon Fall
Dragon Storm
Dragon Soul
Dragon Unbound
Dragonblight

OTHERWORLD ADVENTURE SERIES
Becoming Effrijim
Dragon Revisited
You Sleigh me
Midnight in the Garden of Okay and Meh
All the Jingle Ladies

DRAGON HUNTER SERIES
Memoirs of a Dragon Huner
Day of the Dragon
A Confederacy of Dragons
The Dragon With a Girl Tattoo

BORN PROPHECY SERIES
Fireborn
Starborn
Shadowborn

TIME THIEF SERIES
Time Thief
Time Crossed (short story)
The Art of Stealing Time

MATCHMAKER IN WONDERLAND SERIES
The Importance of Being Alice
A Midsummer Night's Romp
Daring in a Blue Dress
Perils of Paulie

PAPAIOANNOU SERIES
It's All Greek to Me
Ever Fallen in Love
A Tale of Two Cousins
Acropolis Now

EVERYTHING IS FINE SERIES
Improper English
Bird of Paradise (Novella)
Men in Kilts
The Corset Diaries
A Hard Day's Knight
Blow Me Down
You Auto-Complete Me
Tell Them Emily Sent You

NOBLE HISTORICAL SERIES
Noble Intentions
Noble Destiny
The Trouble With Harry
The Truth About Leo

PARANORMAL SINGLE TITLES
Ain't Myth-Behaving

AKASHIC LEAGUE MYSTERIES
Ghost of a Chance
The Stars That We Steal From the Night Sky

STEAMPUNK ROMANCE
Steamed
Company of Thieves

AUTHOR'S NOTE

Because I know many people like to have pronunciations of character's names fixed in their mind before reading, I'll just say that the name Yrian is pronounced EER-ee-un.

Go forth and read with Yrian's name correctly nestled in your brainmeats.

PROLOGUE
YRIAN

"I'm sorry. I'm so sorry, Yrian. I never wanted this to happen. Not this way. Not now."

Amice's voice broke through the abyss that embraced him with tight bands, prohibiting movement.

"What have you done?" The voice that spoke was his, but it seemed to come from a long distance, and he realized that he was hearing an echo of the past. Guilt, the pain of betrayal, and hopelessness crashed over him, threatening to drown him in regret.

Again.

"She did what was needed to be done," a man's voice drawled the answer, filled with amusement that made Yrian want to roar with fury. "And now, I will end your pain. It is the least I can do for a brother."

"Kashi is right," the voice of Amice said, fading as she backed away. "We did what was needed. The dragons ... they are wrong, Yrian. *You* are wrong. You should not be, not the way you were made. The First Dragon tried, but it was a mistake. A deadly mistake. I'm sorry. I'm so sorry."

"They are dead? The sept is gone?" he heard his voice ask, the words spoken a few millennia ago, but the pain just as stark in his breast as it had been when Amice—and Kashi, the betrayer—all but ripped out his heart.

At least that was what it had felt like at the time. Now? He struggled to contain his fire, to force it to his will, to shape and use it, but the guilt from the betrayal washed over him, and he knew it was useless to try.

And to be honest, he didn't care. Not anymore. Why should he when there was no hope?

"This is the one?" The voice was male but was that of a stranger. "Why is the room on fire? I thought prohibitions had been placed on the interior?"

Yrian realized the voice was not one from the past that tormented him nightly, and opened his eyes, turning to look at the people who stood clustered at the doorway of his prison. One was a tall man with washed-out blue eyes, obviously a mage, since he was surrounded by an aura of arcane magic. Two others, both women, stood behind the mage, one clutching a device that Yrian remembered was called a tablet, the other bearing a small container with syringes.

"They are. It was," one of the women said, gazing into the room with overt dismay. "Nothing in here should burn. I … I'll call the team to reapply the prohibitions."

She hurried off, a phone held to her ear.

"No more drugs." The voice that emerged from Yrian was more of a croak than anything else, but he paid no mind to that. "They bring back the past."

"If you would stop attacking the staff when they bring you meals, perhaps you would not need to be drugged," the tall man said, his expression an odd mixture of contempt and wariness.

Yrian couldn't help but smile to himself, the movement stiff as if the muscles in his face had forgotten how to do so. He struggled to sit up, aware that at some point while he was drugged, the attendants had bound his arms to his body with several straps. He made sure to hold the mage's gaze as he allowed his fire to crawl down his body, the sting of it a familiar companion as it obliterated the straps. He took a deep breath, relishing the freedom as he wiggled his fingers to get the blood back into them. "You fear me. Who are you?"

"I fear no man," the mage answered, but he lied. Yrian stood slowly, his head lowered as he locked his eyes on the man, summoning power from the shadows that lurked around all living things.

Arcane magic crackled around the man in a protective shield even as he stepped backward. "There, you see? This is why you are drugged, why you have been deemed a danger to the denizens of this facility as well as the L'au-dela. Have the arrangements been made?"

The second woman, who was more or less hiding behind the mage, peered over his shoulder at Yrian. Her expression displayed fear and what looked very much like hatred. "Yes, Dr. Kostich. The Sovereign has arranged for transport tomorrow. She assures me that fresh Hashmallim have been summoned, and that a suitable gaol in the Thirteenth Hour has been readied to receive this demonic being."

"I am no demon!" Yrian roared, rage filling him and sending him forward on a flood of dragon fire, the pain of it enough to bring him to his knees if he hadn't been so furious at the accusation.

A blue-white arcane light lit up the confines of his cell, knocking him back two steps, but it was enough for the mage to slam the door just as he reached it. Fingers that were now tipped in silver claws curled into fists, the dark gray scales that rippled up his arms warning he'd shifted into dragon form.

He fought the need to destroy, to punish those who dared confine him, to wreak havoc, instead pushing down the violent emotions, knowing he had to soothe the part of his mind that owed its chaos to his dam, and struggled to slow his breathing.

"*Fukka,*" he swore once he had his emotions in control again, invoking his favorite oath from the Norsemen of his past. He knew from experience there was little use to attack the door. It had been especially protected against his powers and dragon fire, most likely due to the fact that a week prior he had almost broken free.

"And now," he said, puffing smoke as he spun around and kicked a merrily burning wooden table against the wall with such force that it shattered into charcoal and wood dust. He glared at his scale-covered arm. "I have to deal with this."

He focused his attention on his form, and slowly, painful second by second, he reclaimed the human body that he had borne since adulthood. The dark scales that seemed to mirror all the colors shifted to an uninspiring tan skin. He gazed at his hands with a curl of his lip, then proceeded to tamp down the fire that still burned around him.

"Next time," he promised himself, glaring at the door. "Next time I will free myself. And then …" He stopped, wanting to swear to vengeance against those who confined him, but they were not the ones responsible for his situation.

No, that sin lay on another's shoulders, and at last, his mind was calm enough that he could make plans.

"Kashi will pay," he announced as he paced the confines of his cell. "The world will suffer by his hands no more. And then I will finally be free."

The pain of the past pierced him like daggers, but he ignored it just as he always had.

This time, he would succeed. He had to, given that the mage was intending on confining him to the Thirteenth Hour. To fail meant the death of the dragonkin.

And he couldn't bear that guilt. Not again.

ONE
BECKET

"I'm a good person! I swear I'm a good person! I just have … argh! … the shittiest luck possible." I'm not proud of the grunt that emerged when I swung the fire extinguisher I'd ripped off the wall of the train station's restroom. "I don't deserve this! I don't deserve *you*! Will you stay dead, dammit?"

"No," the demon snarled, a nasty smile stretching its lips way too wide for the human form it wore. "You cannot destroy me, artificer."

"Maybe not, but I can take you out of the game for a little bit," I said in between pants as I swung the fire extinguisher again, this time connecting with it. The rebound almost knocked me on my ass, while the demon immediately lunged for me.

"Hey, Becket, you'd better hurry or we'll miss the train to Prague—what the hell?" Billie, the band's drummer, froze in the doorway, staring with huge eyes as the demon and I rolled on the (thankfully, just cleaned) bathroom floor.

The demon snarled and tried to slash my face with fingernails that grew into yellowed claws, the look in its eyes filled with glee.

"Hit it!" I screamed, twisting my body underneath the demon, narrowly missing its gouging out one of my eyes, trying desperately both to get out of the iron grip it had on my arms and to knee it in the noogies. If it wanted to wear a male form, I was going to take advantage of any weak spots. "Fire extinguisher! Hit it on the head!"

"But—maybe I should call Skye—" Billie hesitated, and for a moment, I damned the fact I had allowed the demon to sneak up on me.

"Just hit it!" I bellowed, making a monumental effort, at last managing to twist and kick enough I got out from under it, but not before it freed one hand and punched me hard in the eye.

Evidently the sound of my head cracking backward from the blow was enough to send Billie into motion. She snatched up the extinguisher that I'd dropped, and hit the demon on the head, providing enough of a distraction that I could roll away. Although breathless from the altercation, I got to my knees, quickly whipping the strap from my bag around its neck, attempting to throttle it while Billie stood waving the extinguisher in a threatening manner.

"It takes … goddess, I think I may vomit … a lot longer to strangle someone than I imagined," I said, collapsing back when the twisted strap did its job, and the demon slumped forward.

"Is he … dead?" Billie asked, her voice rising on a note of pure panic.

"Demons can't die," I reminded her, frantically trying to get breath into my lungs. I leaned against one of the stall doors, my butt on the cold, slightly damp floor, and felt like a newspaper that had been out in the rain for a week solid. "Well, they can, but it takes someone with serious power to pull it off. This one's form is toast. Unfortunately, it'll be back."

"That's a demon?" Billie's nascent panic attack faded immediately as she set down the extinguisher and bent down to peer at the crumpled form. At that moment, it disappeared into a puff of oily, nasty black smoke. "I've never seen one up close. Are they all that violent?"

I stiffened my wobbly legs as I hauled myself upright, reclaimed my bag, and glanced at the mirror. All it showed was my horrified expression. "They're demons, Billie. That kind of implies they're evil. Crap. We've got four minutes. Are the others on the train?"

"Yes. They sent me to find you." Billie had a slight French accent, her manner of speaking breathy, a trait I'd always admired. "I didn't think you would be attacked in the toilet."

Two women entered as I limped out of the bathroom and made my way toward the platform that contained the overnight train to the Czech Republic, amongst other places. Since it was almost midnight, the train station was blessedly sparse of travelers.

"Demons don't give a damn about things like needing to pee," was all I said as we hurried. I wrapped an arm around my waist, wondering if the demon had cracked a rib. It certainly hurt to take a breath, and I felt like I might vomit at any second, no doubt heightened by the shambling run I adopted toward the train. "I hope it takes that one a while to get a new form, because if they get on the train with us, I'm a goner."

"We'll protect you," Billie said as she boarded, casting a confident look over her shoulder. I didn't say anything to that, knowing there was little the three other women who made up our band could do against demons, especially if Candy and Andy—the big guns, demonically speaking— made another appearance. "And once we get to the CR, we should be safe, what with the festival being run by a troll."

"Vampire," I said absently, collapsing on the bottom bunk of the compartment we were to share, then corrected myself. "Dark One. And I don't know how much they have to do with the actual running of the music festival. It's held on the grounds of one of their castles, but that doesn't automatically mean it's a demon no-go zone. No, thanks, I don't want anything in my stomach until it settles."

She murmured something about staying hydrated and set down the bottle of water on a tiny table. "I'll go tell Skye and Deni that you were attacked, and I smashed the demon's brains in."

I cocked an eyebrow at the fact that Billie—the mildest of our foursome—looked so pleased at the idea of hitting a demon, but since my ribs and swollen eye and just about every other part of me was in pain, I decided it was far better to simply lie still on what was a surprisingly comfortable bunk until my natural healing abilities kicked in.

Just in case the demon reported my appearance, I crafted a new glamour, ready to don when we hit Prague.

By the time we emerged into the glorious sunshine of a late-summer Czech day, my limp was gone, and although my ribs still hurt, I could walk without wincing.

"Train to Brno is in half an hour," Skye said as she stopped in front of where Deni, Billie, and I were sitting. She passed out tickets, and cast a critical look over me. "Brunette doesn't look right on you. You're too pale for such dark hair. Maybe make some glamours with warmer tones?"

I glanced down at my hands, swearing to myself. I had been out of it so much when I made the glamour that I hadn't remembered to change my skin tone to match the rest of the new appearance. "Crap. You're right. I'll fix it once we're on the train."

"Should we form a protective cordon around you, or can you make it to the train without your evil ex sending more demons after you?" she asked some twenty minutes later when we headed for the train. I ignored the spike of guilt that struck whenever the band mentioned my cover story, telling myself that I was doing what I could to make up for the fact that I wasn't entirely truthful with them.

I couldn't be. Not if I wanted to make sure they survived.

"I think I'll be OK, since there were three trains leaving last night, and the demon couldn't be sure which one we were taking, but let me know if you guys see anyone watching us a bit too closely." I pushed down the fear that I might have to stop working with the band if the demons tracked me down again.

An hour later, as we sped southeast to the small town of Brno, where a yearly music festival was held, I touched my hair and asked Skye, "OK, I fixed my skin tone. Does it look right with my hair now?"

"Yes, it is much more agreeable to the eye. And the trousers you picked for the glamour are better than that frompty dress you had on before." She tapped on her phone, bringing up a notes app. "Did you decide on the set? Other than Billie's ballad?"

"My dress was a bit frumpy, I guess," I said slowly, mildly insulted that what I thought of as a perfectly nice sundress had drawn criticism. "And yes on the set list."

The conversation turned to what songs we'd perform at the festival. Deni, Skye's cousin, who with Billie was sitting opposite us, pulled out an earbud and asked, "Did they update the website? Are the rounds announced? And how much do we get for winning a round?"

"They're waiting for everyone to check in before announcing the schedule," Skye said in a soothing tone. "And the money has not changed. It's a hundred euros per band for each win. If we go all the way through the … the …" She paused and glanced at me.

"Brackets," I answered, gently pressing my side. It didn't feel too painful, which meant my healing abilities were doing their job, if slowly. I needed to be able to breathe to sing, though, and I wondered if I shouldn't work up an illusion glamour just in case my voice wasn't enough to carry us through.

"And a thousand euros guaranteed to the top three teams who make it to the end battle," Skye said, her eyes back on her book. "Top band takes home five thousand."

Deni sat back in her seat, a satisfied expression on her face, her eyes on me. "Which will be us, because we have a siren."

"Half siren," I corrected, leaning my head against the window, watching as the scenery zipped by. Some of the little farms we passed set up a deep sense of longing in me, a need to have a place of my own, one filled with peace, and happiness, and animals who didn't give a damn about what magic I could work.

Why couldn't I have been born to normal parents? Why didn't they protect themselves better, so I wasn't left alone at fourteen? And most of all, what demon lord was trying so hard to capture me?

My shoulders drooped as I gave in to worry, miserably wondering what was in store for me.

TWO
CHARITY

"I don't suppose you had any luck breaking into the asylum?" The shadow that moved over my watercolor paper stopped when I spoke. I glanced up and shaded my eyes to admire the man who stood before me. He was so incredibly handsome, my stomach wobbled around. No, I mentally corrected myself. Not man … dragon. Demigod. Sexy-as-hell lover who made my heart sing a thousand songs of happiness whenever he was near.

Avval, the First Dragon, the progenitor of all dragons who ever were, and who ever would be, and incidentally also the love of my life, thought for a few seconds before answering in his usual grave, measured tone. "No. The archimage Kostich is unreasonable, and quite possibly deranged. Archimages often end up so. In addition, he saw through the glamour I used in order to get into the facility. That is most annoying. I will have to order one for my next visit. Your clematis is lovely."

"I bet you say that to all your mates," I teased, setting down my paintbrush in order to stand and kiss him, the sense of rightness returning to my world. He smiled under the kisses I scattered along his delicious lips, his hands instantly on my hips, pulling me close against him.

"I don't believe I have. Neither of them painted, although Maerwyn enjoyed embroidering things. I suppose that is similar. You missed me?"

"More than you can imagine," I said, kissing him like I'd wanted to do for the three days he'd been gone. A flash of surprise and appreciation was visible for a moment in his beautiful eyes.

"I can imagine a great many things, but I will agree that this separation has been onerous. I have missed you greatly, as well. How do you feel?"

"Better," I said, smiling at the way his eye color shifted from silver to a dark blue and then to gold. I still hadn't cracked the entire code, but I knew the colors were influenced by his emotions. When he looked at me, his eyes went gold, bathing me in a warmth that made me want to purr like a cat in the sun. "Thankfully, the worst was yesterday, which means in a couple of days I'll be able to ride you like the dragon you are."

His eyes widened slightly at my not-so-subtle hint; then immediately the gold of his irises turned molten. "I have told you that I am not afraid of blood, but I assumed you were uncomfortable while your woman's time was upon you."

"I was. I am. Well, for another day or so, I'll be a bit bloaty, but after that, all bets are off." I pulled myself away from the lure of his mouth and took his hand, the feeling of his fingers twining around mine bringing me so much joy I almost burst into song. "Tell me what happened with Yrian."

He did. It took about ten minutes, but when he was finished, we sat on a bench in the shade while I chewed it over. "Honestly, Avval, I think I should contact the mates."

"Do you believe they can achieve what I cannot?" he asked, his tone grave as ever, but with an edge that I put down to his frustration with the situation concerning Yrian.

I hesitated for a few seconds. "Not in the sense you mean. I'll admit the first time I joined the mates' group chat, I thought it was just a way for them to gossip, but they have proven their claim that collective brainstorming can be productive. Would you like me to share what's going on with Yrian and the Asile?"

His thumb stroked over mine as two butterflies that were fighting over the gorgeous purple clematis suddenly noticed Avval and immediately flew to him, where they clung to his shirt, gently fanning their wings at him. Butterflies, I'd discovered, loved him, and always perched themselves on him until he noticed and carefully put them on nearby plants. "I don't think it would cause difficulty if you were to do so. Perhaps it is as you say, and the dragonkin may see the problem from an angle different to that which Baltic embraces."

The edge to his voice grew a bit sharper. I tried never to get between his relationship with his descendants, especially Baltic, the youngest of his actual sons, but over the last six months, I'd grown to agree with the mates that Avval was being a little harsh when it came to Baltic. I gave his fingers a squeeze and said, "He tried. Three times, according to Ysolde, who said that Yrian refused his help every time. I don't know what more Baltic could do."

"It should not have taken so many attempts to do what is natural," was all he said. I slid him a look from the corners of my eyes, wondering why he was so annoyed. He must have sensed my concern, because his lips quirked. "You are not pleased by my answer. Have you been listening to Ysolde's opinion of me?"

I laughed at that. "Of course I listen to her. She's one of the mates, and I like her. It doesn't mean I approve of, or agree with, her statements that you deliberately rejoice in dropping cryptic requests that she do something, but I will admit that I'm not sure what's natural about Baltic trying to drag Yrian into the twenty-first century."

"That was not his goal," he answered, and, rising, led me from the garden to the house, pausing along the way to relocate the butterflies onto a flowering orange tree. "Speak to the mates if you desire. I must contact a former Sovereign to locate a better glamour. She always seems to have exceptional ones, and if that annoying archimage can see through the ones I make, then I will simply avail myself of Sally's artificer."

I paused on the way to the small, sunny room I used as a studio. "What's an artificer when he's at home?"

"One who creates glamours. Ah, it is you."

"Yup, it sure is." The dark-haired Asian woman who trotted lightly down the stairs flashed a nervous smile at Avval. "I didn't realize you were back. Should I … er … make myself scarce?"

"Of course not," I said, giving Elle a reassuring smile. She was my bestie and the only person from my past with whom I kept up. "The First Dragon is off to do important dragon things while I contact the mates. You want to join me? They'd love meeting my soul sister."

"Sure," she said, scooting around Avval as he watched with mild amusement lighting his gorgeous—if change-able—eyes. "Sounds like fun meeting your other family."

Avval gave me a little nod of the head. "You will tell me if you need pain medicines."

"I would never keep my crampiness from you," I told him, and blew him a kiss before joining Elle in my studio, plopping down on an overstuffed chair next to her. "I know you're intimidated by the First Dragon, but you really don't have to worry. He's delighted you came for a visit. We don't normally get many people here, so stop feeling like you have to leave us alone together."

"Well, he *is* a demigod," Elle said with a twist of her lips, then laughed and shook her head. "I know, I know—he's not going to smite me on the spot because I didn't take care of you like I should have when we were both in the foster system, but man alive, Charity—he's a dragon god! I don't know any other gods! Of course that means I'm going to watch my p's and q's around him."

I would have scoffed at such an idea but admitted to myself that Avval's presence was naturally one that demand-ed respect, and instead spent an hour arranging to chat with the mates of all the wyverns.

"OK, I get that the leaders of the dragon septs are called wyverns," Elle said ninety minutes later, when we sat before my laptop waiting for the video chat room to open. "And the nonofficial groups are called tribes, and they have mates, as well."

"The tribe leaders are called masters, not wyverns," I reminded her. "There are a couple that are more or less adjacent to the weyr."

She frowned in concentration, glancing at the cheat sheet of names and brief explanations that I had given her. "Got it. I'm just confused as to who are actually the First Dragon's kids, and who are his descendants."

"Every dragon is a descendant, but Baltic and Yrian are the only ones of his actual children who are still alive. Well …" I looked toward the door, and, after a moment's thought, got up and closed it before returning to my chair.

Elle's eyebrows rose at the action.

"He has another child living," I said in a suitably hushed tone, then threw understandable pronoun use to the wind by adding, "But he disowned him thousands of years ago."

"A bad seed?" Elle asked, her eyebrows rising higher.

"Very bad. You've heard of the demon lord Bael?"

She nodded.

"That's him. He was the second child born, and his name was Kashi until the First Dragon stripped him of his dragon nature due to … oh, a whole lot of truly reprehensible things involving much death and sorrow. No one calls Bael by his original name except his older brother, Yrian, who I gather wasn't around when Kashi 'became' Bael."

"Wow, that's just … I mean, everyone knows about Bael," Elle said, blinking a few times. "But isn't he out of commission now? I thought I heard he was stuffed into some afterlife."

"The Egyptian underworld, yes," I said, tapping in a quick message when Aisling texted to ask if we were ready to go. "It's called the Duat, and the First Dragon's brother Osiris runs it."

"Osiris? You mean the actual Osiris? The god one?" she said, gawking at me.

"That's him. And just to totally blow your mind, you've heard of Odin and Freya, yes?"

Her eyes huge, she nodded.

"Freya's his sister. He has a lot of cutting things to say about Odin, but I gather he and Freya are pretty close. She invited us to visit them so I could meet her, but that will have to wait until things have calmed down with the dragons."

Elle shook her head. "I have no idea how you cope with the fact that actual gods straight from mythology are your in-laws, but since you're more or less married to a demigod, I guess it's all par for the course."

"Something like that. Oh, here we go. Aisling usually hosts these, because her wyvern, Drake, is very techy, and has set up a whole system for her to host the mates' chats."

A woman with curly brown hair popped onto the screen and smiled. "Hello, all! I'm afraid we're going to have limited numbers due to the short notice, but I did send everyone the information."

"My apologies for the rushed request," I said, making a face that I hoped accurately expressed my regret. "I wouldn't normally ask for help like this, but it's kind of an immediate problem, so I hoped you wouldn't mind."

"Bee says she's not leaving the bathroom for the next three months," Ysolde said, glancing up from her phone.

I muted myself and quickly told Elle, "That's Aisling Grey in the upper left corner. Ysolde is the blonde. She's Baltic's mate. The woman who just logged on and looks like a nineteen twenties flapper is May, mate of the silver wyvern, Gabriel. Bee is the sister of another wyvern, and another mate, respectively. She and her wyvern, Constantine, are expecting their second child."

"Ugh. I so don't miss those first months," Aisling said with a grimace, then glanced to the side when a big black Newfoundland dog shambled in and plopped itself down next to her.

I unmuted to say, "Thank you all for coming. This is my friend Elle, who has been staying with us for the last ten days, and is very discreet, so you don't have to worry about saying anything in front of her."

"I'm a psychiatrist for angsty spirits, shades, and revenants," Elle said, giving a little wave at the laptop's camera. "So I'm very familiar with nondisclosure as a working concept, and absolutely agree to keep anything heard here to myself."

"We're always happy to know a friend of yours," Aisling said politely, then quickly ran through the introductions. "Not that I want to pressure you to hurry, Charity, but we're leaving for Paris in two and a half hours, and Drake's about at the end of his patience trying to get everything wrapped up here in Hungary so we can spend a month in France."

"In other words, what's up?" Ysolde asked, ignoring the fact that a boy of about four was riding a small bike with training wheels in circles around the couch upon which she sat.

I took a deep breath. "It seems that the First Dragon has been having some difficulty getting to Yrian."

Ysolde frowned. "If that's a dig against Baltic—"

"Not in the least," I said quickly. "I'm sorry for interrupting you, but it's nothing like that. I think the First Dragon understands that there's only so much Baltic can do for his brother. The problem is the Asile itself."

"And that is what?" May asked, obviously making notes. She normally shared secretary duties with Bee, but since the latter was evidently unwell, May stepped in to keep all the mates up to date with the meetings. "A person, place, or thing?"

"The Asile is the name of the … well, I hate to use the term 'mental asylum,' but that's really what it is. The First Dragon said it's a place where the Otherworld confines all the beings it feels have mental or emotional issues. He said that since Yrian had been arrested by the mortal police three different times and subsequently destroyed each of the buildings where he was confined, the Otherworld Committee decided he was a danger to both immortals and mortals, and stuck him in the Asile."

"Gabriel said something about that," May said, tapping the end of a pen on her lip as she looked thoughtful. "We talked about going into the Beyond and reaching him that way, but we weren't sure if Yrian could access it. Do you know if he can, Charity?"

I shook my head. "If he could, the First Dragon would have gotten him out that way. Evidently the Asile people take their security very seriously. Not only do they have those big ghostly scary guys as security, but Dr. Kostich works with the psychiatric team and is more or less in charge of the whole place. He's seen to it that there are so many spells, wards, songs, and even a bunch of banes woven into the material of the building that not only can you NOT sneak in via any altered form of reality, including the Beyond, but you also can't perform magic once you're inside the Asile. Which is why the First Dragon can't simply roll up and take Yrian out with him."

"Wow," Aisling said, glancing to her side when her demon, Jim, shifted next to her. "Dr. Kostich actually used banes and songs to protect the place? Both of those involve dark powers that I assume he would have to stay away from."

I gave a half shrug. "I have no clue about that. I do know that on his last attempt to see Yrian, Dr. Kostich saw through the First Dragon's glamour, and forbade him from entering the building."

"Holy crapbeans," Aisling said, looking again at Jim when it shifted. "Do you need to go out? Or do you have something to contribute to the conversation? You may do so if it will help the situation."

"Heya, everyone," Jim said on a gasp, just like it had been holding its breath.

What sort of a demon chooses a dog as its form? Elle wrote on my notepad that sat on the desk before me.

One that is the son of the being who created Abaddon—aka the mortal idea of hell—while at the same time having the head of the Court of Divine Blood as its mom, I scribbled.

Her eyes widened. *The demon's mom was the head of heaven?*

I nodded as Jim continued. "Heya, Charity. Heya, Charity's shrink. I didn't know you could have visitors at Chez First Dragon. Is it, like, out where anyone can stop by and snuffle the flowers?"

"No," I told it firmly, stifling a giggle at what Avval would have to say if I invited the demon for a visit.

Aisling almost rolled her eyes. "It is rude to invite yourself, as I tell you every time you try to palm yourself onto Ysolde for the food she and Pavel cook."

"They got some good eats," Jim said, smacking its doggy lips a few times. "Soldy would never make me eat that ass-flavored diet food you keep letting the vet talk you into."

"And that's enough out of you," Aisling told it with a little flick of its ear. "No speaking unless it answers a question or is helpful. Sorry, Charity, please go on."

"I'd like to know more about Dr. Kostich forbidding the First Dragon to do anything," May said, still taking notes.

"I don't doubt he'd try, because he's always had the attitude that he rules the Otherworld, but what I want to know is what the FD did in response," Ysolde asked, grunting a little when her son Anduin suddenly leaped onto the couch, hauling a stuffed white dragon that was almost as big as him, slamming it onto her lap with a demand she pet the dragon.

"You can take it as read that he expressed his unhappiness with both the situation and Dr. Kostich," was all I said, but I smiled to myself at some of the pointed remarks Avval told me he'd made, and how Kostich was clearly fuming by the end.

"Good," Ysolde said with a satisfied smile, before shifting the stuffed dragon from her lap, handing her son a plastic sword instead. "Now, what is it you want, exactly?"

I frowned, aware that I might well be overreacting to Avval's unhappiness, but driven regardless to provide him with the love and support he'd lacked for the last six hundred or so years. "I'm not actually sure, to be honest. I just remembered how innovative and productive the mates' collective has been with other problems, and hoped you would put your heads together as to how to get Yrian out of the Asile."

"Hmm," Aisling said, looking thoughtfully at nothing. "I admit that other than having Drake break into the place—which he would do in a heartbeat, because there's nothing that man loves so much as being able to put his green dragon thieving skills to use—other than that, I don't have any ideas."

"I suppose a physical jailbreak is out of the question?" Ysolde asked, a similarly thoughtful expression on her face. Absently, she picked up a second plastic sword, and parried her son's attacks. "Baltic would be delighted to fire up some arcane blasts on the Agile place."

"Asile, and alas, that's also something the First Dragon would do if it would have any effect, which he assures me it wouldn't, due to all the magic woven into the building itself," I answered, glancing at a scrap of paper Elle pushed my way.

Can I help? As a psychiatrist, that is? Maybe I can see Yrian?

"I was afraid of that," Ysolde said with a sigh, still absently wielding her toy sword as Anduin continued to attack. "I'm not sure what else Baltic could do, but I'll ask him."

"Thank you," I said, my hopes sinking as I scribbled my answer on Elle's note. *No, we tried that earlier. The medicos running the Asile don't allow others in to consult unless it's their request for help.*

"I'm afraid I don't have any ideas other than trying to use the Beyond," May said with a little shake of her head.

"Jim?" Aisling asked, nudging her demon. "Does anything occur to you that would help Yrian?

Jim's face scrunched up as it clearly thought on the subject. "It's a question of which you want more … getting into the cuckoo's nest, or getting the first Firstborn out. Which is more important? Because getting in is easy. … It's the getting him out that might be a bit tricky."

"If it was easy to get in, Charity wouldn't be asking us for help," Aisling told it.

"Meh," it said, giving a shrug of its shoulders. "That's nothing a good glamour couldn't handle. Actually … the same could be said for getting Yrian out, too. But it would have to be something special."

"I just told you that the annoying Dr. Kostich saw through the First Dragon's glamour," I pointed out.

"Yeah, but the First Daddy himself admitted that he wasn't very good at glamours," Jim answered, pulling back its doggy lips to smile at the camera. "Right, May? He said that when you guys were in the Duat, right?"

"He did say that, yes," May said slowly, her gaze flickering off to the distance. "But no one other than Bael recognized him, so I don't know how valid his point was. Certainly Gabriel and I didn't see through the glamour."

"He mentioned something about seeking an artificer," I said slowly, biting my lower lip (a bad habit of which I've tried hard to break myself, but it tends to come back in times of stress).

"That would work, except there aren't any around. At least not any that you can find. They hide a lot, what with people torturing their families in order to get them to make the super-duper glamours," Jim said, leaning on Aisling's leg. Automatically, she patted it and gave its ears a fondle.

"You mean if the First Dragon had a stronger glamour, he could get inside the Asile? How would that help Yrian escape?" I asked.

Elle wrote quickly on her notepad and slid it toward me again. *Glamour for your stepson, too!*

That had me raising my eyebrows, but before I could comment, Aisling said, "Wait … can we glamour Yrian?

Could the First Dragon take a glamour in for him? Can you take something magical like that inside? I imagine the wards would prohibit that entering the building."

"Hmm," Ysolde said, scooting down the couch when her son, now dual wielding both swords, attacked the stuffed dragon. "That's a really good question."

"And also a good suggestion by Jim," May said, nodding as she made a note. "So far, I have on my list locate an artificer, determine whether or not someone could smuggle a powerful glamour into the Asile, and ... what else?"

"Ways to get Yrian out if the glamours are a moot point," I said after a few seconds' thought.

"I think we'll have to research glamours a bit more," Aisling said, her brow furrowed as she looked at nothing in particular. "In order to understand their scope. Hmm. I'll definitely pick Drake's brain on the flight to Paris."

"I'll do the same with Baltic, although I assume if he had any good ideas, he would have talked to the First Dragon about them before this. Oh! That reminds me—did everyone get an invitation from Allie to visit her and Christian at their castle? Baltic is prone to refusing such an offer, but I pointed out to him that the reciprocal visit is coming up, and if we were there, the kids would be off dancing at the music festival."

"Reciprocal visit?" I asked, confused.

"Karma's foster daughter, Pixie, is coming to stay with us for ten days while Karma and Adam go to Hungary for the trial of a spirit who attacked Karma," Ysolde answered, shooing her son off the couch when he started jumping up and down on it while waving his swords. "Lovey, why don't you go out to the garden and beat up the imps."

Elle looked horrified as the child yelled with happiness and dashed off with a thundering noise more appropriate to a small herd of water buffalo. *They let their kids kill imps?* she wrote.

"Do you have imps?" I asked, equally startled by Ysolde's suggestion.

"Not in the least, no," she said complacently, smiling at us. "But Anduin doesn't know that. Will you be attending the gathering at Christian's, Charity?"

"I don't think so," I said, glancing at my phone, quickly finding the texted invitation. "Much as it pains me as a siren to miss a musical event—it's practically against the Siren's Code to forgo such things—the First Dragon is very focused on the problem with Yrian, as well as something going on with one of his brother's grandkids, so I doubt if we'll have time. But I will mention it to him and see what he thinks. What about you two?" I asked May and Aisling.

"Oh, we're going," Aisling said firmly, her nostrils flaring slightly as she shot a pointed look at the door that I assumed was meant for her wyvern. "Drake doesn't think it's important we mingle with vampires, but our kids and Allie's are close enough in age that it will be good for them to play together."

"Drake's a bit gaga when it comes to the spawn having contact with non-dragon kids," Jim said before rolling over onto its back. "He wouldn't even let Ash put them into a school with other immortal kids because he said they could be bad influences. Ha! Like the spawn could be worse than they are?"

"I am sitting right here," Aisling said, glaring at the demon. "And if you don't want to find yourself confined to the Akasha for the three days we are at Allie and Christian's home, then I'd advise you to rethink your criticism of my children."

Jim pursed its lips.

"Fine," Aisling allowed, and gave in to its obvious demands for belly scratches. "They are hellions, but they're *our* hellions, and we choose to admire their many good qualities and ignore the ones that sent their own grandmother running after just half an hour's visit."

May and Ysolde both laughed aloud. I had heard tales of the green wyvern's mother, but decided that wasn't my story to tell Elle.

"We're going, as well. Gabriel thinks it's important for us to help the vamps."

"Why?" I asked May, unable to see a connection between the dragons and Dark Ones.

"I don't know," she said, giving a shrug. "To be honest, I don't think he knows, either. He says it's just a feeling he has, and he's obligated to act on it. So we'll be in Europe next week, too. I guess we can meet then and call you, Charity, with any results to our inquiries."

That course of action met everyone's approval, and we signed off.

"That was fascinating," Elle said as we left the room. "I had no ideas that all this intermingling went on between the dragons and other beings. You'll let me know what happens with the son, yes?"

"You're welcome to stay for as long as you like," I told her, catching sight of Avval as he headed in from the garden, his cell phone in hand.

"I know, and I will return, assuming you want me to visit you another time, but I'm as recovered as I ever will be from that rat bastard ex cheating on me with his nineteen-year-old student, and it's time I get back to my plants. I'll take you up on your offer to run me to a portal, though," she added as Avval entered the house, his gaze catching mine.

He gave her a long look, no doubt ascertaining why she felt the need to cut short what I had hoped would be an extended visit, and was obviously reassured that it was her own choice, because he just nodded. "My steward will see to your arrival at your home in …"

"San Francisco. Thank you. Speaking of that, I'd better get my packing done so I can zip out of here after dinner, if that's OK with you two."

I wanted to protest, but bit it back and slapped a smile on my face before giving her a hug. "I'll be up to help you pack in a minute, OK?"

She trotted up the stairs with mild protests that she wouldn't bother me, but I ignored those. Avval watched me closely for a moment before taking my chin in his fingers, tipping my head back to really study my face. It wasn't something I tolerated with anyone but him, and that was only because I could see the love for me shining in his soul. "You will miss your friend. You are lonely?"

"No," I said quickly, turning my head slightly so I could kiss his palm. "Not when you're here. You know I'm an introvert by nature."

"I know this," he agreed, sliding his hand around me, and escorted me up the stairs. "But this loneliness I sense in you disturbs me. We will address it once I have retrieved Yrian from the deranged archimage. What did the mates suggest?"

I told him. He thought for a few seconds, then nodded. "I have heard from the former Sovereign," he said, speaking of the woman who was part of a team that had run the Court of Divine Blood. "She said that the Interweb location where she purchased her glamours has disappeared. I do not understand how something that didn't physically exist could cease doing so, but I do not wish to sit through another lecture from Stewart about virtual."

I was about to ask what virtual aspect he was confused over, but decided that was a discussion for another day. Stewart was an excellent steward, having served with an Irish demigod for many centuries before the First Dragon hustled him over to work for us, but even he had limits.

Sadly, although the First Dragon was superior in many ways, his grasp on all things Internet wasn't particularly strong. It was only since we met that he had taken to using a cell phone, since I'd asked him to keep in touch when he was away doing First Dragon things. "Internet, my love, and that's a shame about the glamour website. I'm pinning my hopes on the mates' collective to locate one."

He smiled at me and I wanted to simultaneously kiss the breath off his lips and have my womanly way upon him.

"Two days," I told him when his eyes did the molten thing again, no doubt in response to my body's obvious de-

sire to seduce him. I had fight my libido to keep from stroking a hand down his magnificent chest. "And then, hoo baby,
you're mine."

His slow answering smile was everything I wanted, and
then some.

THREE
EFFRIJIM

Heya, Amelie! Hope you don't mind me sending you an audio message. Can you play it for Cecile when she wakes up from her post-breffy nap? Also, Ash wants me to tell you that she located the person who you said might have a spell to make my sweet fuzzybutt immortal, but that the dude was really snappy to her and said he wouldn't waste the supplies on a dog. Have you ever heard of anything so ridiculous?

Aisling said that we won't give up, though, so don't lose hope.

OK, here's the stuff that happened over the last couple of days.

It started with a text.

SALLY

Is it true that one of the dragon progenitor's shards is in the hands of a demon lord? Asking for a friend … well, all right, I'm asking for Terrin, because he's tied up helping with a small problem involving some rogue mages who are heading for a very hard time if they don't stop their present course, but that's neither here nor there, now, is it?

ME

Heya, Sally. What demon lord has a shard of the dragon heart? 'Cause as far as I know, only dragons have them, although the blue sept's shard is in the hands of a baddie named Xavier, but he's a dragon. Mostly. OK, it's about half dragon, half demon, but you know what I mean.

SALLY

Ah, that is his name? Interesting. You would think one shard would be enough for him, but evidently he feels otherwise. Still, I'm sure your green wyvern has things well in hand. I will pass along your information to my better half, former-Sovereignly speaking. And now that I've warned you and your dragons, I must go. My bestie, Freya, invited me to swim with dolphins, and you just know I can't refuse that! Plus, Odin will be there, and he's always so fun to tease. I love it when he gets really annoyed and bursts into a cloud of attack ravens. Good times all around!

ME

Just when I think everything is copacetic, you go and drop hints about something happening to the dragons. Is Xavier after Drake and Aisling for something? Their shard?

ME

Wait, I think Drake has two, since Soldy gave him one in order to get him to steal the light blade for Baltic. Is that it? Xavier's going after the other shards? Aisling's gonna freak out, and I won't even speculate how crazy Drake will go protecting his dragons and family. The word "shitshow" comes to mind, you know?

ME

Sally? Is Xavier after the green dragons?

ME

Man, I hate it when you drop tidbits and then go off and do things like hanging with gods and swimming with dolphins.

ME

Also, I have a credit card now, and can pay for a portal to go wherever the dolphin-swimming party is happening. Just sayin'.

I gave Sally a half hour to respond, but when she didn't, I figured I'd better find Aisling to tell her what Sally said.

That's when I got the second text.

UNKNOWN NUMBER

The blood moon must be returned. You will see to it. Desislav the Destroyer hungers for vengeance.

ME

Eh? New phone, who dis?

UNKNOWN NUMBER

I am Lattsa, daughter of Haka, head of the Jabmead Sisterhood. You will see to the return of the blood moon. Refusal will mean the destruction of the dragonkin.

ME

Man, when it rains threats, it pours. Isn't the Jabmead Sisterhood some sort of mercenary band from Finland? I thought you guys were in the Jabmiidaibmu underworld? Did Desi hire you?

LATTSA

Yes, to all of it, although now we reside on a reserve of land in the north of Finland. Do not think to defy me, demon. As leader of the Jabmiid, my roots lie deep in old earth magic. Your destruction, and that of the dragons who refuse to return the blood moon to Desislav, is ensured if you refuse.

ME

Hang on, have to get Google up on another screen, because you're talking about all sorts of stuff that is sus as Abaddon.

ME

Heya, Desi, did you happen to hire a pushy woman in Finland named Lattsa, and if so, can you tell her that she's not gonna win any awards for making friends when the first thing she does is threaten death and destruction without even saying hi?

DESISLAV

I believe your sister said she was going to contact you. Are you safe? Are you well? If the dragons are not able to protect you, you will come to us. Your mother is having difficulty regaining her memory, but perhaps your presence would help. I will send Lattsa to fetch you so that you are not harmed in the war.

ME

Sister? That bossy lady is my sister? You mentioned I had one, but I thought she must be dead or something, 'cause you haven't spoken of her since, and I never heard of her.

ME

Also, I appreciate the offer, but Aisling and Drake and the spawn all need me, so I'd rather stay here with them. But Ash says I can visit you and Parisi whenever I want, so if it would help to make daily visits, I can do that. I have a credit card! Expense is of no concern! Where are you guys? I can get a portal out to have lunch with you today. I like burgers, but I can't have onions or garlic, and raw tomatoes make me gag.

I waited ten minutes, but my dad didn't respond, so I figured I'd ask for a little more info from Lattsa before I found Aisling and spilled all the goss.

ME

So, as far as I know, no one has Desi's blood moon. He said it was destroyed when he gave it up to save my mom and me.

LATTSA

Desislav the Destroyer said it was taken by a dragon named Bael.

ME

Fires of Abaddon! Bael got his relic? OK, that explains a lot … and also brings up about a thousand questions. Let's start with the biggest one: when and where did Bael get the blood moon?

She didn't answer, and I decided I'd held off the bad news for long enough, so rather than pressing for an answer, I took my phone and headed out to the garden where Aisling and Drake were sitting on a couple of Adirondack chairs while watching the kids run through a Slip 'N Slide before leaping into a small pool Drake had crammed into the corner of the yard.

"So," I said as I set my phone down on Ash's lap, "how are you feeling these days, Guardian-wise?"

"What? Dammit, Jim, I don't want your slobbery phone. Where's your drool bib? Honest to Pete, there are times when I wish you'd have chosen a form that's less saliva-based. Ava, no, that butterfly doesn't want to swim in the pool with your brother and sister. Just set it back on the leaf and it will watch you play, OK?"

"What's wrong?" Drake asked, his eyes narrowed on me in a way that made me scoot around to the other side of Aisling, just in case he had any ideas of lighting my tail on fire again. Dude needs some serious anger management when it comes to setting me on fire. "Why do you ask Aisling how she is feeling?"

Aisling, who had wiped my phone, shot a startled glance first at him, then slid her gaze over to me, now filled with speculation. "Yes, why did you ask about my Guardian readiness?"

"Got some texts you're gonna want to read," I said, nudging my phone.

Drake leaned to the side so he could read as she scrolled through them, her expression growing more and more horrified by the second. She didn't even complain when Drake took the phone, obviously sending copies of the texts to his own phone. She just looked at me and said, "What the hell? What the ever-loving hell?"

"Abaddon," I corrected her. You'd think after all these years she'd have that down.

"Xavier is after our dragon heart shards? Why? Drake?"

His phone was already to his ear as he made a call. She got to her feet and moved over to stand next to him, listening, as well. I headed over that way, since Ava, the youngest spawn, was watching me with an expression I recognized.

Kid thinks I'm a pony, and no matter how many times I tell her I'm not, she insists I haul her around.

"—evident that Xavier is planning something to do with the shards. Perhaps he hopes to pull together the dragon heart, although I have no idea what he would achieve by doing so. The First Dragon is sure to have little patience with him, given the situation with Yrian," Drake said when I stopped next to them.

Aisling was busy texting on her phone, but she glanced toward me when Drake wrapped up his call. "I'm going to ask Nora if she's heard any rumblings of trouble, as well as Caribbean Battiste."

"I don't see that the head of your Guardian order will have much intelligence as to dragon happenings, but I would be interested to know if your mentor has heard rumors of an attack on us. Why is this daughter of Desislav messaging you?" Drake asked.

"I take it she's working for him now," I answered, moving around to the other side of Ash and Drake when Ava, having been pig piled on by the twins, squirmed out from under them, her gaze once again focused on me. I tell you, it almost sent a chill down my spine. "She's the leader of some sort of band of mercenaries in Finland who likes old earth magic and stuff like that. She seems to think we have Desi's blood moon relic. We don't, do we?"

"Goddess, I hope not," Aisling said, giving Drake a pointed look. "Is there something you'd like to tell me?"

"Many things, but they are not suitable for ears other than yours," he answered, tapping on his phone. I caught a glimpse of a chat group he had with the other wyverns, and figured he was filling them in.

She nudged him. "Do any of your lairs happen to contain the relic of the demigod who started Abaddon?"

"Inquiring minds want to know," I said, nodding, but just then Ava rushed me, and I had to take off.

I'm really going to hate it when Ash and Drake figure out she's a baby Guardian. That kid is going to summon the Abaddon out of me, I just know it.

Anywhoozlebee, that's what's going on here.

Drake is locking down the house, since his normal standby safe place in the country is about to be renovated because Aisling refuses to live with the antique plumbing anymore.

Ash told me to keep trying to contact my parents, but Desi isn't the best about answering the phone, and only texts when he feels like it, so yeah. That's kinda that.

Smooches to my fuzzybutt, and a head bonk to you, Amelie.

FOUR
MAY

"So, how long have you guys been hosting this music festival?" I asked as we strolled down from the castle's north garden, along a twisty path lined with LED torches that flickered atmospherically in the darkness.

The path deposited us at a broad field now dotted with a variety of temporary structures, including five stages, scaffolding holding lights and sound equipment, and a whole herd of RVs and trailers where the crew and some of the bands holed up for the three-day event.

In addition, a dozen wooden booths selling food and festival souvenirs lined the path from the smaller field that served as a parking lot, while several rows of bleachers lined three sides of the largest stage.

"Almost sixty years, according to Christian," Allie answered, glancing behind where her husband was following. "He didn't actually mention the word Woodstock, but I think he got the idea about then because I recall him saying something about all the mud and hippies. Generally, the music festival is held with the yearly arrival of a traveling circus, but this year, the schedules didn't mesh, so the Battle of the Bands is being held now. Is Aisling angry about something?"

I paused to eyeball the line of dragons, vampires, and assorted children that straggled down the path. "I don't think so, but we can ask her."

Her twins dashed around Aisling and Drake, who were clearly having some sort of an argument, the kids chasing Allie's girls and son, a tall boy who looked just like his father.

"—we do not need a castle. Honest to Pete, Drake, the house in Hungary is big enough and old enough to count as one, not to mention your Paris house. Just because you don't have a home with crenellations and murder holes doesn't mean—what?" Aisling came to an abrupt stop when Allie and I burst into laughter.

"Sorry," I said when Drake flashed a scathing look my way. "I didn't mean to laugh. It's none of my business if Drake fell in love with Christian's castle and wants one of his own."

"He didn't act that way with Dauva," Aisling pointed out when Drake, with a little roll of his eyes, strode forward to where Gabriel was standing with Brom and Pixie, watching all the people stream in and around the audiences at the various five stages.

"That's because Drahanská Castle is unique and desirable by anyone," Christian said as he, too, strolled past. I averted my gaze so as not to laugh at his smug look when he called out, "Perhaps you dragons would like to see my dungeon? I have kept it as it was when I had the castle built seven hundred years ago. It is unique in that respect."

"Oh, that was subtle," Allie said loud enough for Christian to hear. She also must have done some of the mind talking that Gabriel said the vamps could do with their mates, because Christian suddenly whirled around and glared at Allie for a few seconds. She just grinned.

"Ilona! Don't you dare even think of climbing that!" Aisling bellowed when her oldest daughter approached one of the sound scaffolds with a speculative glint to her eye. "Remember what Allie said—she has a time-out space in the playroom where children who don't behave get put.

Keep it up and you'll join Ava and Anduin there. In the play-room, that is, since neither child has misbehaved." The last was spoken to Ysolde.

"Oh, Anduin is almost always in time-out," Ysolde answered as she passed by with Baltic on her heels. "I swear he's worn a groove on the naughty step at home."

"He has my nature," Baltic said with complacence. "He rebels against the constraints deemed important to others."

"Which is just another way of saying he's incredibly stubborn," Ysolde answered, and stood glancing around. "Are we supposed to watch the stages in a particular order, or is it just go where the music sounds good?"

Ilona answered Aisling in Magyar, something I knew drove Aisling nuts, since she had a hard time picking up any language, and her children appeared to have inherited their father's linguistic abilities.

"You know how I dislike it when people say things in languages I can't understand," Aisling told her kids with narrowed eyes. "Remember that the time-out corner awaits any child who doesn't follow the rules."

"Waffle cones!" Brom said, obviously spotting a vendor, his face lighting up just as if he were one of the younger kids. "Would you like one, Pixie? My treat."

"Ice cream! Ice cream!" The chant went up from all the children, and Brom—with only a slightly martyred look—herded all five over to the booth with Pixie wrangling the stragglers.

"Oooh, now, that's what I'm talkin' about," Jim said, following as it tried to pull its backpack around, no doubt to get at the credit card that it had proudly announced Aisling had given it at Christmas. "Heya, Brom, can you float me enough for a strawberry waffle cone? I can't get the zipper open unless I take off the pack, and then someone has to do the snap to put it back on. ..."

"With luck, that will keep them out of trouble for five minutes," Aisling said, also glancing around. "I hope there's some good dance music. Drake is a killer dancer when he wants to be, and I made him promise if there was something suitable, he'd take me for a spin around the dance floor. Or dance grass, as the case may be. Where to start? That looks like a girl group. Shall we support the ladies … er … ladies?"

Seeing as the wyverns were clustered together with Christian as they stood back and surveyed the area, no doubt looking for signs of trouble, we drifted off to the farthest stage, partially concealed by two massive RVs. We'd filled in Allie via the mates-and-friends group chat earlier in the week, so she knew what was going on with Yrian.

"So this evil dragon is after your sept, Aisling?" she asked.

"Supposedly, although it's been three weeks, and we haven't seen hide nor scale of a bad dragon, let alone anyone from Xavier's tribe. My mentor, Nora, thinks maybe it was a mistake, or a way to cause havoc with minimal trouble. Drake, of course, has gone into serious protection mode, which is why he had the security team here for the last few days."

"Christian is pretty good at keeping troublemakers from the festival," was all Allie said in response, but we all shared a smile.

"Have you guys found the artificer you were looking for?" she continued as we moved to the back of a gathering crowd while the four women band members set up their equipment, aided by the roadies and sound crew evidently hired for the event. "Not that I knew what one was, but Christian—who is awfully good with glamours, although he said he wouldn't be able to fool Dr. Kostich—explained to me that they use life magic to craft three different types of glamours."

"Life magic?" I asked at the same time that Ysolde said, "There's more than one type of glamour?"

"According to Christian, the most common glamour is a surface one, which changes the appearance of a person. Then there're will glamours, which affect the moods, emotions, and actions of people within a certain distance of the person wearing it. The last kind, illusion glamours, is evidently the rarest of all of them."

"What do they do?" Ysolde asked as the band took their places.

The four women weren't dressed alike, but each wore some variation of pink and black, the drummer in a catsuit, while one of the guitarists wore what looked like a pair of bike shorts with a tight pink tank top. The second was in what I thought of as a Lolita outfit, complete with pink wig, polka-dot ruffled miniskirt, and thigh-high striped stockings. A woman with thick black braids wrapped around her head, and a black-and-white poodle skirt topped with a pink sweater, was evidently the singer, since she fussed with a microphone for a minute, pausing to chat with one of the technicians.

"Eh?" Allie pulled her attention from watching the band get ready. "Oh, the glamour? They can make people experience whatever the user wants. Christian said he's only seen one of those, and the cost on it was way too prohibitive to consider. Evidently an archimage was selling one to the highest bidder a few centuries ago, but was basically asking for magic far out of the reach of the normal vamp about town. I like that singer's skirt. It's very retro."

"Looks like they're that sort of a band," Aisling said, applauding when one of the crew announced the third round of the tournament was to begin. "I hope it's fifties or sixties music. The kids and I love to dance to that, and it's worth the time to wheedle Drake into doing the twist."

"What's life magic?" I asked Allie when the music began, a boppy dance song that had my toes tapping. I looked across the field to where I could still see the men, now surrounded by the children, as I wondered if Gabriel would like to watch the band, too. "I haven't heard of that, and I like to stay current with all the possibilities."

Allie's expression turned regretful. "I'm afraid I don't know. Christian didn't expound, and I didn't think to ask him—oh!"

The poodle-skirt singer had a fabulous voice, one that had a quality I found hard to define. She sang a song about falling hard for a guy, and how he was blind to her. When she got to a lyric about wanting to shine a spotlight on her love, a brilliant flare lit her up.

"Whoa!" Aisling said, staring.

"That's unusual," Ysolde commented, taking a step forward and narrowing her eyes on the light that shone down from about twenty feet above the singer. "Do you guys see a source for the light? It just looks to me like it's spawning from … well, nothing. It definitely starts higher than the actual lights on the rigging."

"That is odd," Allie said slowly as we all watched. "I think Christian needs to see this. …"

"Is it some sort of magic, do you think?" Aisling asked Ysolde. "A light spell?"

"If it is, I've never heard of it," she answered, moving forward another step.

A flash of movement to the side had me glancing over to see Gabriel and the others heading our way at a fast pace, the kids herded in front of them.

"What's wrong?" Drake asked as soon as he got close enough for us to hear over the music. "The Dark One said his mate is concerned about one of the musicians?"

"OK, that mind-talking thing is seriously cool," I told Ysolde, who nodded.

"It would be so very handy. Baltic, do you see a source for that spotlight?"

The wyverns and vampires all turned to look at the stage. I watched Gabriel as he studied it, his normally placid expression filling with confusion.

"I couldn't see a source," I told him softly.

"That's because it's not there," he answered just as quietly.

"Huh?" I asked.

"It's a glamour," Christian said with a nod toward the singer.

"Glamours can make spotlights appear out of nothing?" I moved forward to stand next to Gabriel. "I've never heard … oh, wait, the illusion ones?"

"Yes," Christian said, his eyes—almost as bright silver as Gabriel's—narrowed on the four band members. The singer hit a high note just then that seemed to soar into the night sky, sending goose bumps down my arms and back as I was filled with a sense of longing and unrequited love.

Instantly, all the men froze. The kids, who were finishing up their cones, were alternately leaping around to the music and throwing glow sticks at one another.

"Is that—it can't be," Aisling said softly. "Not another one."

"Get the children to safety," Drake told her, immediately calling their twins to him.

"Siren?" Allie said, looking at her vampire in confusion. "What's that? I mean, I know about the ones who sat in the water and lured sailors to their death, but—really? They're singers?"

"Take the children inside," Christian told her, his phone to his ear. "Set the security alarm as soon as you are inside. Do not allow anyone else in but us."

"Right, in we go," Aisling said, herding her kids along with Allie's.

"Is she dangerous, do you think?" I asked Gabriel. Brom had immediately moved over to consult his mother and Baltic, holding Pixie by the hand. She looked as bewildered as the rest of us.

"I think Charity should see this," Ysolde said, holding up her phone to film.

"Good idea," I said, and pulled out my own phone, quickly texting Charity to video call me as soon as possible.

"You have history with this siren?" Christian demanded to know of the wyverns. "And you didn't tell me she was in this area?"

"No, and no," Gabriel said, obviously reticent to spill the history of Charity and the First Dragon.

My phone rang just as Allie and Aisling came back down the path at a near run, causing both Drake and Christian to bend almost identical stern looks upon them.

"You left the children?" Drake asked Aisling, clearly outraged, a curl of smoke emerging from his nose.

"They're safe with our nanny, Allie's nanny, and half a dozen vampires guarding the playroom. Holy cow, can that siren sing. Has someone called Charity?"

"This is her," I said, answering the call that burbled, Charity popping onto my screen. "Thanks for calling back. I hope I'm not interrupting anything important."

"Actually, you kind of are. The First Dragon has finally gotten the information he needs about the identity of an artificer, but she's disappeared. He's getting ready to go out and track her down himself. Is something wrong?"

"Do you happen to know this woman?" I asked, and turned the camera to face the stage. I let her see the band for half a minute, then turned the screen back. Her expression mimicked closely that which all of us wore.

"No, I don't, but she sounds … sireny. Is she one? I have no idea who she is. There are only two other sirens, and they are both in protective custody."

"No one here knows, either," I answered, pausing when the song ended, and the audience cheered loudly. "But, as you can imagine, everyone is worried, especially due to the children being here."

"Hang on, let me see if the First Dragon has any insight." Charity obviously got up, because there were several blurry images of her running through a long hall filled with light and flowers before she stopped, and soft murmuring could be heard.

In the meantime, the band started up with another number, this one a soulful song that simultaneously made me want to weep with the beauty of the singer's voice and clutch Gabriel to tell him how much I loved him.

"Go ahead, May," Charity instructed, and I caught a glimpse of the First Dragon looking mildly annoyed.

I murmured an apology for disrupting him before switching the camera to the stage for twenty seconds.

When I turned the screen back to me, it was to see Charity looking to the side, saying, "All right, but are you sure?"

"I hope we didn't anger the First Dragon," I said, glancing at Gabriel, who to my surprise wasn't watching my phone but, like the other dragons and Christian, had spread out to form a loose semicircle around the stage.

"No, I don't mind at all," Charity said to the First Dragon, before adding to me, "We'll be there in a minute."

"What? You're coming here? Both of you?" I moved up next to Ysolde, who was standing with Aisling, their heads together, but before I could ask more, Charity ended the call.

"The First Dragon and Charity are coming," I told them before moving over to tell Gabriel the same thing. I managed two steps before I felt a presence behind me, and spun around to see Charity and the ancestor of all dragons as he stalked forward, his gaze focused on the singer.

All the wyverns—and even Christian—bowed as he passed them, but his attention was wholly on the woman who sang so beautifully.

"I had no idea the First Dragon would take such an interest in a siren," I said softly to Charity. "I feel bad for disturbing you guys. It's not like she's doing anything dangerous."

The First Dragon spun around and looked straight at me, filling me with an odd sense of both joy and worry. Instantly, Gabriel was at my side, not saying anything, but putting an arm around me.

"You are wrong, child of shadows," the First Dragon said to me. I froze, not sure how to answer that comment.

"Dragon sire, if May's call to Charity was inappropriate—" Gabriel started to say, my heart warming at the fact that he was defending me to the most important being in all dragonkin.

"The woman is quite dangerous, although she is not a siren," the First Dragon said, his gaze resting briefly on Gabriel before he turned back to the stage. "She is an artificer, one of such high skill that beings the world over have sought her for years without success. She is the only hope we have of saving Yrian from a future that I cannot prevent."

FIVE
BECKET

I noticed them shortly after our three-song set started. I had seen a few vampires flitting around the music festival, but since they didn't seem to care much about the bands themselves, I stuck to my roadie glamour and just kept my head down until I was needed to perform.

The audience, for the most part, was mortal, but all of a sudden the back of the crowd seemed full of dragons.

"Where the hell did they come from?" I muttered to Deni after the first song, taking a fast couple of sips of water. The pyrotechnics from one of the other competing bands had sent residual smoke drifting our way.

"Who? I think one of the bands just finished, so we're probably getting their audience. Love song next?" she answered, adjusting the strap holding her bass guitar.

"Yes." I gave a mental headshake at my worry and, mindful of the clock and the contest officials watching us, turned back to start the second song, my attention split between using the glamours set for the song and watching the dragons, who now stood clustered at the back of the audience with a vampire.

By the time we swung into the third and final song of our set, I stopped worrying about the dragons and instead kept a horrified eye on a man who wore a glamour so badly created, little tendrils of black occasionally reached out to snap in the air.

"Demon in the audience," I said softly to Billie during Skye's guitar solo. Her eyes widened as she quickly scanned the crowd. "Possibly more than one. As soon as we're done, I'm going to switch glamours."

She nodded as I finished up the song, my gut twisting in a way that had me regretting the cinnamon donuts I'd bought from one of the vendors.

I bowed quickly when the audience, well primed by the fancy effects created by the glamours, erupted into enthusiastic applause. Stripping off the microphone pack, I moved to tuck myself behind a stand of speakers. I wasn't concealed from everyone, but enough that I slapped on my roadie glamour, and hurriedly donned a pair of lavender headphones before hoisting a coil of cable.

The festival crew hustled in to move our equipment and bring in the next band's stuff, so I hopped off the small stage and, with Deni's spare guitar, slowly made my way through the audience, my eyes peeled for the demon.

I hesitated for a second, then, with a glance toward the cluster of dragons, decided to make sure they weren't interested in me, as well.

"—I'm telling you, something isn't right," a woman said as I scooted behind her, trying to keep the guitar case from whapping anyone. "Let me get Jim. It'll know if I'm imagining this or not, but I'm telling you that I'm not."

"A demon?" another woman said, peering around as she limped to the far side of the stage. "Let me ask … oh. Christian says he can feel that one is here, but he can't pinpoint it. He's going through the crowd with a couple of other vamps to find it."

The first woman stepped back and bumped into me, knocking the cable coil from where I had slung it over my shoulder.

"*Mille pardons,*" I murmured in French as she hastily apologized and bent to help me pick up the spilled cable. I jerked my hand away, knowing that even my best glamour could be discovered if I was touched.

"Aisling? Baltic says the woman disappeared when she stepped behind the speakers. Did you find the demon?" a blonde asked as she hustled up, a lanky young man on her heels. "Brom, where's Pixie?"

"She said she could hide in the shadows and watch for the lady," the young man answered, rubbing his arms. "Baltic said to stay with you while he and the First Dragon search, but I don't think I should leave Pixie."

"No, of course you don't have to protect me," the blonde answered. "But neither do I think it's safe to wander around on your own. Perhaps you and Pixie could mingle in the crowds rather than hiding in the shadows? That would be helpful."

The young man, evidently named Brom, murmured his agreement and hustled off.

"I haven't spotted the … uh … bad person yet, but it has to be pretty powerful if I can feel it before I see it. I'll summon Jim and see if it can't help," the woman who handed me the cable said, straightening up to give me a wide smile as I clutched the now-tangled cable to my side. "Sorry again. Here, let me tuck the end under your arm. … There you go."

The two women watched me, obviously waiting for me to leave. I wanted desperately to hear more about what the dragons were up to, since I had no doubt the woman they'd mentioned was me.

"Great," I said under my breath as I turned and headed through the crowd toward the big trailers containing the festival equipment. "Because it's not bad enough that demons are hunting me, now the dragons and vampires are interested. My life blows."

I dumped the cable on one of the crates of equipment, then left the guitar in our corner of a tent used to hold the band's instruments, before pausing to text Billie that I'd catch up with them at the hotel in town where we were staying.

"Now," I said to myself, glancing around the area behind the festival trailers, "to make a timely escape before that demon with the amateur glamour or those pesky dragons find me."

Voices laughing, chatting, and calling in everything from Czech to English, French, and German swam around me as I slowly made my way through the mobs of people toward a gravel drive that led out of the pasture, determined to keep a casual appearance lest I draw any attention.

I strained my hearing for anything more from immortals who might be hunting for me, but as I hurried to the drive, now choked with people heading to the main stage for the last few performances of the night, I saw them.

"Candy and Andy. Great. Just effing great," I said, stopping as my feet felt like they turned to lead, a chill of pure, unadulterated fear skittering down my spine.

"Really? Andy? Man, I remember the time when Andromalius would get spitting mad if you called him by anything but his full name."

I whirled around at the voice, my eyes on the couple who stood behind me, two women in matching tight pink club dresses, but I quickly realized it wasn't they who spoke. Their heads were together as they watched something on a phone before they turned in answer to someone calling to them.

My gaze dropped down to the large black dog that stood next to them, watching me with its head tipped on the side.

"Heya," the dog said.

It took me a minute to realize what I was seeing.

It was a demon. Not a wrath demon like Candy and Andy, but still, a demon—even if I didn't see any manifestations of dark power about it. "A demon is a demon is a demon," I murmured to myself, spinning on my heel, and, as casually as I could, retraced my steps to the equipment trailers. Fewer people were there, with more chances for me to escape.

"Yeah, kinda. I mean, I'm a demon sixth class, so I'm not the same as wrath demons like Andromalius and Furcand, if you get me. Hey, how do you know who wrathies are? You look human."

I ignored the demon, picking up speed as panic overtook me, filling me with dread. How on earth had I missed the two most powerful demons to roam the mortal world, as well as one in dog form? I shook my head at my own carelessness, my heart sick with the knowledge that I was going to have to find another safe place to hide.

Running around the corner of the nearest trailer, I dropped my roadie glamour, since I'd used it before, and was about to apply a new one when I almost collided with two men—dragons—who stood consulting. The nearest one was a few inches taller than me, about six feet tall with dark hair that bore a broad white stripe, dark eyes, and an air of something other about him. The second one was taller, also with dark hair, his pulled back in a small ponytail, his eyes almost as black as his shirt.

I froze when the first one glanced at me, doing a double take that had me instantly backing up, on the verge of flat out running.

"Heya, Balters. Heya, First Daddy," a voice from behind me said just as I whirled around, intent on running.

I tripped over the blasted demon, going down in a tangle of legs with it.

I swore in my mother's native Spanish, and tried to get up. The man with the white stripe of hair held out a hand, but just then I caught sight of Andy at the edge of the crowd, fortunately looking in the opposite direction.

"Shit," I swore, and with nothing else to do, I slipped into the Beyond, the slightly different version of the mortal world, one inhabited by beings of the Otherworld.

Instantly, the noise of the crowd and a band that was warming up faded to a dull murmur, while a sense of everything being slightly off settled around me.

I relaxed a little, knowing I was safe from the demon and dragons, but I wasn't sure if Candy and Andy might not be able to breach the Beyond, so I stood up and headed roughly in the direction of the road leading to a small town where we were staying.

"Ah. It is you. I thought it might be," a slow, sonorous voice said behind me. I whirled around to watch with complete astonishment the two dragons enter the Beyond.

I stood frozen for a moment, my mind too frazzled to do anything but ask, "How?"

"How did we know you were the artificer?" the dragon asked. His voice was deep, but smooth, very smooth, and held a gravitas that made me stand up a little straighter. He studied my face for a moment before answering, "I am the First Dragon."

I had no idea what that was supposed to mean, but I wasn't about to wait to find out. I dashed off into the opposite direction, almost colliding with a woman who reminded me of a 1920s flapper when she suddenly appeared before me. "Baltic? Are you here? Gabriel and I thought we'd—whoa!"

"Does everyone have access to the Beyond?" I couldn't help but snarl, and would have pushed past the woman when another dragon appeared beside her.

"The dragonkin need your help," the man with the presence said, a hand clamping down on my shoulder stopping me from making a getaway.

"Sorry, I closed up shop a couple of years ago," I said, trying to get out of his grip, but by that time, the other dragons had closed in around me.

The man's eyes started changing: first the pupils elongated; then the irises themselves changed from dark brown to hazel and then to pure green. "Your assistance is needed to save my son. Without it, without him, the future of my children is in peril."

My gut clenched again, making me wonder if I was going to vomit all over the pushy dragon.

"I'm sorry," I repeated, shaking my head and twisting until his hand dropped from me. "I wish I could help, but I can't. It's too dangerous."

"This is the singer?" the silver-eyed dragon said, his eyes narrowed on me. "I don't see any sign of a glamour, and she is obviously of another ethnicity."

"Becket Peru," the first one said, and I jerked back at the sting of power that whipped across me when he invoked my full name. His eyes were shifting again, now more blue than green. "Your help is needed. Whatever fee you demand will be paid, but there is no way forward without you."

"No, thank you," my mouth said as my mind screamed warnings to get the hell away from the dangerous man and his buddies, and then before he could grab me again, I flung myself forward toward the woman, slipping out of the Beyond, stumbling over a cooler before righting myself.

Two people watched me with astonishment on their respective faces, but that quickly faded to speculation followed immediately by triumph.

"Artificer!" Candy snarled, grabbing my arm with both hands.

"Got you now," Andy added, fingers digging into my other arm. "Thought you were clever turning yourself into someone else, eh? Not clever enough. My lord will be most happy to see you."

"I have no doubt he will be, but I am going to have to decline, just as I have for your previous attempts to kidnap me." For a second, I thought of bopping myself back into the Beyond, but with the dragons right there—obviously wanting to use me just as the demons did—I figured I stood a better chance with enemies I knew.

I'd escaped them three times before, after all, I told myself as my fingers started to draw a new glamour, one that would distract them so I could escape, but before I did more than start it, Andy jerked my hands forward and used duct tape to bind my fingers together. "None of that! You don't think we're going to fall for you confusing us again, do you? We're not stupid."

The demon dog trotted around the corner, followed by the two female dragons I'd run into a few minutes before.

It stopped, cocked its head, and said, "Hi, Andromalius. Hi, Furcand. I didn't know you guys were still around."

"Demons!" the woman with curly hair said, pulling the dog back as she started casting wards.

The blonde turned and yelled, but I didn't get to hear what she was saying, because Candy jerked me forward by my bound hands while Andy spun around to face the newcomers.

"Effrijim," it sneered at the dog before curling a lip at the woman who flung a ward on it. "You have no power over me, Guardian. I bear the devastation of Bael!"

"What's a devastation?" the blonde woman asked just as the air shimmered and the other dragons appeared from the Beyond.

"Go!" Andy shouted to Candy, pulling a small piece of black rock from its pocket, which elongated into a black sword, the blade of which appeared sooty with demon smoke.

I heaved myself to the side, trying to throw Candy off-balance, but as I did so, the man with the white streak in his hair started casting a spell, his eyes—now black again—narrowed on Candy.

At the same time, the three male dragons leaped forward, two of them on Andy while the third made a flying leap at Candy. He slammed into it, sending the pair of us falling forward, and I felt, for a moment, the flow of energy around me as the white-stripe man pulled it in, clearly about to cast one hell of a spell. To my complete and utter surprise, he didn't blast it at Candy, or even Andy—he flung it at me, and for a moment, I felt as if I was bathed in sunlight, a warm golden glow surrounding and filling me with joy.

I didn't realize when Candy had let go of me, or when the dragon cut the tape from my hands. My brain was too befuddled with the sensation of being filled with golden light, and it was only a few minutes later when I heard the shrieks and oaths that I snapped out of the reverie.

The dragons were fighting the demons, but evidently Candy decided that the odds weren't good and, with a snarled oath that physically hurt (and no doubt took a few years off my life), literally tore open space and, with Andy, disappeared into nothing.

"I really hate it when they do that," the woman with curly shoulder-length hair said, absently patting the demon dog. I glanced around, worried that the mortals had seen the demons disappear into Abaddon, but thankfully, the bands in the last bracket of the night were up, and no one bothered to come around behind the big trailers.

"Are you all right?" the blonde woman asked, watching me with an intensity that made me highly uncomfortable.

I touched my forehead, my brain feeling like it was still reeling from whatever spell had been cast on me. "Yes, just a little confused. Who are you? I mean, I can tell you're dragons, but what are you doing here? And why are you chasing me?"

The last question wasn't one for which I really needed an answer, since I knew full well why any being would make an attempt to capture me, but it slipped out before my still-befuddled brain could rein it in.

"We need to talk," the blonde said at the same time the man with the white stripe of hair put a hand on my arm.

I started to pull away, but before I could do so, the air shimmered and I found myself standing on a lush green lawn surrounded by decorated shrubs and plants, the garden filled with the drone of happy bees, and flowers that nodded in scented air, while above it all, birds sang songs of contentment, general happiness, and lots of braggadocio.

"Whoa," came a voice from behind me. I turned to see all the dragons, the vampire I'd noticed first, and even the demon dog, who whistled as it looked around. Everyone looked as astonished as I felt. "We get to see the First Daddy's house? Cool! Hey, is that an infinity pool? Can dogs use it? 'Cause Newfies love water, and Drake never lets me use his pools except the blow-up one the spawn use when it's hot out, and I always end up getting a toenail stuck in it, and then it leaks."

"No," a dark-haired woman said, sending the demon a pointed look as she moved over to stand next to the man with the white stripe. "Hello, Becket, it is? I'm Charity. This is the First Dragon. He's the creator of the race of dragons."

A skitter of fear had me shivering as I looked at the man next to her. He didn't look like the sort of person who could create a race of beings … until you looked into his eyes, and then it all made sense. "Uh … hello," I answered, my mind back to shrieking warnings at me.

"I'll do the introductions, since it looks like Becket could use a strong drink," the blonde said. "I'm Ysolde, and this is Baltic, the wyvern of the light dragons. That's Aisling and Drake, the latter of whom is the green wyvern, and Aisling's demon Jim. Behind you is May and Gabriel, the silver wyvern and his mate. This is my son Brom and his girlfriend, Pixie. And that's Christian and Allie—they're vampires."

"Dark Ones," murmured the vampire I'd noticed first. He, like everyone else, had a bit of a stunned look about the eyes, but I gathered that these were all leaders, and as such, they coped with being zapped to another realm of existence without so much as a boggle or two.

Unlike me, who was still feeling a bit rattled, what with having been chased, captured, and released to find myself now about to face a god who didn't look particularly pleased to see me.

"We wish to speak about my son Yrian," the First Dragon said, his voice both mellifluous and ponderous. "You are the only one who can help him."

My shoulders slumped.

"Why don't we go onto the patio, where we can all sit and discuss this without getting a sunburn," the woman named Charity said, taking the arm of the First Dragon as she gestured to the side.

"Are we having noms? Because I could totally go for a burger, or maybe some chips, or even popcorn. I love me some popcorn even if Ash has to brush my teeth later," the demon said.

I let myself be guided over to a shady patio done in gorgeous sandstone tiles that matched what appeared to be an Italian villa that spread out behind it, the patio bearing a large table, comfortable chairs, a couple of couches, and even a huge metal firepit in the shape of a dragon.

"Look, it's obvious you know who I am, and much as I appreciate you scaring off Candy and Andy—not that I ever expected to see such a thing, since they are seriously persistent—I'm afraid that I can't help you. Assuming, that is, that you want a glamour. I don't make them anymore."

"Why?" the First Dragon asked, not taking a seat, although all the women did. The men—with the exception of Christian the vampire—stood clustered together, while the First Dragon stood at the head of the table, his arms crossed, his gaze firmly affixed on me.

I tried looking him in the eyes when I answered, because my mother taught me that was polite, but every time I did so, I felt like an insect pinned to a board, leaving my gaze flitting around anywhere that wasn't filled with an actual god. "Because it's too dangerous."

"How so?" Aisling asked, sliding a glance toward the First Dragon.

I didn't want to answer. Hell, I thought for a moment of just disappearing into the Beyond, but the knowledge that the First Dragon could follow me there had me slumping back in my chair. "Because my glamours are too good. I realize that sounds like the worst sort of conceit, but the truth is ... well, they are good. And very much in demand. So much so that every demon lord, mage, and demigod around wanted me to work solely for them. You can imagine what that means."

To my surprise, Charity nodded. "I'm a siren, so I know just how you feel about everyone knowing who and what you are."

"You're a siren?" I asked, staring at her in surprise. "I thought ... my mother told me there were only two others, and they were in the Beyond to keep them out of trouble."

"They are." Charity looked to the First Dragon, before asking me, "Two others? Your mother is a siren, too?"

"She was, yes." I studied my hands, noting absently that my time in the sun during the last few weeks had brought out a new crop of freckles. I realized then that I wasn't wearing a glamour, and panicked for a moment, fearing … I didn't know what, exactly, other than there were very few people whom I let see the real me.

"You are a savant," the First Dragon said, still studying me. I flicked a glance toward him and nodded. He looked thoughtful as he said, "That explains why the demons sought you, but not why you stopped making glamours."

"It's just easier to lean into singing rather than making magic so good that everyone wants a piece of me," I answered, suddenly weary. My entire adult life had been a struggle, one in which the real me was never wanted, only my talents.

"Aisling's a savant, too," Ysolde told me, nodding toward her.

"The Guardian flavor, though, which is why I have Jim," Aisling said.

"It's more really that I enhance her life," Jim told me with a wink.

I stared at it, wondering when my life had taken a turn into a farce.

"Yrian Shadowsworn is held in the Asile," the First Dragon said, more or less ignoring the others to keep his attention focused on me.

It was not a comfortable experience.

"Your son?" I asked.

He didn't answer, instead saying, "He has been deemed a danger to mortals and immortals. The people holding him captive are annoying but, unfortunately, have Yrian in a prison from which I am unable to release him. You must make a glamour that will get him out before they take him to the Thirteenth Hour. According to the former Sovereign I consulted, that event is scheduled for tomorrow. You will make the glamour today, and take it in to him so that he might return to the dragonkin. His help is needed to end the threat to my children."

I knew when I was beaten. There was no way out of this situation that wouldn't end in possible death or at least imprisonment should I refuse. I'm not stupid—I knew that my only option was to bargain a resolution that would benefit me.

"All right," I said, obviously taking everyone by surprise … everyone but the First Dragon. "But I want something in return."

He inclined his head slightly. "Name your boon."

I glanced around at the company, weighing up my chances of actually getting some help for a change. "I want Candy and Andy out of commission."

"Who, exactly, are they?" Aisling asked, her eyebrows raised when her wyvern shot her a pointed look. "Sorry, I didn't mean to interrupt, but as the official demon wrangler of the group, I figured I should ask whose demons they were. I mean, I might be able to help if it's just a matter of banishing them to the Akasha."

The First Dragon was silent, still watching me with those uncanny eyes.

Ysolde tipped her head toward her dragon, who leaned against a pillar looking bored. "Baltic?"

"What?"

"Do you know whose demons those were?"

"Yes."

Silence fell over the group, only the faint drowsy buzzing of bees audible.

"Dragons are seriously the most annoying of beings," Ysolde said, frowning at Baltic. He frowned right back at her.

"Jim? Since the men are being their usual tight-lipped selves and refusing to answer a simple and wholly reasonable question, why don't you do the honors?" Aisling asked, nudging her dog. "To whom do those two demons belong?"

"Eh," Jim said, sending a worried look at the First Dragon. "I don't know if I should say. It's gonna make everyone pissed, and then I won't get a burger, because you'll all be yelling and arguing and picking on me."

"I never let anyone pick on you," Aisling told it, looking outraged before she qualified it with, "I am the only one allowed to do that, except Drake on occasion, and that's only because you've lipped off to him or done something heinous to his favorite leather couch. Now, answer the question, and yes, that's an order."

Jim sighed a put-upon sigh, and lay down on the cool tile floor. "They belong to Bael."

The dragons all froze, all but Baltic, who also heaved a sigh and moved over to stand behind his wife, his hands on her shoulders.

Aisling swore in French.

"Can you do it?" I asked the First Dragon. "Can you take care of them for me?"

"Take care of?" he said in his slow, measured tone. "Define what that means."

"Get them off my back. Make them stop following me all over the US and Europe." I sighed, suddenly feeling as if I were hollow inside, the outer shell all that seemed real. "Distract them with something or someone else so that I can stop running all the time."

"That is not what you want," the First Dragon answered, his eyes dark and watchful, like he was waiting for me to have an epiphany.

My gaze fell to my hands again, and absently, I sketched out a new glamour, one that hid my hair color (a shade of red most commonly called ginger) and facial features. "I'll take what I can get," was all I answered.

Silence fell again, but it was a pregnant silence, one filled with the dragons glancing amongst one another, but no one speaking, clearly giving the floor to the First Dragon.

The august person, for the first time since I'd sat down, let his gaze rest a few seconds on the dragons before it settled back on me. "In the normal course of events, my kin are able to destroy wrath demons, but the two who seek you for their master are different. They have more power than they ought."

"Can Bael do that from the Duat?" Aisling asked. "I thought the whole point of trapping him there was that he couldn't do bad things in the mortal world."

"He is confined, but that does not mean he is powerless," the First Dragon said, asking Baltic, "Did you feel anything about the wrath demons?"

"Only what you did—they were too powerful for what they were," he answered, his expression now looking as thoughtful as the First Dragon's. "But I did not think that Bael could give away power outside of Duat."

The First Dragon was silent for a good two minutes before he spoke. "He should not be able to do so, but I suspect he has found a way around the protections Osiris keeps for his underworld. He has been … distracted of late, and perhaps has not been as attentive as he should be."

"Are you saying that taking down Candy and Andy is impossible?" I asked, the tiny flicker of hope that had lit inside me at the thought of peace sputtering to a smoky end.

"No," he said after a few moments' thought. "It is possible to destroy them, but it will not be as easy as any other wrath demon. The kin will require Yrian's contribution to achieve that goal. I agree to your terms. You will release my son, and in exchange, the dragonkin will protect you from the demons until such time as they have been dealt with."

A little murmur went amongst the dragons, but it was the vampire that surprised me the most. "The Dark Ones have traditionally not involved ourselves much with the business of dragons, but I accept responsibility for the demons' presence at the festival. For that reason, I offer the services of my Beloved and myself. She is a Summoner of great repute, and I have some knowledge of demons and their lords."

The First Dragon looked at him for a long four seconds, but before he said more than, "All help is welcome," the garden and patio and gorgeous Italian villa faded into a slightly smoky-scented night, the harsh stage lights casting deep shadows from the trailers.

"Wow," the woman named Allie said, leaning into her vampire. "That was intense. I've never seen an actual god before."

"Demigod," Baltic and Ysolde said together, then turned to look at me.

I slumped back against the trailer as the young man named Brom loped up, his girlfriend in tow. "Sullivan? Where did you go? We looked all over for you, but everyone was gone. Oh. Is this the siren?" He nodded toward me.

"My mom was a siren, not me. I just inherited good singing abilities, but other than that, yes, it's me," I said with a sudden pulling sense that warned I would need rest soon. It was always so after a performance, especially one where I had to expend the energy to escape into the Beyond. Idly, I noticed that the girl Pixie wore a glamour to hide an extra set of arms, marking her as a poltergeist. The glamour looked like a commonly used lower-grade one, obviously about to wear off. Without thinking, I started drawing a proper glamour.

"The First Dragon took us to his digs," Jim the demon said, wandering over to snuffle Brom. "Hey, is that ice cream place still open?"

"What are you doing?" the green-eyed dragon asked me, his gaze suspicious.

"Creating a glamour," I answered, nodding toward Pixie. "Hers is about to fall off, and I expect with so many mortals around, she wouldn't want her extra arms showing."

Everyone stared at me with disbelief. I held up my hands, the pattern of the glamour glinting faintly in the shadows. "I'll stop if you don't want it, but I figured you'd like something of a better quality than the stuff you get at a glamour shop."

"OK," the young woman said, her black hair piled on her head in a manner that had it bobbing around after she stopped nodding. "How much will it cost? Karma—my foster mother—gave me her card, but I'm only supposed to use it in emergencies."

I smiled at her, and finished up the glamour. "My treat. This should last you a good month before it starts to crack. If you want me to seal it, it could go six months to a year."

"A year?" Aisling asked even as the two young people gawked at me. "You can make a glamour last a whole year?"

"Savant, remember?" I said, eyeing Pixie. "And yes, sealed glamours last longer than normal ones. Mostly, they go for two to three months, but when made by me … well, they last longer. The glamour's yours … unless you don't want one for a month?" The last sentence was spoken to Pixie.

"Is it going to hurt?" she asked, rubbing her arms. "The glamours get a bit irritating after six hours, so I usually have to take them off for a bit."

"My glamours don't do that," I said, eyeing her for a moment, then made a few tweaks to the threads that wound through the glamour. "But if you don't want to wear it …"

"Deus, no! I'd love not having to worry …" She stopped herself as she reached for it, clearing her throat and adding, "That is, I'd like it if you really aren't going to charge me for it, and it doesn't make me itch and get sore."

"Let's try it unsealed, just in case you don't like it," I said, tossing the glamour into the air so it sparkled for a brief moment before drifting down onto her. "It'll last only a month, all right?"

She gasped, an expression of pleasure on her face as she looked down. "It's like … it's like it's not there, but I only have two arms."

"You really are talented," Ysolde said, examining the girl. "I don't even see a hint of it."

"Christian?" Allie asked her vampire.

He took a few steps forward, murmured a "You permit?" to Pixie before moving around her, his eyes narrowed. He cast an odd glance toward me and shook his head. "I see no signs of anything other than a perfectly normal teenage girl."

Pixie looked like she wanted to dispute that statement, but bit back a response when Brom wrapped an arm around her waist.

"Right," I said, wanting nothing more than to fall into the nearest bed and sleep for approximately six months. "I have about twenty minutes before I collapse, and at least one set to do tomorrow for the band contest. Shall we get started?"

SIX
BECKET

In the end, they let me sleep. I think it was when I stumbled over a clod of dirt and did a face-plant that the dragons realized an exhausted artificer was not a productive artificer. At least, that's how I explained it to the rest of the band.

"Are you sure you're safe?" Deni asked after I told her I was going to spend the night at Christian's castle to ensure an uninterrupted night. "You don't really know these people, do you? Could they be working for that demon you saw in the toilet?"

I thought of the dragon demigod, and smiled ruefully at Deni's image in my phone as I snuggled back into the pillows of a surprisingly comfortable bed. "I don't think they are, no. Don't worry about me—these people want me to do something for them, so they aren't going to let anyone nab me."

At least, not until I'd sprung the dragon lord's son. I pushed aside the thought that they might not eliminate Candy and Andy from my life, clinging to the fact that I had an agreement with the First Dragon.

"OK, but will they understand that we have to perform tomorrow? You did see that we made it through to the next bracket? We're only three wins away from taking the big money! Skye says we should have no problem so long as you keep up the effects. None of the other bands' glamours are as good as yours."

I smiled at her obvious excitement and spent a few minutes talking about the contest before promising her I'd be back for the afternoon set.

Just as I was about to get up so I could peel off my clothes, someone knocked at my door.

"Christian had your things brought from the hotel," Allie said, handing me my bag. "I hope you don't mind—personally, I would have asked you if you wanted your things rather than just taking them, but you know how men are. Regardless, I hope you'll be comfortable." She glanced around the room, clearly worried I wouldn't like the digs.

"I'm sure this is the worst sort of ungrateful, but honestly, I'm so tired, I could sleep on the floor, so a comfortable bed with a down duvet is heaven. And thank you for my clothes."

She toddled off shortly thereafter, and I crawled into bed, my body feeling like I'd been run through a particularly prickly hedge a few times. To my surprise, I fell asleep almost immediately, and woke up only when I had an uncomfortable feeling I was being watched.

I opened my eyes to find three children standing at the foot of the bed.

"Hrn?" I asked, shoving my hair off my face, immediately pulling on a glamour to hide my true appearance. "Who are you? What are you doing here? Do you belong to the vampires?"

"We're Dark Ones," the boy said. He looked to be about thirteen or fourteen, while the two girls were obviously twins, and a few years younger.

The girls nodded.

"Papa said you were dangerous and that we weren't to go near you," the boy continued. "But the twins insisted, so I came with them to make sure they didn't bother you."

I pulled myself up to a sitting position, making sure the tee I slept in hadn't ridden up. "And I appreciate that fact, although I'd argue that coming into my room to watch me sleep like something out of a creepy Japanese horror movie isn't the most restful of thoughts."

They all grinned. I was about to reply when I heard raised voices from somewhere nearby, and the sound of running feet on the passage outside my room.

I sighed to myself. "I suspect your absence has been noted."

"Yeah," the boy said, giving his sisters a very pointed look. "That's Papa yelling."

"That's Papa," one of the girls agreed.

"Yelling," the second one said. Then they both whirled and dashed to the door, pausing to bellow, "We're here, Papa! The siren lady is awake now."

"I am so sorry," Allie said, appearing in the doorway, sending a potent glare at her kids before herding them out. "I am mortified that a guest in my home would have to put up with such naughty children. Jakob, you know better! As should your sisters. Your father and I forbade you to disturb Becket."

"I made sure they didn't bother her," the boy protested as his mother more or less shoved him out of the room, just as Christian appeared in the doorway.

If I thought Allie had a glare for her kids, it was nothing compared to him. His eyes damned near glowed silver at the children, his jaw working a few times before he glanced in to me.

"The dragons are waiting for you. Drake's plane is ready to fly to Paris as soon as you have breakfasted."

It was an obvious hint to get moving, and knowing I had no way out but to comply, I nodded and, after spending a minute reassuring Allie that I wasn't in the least bit traumatized by her kids watching me sleep, managed to get a fast shower and make it downstairs fifteen minutes later.

"We flew the kids home last night," Aisling said almost a half hour later as we boarded a sleek-looking private jet at a nearby airport. "Drake was having a hissy fit about the demons being around, and the possibility that some dragons might be working with them, so we thought it better to tuck them away at our Paris house."

"I do not hiss, either in fit form or in a general sense," Drake said as he took a seat next to Aisling. I said nothing when the other dragons filed in after him. I figured they had to be there to protect me in case Candy and Andy figured out where I was.

Christian leaned in through the door and said, "I have contacted a Guardian who is a Beloved. She is on her way here to ensure that no demons blight the castle. If you have need of me in Paris, let me know. I can be there quickly via a portal service."

Drake and the other male dragons all nodded at him.

I stopped Christian before he left. "I hate to ask for a favor, but my bandmates will be at the festival to check out the competition. Can you make sure they're OK? I don't think Candy or Andy would bother them, but—"

"They will come to no harm," he answered, glancing at his watch. "I have spoken to the festival organizers, and they pushed your performance from afternoon to the last slot in the evening. That should give you time to release the dragon and return."

I thanked him, texted Skye an update and reassurance that I would be present for the performance, and then settled in for the short flight to Paris, trying to calm my mind as I worked up a couple of glamours.

"We were thinking that Jim should go with you into the Asile," Aisling said about twenty minutes into the flight. The dragons had been clustered together, talking over the situation.

I stopped the glamour I was tweaking and looked at the dog.

It winked at me.

"Why?" I asked.

"Despite what you may think, Jim can be helpful," Aisling said, giving it a little fondle on the head. "Especially if I give you temporary management of it."

"I suppose that couldn't hurt, although I'm not sure how helpful a demon would be in dog form," I said, studying Jim with some misgivings.

"I can order it to human form," Aisling offered.

Jim made a face, but said nothing.

"You can talk if you have something helpful to say," she told it.

"Man, I really hate it when you do that," it said with a big gulp of air. "It always makes me feel like I can't breathe. Heya, Beckles. You don't want me in human form, do you? 'Cause that always blows."

"No, I don't want you in human form," I said after a moment's thought.

"You don't?" Aisling asked. "If it's the endless, nonstop complaining that Jim is prone to when ordered to human form, you don't have to worry. I'll order it to keep mum about that."

"See?" Jim said, plopping down next to my cushy chair. "Even the Beckster doesn't want me in human form."

"Oh, I do, but not a form you pick," I answered, quickly starting a new glamour.

"Why not?" it asked, leaning against my leg, leaving a slime trail on the black leggings I wore with a tank top and open gauze tunic decorated with colorful Peruvian animal art.

"Jim! I'm so sorry, Becket," Aisling said, snatching up a cloth and mopping up my leg before ordering her dog to go sit in a dog bed placed at the rear of the plane.

"The answer is because you are a demon, and people versed in demons—as I assume the guards at the Asile will be—would recognize any form you take as being demonic in nature. They won't see through the glamour I make for you, though," I answered, my hands dancing in the air as I took bits of energy that drifted around all living things, and bound it into the glamour.

"Oooh, smart thinking," Ysolde said, and, after a look at her husband, added, "Baltic and I had a thought this morning about how to get you into the Asile place."

"I figured I'd just use a glamour, too," I said with a little shrug, tucking away Jim's glamour to make a backup for myself. I preferred to have a selection available should I need to get away from anyone who posed a danger to me. "They won't see through it, I assure you."

"Yes, but you still have to have a reason to get inside," Ysolde said.

"Oh, I see what you mean—that even if Becket wears one of her awesome glamours, the guards might not let her in unless she has a reason?" May said, glancing around at the other dragons. "Should we brainstorm some ideas?"

"You don't need to," Ysolde said, smiling at her dragon. "Baltic had an excellent suggestion: that we make you—temporarily—the weyr representative to the Otherworld."

"And a weyr is … ?" I asked, finishing the glamour.

"The collective of dragon septs," Ysolde answered, picking up her phone. "Damn. Brom says he and Pixie just caught sight of a demon at the festival. Ah, there's a text from Allie saying the same thing, but that the vamps had captured the demon and destroyed its form. Evidently it was a lesser type."

I had a moment of feeling bound tightly, so constricted I couldn't draw a breath. There were more demons after me? My stomach turned over, making me thankful I had forgone breakfast.

"I'm glad the demon wasn't a big deal, but holy crapballs, that's brilliant, Ysolde," Aisling said as the male dragons all looked thoughtful, all but Baltic, who wore what I was coming to think of as his standard enigmatic expression. "The bit about Becket being a rep, not the demon."

"Why is it brilliant?" I asked, rubbing a growing headache at the back of my head.

"Because Yrian's a dragon," she answered, looking pleased. "It makes absolute sense for our rep to make sure he's being treated well. But can we do that? Doesn't it take a *sárkány*—that's a weyr meeting, Becket—to designate someone?"

"We can do it with a simple majority vote," Drake said, glancing at the other two wyverns. They nodded, and Drake tapped on his phone before saying, "Kostya agrees to the temporary change. If Becket is willing, then we can proceed without any further issue."

"I'm not sure what your rep is supposed to do," I said seven minutes later, after I swore to champion all things dragon to the L'au-dela, and was duly appointed as their ambassador. "But if you think the people at the Asile won't kick up a fuss about it, then I'll do my best."

"You can go in without a glamour," Aisling said, glancing at my hair. I was currently wearing an appearance that closely favored my Spanish mother. "Just in case they can tell that you have one on, that is."

"They won't," I said, not in the least bit worried about anyone detecting my true self. "I used to make glamours for the Sovereign to wear in Abaddon, and she said no one ever saw through them."

"You're the one who did that?" May asked, looking astounded. "I always wondered how Sally could march around being a demon lord without anyone noticing that she was also one-half of the Sovereign."

"So, you'll go in as yourself, our ambassador, and Jim will help in whatever glamour you put on it," Aisling said, giving her demon dog a meaningful look. "We'll wait outside the Asile in case you need help once you get Yrian out, and to keep any demons away should they find out where you are. Does that sound right to everyone?"

Murmurs of agreement drifted around the plane. There was a little discussion as we circled Paris before landing, but as it was mostly logistics of travel, and the dragons organizing protection of me from Candy and Andy, I didn't pay it much mind.

I did approve, however, when two redheaded men met us at the plane, both of them positively bristling with swords, morning stars, and a couple of big battle-axes, passing them out to the dragons.

"Is something wrong?" The question, offered in a soft voice, dragged me out of the contemplation I'd fallen into on the two-hour drive to the building known to the Otherworld as the Asile. May, who sat opposite me in a lovely antique Rolls that belonged to Drake and Aisling, looked concerned as she continued. "I'm sorry if I was disturbing your concentration, but you look upset, and I wondered if you were worried about us protecting you."

"No, I'm not upset. Just mulling over everything in my mind." I sorted through my thoughts, my fingers absently starting another glamour, this one a backup for Jim. I was a big believer in backups. "Am I correct in thinking that Yrian has a lot of power?"

Silence fell in the car, with just about everyone looking at Baltic.

He raised one eyebrow, but said nothing.

"Please don't make me elbow you in front of everyone," Ysolde told him.

His lips twitched.

"You're a big boy, Baltic," Aisling said, one possessive hand on her dragon's thigh. "I think you'll survive doling out a little info."

He looked like he wanted to dispute that fact, but after a moment of looking profoundly martyred, he said, "He is the first of the Firstborn, son of a fury and a demigod. He has power, yes."

"Iceni was a fury?" Ysolde asked him, looking surprised.

"Who—" I started to ask.

"Iceni was the First Dragon's mate, and mom to all the Firstborn children other than Baltic, whose mom was a dragon," May told me.

"That is not correct," Baltic said, his expression now thoughtful, as well. "Yrian and ... another of the Firstborn were the children of a fury. The First Dragon was with her before he found Iceni, who bore two more sons and a daughter."

"A fury? Those aren't around anymore, are they?" Aisling asked Drake, who shook his head.

"Not in the mortal world, no. I assume they are in the Beyond or some underworld," he answered.

The dragons continued discussing that while I considered my options. I waited until there was a break in the conversation before saying, "My concern is not so much with who Yrian's mother was, but whether or not he had the sort of power that meant I couldn't easily hide his essence, if you will. Beings of power are harder to glamour."

"You just said no one could detect your glamour," Gabriel said with a little frown.

"I said the people at the Asile wouldn't be able to do so, but I am not the son of a demigod and a fury, with what I can only imagine is a lot of power of his own. I'm concerned that if he's all that and a pickle on the side, then someone devoted to security might be aware that a being of unusual abilities was hidden by the glamour," I explained.

"But you did just fine with Sally," May protested. "Like you mentioned—no one in Abaddon ever caught on to her true self, and she had a crap ton of power at that time."

"Yes, but she gave me a fetish." I dug through my memories of ten years or so in the past. "I drew on that when creating the glamours, and that gave both it and Sally the oomph she needed to pass as a demon lord. I don't suppose any of you have something like a talisman or juju owned by Yrian?"

No one answered me.

"I didn't think so," I said on a sigh, and looked out of the window at the passing scenery. We were well and truly in the French countryside now, with the sun pouring down onto red-tile-roofed villages, crumbling châteaus, and verdant hills spilling down to silvery rivers.

As we curled around a road that wound upward, I realized the cream stone building that sat atop had to be the Asile itself.

"That doesn't look like a mental hospital," Aisling said as everyone peered out at the building when we crested the hill and pulled into a cobblestoned parking area. "It looks like Drake's château in the south."

"I assume it was a château before the Committee took it over for the L'au-dela," Drake answered, holding out a hand for Aisling as we all piled out of the car. "Nonetheless, I believe the artificer has a point."

I got out slowly, feeling like I had ants crawling all over my skin. I recognized a particular symptom common to artificers, and moved around so that the car was between me and the building, the urge inside me building until I knew I had to do something.

"Becket?" May asked, glancing toward me.

"Sorry. I have to discharge," I told them, with a deep breath, focused. "I'll try to do it quietly. Just ignore me for a few minutes."

"Discharge what?" I heard Ysolde asking as I closed my eyes for a moment, allowing the music that always seemed to be simmering in the back of my head to come forward.

My brain randomly picked a song that had sufficient energy to let me discharge the buildup of magic that was inherent to weaving so many glamours in a short amount of time.

The music crashed over me, and I started singing softly to myself, my body moving to a stomping beat that I found most efficient for this purpose.

For the next three minutes, the only sound was the distant drone of traffic, chattering birds, my whispered song, and the occasional scuff of my shoes on cobblestones as I danced out my discomfort. I kept my gaze on a tree in the distance, forcing the buildup of magic out of me and back into the world, where it would rebind itself with the life force of living things.

"Is she singing 'Run the World'?" I heard Aisling ask Ysolde.

"I think so. She's very good at dancing. I wonder if she knows that ballerina who helped us out with Jim's parents," she answered.

"She even sounds like Beyoncé," May told her dragon. "This is amazing. I wonder if I should film it for Charity?"

I lifted a hand to shake it at May before finishing up the discharge (and song). Thankfully, she understood and put away the phone she'd pulled out.

The ladies sang the last chorus with me when I shook out the remnants of the magic buildup.

"It's too bad Becket isn't a dragon," Jim said when I turned back, feeling much more like I could cope with life. "If she was, she could join the Mates Union, and you could have a girl band."

"I already have a band," I said, giving everyone a rueful smile. "Sorry about that. Singing always helps me focus, and moving my body lets me purge the extra magic that builds up when I create glamours. Is that ... is that what I think it is?"

The dragons, who had all been facing me as I did my little song and dance, turned back toward the Asile. We were parked at the narrow end of the building, one that consisted of a covered entrance, double Gothic-arched doors, and, higher up, narrow windows that looked like they had the original glass still installed.

But it was the darkness that oozed around the corner that stopped me cold. I realized after a moment of staring at it that it was a being.

A cowled and faceless being, extremely tall and draped in black flowing garments that seemed to move without any help from a passing breeze, headed toward us. The terror that rolled off it had me fighting to keep from bolting down the winding road.

"Oh lord. Hashmallim," Aisling said, taking a step closer to Drake. "Er ... do we say hello?"

"Absolutely not," he said, moving in front of her, obviously blocking the Hashmallim from seeing her. "We have nothing to do with them other than bringing the weyr ambassador here."

That was my cue, but I really didn't want to step up to the big scary dark thing. I reminded myself that there was nothing it could do to me (other than possibly scaring me to death) and, steeling my shattered nerves, slowly made my way to the entrance where the Hashmallim lurked.

"I am Becket, the dragon ambassador to the L'au-dela. I wish to see Yrian Shadowsworn, a dragon you have in your custody," I told it.

Little bits of its gauze robe drifted, reaching out as if to touch me. I stepped back and, channeling my mother at her most arrogant, lifted my chin and tried hard to send a scathing look down the length of my nose.

"You are no dragon," came a voice from the blackness inside the cowl. It sounded like rocks grating on other rocks, making me want to rub my arms against the goose bumps that blossomed in response.

"I don't have to be," I said, repeating the excuse that had been discussed on the flight to France. "I am recognized by the weyr as being their representative, and as such, I have the right to ascertain the welfare of Yrian Shadowsworn. You will take me to him immediately."

The Hashmallim said nothing for a minute, but its form moved in a way that had me thinking it was considering the dragons, all of whom had formed a semicircle behind me.

"Wait," was all it said before it drifted to the doors, disappearing inside with an almost silent *whoosh*.

I slumped, clutching a bit of wall, feeling like I'd just run a marathon. "I feel like I'm made of pasta. Soggy pasta," I said, turning back to the others.

"Don't blame you. The Hashies are masters of intimidation. But if you sing 'My Humps' to them for thirty-six hours straight, they'll cave. Well, most of them. There's a couple that I don't think can be broken," Jim said.

"Do you want to put Jim's glamour on now?" Aisling asked, casting a nervous glance at the door. "Maybe we should go to the other side of the car, so anyone who's looking out won't see."

"I'm thinking not," I said, following when she moved around the car and, with a few words, and a ward drawn on my hand, gave me temporary powers over her demon.

"No talking unless it helps Becket," Aisling told the demon, giving it a swift pat. "Be as helpful as you can, and yes, that's an order."

Jim rolled its eyes, but said nothing.

"I guess we'll give this a go," I said, squaring my shoulders.

"One minute," Baltic said, tucking away his phone.

Beyond him, light seemed to gather like a mass of tiny fireflies, forming itself into the shape of a man who stepped forward with a frown directed at me. "You are correct."

"OK," I said, more than a little startled by the First Dragon's statement. "Er … about what, exactly?"

"You will need this." He brushed his thumb across a spot on my forehead, then disappeared in another sparkle of fireflies.

"Holy *merde*," Aisling said, her eyes huge as she stared at me. "That's the First Dragon's … what, personal blessing?"

"I guess so." I rubbed at the spot on my forehead. It felt a little hot, but didn't hurt. In fact, the warmth from it seemed to be seeping downward through me, filling me with a sense of confidence.

"He did the same thing to me a few years ago, when Baltic and I found each other again," Ysolde said. "It's definitely his blessing."

"That's good, because I'm going to need the oomph." I shot a quick glance toward the entrance, and made a sudden decision. "Since a Hashmallim has already seen Jim, we'll try this with it in its natural form."

The dragons didn't like that much, but when the Hashmallim reappeared, they said nothing. Big Scary was accompanied by a blond woman in an impossibly crisp white doctor's coat. The Hashmallim moved off the way it had come, disappearing around the side of the building as the woman approached me, a tablet in her hand.

"I am Dr. Debruin. I understand you wish to see one of our patients?" she asked, tapping on the tablet as she spoke. "You are the dragon representative?"

"I am," I said, gesturing toward the others. "Newly appointed, but as you can see, I am here with the full authority of the weyr. Please take me to Yrian Shadowsworn so that I may verify he is receiving proper treatment."

Her lips thinned. "Now is not convenient. The patient is scheduled to be removed in"—she consulted her watch—"approximately forty minutes. You should apply to the Court of Divine Blood for permission to visit him once he has been placed into their custody."

"That is not acceptable," I said, and, without looking at either the dragons or their demon, gave a toss of my head and strolled through the doorway. "I do not have time to waste waiting for others. Jim, heel."

"I'm afraid—" the woman started to say, but by then Jim and I were inside, and she had little choice but to follow us.

The entrance was a narrow hallway that opened up into what must have been the original reception room, with a gray marble floor, paneled walls bearing somewhat tatty-looking tapestries, and a split staircase that curved upward to the landing above. A heavy table sat to the right of the room, occupied by a young man who typed industriously on a laptop.

"Madame!" the blonde doctor protested as I stopped at the foot of the staircase. "It really is not an opportune moment, as I have just told you. The patient will be moved shortly—"

"That leaves ample time for me to check on him," I interrupted with a ruthlessness that had me mentally squirming with discomfort. "I assume his room is upstairs?"

Dr. Debruin evidently had enough of me, because she thinned her lips, crossed her arms, and said, "Yes, but I'm not going to tell you which room."

"That's OK," I said with a little smile, and started up the stairs, with Jim on my heels. "I have Jim. Can you find the room containing Yrian?"

"Sure, unless this place is loaded with dragons," it answered, and hurried up the stairs, its tail waving happily as I raced after it. We both ignored the protestations of Dr. Debruin, although I did whisper to Jim, "We'd better be quick. I have a feeling she's going to call in those Hashmallim dudes to give us the boot."

"It's OK—he's down here," Jim answered, galloping down a long carpeted hall. One side of it was a bank of windows that looked out onto the valley below, while the other was lined with doors bearing discreet signs with names.

Jim stopped before a door that was so heavily scribed with wards and other protections, I was astounded it could be opened.

"*Mierda,*" I swore, wondering if I could put on a fast will glamour that would make the angry doctor open the door.

"Dude," Jim said in a near drawl, tipping its head as it looked at me.

"What?" I asked, looking from it to the door.

It said nothing, and I had a faint memory of the laws concerning demons. "Demon Jim, I command you to answer my questions."

It heaved a dramatic sigh, and I swear I heard it mutter something about Aisling not being the only clueless person around. "Take a closer look at those wards."

Another profanity was on the tip of my tongue, but I bit it back. "Look, we don't have time for this—"

"They keep the person in the room from leaving ... not anyone from getting in," it pointed out with a cocked eyebrow.

I looked back at the door. Dammit, the demon was right. It wasn't even locked, since obviously the people in charge at the Asile relied upon magic to keep their occupants contained. "Stupid, stupid people," I murmured as I opened the door and looked inside.

I don't know what I expected to see, perhaps a drooping man with the long hair and beard of someone who'd been deemed crazy and locked away, but the man who was in the act of striding across the room, his hands busy as he sketched spells in the air, fire trailing behind him, was not that. Not at all.

He spun around, his eyes glowing golden just as the First Dragon's had earlier.

He also had a stripe of white in his dark hair, but rather than his hair being a tangled mess, it was cut short in a style that I connected to the 1930s, the front part of it swooping back in a slight wave that made something in my stomach tighten.

"Who are you?" he asked, spinning around to face me, his dark brown brows pulled together in a truly magnificent scowl. His eyes narrowed on me. "You are no dragon, yet you bear the mark of the First Dragon."

I shot a fast glance down the long hallway. Noises could be heard coming up from the stairs.

"No, I'm not, but they sent me to get you out, and we have to be really quick because that sounds like one of those terrifying Hashmallim on its way. Stand still so I can apply this glamour on you."

He shook his head as I gathered up the glamour I'd made for him, holding it for a moment and imbuing into it the warmth of the dragon blessing before tossing it on him.

Or rather, I tried. The glamour didn't leave my hand.

"You better hurry up. That's not just one Hashie—it's a whole herd of them," Jim warned, backing up until I was between it and the landing.

I examined the glamour, but nothing seemed amiss with it, so I tried again to fling it on Yrian.

It refused to be applied.

"Shit," I said, looking to the left when a wave of terror rolled down the hallway. Dark shapes appeared and started oozing toward us.

"You can't apply glamours here," Yrian said, his eyes still narrowed, glittering like gold in the noonday sun. His lips twisted as he gestured toward the wall. "They've made sure of that."

"Come on, then," I said, holding out one hand while my other started drawing a will glamour that I hoped would allow us past the Hashmallim.

"I can't. I've tried. They've warded the space," he said on a near snarl, the fire that had been following him now a pool at his feet.

Panic rode me hard. I glanced toward the Hashmallim—three of them—as they approached, and made a snap decision. I leaned forward, saying softly, "I'll be back. Don't lose hope," before I closed the door and spun around to face the three horrors.

"I told you that now was not convenient," came the terse voice of Dr. Debruin, who moved into view when the three Hashmallim circled Jim and me. "You will leave now!"

"Fine," I said, wishing they were looking elsewhere so I could slap on my will glamour. "But the weyr will lodge a formal complaint with the Committee about this treatment. I am an official ambassador! I will not tolerate such actions against the dragonkin!"

I stepped forward, praying to any deity who was around that the nearest Hashmallim let me pass, and to my great relief, it did, but only once I was close enough for several strands of its garment to reach out for me.

I slapped them away, trying to glare into the blackness in the cowl where its face should be, before snapping an order to Jim to follow me.

We made it outside before I had to stop and double over, my stomach revolting against the absolute wrongness of the Hashmallim.

"Where's Yrian?" I heard Aisling ask as the dragons gathered around me.

"We have to leave," I said as soon as I was sure I wouldn't vomit, looking at Drake. "Do you have another car here?"

His gaze sharpened on me for a few seconds before he answered, "In this town? No. But I can procure one."

"Do it. Something a big shot would use." I looked back at the entrance of the Asile, but the doors remained shut. "And we're going to need it in the next ten minutes."

I don't know how he did it, but by the time we had all piled back into the car, driven down the hill to the valley below, and made it to the nearest town, a sleek black sedan zoomed out to meet us.

Jim filled everyone in on the ride to the car while I madly created two more glamours, pulling hard on the dragon blessing to give them extra wattage.

"Right. This is going to be a bit dicey, but it's the only thing I can think of. I'd suggest you meet us back at the Asile in five minutes. That's about as long as my glamour is going to last in a place so heavily warded against magic," I told the dragons as Jim and I climbed into the back of the sedan. One of the redheaded bodyguards took up the position as driver.

"I'm amazed you can do anything in there if it's as impossible as Jim says," Aisling commented, giving her demon another pat on the head. "Just don't do anything dangerous."

"Yeah, I got my coat into peak condition, and I'd hate to get it scorched or anything," Jim said from where it stepped on the window's button, and stuck its head outside.

"Fingers crossed, everyone," I said, trying to summon up enough concentration to craft a will glamour that would ensure everyone in the Asile would not think twice about fulfilling my orders and commands, even if only for a short time.

"Man, if you're gonna rely on superstition—" Jim started to say, but stopped when I turned in the seat and tossed the glamour on him.

The driver jerked the wheel in response to the back seat suddenly being filled with a Hashmallim, but luckily, Jim's voice emerging from the depths of the horror had him pulling back onto the road, and zooming up the hill. "Dude! You Hashied me? Where's my package? Aw, man, I don't even have hands in this form! I'm just all black ooze and emptiness."

"No speaking unless you can do a tolerable impression of rocks grinding on each other tinged with enough horror to make a slasher-movie fan delirious with joy. Hang tight, driver, another glamour incoming."

The redhead cast a wary glance in the rearview mirror, but said nothing when I slid the second glamour on myself.

"Niiiice," Jim drawled as we stopped before the entrance to the Asile.

"I sure hope so, because otherwise, I'm out of ideas."

Fortunately, no one was present to see Hashmallim Jim emerge from the car, and at a gesture from me, it moved over to the corner of the building where I'd seen the first one. I pounded on the door, tightening the glamour until it sank into my head and neck, allowing my very atoms to be changed by it.

"Dr. Kostich!" Surprise flashed over the face of Dr. Debruin as she opened the door, her eyes puzzled until Jim glided over to loom behind me. "You're early."

"I've heard a rumor there are dragons in the area," I said, hoping the glamour got the cadence of Dr. Kostich's voice correct. I'd only seen videos of him before now, but knew the will glamour should smooth over any minor defects in my impersonation. Accordingly, I pushed past the doctor and entered the building, striding to the hall as I tossed orders over my shoulder. "I want the documents pertaining to this troublesome dragon. Where is he? Hashmallim—fetch the prisoner. You, guard, take a group to search the grounds and verify no one is lurking thereabouts. I wouldn't put it past the dragons to try to rescue their dangerous kin. Why are you still standing here? Go fetch the documents! The Court won't accept him without the transfer order."

Behind my back, I applied the will glamour, a little skitter of nerves causing me a moment of doubt, but that was eased when the doctor, with a slightly glazed look to her eyes, murmured something about fetching the paperwork from her office. She scurried off to do so before I bent Dr. Kostich's eye on the guard who stood at the reception desk. One raised eyebrow was all it took before he left to do as I ordered.

A faint machinelike drone drifted down the stairs from the floors above, no doubt from the cleaning staff. I waited until the guard disappeared outside before bolting for the stairs, Hashmallim Jim hot on my heels. As we reached the top and turned to go down the passage where Yrian was held, I stopped in surprise.

Half of one of the walls was completely destroyed. And then there was the fact that the entire hallway was on fire.

"Is that—" I started to ask.

"Yup. Dragon fire. Looks like Yrian didn't want to wait around for you. He must have let off a doozy of a blast to destroy his room like that."

Just as it spoke, a loud siren sounded from below at the same time a gaggle of people in white coats emerged at the opposite end.

"Where is the prisoner?" I bellowed to them, not trusting the dragon fire.

"He is trapped below, in the ballroom," one of them called back, moving aside as a new person arrived with a fire extinguisher. "The Hashmallim are just outside, though."

I didn't wait to find out more. I spun on my heels and raced back down the stairs, turning to follow the hallway that led off at right angles.

A second siren joined the first, making my head hurt from the tone and decibels, but Jim and I ran along the building, throwing open doors as we passed. Another group of people was huddled in one of the offices, shrieking when I flung their door open.

"Where is the dragon?" I snarled, feeling Dr. Kostich was the sort of person who did that sort of thing when he was thwarted.

One of the women pointed to the right.

"Stay here where you're safe," I yelled, and dashed off to jerk open a set of double doors. Inside, Yrian was wielding a chair like it was a weapon, fending off two Hashmallim, the room also alight with fire.

I was about to yell for the Hashmallim to back off, but at that moment, Yrian—with a battle cry that raised the fine hairs on the back of my neck—lunged forward and slammed a wall of fire into the nearest Hashmallim, causing it to reel backward.

"Jim, get the one on the right," I yelled, and ran forward, pulling every last bit of power that I could out of the life force of beings around us, and from the dragon blessing, blasting the two Hashmallim with it. One of them, the one Yrian had attacked, went down with a screeching cry that damn near made the skin crawl off my body. Its terrifying form melted into nothing and disappeared, leaving behind only a small mound of gray ash.

Yrian turned to see who was helping him, and stumbled at the sight of Jim and me, but I could feel his gaze on my forehead for a second before he turned back to the remaining Hashmallim.

"Again!" he commanded, and lowered his head as he raised his hands, obviously gathering his own power.

I gave a quick assessment to my skills and staggered forward a few steps, trying to gather to me enough power to destroy the Hashmallim's form, but my body felt boneless and hollow.

Jim rushed past me to obey my order, but I caught at its sleeve, pulling it toward me despite my mind shrieking warnings. "I have to break your form. I'm sorry," I told it, ignoring the jerk back it made as I did something I've only done twice before—I smashed the glamour to smithereens, thereby releasing the energy stored within it.

For a second, Jim reverted back to its doggy form, its eyes huge, and then it was gone, leaving an oily black mark on the ground. I made a mental promise to apologize later, but first ...

The Hashmallim lunged at Yrian, sending him flying backward through the wall into the room beyond. I made a leap I hadn't known I was capable of performing, but before I could reach the Yrian-shaped hole in the wall, he reappeared, now in the shape of a dragon covered in scales that seemed at first to be a dark gray, but the light shifted along them in a way that reminded me of water on the black sand beaches of Hawaii. I stood mesmerized for a few seconds before I remembered we were in a fight for Yrian's life.

The fact that he had destroyed the form of a Hashmallim was astounding. That he should have enough power to take out a second one alone was out of the question. I quickly spun the energy from Jim's glamour into one that would make the Hashmallim compliant, and just as Yrian rushed the Hashmallim, a massive explosion of fire bursting around and through us, I flung the glamour.

The Hashmallim stopped moving, frozen.

"Quickly!" I yelled at Yrian, who paused in midstride, confusion crawling across his dragon face. "That's not going to hold for long, because I'm about out of energy. We have to get out of here."

"That's exactly what I was doing," Yrian snarled, but, to my relief, followed when I lurched toward the door, begging my legs to hang in there long enough for us to get to the car.

He must have noticed, because when I stumbled and went to my knees, he scooped me up with one arm, clamping me to his side and more than half dragging me down the hallway to the entrance.

Voices yelled over the continuing sound of the sirens, and people scattered as we headed for the exit, where a number of people were rushing about, waving hands, and crying for explanations.

Yrian didn't so much as slow down—he simply plowed through the people, scattering them like bowling pins.

"There's a car outside for us," I managed to get out as I freed myself from his hold, yanking open the door. "It'll take us to your—"

The words stopped at the sight that met our eyes. The entire parking area seemed to be filled with people—mostly dragons—along with four different Hashmallim, a handful of human guards, and what I figured were a couple of mages, since they stood in the back and were flinging balls of arcane at the dragons.

To my surprise, Ysolde was doing the same to the mages, although hers seemed a bit off, since halfway to the target, her arcany changed into bananas, a couple of grapefruit, and even a pineapple.

Her husband held a sword in one hand and was throwing arcane blasts at the mages with the other.

"I thought dragons couldn't use arcane magic?" I couldn't help but ask as Yrian swore and shifted into human form.

"Firstborn can," was all he said before he started forward toward the nearest Hashmallim.

"No, no, no," I said quickly, and grabbed at his shirt, taking us both by surprise by using his momentum to send him swinging to the side toward the sedan. "I'm not going through this again. We have to get you away before more Hashmallim come!"

"My kin need me," Yrian snapped, twisting around to try to pry my hands off his shirt. "I will not abandon them."

"I do not have the time for you to be all heroic and shit," I said in a near snarl, slamming him with a great big impulse push. Although I wasn't a full-blooded siren, I had a sometimes tenuous grasp on mental pushes, and I pushed now like I'd never pushed before.

Yrian glared at me. "Stop yelling in my head! Release me so that I might aid my kin."

"Not now," I yelled, shoving him another three steps until we were at the car.

"Go!" I heard Baltic yell, his head turned toward us. "Get him out of here!"

"You heard the man—oh, no, not now."

A car crested the hill and pulled up alongside the sedan, a man emerging from it with a disbelieving expression that turned to outright confusion when he turned from watching the dragons battle the Hashmallim—they had one destroyed, but the other three didn't look like they were going anywhere soon—to Yrian and me.

Dr. Kostich blinked twice at the sight of us; then his face screwed up in anger and he started shouting orders.

I didn't wait. I hit Yrian both with the will glamour I'd been automatically weaving since we left the Asile and with every last ounce of dragon power I held, sending him staggering forward into the car and onto the back seat. I pushed him until he doubled up, slamming closed the door before flinging myself into the driver's seat.

"Stop him! Stop that pretender! He is not me and he is taking the insane dragon!" Dr. Kostich yelled, but at that moment, a banana struck him on the side of his head.

I jammed my foot on the accelerator, mentally thanking the redheaded dragon for turning the car so it was ready to leave, and was halfway down the hill, fishtailing madly, when Yrian managed to get himself upright.

"Woman!" he bellowed, filling the car with fire. "Stop this vehicle! I have never run from a fight, and I will not start now!"

"You're not running; you're escaping, you idiot! And a whole lot of people, including your dad, went to a great deal of trouble to make this happen, so stop trying to climb into the front seat. You're going to make us crash if you try that again."

He stopped attempting to take hold of the steering wheel, but managed to get himself into the front seat next to me without actually sending us plowing off the road into the granite wall of a cliff that lined part of the road down. "Why did you have a demon pretending to be a Hashmallim? And who are you?"

"Becket," I said, spinning the wheel when two more cars careened up the road, one of them slamming on its brakes as we sped past.

"Is that your surname or first name?" he asked.

"First name. Can you get rid of this fire, please? It's kind of irritating, and I wouldn't want it to make the gas tank explode."

Yrian shot me an oddly calculating look for a few seconds before glancing at my legs and feet, which were covered in dragon fire. It died down to nothing just as we reached the bottom of the hill, but the screeching sound of a car trying to make a U-turn on a narrow road hadn't escaped me.

"Do not give me commands," Yrian said in a grumpy tone that somehow made me want to laugh. He shot a look behind us, his jaw working. "I do not run from battle."

"I'm sure you don't under normal circumstances, but this isn't your fight. Your relatives will be OK. They assured me they have a treaty with the L'au-dela, so they won't be harmed. I sure hope there are no mortal police on this road."

"Why?" he asked, facing forward again.

"Because we're going to break a whole hell of a lot of speeding laws," I answered, following a windy bit of the road with reckless speed. Ahead of us a few miles away, the town sat on the edge of a river.

Unfortunately, the two cars that had been going to the Asile were hot on our tail, and evidently, their cars had more power than ours, since they were creeping closer with each passing minute.

"Where are you taking me?"

"Paris." I tightened my fingers on the steering wheel as we came to a straight stretch of the road, pushing the car to speeds I would never even think of approaching under normal circumstances. "Your family said that if the worst happened, there's a portal shop in the town ahead of us. It's going to be tight, but we should make it before Dr. Kostich and his friends realize where we're going."

"Paris?" Yrian sat back, and to my surprise smiled. "Excellent. I will wreak my revenge there."

I swore to myself, wondering if getting Candy and Andy off my case would be worth getting tangled up with dragons.

SEVEN
YRIAN

"Effrijim, I summon thee."

Yrian emerged from the toilet to find the woman named Becket standing in the waiting room of the small and dingy portal shop to which she'd driven him, obviously summoning the demon who had accompanied her into the Asile. He had no idea why she thought a demon could be of assistance, but was willing to let that point pass, assuming she gave him answers to the questions that were even now plaguing him.

"Woman," he said in preparation for unburdening his curiosity.

"Dude," she said in a drawling tone that prickled along his skin like several small burrs. "I have a name. It's Becket."

He gave her his loftiest look, one that used to leave youngling dragons cowering in terror. No, he corrected himself the second the thought flitted across his mind. Not cowering. Dragons did not cower. Stepped back deferentially, that was more like it. "Your name is odd. Is it even a woman's name?"

"Oh, you do not want to pull the weird-ass name card, *Yrian*," she snapped back, giving him an insolent look in return. Not even the oldest of his kin had ever done so. Only the First Dragon subjected him to such things, and this woman, this artificer who bore the First Dragon's mark, certainly was not qualified to treat him thusly. "And if you really want to get into a discussion about the patriarchy's view on feminine names, and why it's misogynistic, I will, but it's going to have to wait until this demon is summoned. Effrijim, I summon thee. *Again.*"

"Why are you summoning it? And how does this portal work?" Yrian had moved across the room to stare into a dimly lit smaller room dominated by a mass of twisting black and purple that seemed to float in midair. "We did not have such things in my time, although I understand much has changed since then."

Becket gave him a considering look as she moved over next to him to peer into the room. "It'll take us wherever there's another portal shop. The green dragons say you are welcome to stay with them in Paris, so that's where you're going. Dammit, where is that portal operator? The assistant said he was just around the corner, but it's been three minutes, and Dr. Kostich is sure to guess we're going here. Gah! It's already almost two. I have to get back to Brno in the next hour, or we'll miss our rehearsal spot."

As she spoke, she glanced at a small phone device similar to one Yrian's youngest brother had given him, but it had been destroyed when he exploded the room in which he'd been held captive.

He regretted the loss of the device, having enjoyed it greatly—especially the many videos of cats dancing—although he didn't quite understand the type of magic that fueled it.

"I wish to have another phone device," he told Becket, ignoring her question, since he had no knowledge of the portal operator. "You will help me find a purveyor of the Internet magic so that he can create a new one for me."

"I mean, how long does it take to get a freakin' sandwich? Effrijim! For all that's good and green, I summon you! Wait, what? Internet magic?" Becket stopped frowning at the portal and turned it on him instead. "Just how long have you been outside of the mortal plane?"

"The First Dragon says it has been sixteen hundred years, although I have difficulty believing that. It seems like twelve hundred, at best."

She blinked a couple of times at him, drawing his attention to her eyes. They were large, and a delightful shade of blue that made him very aware of her female self. "OK. I guess some things in modern life would seem like magic to you, but I can assure you that cell phones aren't made up of anything but metal, plastic, and glass. Stay here. I'm going to make sure Dr. Kostich isn't outside waiting to pounce. Effrijim!"

She hurried out of the room, trying to summon the demon again.

Yrian pursed his lips prefatory to considering his next move, but at that moment, the demon dog popped into the room with him, shaking before it sat down and tipped its head as it studied him.

"Heya," it said.

"A demon is of no help to me," he told it by way of a greeting.

"Yeah, lots of people say that, but then something happens, and whammo, yours truly is suddenly your best friend. Where'd Beckers go?"

"*Becket,*" he said, annoyed with the flip way the demon referred to her—and ignoring the fact that a minute ago he'd questioned her name—"is getting the portal operator. Ah. That must be him. What practice are you conducting?"

The last question was asked of Becket, who had returned accompanied by a slight man with brilliant green hair, bits of metal piercing many spots on his face and ears, and a parrot perched on his shoulder.

"Huh? Oh, it's my band's practice. Jim! There you are. I've been summoning you for the last five minutes. I assume you'll travel with Yrian through the portal. We've got to hurry. I paid Simon here to close up the shop for lunch, but that's only fifteen minutes more, so we need to get Yrian to safety, and my butt to the Czech Republic, before our time is up. I don't trust that Dr. Kostich further than I could hurl a behemoth."

"He gets pissy about things like prisoners escaping," Jim said, nodding.

"You're a dragon?" the green-haired Simon asked Yrian, squinting at him in a way that had Yrian straightening his shoulders.

"I am Yrian Shadowsworn, the Firstborn," he said simply, allowing a little of his fire to escape, stifling the flinch of pain that always accompanied such things.

"OK, but …" Simon's face screwed up as he obviously thought. "Dragons don't do well portaling, right? At least, that's what the ones that use the Paris shop say. I used to work there until they opened a new one because the old portal collapsed on itself. They always had some special wine for the dragons that came through."

"Dragon's blood," Yrian said absently, his gaze on Becket.

He had to admit, it wasn't hard at all to look at her, not once she'd removed the glamour of the mad mage Kostich. She had copious amount of curves, a heavily freckled heart-shaped face that made him feel things he hadn't felt for many hundreds of years, and a quirky mind that he admitted held him highly intrigued.

"That's the stuff. You got any on you?" Simon asked them.

"No. I had no idea you needed wine, or I would have mentioned it to the dragons," Becket answered, glancing behind her nervously as if she expected to see the mage burst into the room. "Is it vital? That is, can you send Yrian through without it?"

"I like dragon's blood," Yrian told Jim.

"Yeah, Ash always keeps a few bottles in the London, Paris, and Budapest portal shops just in case they have to use them," it answered, nodding and snuffling Simon's shoes.

"As it happens, I have half a bottle that was left by some blue dragons the last time they came through," Simon said, turning around and heading for the outer room. "I can get it if you like."

"Hurry, please," Becket told him, glancing again at her phone. "I just hope your dad and the vampires cleared the area."

"Paris?" Yrian asked, confused. He didn't like the emotion. "Why would Dark Ones be helping the First Dragon? Dragonkin do not involve ourselves with them."

"Maybe you didn't in the past, but you do now. Or at least, a few of your family members do so. And I wasn't talking about Paris. My band—musical band—is playing in a town named Brno in the Czech Republic. Your father and I made an agreement whereby I'd get you out of the Asile, and he'd make sure your family members force a couple of demons to leave me alone."

For a moment, a pang of guilt stabbed deep into Yrian's gut. That others—most notably the First Dragon—had to intercede on his behalf was galling. He was the Firstborn! He needed aid from no one!

That thought died even before it was fully formed. Obviously, he very much did need aid, since he hadn't been able to get himself out of the Asile prison. "Although I would have, in time," he said aloud.

"Would have what?" Becket asked, tapping on her phone, no doubt sending one of the sorts of messages that took him an entire two weeks to master.

"Escaped the prison. Why are demons bothering you?" He cast a pointed look toward Jim, whose eyes grew round as it scooted behind Becket.

"Given that you more or less blew out a heavily magicked wall that should have been impervious to your powers, I can see where you feel like that. And the demons were sent by a demon lord."

He just looked at her, waiting.

She apparently understood, because she made a *tsk*ing noise and put away her phone. "I'm an artificer savant. Everyone wants me, and yes, I realize that makes me sound horribly conceited, but that's why demons are tracking me. There were two in Brno that are particularly difficult to avoid, and I just hope they haven't come back."

"They're wrathies. They'll be back," Jim said, absently sucking a tooth as it glanced around the room.

"Wrath demons seek you?" Yrian asked, a swell of emotion taking him by surprise. He suddenly found himself enraged on her behalf. How dare demons bother her? She had clearly devoted herself to helping others, and what was her payment for such kindness? Demonic pursuit. A surge of protectiveness triggered his fire, which he fought down with pained determination. "Which ones?"

"Candy and Andy," she said, tapping on her phone again when it burbled a short musical sound.

He missed his phone device even more. His meowed when a new dancing-cat video was available.

"Better known to the rest of us as Furcand and Andromalius," the demon said.

Horror crawled up Yrian's back, instantly pushing him fully into protector mode. "Those belong to Kashi," he said, his voice coming out a near snarl.

"Whoa," Jim said, backing up until it ran into the wall.

"Ack!" Becket yelled at the same time, slapping at the fire that roared out of him, spreading quickly across the tile floor, and up her legs. "What is it with you and fire? I thought you guys had better control of it?"

"It's not the easiest thing in the world to harness," Yrian said through teeth gritted with determination. He fought to leash his emotions—and thus his fire—his mind automatically going to the memory of the first time he'd seen Amice. That normally centered him, giving him the strength to battle the elements that warred within him, but for some reason, the sight of Becket standing at the door to his cell was what came to mind.

"Really? The other dragons don't seem to have a problem with it. At least, not that I noticed," Becket replied, turning her attention to him as she put away her phone again.

"They are not the Firstborn."

"One of them was. Baltic. He's your brother, isn't he?"

"He is a Firstborn, not *the* Firstborn," Yrian said, taking a deep breath as the fire slowly dissipated. "We have different mothers. His was a dragon. Mine is a fury."

Becket gawked at him, incredulity written all over her freckled face.

He decided he liked that face, liked the fact that she didn't mask her emotions. Amice hid her emotions in deference to his, preferring to keep her feelings and thoughts secret from all … until the day she didn't.

I'm sorry. I'm so sorry, Yrian.

"One of your dragons mentioned something about your mom being a fury, but I was making glamours, so I didn't really take it in. Your mom was the elemental-beings sort of fury? I thought they went away a few thousand years ago. Just how old are you?"

He shrugged. "Many millennia. I do not know how many. Does it matter? The First Dragon impregnated my mother, a fire fury, bringing the element of fire to dragonkin."

She looked thoughtful before asking, "But your surname is Shadowsworn. Does that mean you have some affinity to shadows? Wait—forget I asked that. You have to stop distracting me with fascinating tidbits about your life. We need to get you to Paris now, before Kostich finds us."

"You find my life fascinating?" he couldn't help but ask, startled and gratified at the same time. Even before the time he'd retreated to his griefscape, no one had ever declared his life fascinating, not even Amice. Chaotic, yes, but fascinating? It was an odd sensation.

Becket whapped him on the arm. "Are you kidding? You're, what, the second dragon who ever existed? Yeah, I think it's safe to say that your life is fascinating."

"You are an artificer," he pointed out, feeling that he should reciprocate interest in her. It wasn't at all difficult—she had a way of filling his mind that should have stirred concern but, for some odd reason, instead seemed simply to be the way things were meant to be. "You must live an interesting life."

"I wish," she said with a grimace. "Mostly, it's all about protecting myself and hiding from baddies who want to use me for their own purposes. OK, enough chat. I can almost feel Dr. Kostich out there looking for us."

The decision was made even before he was aware of it. "We will depart now," he informed the portal attendant, who had returned with a dusty bottle of wine. "We will go to Brno."

"*I'm* going to Brno. *You* are going to Paris," Becket insisted.

"The First Dragon promised you protection by kin. I am kin. I will protect you," he said, ignoring the fact that as of a few hours prior, his sole focus had been escape in order to aid the dragons against a threat that had yet to be explained to him. "We will go to Brno."

"But …"

"Configure the device," he told the portal attendant, who handed him the bottle. "We go to Brno."

"Okey doke," Simon said, going over to a small desk where he tapped on a keyboard. "You may want to take off your shoes, and wrap your arms around yourself just before you step into the portal."

Yrian looked at first the bottle and then Becket. He pulled off the cork and offered it to her. "Would you like some?"

"Wine?" Her nose wrinkled in a way that he found utterly delightful. He didn't bother to wonder about the fact that he'd never before found such an expression enticing, not even on Amice. It was simply another one of those things that just were. "I guess it's technically after noon, so a swig wouldn't hurt me."

He watched her closely as she gave the mouth of the bottle a quick wipe with the sleeve of her shirt before lifting it to her lips.

"You know—" Jim started to say as she took a sip.

Yrian caught the bottle as she dropped it when she doubled over, her hands on her knees as she coughed and sputtered.

"—you might not want to do that … too late." Jim sauntered over to the portal, casting a glance back over its shoulder at them. "Good thing you're a wyvern's mate, or I doubt if you'd survive that. Welp, going through now. I'll call Aisling on the other side and tell her where we are."

"What …" Becket coughed a few more times, dragging in great rasping breaths. Yrian patted her on her back until she grabbed the front of his shirt and used it to leverage herself upright. Her face was red, her eyes streaming, and she sounded like she had been gargling lava when she said, "What the hell was that?"

"Dragon's blood," he answered, studying the label. He had learned much in the two years that he had been in the mortal world, not the least of which was reading and the English language. He was proud of the fact that he was now all but indiscernible from a modern dragon. "Bottled in 1927. A good year."

She wiped at her eyes, shooting him a glare from the corners of her eyes as she finally released her hold on his shirt. "You've been here for what, six months? You can't possibly know what sort of year 1927 was."

"I have studied many videos on the Youbtoo," he said with dignity. "And I left the griefscape two years, one month, and seventeen days ago. I am as proficient as any other dragon."

"Mm-hmm," she said, but didn't look either impressed or like she agreed with his assessment. "Regardless, that wine packs a hell of a punch. Let me have another sip of it. I feel like I'm going to need it."

He offered the bottle and watched her carefully, prepared to help if she needed it, but other than her eyes widening and a couple of deep gasping breaths, she was fine.

He took a deep drink from the bottle when she returned it, relishing the rush of heat from the beverage as it seemed to course along his veins, invigorating him, and filling him with a sense of well-being.

"That really is something else." She had taken the bottle, recorked it, and, after pulling off her loose tunic, started to wrap it around the bottle before she paused and looked toward the portal. "What did Jim mean I was a wyvern's mate? Wyverns are dragons. I'm not a dragon."

"Mates do not have to be dragonkin. Wyvern's mates are always another race." He removed his shoes, placing them in a small container offered by the attendant, then stood by the portal, waiting for Becket.

"That implies you think I'm one of the latter group," she said, her gaze searching his for a few seconds. He had no idea what she sought, but he had an itchy feeling that he needed to be acting, not standing around being enticed by her delectable self.

"You took my fire," he said, wondering how she could not realize the significance of that. He knew full well what his father would say about that fact, but that was of no matter. He had chosen many millennia ago to live his life as he thought best, often bringing him into conflict with the First Dragon. "Only a mate can do that, and as I am a wyvern, you are thus a wyvern's mate. I wish to leave. I have many things to do once I attend to Kashi's demons."

She looked like she wanted to argue, but instead glanced back toward the entrance and, with the bottle held close to her body, stepped into the portal.

Yrian nodded at the attendant before he walked into the mass of twisting purple.

And that's when the world seemed to come apart into an infinite number of particles before slamming back together in a way that left him face down on the floor, his body screaming, his fire threatening to explode out of him, and his brain whirling.

Sounds rolled around him, but his wits were too scattered to make sense of them. He tried to move, but his body felt like it was encased in lead. Something soft touched him, rolled him over, and more or less patted down his body, but he was unable to react for many long minutes.

When he finally did open his eyes, it was to find the demon dog sitting next to him, watching with amused eyes.

"Hey, Beckleberry, he's awake," Jim announced.

A shadow fell over Yrian. He tried to sit up, but his limbs didn't seem to want to enact that thought.

"Thank the goddesses, you're OK. I was trying to find a healer, since you've been out for a good seven minutes. Here, take a little sip of your fancy dragon wine." Becket knelt beside him, pushing Jim aside as she gently lifted his head and held a paper cup to his lips. "You really scared me collapsing like that. I was trying to figure out what I was going to say to your dad that wouldn't end up with him smiting me on the spot for killing you. There you go … now you're getting a little color to your face. Should I ask you how you feel?"

"Grn," he said, his mind slowly shaking off the stupor brought upon by the portal. "Flrr."

"Yes, you're on the floor, but that's only because you're, what, six three? Six four? Too big for me to hoist onto the couch. Are you OK, Yrian?"

His eyes focused on her, warmed by the concern written on her face. She offered him the cup again, and for a moment, he embraced the fire of the wine before struggling to sit up. He didn't have time to sit around and admire her. "No. But I will live. Where are my trousers?"

"They didn't seem to come through," she said, her gaze flickering to his lower half for a few seconds. "You have really nice legs. Oh goddess, that was inappropriate, wasn't it? I'm sorry."

He looked at the limbs in question. "They are just legs."

"You may think so, but your thighs are …" She coughed and cleared her throat, standing and offering him her hand. "Sorry again. I'm not normally so obnoxious. I'm going to blame the portal. Let's get you up."

The portal attendant, a round woman in a hot-pink jumpsuit, moved in on his other side to help right him.

"Dragons always do have troubles," the woman said in a German accent. "But you made it with all your arms and legs, and that is always good, yes? I will go look in the found-objects box to see if there is a pair of trousers to fit you."

Yrian wobbled for a few seconds as he stood up, but another—much longer—drink of wine had his mind clearing and his body ceasing its screaming objections.

Five minutes later they exited the shop, and Becket directed them to a car that was waiting.

A man and a woman stood next to it.

"We made it," Becket told them as she approached.

"So Aisling said," the woman answered, eyeing him. He studied her for a moment, then transferred his gaze to the man next to her. "Hello, Yrian. I'm Allie. This is Christian. He's the head of the Moravian Council."

"Dark One," Yrian said, giving him a curt bow. He would have made a proper one, but he had a horrible suspicion that should he try, he might end up toppling forward.

The vampire bowed in return. "It is our pleasure to welcome you to Brno, but I believe it would be safer for Becket if we were to get her off the street."

"Have Candy and Andy returned?" she asked, her normally silky voice now pinched as she climbed into the back seat of the car.

"No, but we've caught three other demons lurking around the area," Christian said as he and his mate entered the car after them.

It was of the style that had facing seats, just like one his brother had made available for him, but that vehicle had been defective and ran into various road signs, barriers, and occasionally buildings before Yrian deemed it unusable.

"Their forms were destroyed," Christian continued, "but the Guardian we brought in to help says they all belonged to the same demon lord."

"Kashi," Yrian said, nodding, then stopped himself. "No, my youngest brother says he uses another name since the First Dragon stripped him of kinship."

"Bael," Christian answered, his lips twisting in a grimace.

"That is it, although I cannot think of him as anything but Kashi. Baltic said he was confined to the Egyptian underworld. Has he escaped?" Yrian absently cracked his knuckles, his mind fighting its way through the haze caused by the portal to focus on what needed to be done.

After he saw to it that Becket was protected, that is.

"I believe not. The dragon progenitor implied he was still confined to the Duat," Christian answered.

"Looks like everyone is flying back this way," Allie said, having studied her phone for a few minutes. She glanced up at them. "Since it's probably not safe for either of you to hang around an easily accessible hotel, we'd be delighted to have you stay with us at the castle."

Yrian slid a look toward the Dark One. He looked anything but delighted. Yrian realized with amazement that the odd sensation in his chest was the urge to laugh. He was scandalized by the very idea.

"What's wrong?" Becket asked, leaning in to ask in a whisper. The Dark One and his mate were distracted by something on his phone, so he answered just as quietly. "I am Yrian Shadowsworn. I do not laugh."

Becket's eyebrows rose a fraction. He liked her eyebrows. They were a dark russet, darker than the coppery hair that she liked to hide with a glamour, just as she hid her freckled skin. He really liked her freckles. He had the worst urge to cover her face in kisses, just to see how those freckles tasted.

"OK," she said, then added, "That's a shame, really. I think a sense of humor is an attractive quality in a man. Sexy, even. Are you going to answer the vamps?"

"Dragons do not seek aid from Dark Ones," he told her, loud enough to be heard by the others. He inclined his head toward Christian. "I appreciate the offer of succor, but I have no need of it. I do not fear demons, wrath or otherwise."

"Bully for you," Becket all but snapped at him before turning to Allie. "And here I'd always heard dragons had impeccable manners. If your offer extends to me again, Allie,

I'd be thrilled to the tips of my toes and back to stay with you. Yrian may not worry about demons, but I definitely do."

"Why are you angry with me?" he couldn't help but ask her, trying to puzzle out why she was suddenly as bristly as an aurochs's tongue.

"Dude!" she answered, shooting a fast look at the others before settling a frown upon him. "I realize you've been out of the mortal world for almost two thousand years, but surely even in your time there was such a thing as common courtesy?"

"I thanked them," he said, pointing at the Dark One, who was now, he noticed, wearing a nobly martyred expression. His mate had a hand over her mouth to obviously contain giggles. "I was courteous."

"Your idea of courtesy and mine differ greatly," was all she said before she crossed her arms and looked pointedly out of the window.

He was annoyed with being so ignored, but couldn't think of a way to demand she stop refusing to look at him without appearing in a bad light. To his surprise, the Dark One, after a few minutes' study of both Becket and him, gave him a sympathetic look.

Before he could try to figure out what that was about, they arrived at a massive castle that sat atop a low hill. In the fields below, several tents, trailers, and stages lurked, with throngs of people streaming into and out of the venue.

"When do you sing?" Yrian asked Becket when they alighted at a magnificently carved stone door.

She glanced at her phone. "Our rehearsal time is in an hour, but our next actual performance is going to be later tonight. Christian had it moved back in case it took longer to get you out than we anticipated. Why?"

"I wish to see you sing," was all he said before he followed her into the castle. He realized that although he would prefer to keep Becket away from the vampires—solely for her protection, of course—their domicile would be likely to have some form of security, and since he had to split his time between protecting her, finding the wrath demons that threatened her, and figuring out what Kashi was up to, it was better that she stay in the castle.

Accordingly, he said to Christian, "I have changed my mind. I will accept the succor you offer to Becket and me. I may have to follow the wrath demons, and it would ease my mind to know she is safe here."

"We're going to have a little chat about you being Mr. Bossy Boots, but right now, I need to get changed and get my behind down to the practice stage. Am I in the same room, Allie?"

"You are, minus my children, who have been forbidden to bother you." She slid a glance toward Yrian. "And Yrian, of course. Let me show you to your room. It's just down the hall from Becket."

He shook his head. "I will stay with her. I can't protect her if I am not present."

"You are so not going to make decisions for me," Becket said in a voice that seemed to be made up of sharp, stabby bits. "The First Dragon said that you guys would take care of Candy and Andy for me, not that you would become the Dictator of Becketsville."

"And if the wrath demons made it into your room in deep night, would you be able to defeat them while I was asleep in another room?" he asked, wondering that such a intelligent woman wouldn't see how necessary it was that she remain at his side.

"I doubt if a wrath demon could make it inside," Allie said as her mate, with a roll of his eyes, headed off in answer to a call. "Christian has the castle protected every week by a professional mage service, in addition to which a Guardian comes out every ten days to refresh the wards."

"These wrath demons are not like others," Yrian told her. "They could get past your protections. Becket? Would you be able to protect yourself?"

Her jaw worked a couple of times before she said, "Not as well as I could with you there. All right, I admit that you being in the room is going to be safer, but I really dislike being told what to do."

Allie looked worried. "Is there something else we should do to protect the children?"

"Yes. Place guards at all the entrances," he answered. "Where is our room? I wish to ascertain how easy it will be to defend should an attack come tonight."

It was obvious that neither Becket nor Allie liked what he said, but they duly showed him to a pleasant, well-lit room dominated by a large bed. He ignored it to check the window protections, seeing three different wards on it to guard against beings of dark magic. The door was also protected, although not as heavily. Given that they were two floors up, he judged the windows safe, but pointed out the door could use more protection.

"I'll have our Guardian friend add in extra wards tonight," Allie assured them, pulling out her phone as she hurried out of the room.

Becket looked at him.

He looked at Becket.

They both turned to look at the bed.

"I'd like to point out that this is my room, and you're just a guest in it, but since I'm also a guest, and you'll be protecting me from Andy and Candy, I guess you can have the bed," she said with a half smile. "I'll sleep on the window seat."

A little kernel of warmth blossomed in his chest at the gesture. Absently, he rubbed the spot as he answered. "I will be standing guard, so you will use the bed. When do you need to go out?"

"Probably now," she said on a sigh as she glanced at her phone. "I just need to change. The others are asking for me, since our rehearsal time is in twenty minutes."

"I will accompany you there," Yrian said, wishing again he had his phone device so that he might contact his youngest brother. He needed to speak to Baltic about not only extra guards for Becket but also information about Kashi. He made a swift decision and turned to exit the room, saying over his shoulder, "I will meet you downstairs in five minutes."

"OK, but you can knock off the bossy crap anytime now," she called after him, closing the door with a bit more force than was polite.

That fact made another one of those laughter bubbles rise within him. He wondered at that for the time it took him to go to the ground floor, locate the Dark One Christian, and make a few arrangements with him before meeting Becket at the front door.

He wasn't interested in a woman, he told himself as he walked her down to the music-festival area.

Especially not a mate. He'd had a mate once, and look how that ended.

Death. It ended in death.

And more than a millennium paying penance for his sins.

"This is Yrian." Becket ran through introductions to three mortal women, all of whom studied him with curious eyes. "He's … uh …"

"You have a boyfriend?" one of the women said, the one with two pink blobs of hair on the top of her head. "You didn't tell us you had a boyfriend!"

"No, we're not together," Becket said hurriedly, giving him an odd sidelong glance. "Not in that way. Not romantically. He's … er …"

Yrian remembered a movie he had watched on his much-lamented phone. "I am your bodyguard."

"Yes," she said quickly, flashing him a fast smile before turning it on her friends. "He's protecting me from you-know-who."

The women seemed to lose interest, although one of them sent him a warm look that he had no trouble interpreting.

"You will stay here," he told Becket. "The Dark Ones over there will watch out for any demons while I'm away. You will not leave their presence."

Becket sighed a highly martyred sigh, just as he'd suspected she would.

What he didn't anticipate was her grabbing his arm and more or less hauling him a short distance away so she could speak in a hurried whisper. "OK, first of all, there are mortals everywhere, including within earshot, so please don't be yammering on about demons and vampires where they can hear. And second, and this is a big second, stop feeling like you can boss me around. I appreciate that you are trying to fulfill your dad's promise to protect me, but I'm not an imbecile, Yrian. I can take care of myself."

He cocked an eyebrow at her.

She swore under her breath. "Yes, all right, there are times when I could use help, but that does not mean you get to go all dictator on me. I will stay here, but only because we have to rehearse tonight's set, and then we like to watch other bands to see what the competition is doing in case I can work up some new glamours. Where are you going to be while we're rehearsing?"

"The Dark One told me there is an Internet magician in town who can provide me with a phone device. I must have one so that I can contact my kin. Also, I miss the dancing cats, and wish to see what new videos are available."

She gawked at him for a second, then slid her hand across her mouth. "I didn't peg you for a dancing-cat-video sort of guy, but I can see where you would want a phone."

"Do you not like cats?" he asked, unable to imagine anyone who wouldn't enjoy the videos that had kept him sane during the long months of his imprisonment. "There are some excellent videos with cats that belly dance I was hoping to show you, but if you would prefer not ..."

"I'm more of a dog girl—I have a weakness for pugs—but I enjoy a good cat belly-dance video, too," she said, her lips doing an odd sort of twitching that he put down to excitement at seeing his favorite videos.

"Stay within the sight of the Dark Ones," he said, nodding toward the three men and one woman who had appeared to their left. "They will guard you until I return from the Internet mage."

She murmured something about not being an idiot, and hurried off with her bandmates to a stage on the far side of the field, the four Dark Ones on her heels.

He found the driver Christian had told him would take him into town, and spent a pleasurable half hour talking with the Internet magician about new phone-device possibilities, emerging from the shop with not only a phone but also a tablet device, the latter of which had a lovely big screen with which to view his videos. He was quite pleased with the new addition to his collection of Internet, and looked forward to showing it to Becket.

"Wait," he told the driver, a Dark One by the name of Wolf. He stood next to the car Christian had put at his disposal, awareness pricking a line down his back. He spun around, his eyes searching the passing people and vehicles until one screeched to a halt next to him. "Ah. It is kin."

The window rolled down to reveal the face of his youngest brother. "Did the artificer haul you through a portal?"

Yrian grimaced, running a hand over his hair. Ever since he had been through the portal, it had a tendency to stand on end. "Yes. She did not tell me it would almost kill me."

Baltic's expression displayed abject horror, no doubt matching his own. "They are extremely unpleasant. We have much to discuss. Drake has called a *sárkány* and asks that you attend."

He inclined his head. "Becket and I are staying with the Dark Ones."

"So are we," one of the mates called from inside the car. Judging by the manner in which she was pressed against the green wyvern, Yrian assumed she was part of that sept. "Although now that Archer, Thaisa, and Hunter are on their way, I'm not sure where they're going to sleep. The town's hotels are full. I hope Allie can find room to fit them in. She said they had eighteen bedrooms, and no, Drake, we do not need a castle."

Yrian didn't understand what was so funny that had the women laughing, but he decided it was something he would determine later, when he had time to fully bring himself up to date with the lives of his kin. "I must return to Becket, but I will ask the Dark One's mate if she can house your friends."

"Archer and Hunter are dragon hunters, not friends," Baltic said before rolling up the window.

Yrian wondered what he meant, but figured that, too, would be something he ascertained in the future. Right now he had to take his new phone to show Becket.

"We return to the castle," he told Wolf as the long car containing the dragons drove on.

He ignored the fact that he had no reason to want to share his joy with her. It, like so many other things, simply was, and he accepted that fact in order to focus on what was most important: destroying Kashi before more death resulted.

A stab of pain bit deep into him, a pain he pushed away. He simply would not allow Kashi to destroy him again.

He would keep Becket safe at all costs.

EIGHT
BECKET

"I don't think poor Allie was prepared for all of us," Aisling said softly to Ysolde, May, and me.

"This is my fault," I said, feeling guilty as the castle hall was filled with not just other vamps and a whole bunch of dragons, but now also my bandmates, who had hinted broadly that they would love to see inside until I asked Allie if a brief tour was possible.

"Of course," she said, looking a bit glazed about the eyes when we all rolled up, complete with my vampire guard escort.

All the ladies turned to look at the newest arrivals, who were greeting Christian.

"That's Archer with Thaisa, his mate," Aisling said, nodding toward them. "His twin is Hunter. Their dad is the guy who is evidently trying to destroy the dragons, although no one knows why."

"Or at least the men aren't telling us why," Ysolde answered, shooting Baltic a pointed look.

He didn't so much as bat an eyelash at it. He stood somewhat apart from the other dragons, his arms crossed as he watched them.

I turned to look to my right. Yrian stood in almost the same pose, wearing an identical expression of watchfulness.

Allie went forward to greet the newcomers as Ysolde went to her dragon, sliding an arm around his waist and leaning in to bite his ear.

I moved next to Yrian as a sense of yearning gripped me, making me feel things I hadn't felt in many years.

"Why are you standing over here all by your lonesome?" I asked him when I reached his side. "These are your family, aren't they? Or are the new guys not dragons? They look like dragons to me, but I admit that I'm not very conversant with your people."

His gaze shifted to the newcomers. Absently, I noticed that the gold of his eyes was now dulled, more of an old gold than the shiny brightness I'd seen before.

"They are …" He hesitated. "Not kin and yet they are. I would ask my youngest brother about them, but he indicated that the green wyvern was calling a *sárkány*, so I will get my answer there."

"What's a *sárkány*?" I couldn't help but ask, telling myself that I didn't need to involve myself with dragon things any more than was necessary.

That thought was dismissed almost immediately. I liked the dragons. I liked the women, and while the men were rather intense and intimidating, Yrian wasn't in the least bit like them. He was warm and protective and fascinating, and a hell of a fighter to boot.

"It is a meeting of septs." He pulled out his phone when it meowed at him. "Ah. The Internet mage informs me that he found a laptop for me. I have not had one of those before, but he told me it was better even than the tablet."

"You bought a phone and a tablet?" I asked, fighting to keep from smiling. For a man who'd spent almost the last two thousand years out of the mortal world, he sure did love his YouTube cat videos. The fact that he found so much delight in them warmed me to my toes. It was just one of the many contradictory facets of his personality … a personality that I was finding more and more attractive as each minute passed.

"It was necessary," he said with a serious mien that also made me want to laugh.

"I'm sure it was. So, you're having a meeting with your dragon buddies? When is that? Not that it's really any of my business other than wanting to make sure I have someone around me when we're performing," I asked.

He glanced at his phone. "You have three and a half hours before you must sing?"

"About that, yes."

"Then we can have the *sárkány* now. I will inform my youngest brother," he said, surprising me by taking my hand when he marched across the hall to where Allie, Christian, the ladies, and the dragons were now in a cluster.

My bandmates, after seeing the sights in the main and upper floors, were excited to go off with the housekeeper to see what Allie had said was a nice collection of art Christian housed in the basement, so it was just dragons, vamps, and me.

"Are we having fisticuffs?" Christian asked when we stopped next to him. He glanced at the dragons. "You are six. I will ask another guard to join us, so that we might make easy teams."

"Fisticuffs?" I asked before I realized it. I looked at Yrian. "Why are you guys going to fight? I thought you were all friends?"

"It's not like that," Aisling said at the same time May answered, "Dragons get a bit testy when tensions run high, and it helps calm them down if they can have a rumble."

"Mayling!" Gabriel said, outrage dripping from the word. "Wyverns do not get testy! It is simply that our primal selves occasionally get the better of us, and physical exertion helps alleviate that."

"Uh-huh," Aisling said, automatically taking the suit coat that her husband peeled off. "That's why you guys take advantage of any dragon get-together to beat the stuffing out of each other. Drake, so help me, if you lose another one of your real teeth, I will have many things to say to you."

Drake looked like he wanted to roll his eyes, but he simply muttered something in Magyar, and proceeded to remove both his tie and cuff links.

"What is this?" Yrian asked his brother.

Baltic, who was also divesting himself of his coat while rolling up his sleeves, said, "We fight. The mates insist on human form only, no weapons, just fists." He smiled, his gaze on Gabriel. "They are enough."

"It sounds barbaric," Allie said as her vampire was stripping down, removing his coat and a fancy vest, his tie, and a couple of rings. "But it's honestly kind of mmrowr. No one gets seriously hurt, and Gabriel is a healer, so if someone does break something, he can help it heal. Christian was hoping he and the others could get down and dirty, and had a small section of the side garden blocked off from the public just for that purpose. We even got in some of that killer wine the dragons love, since they seem to favor it for recovery time."

"Recovery—Yrian!"

"What?" he asked as he handed me his phone, then stripped off the jacket and shirt he wore, leaving him clad in nothing but his shoes and a pair of black jeans. I stared at his bare torso, my mind staggering to a halt, while my tongue felt like it cleaved to the roof of my mouth.

Holy shit, the man had the chest of a Greek statue, all pectorals and a ripple of muscles that disappeared into his jeans.

He had a six-pack, an actual six-pack. My mind had a hard time getting past the idea of a man who had lived in his own griefscape for sixteen hundred years and still had the ability to maintain a six-pack, biceps that turned my knees to jelly, and shoulders that made me—not at all a petite person—feel delicate by comparison.

And then he turned away in order to toss his shirt and jacket onto a bench.

A glorious, full-color tattoo of a dragon coiled down his spine.

"Oooh, pretty," Aisling said, catching sight of it.

"Wow. That really is," Ysolde said, then slid a glance toward her husband.

"No," he told her.

She smiled, and leaned in to whisper something in his ear.

"Becket?" Yrian asked, clearly waiting for me to explain my protest.

I moved behind him to look again at the tattoo. It was a piece of art, with shadowed shading on the scales that somehow held muted colors. "This is absolutely gorgeous. I've never seen such an artistic tat. Where did you have it done?"

"Mongolia," he answered. "My mate arranged for me to have it. I wished to have the image be of her, but she insisted a dragon was more fitting."

There was something about the set of his jaw that said the memory wasn't a happy one.

"The battle arena awaits," Christian announced, gesturing toward my four guards. The three men had stripped down to just pants, while Annaliese peeled off her shirt to expose a sturdy sports bra. She flexed her fingers a couple of times as she eyed the dragons.

"Did you need something of me?" Yrian asked me as Christian suggested teams of two.

"No, I'm just a bit taken aback that you're so ready to fight your own family."

He thought about that for a moment, then gave a one-shoulder shrug. "We are primal beings. I used to practice on a pell when my humors were out of sorts. This sounds like it is similar, with the added bonus of honing battle skills."

I had a vague memory of a historical romance defining a pell as a sort of target dummy for swordplay, so said nothing else, just held his things while he turned back to the others.

"There's six of each group," Ysolde said as she accepted one of the bottles of dragon's blood. "Why don't you guys make it a bit more fun and have a vampire and dragon pair up? That way you can't blame one group for beating up the other."

I could tell no one really liked that idea, but in the end, it was settled that it would be the fairest way to hold what I was beginning to think of as a massive pissing match.

Yrian eyed the vampires. "I will take you as a partner," he told Annaliese.

"You will, will you?" I asked, suddenly feeling cranky as hell.

"Yes," he said. Annaliese sized him up for a few seconds, then nodded and headed toward the door.

"Why?" The word popped out before I could stop it. "Do you fancy her?"

"Fancy?"

"Want her. Do you want her?" I asked, my voice taking on a hint of the Hashmallim's rock-grinding-on-rock tone.

"Yes."

I fought the urge to punch him in the nose, curling my fingers into fists to stop myself.

"She looks ruthless," Yrian continued, his expression pleased. "She will have no mercy on the others."

"Is that the only reason you want her on your team?" I hated that I had to ask the question, but it came out nonetheless.

In the back of my head, my inner narrator was having a field day with why I cared, but I ignored her as I was frequently wont to do.

She was way too snarky for my comfort.

"Of course," he said, his gaze on the others present. "She may not wish to attack Christian, but I will take care of him."

Christian must have heard, because he paused in a comment to Baltic, who evidently was his partner, and shot Yrian a fulminating glare.

Yrian smiled.

My heart felt like it leaped and did a somersault at the sight of it. Dear goddess, the more I was around him, the more I noticed just how sexy he was.

"It's a good thing we sent Jim home to Paris, or it would be demanding we film the shindig," Aisling commented as we all traipsed out of the castle to a small side garden surrounded by high hedges.

"I feel the same about having Brom and Pixie go off for date time rather than attend the *sárkány*. They'd just want to fight, too, and I know everyone would have to be careful not to hurt Pixie. And just so you know, I'm absolutely going to film, but it's for those times when Baltic has to go away, and I feel the need to see him beat the tar out of Drake and Gabriel," Ysolde said with a bright smile at everyone.

The two men in question looked martyred for a few seconds; then everyone broke into pairs and spread around the garden in a rough circle.

A row of chairs had been set out, along with a table with several glasses, a collection of appetizers, a few bottles of assorted alcohol, and even champagne on ice. I recognized two familiar bottles, and wondered if anyone would think it rude if I asked for a hit of the dragon's blood wine now, but decided I could get through the confusing mess of emotions that Yrian seemed to stir inside me without it.

"I believe ten minutes is the usual time allowed?" Allie said, glancing at the ladies, who had all moved over to the table and were loading up tiny plates with the snacks.

"We try to keep it to that time, since any longer and they lose all the benefit of working out their frustrations," Ysolde said around a mouthful of food. "Good lord, these baked feta crostini are delicious. Allie, Pavel and I are going to want the recipe so we can serve this for the next *sárkány*."

"I'll text it to you," Allie promised, then turned back to where everyone was waiting. "Right, ten minutes. No fire, no fangs, no ... er ..."

"Human form only," Aisling called, moaning softly when she bit into a salmon cake. "Also, please send me the recipe for this. Does it have lemon and sriracha? May, you have to try this."

"Oooh, that sounds divine," she answered, quickly picking up two of the salmon cakes. "I'll save one for Gabriel. We love sriracha."

"That's right, human form only, not that vamps have any other form, but still," Allie said, turning back to the circle, pulling out a whistle.

"We could change form if we wanted to do so," one of the guards said, glaring at Drake, who glared right back at him. I had a feeling they wouldn't be the best team, and instead considered Yrian. Annaliese was speaking to him, her hands dancing in the air as she gestured across the circle, obviously making plans. He nodded, but his gaze was on me.

I felt alternately hot and cold, my emotions going into overtime with speculation, curiosity, and what felt like a whole lot of sexual interest.

"May I suggest that we also remind Yrian that no god-like powers be used?" Ysolde asked, scooping some chicken larb onto her plate. "Baltic knows he can't use any magic, so it's best that Yrian adhere to that policy, as well."

"That makes sense," Allie agreed, lifting the whistle to her lips. "No magic, no powers. Everyone ready? And … go!"

The entire circle imploded on itself, all the participants rushing forward until there was basically a massive pig pile of people flailing, thrashing, kicking, and subsequently grunting with pain.

I stared in horror for a few minutes at the sight of it all, turning back to the women. "This is barbaric!" I told them.

Aisling, who had set down her plate to applaud when Drake sucker punched Baltic, gave me a wry smile. "I know it looks horrible, but it actually does them a lot of good, and no one gets seriously hurt. Dragons have a remarkable healing ability, and as Allie said, Gabriel is available to heal anyone who gets too hurty. Hey! I saw that, Christian! No fangs means no fangs!"

Christian said something quite rude in Czech, but since I gather it was just a general statement and not directed at Aisling, the battle royale went on.

I flinched every time Yrian was attacked, but after a couple more minutes, I realized something astounding—he was clearly enjoying himself. His eyes were so bright they almost glowed gold, while he and Annaliese worked with amazing harmony to take down the others, one pair at a time.

"Yrian was right about her," I said, watching as Annaliese and he attacked, and took down, Gabriel and his vampire.

"Who? Oh, your guard?" May stood next to me, sipping champagne, wincing when Yrian flung himself onto Gabriel, his fists bloody, but his expression obviously one of satisfaction. "Yeah, she's pretty tough. Maata, one of Gabriel's elite guards, is female, too, and there is no way I'd ever want to get on her bad side. She's beyond badass. Nice one, Gabriel!"

"You may think it's nice, but now he's got blood in Archer's pretty hair," Thaisa said as she moved over to stand with us. I eyed her for a moment. She had what I assumed was a genetic trait that left her with oddly colored eyes, and a stripe of white on her eyelashes and eyebrow, narrowing into a faint line in her hair. She flashed me a smile. "I know what it's like to be the new kid on the block. My best advice is to ask questions when things confuse you. The men hate answering questions, but thankfully, all the mates share info."

"The new kid?" I asked, confused.

"Being a mate, I mean," she answered.

"I'm not a mate," I said, shaking my head, but whether it was at her comment or my own misguided emotions, I refused to consider. "I'm an artificer."

"Right, but you're with Yrian, aren't you?" she asked.

"Not in the way you mean—holy shit. He really is something, isn't he?" I watched in astonished admiration when Yrian spun, kicked, and tackled the others in a manner that left me nigh on giddy with sudden lust.

"They all are," Thaisa said, smiling broadly.

"Now I know I'm insane," I murmured to myself, and took the glass Allie offered.

"Five minutes!" she shouted over the sounds of the fray, holding up a bottle of champagne. "Anyone need a refill?"

All the dragon ladies held up their glasses.

Near the end of the allowed time, the fighters broke up their pairings, and it became a free-for-all.

"That happens," Ysolde told me when she caught sight of my expression when Annaliese jumped Yrian, and they both tumbled to the ground when Drake attacked Yrian at the same moment. "The last few minutes they go solo. Don't worry—no one looks seriously hurt, although it would appear Drake is bleeding from his mouth, and we all know what that means."

"He'll end up with another fake tooth," Aisling said with a sigh.

"I think Archer may have done something to his knee," Thaisa said, not in the least bit concerned. "He's limping after his brother, and it looks like Hunter's fingers are broken, which is why he's running away rather than fighting."

"I am not running away!" the dragon in question bellowed. "I don't run away from anyone, let alone Archer. Dammit, stop chasing me, so I can fix my fingers!"

"They have really good hearing," Thaisa said, giving her brother-in-law a little wave.

"They do, but I really want to discuss what Thaisa said." Ysolde's eyes were on me, making me feel all shades of awkward. "Do you ... er ... for the lack of better phrasing, like Yrian?"

"Of course I like him," I said, tamping down the emotions that wanted to rise. "He's a nice man."

"He is?" May looked across the carnage. About three-quarters of the dragons and vamps were now on the ground, most moaning, while the remainder lumbered around slowly and painfully, still trying to continue the fight. I was oddly proud of the fact that Yrian was one of the two standing dragons, his brother being the other. Christian and a Spanish guard named Jesús were the upright vampires, but as I watched, Jesús went down when Drake lashed out with a leg.

Allie blew the whistle. "Time's up. Vampires will find blood inside in the fridge. Dragons, the dragon's blood is flowing."

"Literally," Ysolde said with a little giggle as the ladies

all went onto the field of battle and helped their respective men over to the chairs.

"I would say I was dead, but I hurt too much for that to be true. Can someone pick me up and pour me into the nearest chair?" the dragon named Hunter said from where he was struggling to sit upright.

Christian and Baltic obliged, half dragging him over to the chairs, where Aisling handed him a glass of wine.

Yrian took two steps toward me and went down to his knees. I was moving before I even considered what I was doing. "Are you OK? You don't have any blood on you."

"You haven't seen my back," he said, accepting the glass of wine I had picked up for him. I moved around to look at his back, my eyes wide with horror at the sight of a line of four deep gouges down the middle of his beautiful dragon tat.

"What the hell?" I asked, pulling a tissue from a pocket to try to mop up the blood that leaked out of the slashes. "Who did this to you?"

Archer raised a hand. "Dragon hunters don't normally shift, but my claws came out when Yrian broke two of my ribs. I apologize for that. No, Thaisa, don't try to lift that arm. It'll take me a bit to heal the ribs."

"I thought the rules were made quite clear. No dragon form, just fists," I said in a stiff tone directed at Archer, but as he was at that moment leaning back in his chair, a pained expression on his face while Thaisa mopped up various cuts and scrapes, I figured he was feeling the weight of his actions.

"Do not enrage yourself," Yrian told me when I helped him over to a chair and poured him more wine. "It was not done maliciously. Did you enjoy the sporting?"

"Are you insane?" I asked him, still dabbing at his back, although thankfully, the blood had stopped, and the slashes were beginning to scab over.

"You admired me," he said, his eyes glittering. "I saw you watching me."

"I admired the way you and Annaliese worked, yes," I answered, reluctant to discuss my emotions. "You made a good team."

"I told you she was ruthless," he agreed, his voice thick with satisfaction. "Why do you think you aren't a mate?"

I stared at him in utter surprise for a moment. "You heard us talking?"

He nodded, draining the glass of wine. "You took my fire. You are a wyvern's mate."

"Look, I appreciate that you are sexy as all get-out, but I am not looking for a man. I have enough going on in my life to even think about trying to cope with a relationship, especially with a dragon."

I could swear I saw a flash of pain in his eyes, but it was gone before I could be sure. I felt like the biggest heel in the world.

"That came out wrong," I told him, wanting to apologize, but knowing my life was way too fraught with danger to consider even a brief fling with him. "It's not anything to do with you, Yrian. You're gorgeous, and quirky, and really, really interesting, but having the entire Otherworld after you tends to put a crimp on romance. Are you feeling better? Your back is healing. I hope those scratches won't mess up your tattoo."

He said nothing, just gave a slight grunt when he got to his feet, allowing me to help him put on his shirt and jacket.

"That went well, I think," Allie said a few minutes later, when the combatants had recovered, and were more or less able to stand. "I hope everyone enjoyed themselves."

"Other than adding more to our dentist's retirement fund, Drake had a lovely time," Aisling said, one arm around her dragon as he limped back into the castle.

"Baltic obviously had great fun until his brother pounced and did something to his shoulder. Gabriel, could you look at it, please?"

I glanced at Yrian. The faintest hint of a smile curled the corners of his lips.

"Bad dragon," I told him softly, smiling to take the sting out of it.

"Yes," he answered seriously, his brows pulling together. "But that is because the First Dragon had not yet conquered dragon fire when I was born."

"Huh?" I would have asked him to explain—since he clearly had control of his fire—but at that moment Allie spoke, handing Ysolde the remaining bottle of dragon's blood.

"Christian said you can use the library for your meeting. That should give Becket time before her performance."

"That's nice, but I don't have anything to do with the dragon stuff," I said, following when the rest of the dragons (slowly, and with some stifled moaning) traipsed into the castle after Allie and Christian.

"You will attend with me," Yrian said, surprising me by taking my hand in a firm grip.

"I'm not a dragon," I pointed out, but allowed my inner narrator to squeal softly to herself over the hand-holding. "I have no reason to be there."

His voice had a flinty edge to it that had me wondering if he was annoyed with me, or the deal his dad had agreed to with me. "The dragonkin owe you a debt. You will not be unwelcome."

I had different ideas about how the other dragons would take me intruding on their private business, but figured they could set Yrian straight on that subject.

Allie paused at a set of engraved mahogany doors. "This is the library. Dinner will be after Becket's band performs, but there'll be snacks available in the lounge next door, in case anyone gets hangry."

"I'm so full of salmon and feta, I couldn't even think of more food," Ysolde told her. "But I am taking pictures of everything to share with Pavel. He's thinking of starting a food blog."

"You dragons are so interesting," Allie said, herding her children—who had appeared at the mention of snacks—

ahead of her into the lounge. "You have so many interests. Vampires are pretty much only focused on saving other vamps. They definitely need more hobbies."

We entered the library. The other dragons were already there, and looked over when Yrian and I entered, the men giving me what I thought of as a bit of a stink eye, all but Baltic, who instead watched his brother as the latter gestured me toward a comfy armchair.

I took a wooden chair instead, ignoring the look Yrian bent upon me before he, too, sat down.

"Is there something you would like to tell the weyr?" Baltic asked him.

"Yes," Yrian said, settling into the chair. I assumed the ladies were correct in that he had already healed up the slashes on his back, and had a few moments where I dwelt with much pleasure on the intricate tattoo he bore. I didn't realize until that moment that I had a weakness for men with big dragon tats on their backs, but evidently that was now a thing. "I must pursue Kashi and destroy him. During those times, I will rely upon the dragonkin to guard Becket."

I gave him a stiff smile. "I want to remind you that I can take care of myself, thank you, but since Candy and Andy are still hunting for me, I won't say it."

Yrian's brows pulled together as he turned to me. "You just did do so."

I whapped him gently on his arm. "It's called irony."

His eyes narrowed in thought for a few seconds; then his brow cleared, and the corners of his mouth quirked. "Ah. I see. You were being amusing."

"Not really," I said with a sigh, and held out a hand when Aisling and Ysolde were both handing out more glasses of wine. "But I appreciate you giving me the benefit of the doubt. Yes, please, Ysolde. I don't normally drink before a performance, but I think this time I'll risk it."

"Er …" Ysolde hesitated, glancing first at Baltic, then at me. "This is dragon's blood, Becket. Not normal wine. You're not mortal, are you?"

"Not as such, no."

She continued to hesitate. "It's just …"

"Give it to her," Baltic said, his eyes now on me.

She did so, and everyone watched as I slowly lifted it to my lips, wondering if I was breaching some rule of dragondom by drinking their fancy wine. "Bottoms up," I murmured, taking what I later realized was a foolishly large sip.

Once again, fire seemed to roar through my body, setting every atom alight until all I could hear was a rushing noise, while the air in my lungs seemed to vaporize. I gasped, desperate to both put out the inferno inside of me and get some oxygen into my body, and for one horrible moment, I wondered if I was quite as immortal as I assumed. But the second spots started to dance across my vision, a hand was placed on my back, and with that touch, the inferno became something else. It was … tamed. Instead of trying to destroy me, it filled me with a sense of power and invincibility, one that coursed through my veins giving me a cockiness that was at odds with my normally hidden personality.

"Again, I am so glad Jim is visiting Amelie, because if it was here right now, it would be making endless comments about the proving of a new wyvern's mate. Also, holy cow!" Aisling looked a bit stunned.

"Just so you know, Becket, dragon's blood wine is lethal to mortals and pretty much dangerous to anyone who isn't a dragon mate," May explained, then smiled. "And it turns out to be an excellent way to determine wyverns' mates. Both Aisling and I drank it before we knew it was so dangerous."

"Drake knew it would kill me if I wasn't his mate," Aisling said with a complacence I admired, "but luckily, he is very astute and knew I had to be a mate."

I dragged in a deep breath now that the fire inside me was dying down, my head turned to Yrian so I could ask softly, "It was bad before when I took a smaller sip, but this … is this what your fire is like?"

"Yes," he said, his hand now rubbing my back in an impersonal way, but my inner self didn't care. It just relished the touch, making me want to arch my back and purr like a satisfied cat.

"*Now* do you have something to tell the weyr?" Baltic asked Yrian.

"I have many things to say, yes," he answered, his expression serious, but I had a suspicion he was deliberately misinterpreting his brother. Since I didn't want to deal with any errant emotions, not while Candy and Andy were obviously still on the hunt, I didn't say anything, just took another— much more cautious—sip of the wine while Yrian continued. "You said Kashi reproduced and his son is a wyvern. We will use him to lure Kashi forth. We will now arrange our plans for his destruction."

Drake had set up a large tablet on a sideboard, and as Yrian spoke, several people logged on to a video call for the meeting. As Yrian finished, one of the men looked simultaneously horrified and furious. He had shoulder-length dark-blond hair, and eyes that were a dulled version of Yrian's shiny gold. "Because that's what I need right now—a deranged Firstborn trying to sacrifice me to Bael. My mate is with child! I'm not going to leave her and our daughter alone, so whatever plans you have for me, Yrian Shadowsworn, can be rethought. I am no sacrificial lamb!"

"You were once," Ysolde murmured, making her husband stifle a snorted laugh. Ysolde glanced at me and made a rueful face. "Sorry, Becket, that's tantamount to a private joke. Constantine sacrificed himself due to killing his wyvern, but he was insane at that time, so no one is holding it against him now."

"That wyvern was my mother's sire," Baltic reminded her.

She patted his hand before twining her fingers around his. "Yes, but that was several hundred years ago, and now that Constantine is resurrected, he's no longer crazy, so all is well."

I gave Yrian a long look.

"What?" he asked.

"You have an interesting family."

"And you do not?" he countered.

I thought about that for a few moments while the dragon named Constantine argued with Baltic about some events in what was apparently the distant past.

"You have a point. Do you think I'm your mate just because I drank some wine?" I asked Yrian.

"No," he answered, and a little stab of pain shot through my chest. "I think you are a wyvern's mate because you took my fire. Do you wish to be my mate?"

"I met you approximately eight hours ago," I pointed out. "I may be many things, but the type of person to fall madly in love with someone within that time frame is not one of them. Why, do you want me to be your mate? I thought you had a mate? Someone told me dragons only have one mate in their lifetime."

"Most do, but some, like Baltic and I assume Yrian, are special, and they can have more than one," Ysolde told me. "Drake's grandmother was also able to have a second mate, which is why he and his brother are wyverns of different septs."

Evidently, she, too, had excellent hearing.

"We will call the *sárkány* to order, since we have much ground to cover," Drake informed everyone, his gaze on me for a few seconds. "And since we have asked Yrian Shadow-sworn to attend, we welcome his mate, as well."

"I know full well you guys heard me talking to Yrian, so I'm not even going to argue the point that I am not his mate. In addition, I'll remind you the only reason I'm here is because your ancestor promised me aid in getting rid of Candy and Andy." I gave the look Drake sent me right back to him. "Also, it's rude to listen in to conversations conducted in an intimate volume."

Yrian looked so righteous that it made a giggle rise inside of me, but due to the obviously serious nature of the meeting, I kept it from emerging. "Becket is correct. We are here to discuss her protection."

"On the contrary," Drake said, sitting down after making an adjustment to the tablet, which was now filled with a bunch of faces. "This *sárkány* has been called to address the issue of Xavier and, to a lesser degree, Deus."

I wondered who they were, but before I could ask Yrian, he frowned and shook his head. "The First Dragon told me dragonkin were in peril unless I rejoined the mortal realm. Only Kashi could pose that sort of threat. It is for that purpose I am here."

The dragons all started talking at once, everyone arguing that he was mistaken.

"Bael is in the Duat," Drake told him after calling the meeting back to order. "There is no reason to fear his influence on our lives, or indeed anything in the mortal world."

"I agree that he is the biggest danger to dragonkin, but is he not powerless now?" Constantine asked, scowling from the tablet at Yrian. "He can't get out of the Duat, after all."

"He can," Yrian said simply, nodding toward me. "Becket is his way out. Why do you think he has sent his wrath demons after her?"

Another dragon on the tablet sputtered something about Bael stirring up trouble despite having no power here, and all the other dragons nodded their agreement.

All but Baltic, whose gaze was on Yrian and me for an entire minute before he said, "Do you think she has that sort of power?"

Everyone turned to look at me. Nervously, I took a sip of wine before remembering just how traumatizing it was. This time I managed to get it swallowed without bursting into flames and expiring on the spot. I didn't even gasp, although for a few seconds I felt like my lungs had collapsed.

"On her own? No. But with Kashi's help, her glamours could negate the magic keeping him bound to the Duat," Yrian finally answered.

"Like how your dad helped me with your glamour?" I asked. He nodded. "But this is a demon lord we're talking about, right? That's dark power. Artificers don't run on that.

We pull energy from the life force, not the opposite. I don't see how he could give me the oomph I would need to let him escape."

"He would find a way to use and destroy you," he said in such a matter-of-fact tone that it took me a couple of seconds before the words hit me.

"That's the first correct thing you've said," Constantine announced, leaning into his camera until his eyes filled the screen. "Bael will use up every ounce of power you have, and then destroy you without a second's hesitation. If you value your life, stay away from him. Stay out of the Duat."

I disliked being told what to do, but didn't want to make a fuss over something that truly wasn't going to affect me, so I kept silent while the other dragons reinforced the statement that Bael was not the issue.

"We have had word that Xavier is focusing his attention on the green sept," Hunter said. He had a light Irish accent, and a casual manner of speaking that made him seem anything but serious, but the grim light in his pale-green eyes told another story. "We do not know how or even why he has singled them out, but the threat is very real, and is the reason why Xavier must be located and stopped."

"Dragons have warred since before I created the septs," Yrian said in a dismissive tone. "If you insist on my aid in ending the fight between this Xavier and the weyr, I will do so, but only after Kashi has been dealt with."

Archer and Hunter exchanged glances; then Archer said, "Xavier is our father. We believe he is working with Abaddon, for what purpose—other than the destruction of dragonkin—we do not know. But be assured that he is far more of a threat to us than Bael."

"This dragon war—" Yrian started to argue, but Aisling cut him off.

"Did he say he *created* the septs?" she asked her husband. "As in … created? I thought the First Dragon did that."

"He was busy elsewhere," Yrian said with a slight shrug. "I decided that since the kin were warring amongst themselves, we needed a way to work together. My sister and two brothers agreed to become wyverns to septs, and following that, I organized the weyr to benefit dragonkin. The First Dragon created the dragon heart for the purpose of binding all dragons to the weyr, and distributed the shards accordingly."

"Holy *merde*," Aisling said, her eyes wide as she watched Yrian.

I knew how she felt, and acknowledged the wholly unnecessary surge of pride at the idea that Yrian had so much impact on the growth of his family.

"Nala is the mother of Xavier," Archer said, the words dropping like lead.

Next to me, Yrian stiffened.

I sent him a quick glance, but his expression was frozen, although his eyes had narrowed on Archer when he asked, "What sept was this Xavier from?"

"Blue dragons," Hunter answered. "Our mother, Raisa, was a green dragon when he abducted her and impregnated her in his attempt to create the race of dragon hunters."

Once again, he and Archer exchanged telling looks.

"It didn't work," Thaisa said, giving her dragon a little smile. "At least, not until we broke the curse that kept the two of them unbalanced."

My attention was on Yrian. He didn't seem to be breathing.

I leaned in close and whispered in his ear, "Who is Nala?"

His head turned, his eyes now dark with obvious pain and distress. "My youngest daughter."

"You have kids?" I asked, for some reason astounded by the idea that he had children. I mentally lectured myself that of course he had children—he'd had an official mate, one who helped him create more dragons, not a weird artificer with a penchant for quirky men with dragon tats.

"I had four daughters. Three died. The fourth survived, but I placed her into hiding before I retreated to my griefscape," he answered, but I could almost feel the pain in him.

I put my hand on his, giving his fingers a supportive squeeze. "I'm sorry. Even if it was a long time ago, I'm sure you still feel their loss. Is Nala still alive?"

He turned to look at Archer, a question in his shaded eyes.

The latter shook his head. "The castle she held was under siege by mortals, and she was killed in their attack around 800 CE."

I rubbed Yrian's fingers, my heart aching for him.

He was silent for a few minutes while the others discussed what Xavier could want with the green dragons, but eventually squared his shoulders and addressed the others. "What you tell me is regrettable, but it does little to change the situation facing us. Kashi is more powerful and poses a bigger threat, not just to Becket, but to dragonkin. You think he's helpless in the Duat., but that is not the case."

"Sorry I'm late. Again. We have a new steward, ironically named Stewart, who is a very nice man, but he's horrible about arranging me transport out of the Beyond to wherever a sarkany was being held. Hello, everyone." Charity entered the room, a notepad clasped in her hands as she greeted the dragons. All the wyverns stood and bowed, including Yrian, who fetched another chair, placing it on my far side. I figured that since no one objected to her presence, she must be a normal member at the meetings. "The First Dragon is away helping one of his brothers with a problem, so I'm here to take notes for him. Did I miss anything I should tell him?"

"Nothing other than the fact that Yrian created both the septs and the weyr, which I think is pretty amazing," Aisling said, her eyes still big when she looked at him.

"Oh, I didn't know that." Charity hesitated, then set down her pen. "But I'm sure the First Dragon does, so feel free to proceed."

"And then there's the fact that Becket is Yrian's mate," Ysolde pointed out, smiling at us.

"No," I said firmly.

Yrian cocked an eyebrow at me.

"We are not discussing this now," I told him, his eyebrow, and Ysolde. "There's too many other things going on to distract ourselves with who may or may not be a mate."

"Just so. Charity, we were explaining to Yrian why his help is needed in dealing with Xavier," Drake said, obviously trying to take control of the meeting again.

"Who it turns out is Yrian's grandson. Oh!" Ysolde's eyebrows rose as she looked at her dragon. "That means he's your grandnephew, and Constantine's cousin."

"Just what I need. More murderous family," Constantine muttered.

"After discussing the situation with Bastian, we have agreed that it's likely Xavier wants the shards belonging to the green dragons," Drake continued.

"You have more than one shard?" Yrian asked, a little frown pulling down his eyebrows.

A sudden urge to smooth out the wrinkle between his brows was so overwhelming, I actually lifted my hand before

As soon as I realized what I was doing, I tucked my fingers under my leg, determined to keep my misbehaving libido in check.

"Yes," Drake said, looking away.

"He has our shard, the one given to the black dragons," Ysolde told Yrian. "I gave it to him in exchange for retrieving Baltic's mage sword."

"Without bothering to ask me if I wanted you to do so," Baltic said with a glower at her.

She just smiled in return. "Shortly after which, the sword was lost to the mages and handed over to Bael."

A slight commotion emerged from the tablet, where a woman was now sitting next to Constantine, arguing with him.

"It's not your fault, so stop martyring yourself. Becket? Hello, I'm Bee, and I'm Constantine's mate. Just so you know, he feels absolutely horrible that he couldn't get the light sword away from Bael, but since he only just managed to save me from almost certain destruction, he needs to cut himself some slack. Besides, it's not like Bael can use the sword. Not while he's in the Duat."

"The weyr must pull together to face Xavier," another blond dragon on the tablet said. This one had an Italian accent. Next to me, Charity wrote something on her notepad, and then surprised me by sliding it toward me.

His name is Bastian. He used to be wyvern of the blue sept, but he left the sept to save his mate, Phyllida.

I mouthed a "thank you" to her.

"The tribes—those who are friendly—have been talking about setting up our own version of a weyr," Archer said slowly, but his expression was troubled. "I don't like the idea of having two entities overseeing dragonkin, but I suppose it can't be helped."

"Why?" I asked before I realized I'd spoken. Hastily, I added, "Sorry, I know I'm just a guest here. Ignore me."

"You are more than a guest, and you will not be ignored," Yrian said, taking my hand again.

"Why do we not want two groups?" Archer glanced around the table. "It defeats the purpose of the weyr, which is to make the dragonkin collectively stronger."

"That is part of the reasoning behind the weyr," Yrian said, now looking thoughtful. A little shiver of pleasure rippled down my back when his fingers absently stroked mine. "Keeping the weyr safe from any dragons who wanted to rule over all the kin was another reason."

"So, fundamentally, your weyr is a collection of dragons who agreed to work together for the betterment of the dragonkin?" I asked, the problem solver in me wanting to work out a solution. "That doesn't explain why some of you guys would make your own weyr."

Tribes, Charity noted on her pad, *are groups of what are sometimes lawless dragons, but some are sept-adjacent. Tribes aren't all one type of dragon, like the septs. Archer and Hunter each lead a tribe.*

"Tribes are only granted membership in the weyr if they hold a relic with suitable provenance to verify it had been in their possession for a reasonable amount of time," Drake explained. "We recently reformed the rules regarding admittance to the weyr in order to safeguard it from an influx of tribes who would wreak havoc."

"We were going to approach the First Dragon about changing the articles founding the weyr to allow us to include those tribes who agree to our tenets, but evidently, we should be asking you, instead," Gabriel said, looking at Yrian.

"It's your weyr," I said, confused as I looked amongst the dragons in the room. "Why can't you guys make that a rule?"

"We can change only minor aspects, not those impacted by the magic woven into the creation of the weyr itself," Drake answered. Now all the dragons were eyeing Yrian. "We—the dragonkin—are bound to the articles of creation. The most we can do is reform it within the bounds of the articles."

"Did you do that on purpose?" I asked Yrian, intrigued by just how intricate were dragon politics.

"Bind the kin to the articles?" he asked, then answered before I nodded. "It was the only way to keep them from warring. They had to be bound to the articles, or they would not be a part of the weyr. In the end, all agreed."

"Smart," I said, admiring how he'd obviously worked so hard to get his family to pull together instead of going their own way.

Yrian looked surprised for a moment, then pleased.

"As the creator of the weyr, you could break the articles without repercussion. Would you break them so they can be reformed to reflect our current reality?" Archer asked him. I had a feeling he just asked a question that everyone had wanted to ask but hesitated to do so.

It drove home how much respect Yrian commanded ... that or they acknowledged just how powerful he was in his own right.

Yrian said nothing for a few minutes, frowning at the table as he evidently worked his way through the suggestion.

"I hesitate to do so," he finally said, his voice almost as

measured as that of his father. "Not because I wish to deprive your tribes of the support provided by the weyr, but because the articles themselves carry immense power. To break them is to release that power, and I have no idea how it would affect both the mortal and immortal worlds. Even if breaking the articles did no harm, it would attract the notice of Kashi and this Xavier who is warring with you … and both would use it to destroy kin."

"Baltic said the articles couldn't be broken just for that reason," Ysolde said, her expression somber. "But surely, there must be a way that a codicil or something like that can be added to them? The articles, that is. Something that would let the tribes without relics join us."

"Perhaps the answer is to locate the relics, rather than trying to change the weyr itself," Gabriel suggested.

"There are none that aren't already being held," Bastian said. I noticed he'd been joined by a dark-haired woman with watchful eyes. "But Phyllida had a question I could not answer—would it be possible for the First Dragon to create relics for our tribes in order to join the weyr?"

Yrian was shaking his head even before Bastian finished. "That is not how it works."

"The relics were formed in the act of creating the dragonkin," Baltic added, his expression matching my suddenly glum spirits. "Once those were created, all others were lesser, not as potent or powerful, and having little to no importance."

"My youngest brother speaks the truth," Yrian said, leaning back in his chair. "Only the dragon heart, Firstborn talismans, and Iceni's ringsels are true relics. All others are related, but not powerful enough to bind them to the weyr."

"And Iceni was … ?" I asked, the name familiar, but regardless, I wished I had a notepad of my own to take notes.

"The Life Mother," Yrian answered. "She was the First Dragon's mate."

"She gave birth to three of the six Firstborn," Constantine added. "After she perished, her ashes were bound to the ringsels. The First Dragon gave them into the protection of various lords of equally various underworlds."

"But they're precious to you guys, right?" I asked the table in general.

All the dragons nodded.

I turned to Yrian. "So, why didn't your dad give them to you guys? If they are that valuable, it seems odd that he'd give them to someone who wasn't a dragon."

"That was the reason he did so," Yrian answered. "They are powerless to anyone but dragonkin, but since Iceni's murderer would have moved the stars in the sky to get ahold of them, the First Dragon put them out of his reach by working with the Sovereign to create the thirteen Hours, and secured the ringsels with the Hours' lords."

I mused over that while the dragons discussed finding the existing ringsels.

"If we can't have new ones made, and we can't break the articles of the weyr, then we'll just have to find the relics being held in the Hours," a dark-haired man said in a Slavic accent, his manner of speaking him leaving me feeling like he was almost biting off the ends of the words.

That's Kostya, Charity wrote on her notepad. *He's very dramatic. He's also Drake's brother. The mates have a drinking game related to his drama-llama moods.*

Drake looked suddenly much happier. "Naturally, the green dragons will make available our services in order to liberate the ringsels from their respective guardians."

"We might try talking to the lords of the Hours first," Bastian suggested with a little smile toward Drake. "They may be agreeable to return the relics, especially if Yrian is on hand to reassure them of the fittingness of our request."

Drake made a face at that suggestion.

"Xavier and Deus tried that," a man on the tablet said. He sounded Greek, but was also blond. "They tried to get the ringsels, but the Hours' lords couldn't be forced to give them up. That was part of the protections written into the creation of the Hours, themselves. We heard that Xavier was in a rage once he realized they were beyond his reach. Sadly, that means they are out of ours, as well."

Charity nudged the notebook toward me. *That's Feo. He used to be with Xavier's tribe, but left due to not being a monster. He leads the Fire Tribe now.*

"Sounds like we need to talk to Finch and Christian," Ysolde said, and the other ladies nodded.

Finch = Christian's nephew. He runs one of the Hours with his wife, Tatiana, Charity wrote.

"What if the First Dragon were to ask the Hour people to give the ringsels back?" May asked.

The room fell silent, all eyes now on Charity.

She pulled out her phone and tapped on it while saying, "I'll ask him, but I doubt if it's that easy. If it was, he'd likely have gotten them back. Oh. He's already answered." She smiled at Yrian and me. "He says that's why he ensured that Yrian was freed—he is the help the dragonkin need."

"I had a feeling he would say something along those lines," Ysolde said, her hand on Baltic's leg. "He's forever doing that sort of thing. I hope he doesn't drop mysterious quests on you the way he did me, Becket, because it's enough to drive you insane."

I slid a glance toward Yrian's thigh sitting right there next to me. I cherished the memory of him in the portal shop, standing in nothing but a pair of briefs and a shirt, his glorious legs right out there where I could best admire them. Heat flashed through me, and before I realized I was doing it, I tamped out the fire that blossomed at my feet.

I allowed myself to indulge in a little introspection while the dragons discussed their options, wondering if the connection growing stronger with each passing minute meant I really was Yrian's mate, or if I just hadn't had a roll in the sack recently. I counted back, realized it had been almost five years, and gave a mental sigh.

It was most likely libido and nothing more.

And what a depressing thought that was.

NINE
YRIAN

Yrian was on fire.

Literally.

"Sorry, is that you or me? It was me earlier, which, no, I don't think means I'm your mate, but perhaps it's something to do with having a sympathetic link? Regardless, I'm not sure Allie's carpet is fireproof," Becket whispered.

Yrian stopped imagining her lying on his bed, her lovely red hair spread across the pillow, and all her silky, freckled flesh laid out for him to worship, looked down, and realized that the near erection he sported also triggered a merry circle of dragon fire around their chairs.

"That is my fire, and we will discuss the mate issue at a later time," he answered, clamping down hard on both his errant fire and the sexual interest that increased with each moment she sat next to him, being tempting.

"Just so you know, I really dislike people telling me what to do. Also, I need to go. My bandmates are getting testy because they want me to watch the other bands, so I'm going to scoot. I'm sure I'll see you later." As she spoke, she rose and, with a quick apology to the others, headed for the door.

He followed her, ignoring the looks from the kin.

She stopped as soon as she left the library. "What are you doing?"

"Escorting you," he answered, wondering why she thought he'd allow her to venture out unprotected. Even if the First Dragon hadn't promised that the dragons would protect her, he would never risk her safety. Not with Kashi's minions searching for her.

"But you're vital to the meeting your family is having," she said, and actually put her hands on his chest and gave him a push, no doubt intending on shoving him back into the room.

He didn't move, just lifted one eyebrow at her. "Like you, I don't take well to being forced into action. If you wish to feel my chest, I am agreeable, but this pushing action is not tolerable."

She glowered at him for a few seconds; then suddenly, her expression cleared and she smiled.

She had a faint indentation on one cheek that pleased him. "Point taken. I wouldn't like it if you got pushy with me. As a reward, I'm going to tell you something that you're going to love."

"Your legs?" he asked. "Or your breasts? I like both. Also, your hips are quite pleasing. They have a width that makes me feel ..." His eyes narrowed as he tried to put into words just how her hips affected him.

She seemed to be having trouble breathing, her breath coming in short inhalations, her eyes dilating in a way that made him think of bedsport on a lazy summer day. "It's not about any of that. You like my hips?" she asked, her voice more breath than actual sound. "I like yours, too. And your thighs. I really like those. Did you have a horse in your grief world? Because you have the legs of a man who does a lot of riding."

"I did, but he died. I miss him," Yrian said, remembering with mingled fondness and sadness his faithful Gallie. He'd lived much longer in the griefscape than he would have in the mortal realm, but time caught up to him after a few hundred years, leaving Yrian absolutely alone. "What do you have to tell me if it isn't about your breasts and hips?"

She reached into his pocket and pulled out his phone device, tapping on it until she held it up to him.

"'Chonky cats,'" he read on the video page. A plethora of videos appeared beneath the words. "What is 'chonky'?"

"It's a modern term meaning chunky. Or downright fat. And if you're one of those people who bitch at chonky-cat videos by yelling about how unhealthy it is, then we are not going to be friends." She gave him a pointed look that, to his great amusement, he felt down to his toenails. "And thank you for the offer of an escort, but that's Annaliese and Jesús just by the door, and I'm willing to bet you they are waiting to walk me down to the performance area, so you can go back and help your family."

He didn't like the idea of leaving her care to others, but realized he had little choice. "There is truth in what you say. My kin has need of my help, and I have sworn to do what I can for them. Very well, I will see you later. Do not leave the area, or separate from your protection."

"OK, this is an example of the bossiness I mentioned earlier. Go do your thing, and I'll see you later."

She left before he could give her another five minutes of warnings, but both Dark Ones gave him a nod to let him know they would guard her well.

The rest of the *sárkány* was engrossing but, at the same time, infuriating. The wyverns continued to insist that Kashi was of no concern, and that he needed to aid them with the dragon Xavier.

"It comes down to this," the green wyvern said at the end of another hour of discussion. "Xavier is of direct threat to not just my sept but the weyr and other tribes, while Bael—who, yes, we concede has far more abilities in the Duat than he should, or with which we are comfortable—is the lesser of two evils."

A wordless protest emerged from the tablet, Kashi's son clearly objecting.

Yrian was sympathetic; Constantine seemed to be the only dragon present who understood just how dangerous

Kashi was and the folly that the kin were encouraging by designating him as a lesser concern.

"Will you help us?" the silver wyvern asked, and Yrian felt a familiar trap closing around him.

"Once, I allowed myself to be distracted," he said slowly, his gaze on the wood grain of the table. It was pleasing, but not enough to drive away the sense of dread and despair that came with the request by the wyverns. "That ended in the destruction of the shadow sept, my mate, and Iceni."

Silence fell at his words, and despite the distance, faint music could be heard from the field below the castle. He had a sudden urge to be out there with Becket, listening to her, watching her, and sharing cat videos with her. He wanted to hear her sing, and see how much of her mother's abilities she had inherited.

He just wanted to be with her.

"I'm afraid we don't know the events you are referencing," Drake said, glancing around at the other wyverns. All of them but Baltic shook their heads. "And with all due respect, that had to have happened more than a millennium ago, and the weyr is in peril *now*."

Yrian thought about what they were asking of him. His gaze met that of Baltic. It had been two years since the latter had met him at the exit of his griefscape, and during much of that time, Yrian struggled with the madness inherent both in being separated from dragonkin and in grappling with the modern mortal realm. Baltic had aided him as best he could, Yrian now realized, although he hadn't been so understanding in the past.

"I apologize for the manner in which I dealt with you," he told Baltic, getting to his feet, his precious phone in hand. "I was mad for a while."

The corners of Baltic's lips twitched, but he bowed his head in acknowledgment of the apology.

"I will not, however, allow more innocents to die because my attention was focused on the wrong threat. Kashi is infinitely more dangerous than Xavier. It is he whom I must attend to first. Then I will help you resolve the issue of the tribes, the weyr, and Xavier."

Several wyverns protested. He hesitated at the door, his gaze once again on his brother. "You know of the events surrounding my destruction?" he asked.

Baltic gave an abbreviated nod.

"You may tell them," he said, then marched out of the room, and castle, heading down to the field where even now the music swelled and lifted in the late afternoon air.

"What are you doing here?" Becket asked seven minutes later when he found her seated on a blanket with another woman. He recalled the latter's name was Billie, and she was part of Becket's band. The former had twisted around to look up at him, one hand shading her eyes from the lowering sun. Her glamour was the same one she'd worn that morning—dark hair and eyes, and no freckles.

He missed those freckles.

"My youngest brother is explaining to the weyr why I must put Kashi first. You do not need to move—I will sit on the grass." The last was said to the other woman, who grinned and told him she wanted to go watch some friends perform before leaving. Yrian sat next to Becket, his gaze automatically searching the crowds for signs of demons. "Why do you hide your appearance?"

She looked momentarily startled, and it took almost a full minute before she answered. "I started using glamours as protection when I was young. My mother warned me that I needed to hide my true self so that people wouldn't take advantage of me. Or, worse, use me to harm others. Does it bother you?"

He thought about that while absently watching a couple of blue dragons skirt the edges of the crowd. "Not in the sense I think you mean. I do not mind any of the appearances you don, but I also like the one natural to you. I like your hair and freckles."

She touched the thick black braid that wrapped around her head. "Have a thing for redheads, do you?"

"I didn't know that I did, but perhaps it is so," he answered, noting the arrival of three green dragons. "My daughter Nala joined the blue sept after I retreated to the griefscape. Some of her kin are over there behind the food stall."

She craned to look around him, her arm brushing his as she peered at the green and blue dragons, now clustered together. "Do you want to tell me what Baltic is spilling to the others about your past? If I'm being nosy, just ignore that question."

He examined her face. "My brother Kashi corrupted my mate, Amice. She betrayed me. With the help of our mother, Kashi slaughtered all of the members of my sept, two of my four children, and Iceni, the Life Mother."

The band playing reached the end of their song just as he finished speaking.

For a few seconds, the air was full of applause; then silence drifted softly down upon them as the band left the stage for the next group.

"Your brother did that? The demon lord Bael?" Shock was evident in Becket's expression, but that quickly melted to one of sympathy as she carefully leaned to the side and gave him what he considered a far too impersonal hug. "What happened to your wife … er … mate? Regardless, I'm so sorry. I know this was a long time ago, but it's still a horrific tragedy. No wonder you want vengeance against Bael."

"I don't want vengeance. I want him destroyed so that he cannot harm anyone else," he answered, the familiar sense of being encased in ice creeping over him … at least it did until she leaned in closer, her breast pressed against him in a manner that threatened to end in another erection and circle of dragon fire. "Amice bound herself to Kashi after the death of the sept. He killed her, of course, and dragged her mutilated corpse to lay at my feet. I took her into the griefscape along with all the members of my sept whom I failed. I could do no less. She wasn't to blame, not really. Kashi wanted to destroy me just as he wanted to destroy our siblings, but they were still under the protection of the First Dragon, so he struck at me, instead."

"Jesus tap-dancing Christ," she swore, her upper body now pressed against him in a manner that left him in profound admiration for her curves. "Like it couldn't get any worse? Yrian, I may not have known you for long, but I can tell you are a protector, someone who clearly devotes himself to the care of others. You aren't to blame for your sadistic brother's actions. And I'm sorry, but your dad was an asshat for not protecting you, too."

He mulled that over for the time it took Becket to release him, his body mourning her removal. "The First Dragon is many things, but I do not think asshat is fitting."

"You just said he let your insanely homicidal brother kill off your sept and wife while protecting the rest of your family. That's asshat territory right there," she insisted, her expression dark with sorrow.

"My siblings were still young, and I had just formed the weyr. Kashi was furious with the First Dragon because he wasn't allowed to form a sept of his own. It was needful that they—my two brothers and sister—were protected from his wrath. The First Dragon knew I could stand against Kashi, while they could not." His gaze dropped to the grass, regret swamping him just as it had for every day of the last sixteen hundred years. "He was proven wrong when I went to help my sister, not knowing that Kashi had lured me away in order to destroy my sept. It's why I will not allow the same to happen again."

"You think Bael is behind this Xavier dude attacking Aisling and Drake's sept?" she asked, but he was pleased when she scooted over until her hip was pressed against him, one hand now rubbing his back in an obvious attempt to drive him to the very limits of sexual need.

"No, I meant that I will not abandon your protection by being diverted to ending the threat of Xa—" He stopped, her words penetrating the miasma of guilt that rose with his explanation of the past.

"What is it?" she asked softly, her breath brushing his ear in a manner that had him instantly hard and wishing that they were in her bedroom with the massive bed. "Do you see Candy and Andy?"

"No. It's what you said." He was silent for a moment. "I hadn't considered that Kashi may be behind the distraction of Xavier, but you may have seen through the deception my brother always wrapped around his actions. For what purpose would he do so?"

"Obviously, he knows you're back, and he's being a jerkwad," Becket answered.

Yrian's mind was still dealing with the new idea regarding Kashi. "The green wyvern said his guards were arriving to help protect you. Would you be able to make six or seven glamours quickly?"

She looked curious, but rather than asking why, she thought for a few seconds, glanced around, then turned her body toward him, leaning against his shoulder as if she was cuddling. But hidden by their bodies, her hands started weaving in the air, little glints of light flashing briefly as the energy she used was formed into glamours. It took her only five minutes before she sat back, a small stack of the flattened disks that were glamours on her lap before she handed them to him. Her phone device chimed a bell at her just as she did so. "I hope these help. I've got to run and get dressed. Our set is in forty minutes—are you going to watch?"

He dragged his mind from the dark thoughts concerning what Kashi could possibly want with the dragon Xavier, and instead rose when Becket got to her feet, feeling a blossom of warmth in his chest at the shy smile she offered.

On impulse, he took her arms, pulled her up to his chest, and kissed her. She stiffened for a few seconds, then relaxed against him, her lips parting under his, allowing him to dip into the sweetness of her mouth. His mind was flooded with need, want, desire, a smidgen of guilt, and a whole lot of lust. He tried to remember the last time he had even thought about having sexual congress, and realized he hadn't ... not since Amice had turned against him. She had been every-thing to him at the time, and even though her betrayal of him and the sept was a deep scar on his soul, he remembered the time when she held his heart.

And now here was Becket, her body deliciously soft against his, fitting into him in a way that did much to assuage the ever-present guilt.

"Holy cheese on toast," she said when she managed to pry her mouth from his. She panted, her eyes misty with emotion, and for a few seconds, he saw past her glamour to her true self. Her freckled cheeks glowed with a blush, her pale-blue eyes sparkling like topazes in clear water, her breasts heaving in a manner that had him almost to the limits of his control. "For someone who has been alone for sixteen hundred years, you sure as hell know how to kiss."

"You are very good at it, too," he said, feeling it only right to acknowledge her part in the proceedings. "I particularly enjoyed that wiggle you gave against my rod. Do you wish to engage in bedsport?"

She stepped back out of his arms, his body singing a dirge over that fact. "Can I just say that I love the fact that you are such a fascinating mix of a modern man with a fine appreciation of cat videos, and someone who was around several thousand years ago. I assume bedsport is sex? If so, then of course I want to go to bed with you. Just look at you! You're gorgeous! Your eyes damn near glow, they're so golden. Your hair makes my knees weak, especially that white swash, and the rest of you is downright droolworthy. But as I said earlier, I'm not the *jump into bed with the first handsome dragon I meet* sort of girl, so although right now I can't think of anything more I'd like to do than kiss and touch and taste you, I'm not going to. Maybe later, after we've had some time to get to know each other, but not now. Besides, I really have to go, or Skye will have a hissy fit. I'll see you after our set, yes?"

"Yes," he said, flattered by her praise, while at the same time wanting to catalog everything he liked about her. He decided he'd save that for later, when she would be more receptive to such things.

She pressed a finger to his lips, her eyes sparkling at him under the setting sun; then she was off.

It took him a good ten minutes to will his erection to a state more conducive to comfort, at which point he handed over the glamours to one of the patrolling Dark Ones with instructions to give them to the dragonkin, then wandered over to a food tent where he purchased and consumed three cinnamon pastries before returning for a fourth, which he carefully wrapped in a napkin and placed in a pocket for Becket.

He was considering a stall that sold brightly colored dresses and skirts, trying to remember how much of the money that Baltic had given him he had remaining, when Gabriel approached. He looked different, but once he was near, Yrian could feel the nature of the dragon beneath the glamour.

"Is something wrong?" Gabriel asked, his now dark eyes wary as his gaze skittered along the streams of people; some were just arriving, while others took advantage of the break to utilize the toilets and various food stalls.

"That is an odd question. In what way is something wrong?" Yrian asked, studying the wyvern. He'd learned how the black sept had been sheared in two by the once-mad Constantine, and that the silver dragons were, until recently, the youngest of the kin, but there was something about Gabriel that had him feeling the silver dragons were lucky in their wyvern.

"For one, you sent glamours in for us with the instructions to put them on before we left the castle. Is there someone you feel we need to hide from? The two wrath demons?" Gabriel answered slowly, his gaze still moving amongst the mortals. Yrian noticed the green and blue dragons were no longer visible.

"I have not seen or felt the wrath demons, but there are blue and green dragons here," he answered.

"Drake's guards, yes … although blue dragons? Bastian didn't mention having tribe members in the area." Gabriel rubbed the back of his neck, still obviously searching the masses of people thronging past them. "Something is definitely off. I'm prickly, like the air is full of static. Since you are the Firstborn, I thought you might feel it, too. Is that why you have us wearing glamours?"

"Your mother is a shaman?" he asked, having a vague memory of his youngest brother explaining who were the current wyverns.

"Yes." Gabriel's back twitched, a gesture that had Yrian feeling oddly disconcerted. He didn't feel the static mentioned, but now he was feeling a bit edgy.

"That is a form of earth elemental. My mother is a fire fury. They are not in tune with any element but their own, and thus, I do not have the awareness of the environment that your shaman mother gave to you. However, it is almost time for Becket to perform. I will ensure the others pose her no harm."

Gabriel looked confused when Yrian caught the echo of the announcer mentioning the next set and hurried off to the stage area.

"What others?" Gabriel called after him, but he didn't wait to explain. It was far more important that Becket be protected.

TEN
BECKET

"We just have to make it through these covers—then we'll be in the final three. And I can't see how we can mess up. Billie's version of Lady Gaga is spot-on, and Becket has the other two songs rocking hard. No, we're definitely going to make the final. The Tres Leches failed miserably and are out. Did you see them, Becket, or were you too busy snogging your new boyfriend?" Skye asked.

"He's not my boyfriend, although … never mind. I'm not going to deal with the fact that the man is so sexy he could drop a nun at thirty paces. I didn't see the Spanish band, but it's interesting they didn't do well with their cover set." I emerged from the tent given over as a dressing room, wriggling my toes in an attempt to make my heels more comfortable, smoothed a hand over my short, flirty red dress that would not have been out of place in a popular club, and settled into my glamour. I'd kept to the same one I'd used before while performing so as to not confuse the judges or audience, but I was a little nervous being out on the stage wearing it, since I was just with Yrian, and any demons around might have seen us. "However, I don't like counting my chicks before they hatch, so I'm going to do my best to wow the audience regardless of how bad the Leches did."

"The two German boy bands are out also, did you see?" Billie, clad in short red satin shorts with a matching bustier, did her usual preperformance calisthenics, mostly touching her toes, and doing an odd marching-in-place exercise that made my feet hurt just watching her.

"Am I the only one with pinchy shoes?" I asked, glancing at the others. Deni wore thigh-high boots, while Skye looked like a red catsuit had been painted on her. Neither one of them appeared the least bit uncomfortable. "Great. I am."

"You have to suffer for art," Deni said with a half smile. "That is what my father always told me, but he was a crap artist. Should we warm up again?"

"I don't think we need to," Skye said, watching the crew as they fetched the guitars after having set up Billie's drum kit. "The rehearsal that Becket managed to make was enough."

"I'm sorry that I was delayed by a problem, but since the people involved with that problem are keeping me—keeping all of us—safe, I'm going to be grateful rather than pissed. Shall we mantra?"

We stood together in a circle, arms around one another as Skye intoned the "we are awesome, we are winners" invocation to the goddess that the band swore by before performances. I was less confident in it, but kept my thoughts to myself, and simply gave myself up to the joy that was singing with the band.

The biggest stage was used for the day's final nine performances, of which we were the last. I was happy to see that the crowd, rather than dispersing for the night, was the largest we'd had yet. The tall event lights made it difficult to see out into the audience, but as we were walking across the stage, I caught sight of a clutch of familiar faces.

Ysolde, Aisling, Thaisa, and May stood together, completely surrounded by Christian's security team. Even the stage lights couldn't hide the fact that the ladies looked annoyed, no doubt due to having been herded together on the orders of the wyverns. I gave them a quick wave before moving out onto the stage proper.

As I took my place at the microphone, I had a fast look around, but didn't see any of the dragons other than Ysolde's son Brom and his girlfriend. I was disappointed not to see Yrian, wondering if he had used one of the glamours I created, but as soon as I stepped out, I saw him. He was at the end of the runway that extended from the main stage, standing with his arms crossed, looking so impossibly gorgeous I wanted to race down the runway in order to kiss him again.

"Your dragon friends out there?" Skye asked as we took our places.

"Yes, but Yrian had me make them glamours. I imagine they're out in the audience watching for demons." We both turned when the emcee announced our band.

"Give it up for our last band of the night: Unstoppable Beings!" the man yelled into the microphone over the crowd's noise at seeing us. "Straight from France, and currently in fifth place in the rankings, let them know how you feel!"

The cheer that followed was our sign to go, and after taking a deep breath and flashing a smile at Yrian, who didn't see because he was glaring off to the right, I took the microphone, gathered up my glamours, and started to sing.

The crowd was so reactive that I didn't need the glamour that encouraged people to dance, but I used it during Billie's song regardless, having seen two other bands use similar ones earlier. By the time we started into the last song of our set, a cover of a Sia song that always made my toes tap, a hint of something not right filtered onto the stage.

I was singing and flinging out glamours that had a rain of silver stars falling onto the crowd when I noticed that Yrian was no longer at the end of the runway. I was about to start down it, throwing more star glamours as I made my way, half-blinded by the big stage lights until all I could see of the audience was a black blur of shapes bopping up and down along to the tune.

I finished with big explosions of silver blasting upward from the stage, lighting up the entire field for ten seconds with brilliant flashes reminiscent of lightning strikes.

To my left, I saw three men running toward the stalls, men I recognized as wearing my glamours. They were followed by a handful of vampires.

My stomach turned over at sight. There was only one thing that would cause the dragons to leave their wives, and that was Candy and Andy.

As I returned to the main stage for our bow, I searched for signs of Yrian, but he was nowhere to be seen.

More concerning was the fact that Christian now stood with the women, along with Jim the demon dog, and Pixie. Two of the four guards peeled off with Christian when the latter went dashing off in the opposite direction of the wyverns.

"That went so well, didn't it? I think it went well. Did you see how they were dancing even before you glamoured them?" Billie almost skipped next to me as we hurried off the stage to the changing tent.

"I don't want to count my chickens early, like Becket said, but we kicked ass!" Deni said.

All three of my bandmates talked at the same time, excited, amped up on performance adrenaline, and just overall thrilled that the set had been received so well.

I was silent as I hurriedly stepped behind a privacy curtain and changed into a pair of leggings, a black tunic, and a blond glamour that was as opposite from my stage appearance as was possible.

"You guys were absolutely brilliant," I said as I emerged.

"So were you," Billie said with a giggle before taking her place behind the curtain.

"I don't think I've ever heard Billie sing better, and you two were beyond kick-ass and into the realm of legends," I told Deni and Skye. "But if you don't mind, I'm going to scoot. Something's up with the dragons, and if it's my stalkers, I'd rather get out of the public eye."

"We'll text you the time for the set tomorrow, but it won't be until after noon, so you'll have time to enjoy your boyfriend," Skye said with a slight acid tone to her voice. I said nothing, well aware she was still salty about her partner breaking up with her a few months before.

"Thanks, I appreciate the heads-up. Brilliantly done, ladies! We'll knock everyone's socks off tomorrow!" I gave them each a hug before hurrying out of the tent, my mind worried, my stomach unhappy, and my toes still angry about the heels.

Just as I rounded the stage, Allie took off to the left in a fast trot. I went straight for the ladies who now looked downright angry as they obviously argued with the vampire guards.

"What's happened?" I asked as I ran up to them, one of the vampires immediately blocking my view of the women. "Is it Candy and Andy? Where's Yrian?"

"Becket?" Aisling asked, peering around the bulky vampire. "You look so different!"

"I didn't want to wear my performance glamour," I said softly, looking around to make sure no one was close enough to hear. The crowd was filing out more or less without issue, although there were always a few stragglers who had to be encouraged to return to their lodgings. "Are more demons here?"

"No," Aisling said grimly, squeezing herself between two of the vampires. "Dragons. Bad ones. Jim, come with me. You may speak, but only if it's of importance."

"Like I got anything to say that isn't a pearl of wisdom? Heya, Becklestein. Loved that last song. Did you know when you twirl you can see your undies? Well, maybe *you* can't see them, but those of us on the ground can."

"Jim!" Aisling pinched the dog's shoulder. "We do not mention other people's underwear. Becket, I think everyone would be happier if you stayed here with Christian's men. I'm going to see what's happening, and remind Drake that I'm not a Guardian savant for nothing!"

"I'll come with. I can cast a few spells on whatever drag-on is causing issues," Ysolde said, likewise squeezing out of the vampire cordon. She hesitated a second. "Pixie—"

"I'm coming, too," the young woman said, a pugnacious expression on her face. "It's dark out. No one will see me when I hide in the shadows. I can spy and tell you where the baddies are."

Ysolde didn't look any too happy about it, but sent a meaningful glance toward her son, who gave her a quick nod of understanding as he took Pixie by the arm, and they hurried off toward the trailers and food stalls.

"And that's my cue to go to the shadow world, I think," May murmured before she blipped out of sight. I considered following her to the Beyond, but couldn't leave Yrian. What if he needed my help?

"Well, I'm not going to stay here by myself," I told the ladies, ignoring the objections by the guards when I followed the others.

"You're the one who needs the most protection," Ysolde pointed out. The guards moved alongside us, clearly deter-mined to do their best to keep us safe. "Yrian will go mental if you are harmed. Oh, hell. That sounds rude. Obviously, we would all be distraught were you to come to harm—"

"It's OK," I told her, worry quelling any amusement at her unintended gaffe. I searched the few remaining peo-ple on the field. Most of the attendees had left, and no one who remained appeared to be a dragon, or someone who was wearing a glamour. It was just a few mortals laughing, singing, and chatting loudly as they streamed past the stalls, heading for the parking lot and shuttles to nearby hotels. "I know what you mean, and I would agree, but this is a new glamour."

Jim cocked its head at me. "Yeah, but you're still a girl, and all the demons are looking for a girl."

"Hmm. Good point." I took advantage of the group pausing at a (now closed, much to Jim's sadness) ice cream stall, and whipped up a quick glamour for myself. "Glamour incoming," I warned everyone, and ducked behind the stand to apply it.

"Whoa. That's …" Jim blinked at me.

"Yeah, I know, but it's the only man I could think of who wasn't present," I said, trying to remember the First Dragon's exact speech cadence. I'm sure it was highly disconcerting to everyone to see what they thought was the dragon ancestor but hear my voice emerging from his mouth.

"What a good idea to use his form. The dragons may recognize his appearance, but I'm willing to bet they'll give you a wide berth, because they won't want to tangle with him," Aisling told me; then she pointed at a flash of blue light that exploded from behind two of the big trailers. "Is that an arcane blast?"

"Yes," Ysolde said with a heartfelt sigh. "It means someone has suitably pissed off Baltic until he resorted to magic. We'd better go see how many of Xavier's crew are here."

"Hey, look, it's the First Dragon," Jim called as we all rounded the corner of the trailers. The scene laid out in front of us was so horrifying—Yrian and his family were fighting at least a dozen others—that we all paused for a moment to take in just what was happening.

"Jim!" Aisling snarled the word in a near whisper. "Don't call attention to … er … the First Dragon."

"It's like you said, they won't bother her if they think she's a badass demigod who can wipe up the ground with them," Jim whispered back.

Yrian had somehow managed to possess himself of a massive two-handed sword, a fact that had me boggling for a moment until I remembered the arsenal the vampires had made available.

The other wyverns were equally armed, although I noticed Gabriel and Drake were dual wielding maces, while Archer and Hunter had swords that glittered with gems and runes.

"Is that who I think it is?" Ysolde asked even as her hands danced in the air, obviously working up some magic.

Aisling leaped onto a stack of instrument cases, likewise drawing wards and flinging them out toward the melee. "It's Deus, yes, and I'm willing to bet the big guy in the back is Xavier, Archer and Hunter's father. Jim, stay out of their way!"

I didn't know which dragon belonged to what sept—or tribe—but Yrian and Baltic were fighting back-to-back with a group of five dragons. Baltic held a sword in one hand, while the other was splashing arcane magic around.

"Go help them," I ordered my protective guard. "They're outnumbered!"

Jesús, the nearest vamp, looked incredulous. He gestured toward the fighters. "They're all dragons."

Drake snarled something rude in Magyar when a dark-haired man suddenly appeared behind him and ran him through with his sword.

"Oh, you did not!" Aisling bellowed, and would have run toward her dragon but Ysolde grabbed her as she passed.

"He's OK. See? Gabriel and Baltic have beaten Deus back. Oh, nice one, Baltic. I bet he has trouble growing whiskers on that side of his face after that arcane blast."

"Go help them! They can still be hurt," I insisted to the vampires, feeling like screaming.

I wanted badly to help Yrian, but at the same time, I was wary of anyone deciding to go for the First Dragon. At the best, all I could do to escape harm was slipping into the Beyond, and after the two days I'd had, I didn't have much faith in it as the place of protection I had previously assumed it was.

"Christian told us to protect you," another vamp said, looking as stubborn as the other three.

"Where is he?" I heard May ask as she materialized next to us, out of breath, and wiping two bloody, wickedly sharp daggers on a flyer she picked off the ground.

"He and the others are taking care of the demons that swarmed in just as you finished," Jesús answered, waggling a falchion. I noticed the rest of my team was equally equipped with bladed weapons, although one had a Taser that I thought seriously about asking to borrow.

Aisling climbed to the top of the trailer, running to the end so that she was just above the battle, and flung wards out so fast I couldn't even see them land.

"Stay with the vamps," Ysolde told me, and also climbed the trailer, her hands full of blue-white magic. "Brom?"

"Over here. Should I stay with Pixie?" He appeared behind us, a two-handed axe in his hands. "She's got no one to protect her."

"I don't need protection! I'm a polter!" The outraged voice came from the inky shadows cast by the stage lights.

"Stay with Thaisa and Becket," Ysolde ordered her son, and moved to the end to join Aisling.

"I don't need protecting, either," Thaisa protested, but no one paid attention.

"I am not the *stay behind and let other people fight my battles* sort of a person," I told Brom, looking around frantically for something I could use as a weapon. "I don't suppose anyone has a bow? I used to be a pretty good archer when I was in college."

"No bow, but you can borrow Allie's sword," Annaliese said, handing me a short sword with lovely green gems in the quillons.

"Thanks. Let's see if we can't cause a little havoc," I said, throwing caution, common sense, and even self-preservation aside as I charged forward to the whirlwind that was the battling dragons.

The vampires all protested, but followed when I lunged at the nearest dragons, aiming for arms and legs, since I didn't want to kill anyone, just disable them.

Ahead of me, Yrian was now fighting three dragons by himself, but other than a slash on his arm that bled heavily, he looked like he was holding his own. He kept two of them busy by splashing fire over them, which had both men screaming and dropping to the ground to roll around in an attempt to put out the fire.

"I thought dragons weren't hurt by their fire," I said, moving back to the fringe of the fighting, just below the spot where Ysolde was throwing arcane balls at the dragons. Only a few landed, but oddly enough, several turned to fruit and bounced harmlessly off their intended victims.

"They aren't, but Baltic—oh, you bastard, now Baltic is going to have to get his hair cut!—Baltic says that Yrian's fire is different than normal dragon fire. By the rood! What is Xavier doing?"

"Running away," Archer snarled as he gave a valiant heave and tossed aside the two dragons who were trying their best to decapitate him with massive axes.

"As usual," Hunter added, leaping over a dragon as he fell, and racing forward to tackle the man who clearly was their father. "Yrian! A little help to keep that bastard from slipping into the Beyond!"

"Yrian?" Xavier asked, one hand dancing in the air, smoky black symbols of a spell glowing briefly before disappearing. Protected as he was by a shield of dragons, he glanced over the scene, pausing on me with narrowed eyes that immediately made me want to run to the Beyond.

A roar went up, one that seemed to scrape the night sky, and suddenly, a wave of fire boiled forward, knocking down everyone in its path.

Xavier hissed something in a language I didn't understand; then he was gone, having turned and fled into the night ahead of Yrian's fire.

Since the other dragons—both friendly and otherwise—went down in the wave of flames, only Yrian was upright to chase him. He stumbled when I leaped forward to help, his eyes furious when he realized it was me. I made a mental note to ask him how he knew I wasn't his father, since my glamours should pass muster so long as he wasn't too close to me, but ignored that question along with my remaining caution, instead running after him.

There were still mortals in the car park, long lines of vehicles pouring out onto a narrow road, and to my relief,

Yrian didn't blast everyone there in an attempt to stop Xavier. I caught up to him on the edge of the road, panting as I asked, "Did he get away? Dammit, I really need to get back onto a treadmill."

"Yes, he merged into the crowd of mortals," Yrian said, turning to land a glare on me. "Why do you appear to be the First Dragon?"

I gave a half-hearted shrug, still trying to catch my breath. "I figured it was safer if Candy and Andy were here. Also, how can you fight like you did, then run all the way out to the road and not even be breathing hard?"

"You are female," he said, taking my arm and heading us back toward the stage area. "Females are weaker than males."

I stopped and punched his non-injured arm. "I don't know where you got that bit of crap, but I can tell you right now that it won't fly. Not here, not now, and most definitely not with me. Women are so much stronger than men. We cope with blood and pain every month. We can form new organs to grow babies. And we keep the human—and other—races alive."

He made a scoffing sound that made me want to punch him again. "I will grant you the other examples, but as for the last, you must have a male to procreate."

"You think so?" I made the meanest eyes I could at him. "If I wanted to, I could get pregnant without ever seeing a man. And just for the record, Mr. Two Thousand Years Old—"

"I don't believe that age is correct," Yrian interrupted. "My youngest brother mentioned something he called the Bronze Age."

"Fine, then you're, what, five thousand years old? Regardless, if you ever want into my pants, you are going to need an attitude adjustment."

He took the hand that I had yanked away at his misogynistic statement. "Are you as physically strong as me?"

"No, of course not." I tried to pull my hand back, but he just twined his fingers through mine and continued back toward the staging area. "I'm not an idiot, Yrian. I know that men are frequently—although not always—physically stronger, but that is only one type of strength. In all other ways, your supposition is false. And rude. And annoying."

He was silent for almost a minute as we returned to where the others were just now picking themselves up off the blackened grass. "Very well, I concede your point, but only if you would explain to me why you believe I want to wear your pants."

"Huh?" I watched as the women and my vampire guard, all thankfully out of the splash zone, were checking the downed dragons, part of Xavier's attacking force.

"You said if I wanted into your pants, I would need to change my mind."

I whispered, "It's a colloquialism. It means sexy times."

"Bedsport?" His eyes went molten.

"Yes. Let's see how many people you decimated. I hope none of your family are hurt." I hurried forward, noting that although the wyverns all looked red and blistered, they were all alive. A few of the invader dragons rolled around on the ground moaning.

"What can I do to help you?" May asked Gabriel as we approached.

"Nothing." He was sitting on a crate, his head down, blisters evident on his arms and hands. "I just need a few minutes to concentrate on healing."

"Is there something we can do?" I asked, frustrated by so many things that, for a moment, I wanted to sit down and cry. Or scream to the stars. Or throw myself into Yrian's arms and hide away from the world.

My inner narrator was startled by the last thought, but immediately approved it and moved it to the top of our to-do list. I nixed that, reminding myself that I couldn't lecture a man about how strong women were one minute and, in the next, cling to him in order to hide from life.

"The urge to say Yrian's done enough is strong," Aisling said as she fretted over Drake, whom she helped to a nearby picnic table where Thaisa had Archer, with Hunter slowly dragging himself over to sit with them. "But I won't say it because Drake will lecture me later about unseemly mate behavior in front of the weyr. I'm glad to see you managed to heal where that blue dragon gutted you with the sword … oh, sweetie, no! How can you lose a tooth to fire? That makes two for the day. You're going to have to eat ice cream for a week."

"I am a wyvern. I don't lecture," Drake said, obviously trying for a dignified response, but his voice more of a croak than anything else. "I guide you to what is proper and right in a mate, and stop, Aisling. The tooth next to the one that exploded is loose, and you are making it worse."

She stopped trying to stuff a tissue into the bloody spot in his mouth, murmuring an apology.

"I think you guys could do with more of that spicy wine—Yrian, what are you doing to that poor man? He's burned to smithereens!" I had turned while speaking to see why Yrian was not offering to help his family, only to see him dragging one of the moaning dragons upward with one hand (causing my inner narrator to squeal to herself about just how very manly he was), before hauling him over to another picnic table, this one loaded with extra cables.

"That's Deus," Hunter said, lifting his head from where he was now flat out. "Also a son of Xavier. I'm surprised he didn't disappear into the Beyond with the sire."

"He didn't go into the Beyond," I said, moving over to Yrian's side. He was looking around for something, and I realized he wanted to bind Deus's hands.

"Are you sure?" Baltic lifted his head from where he, too, was obviously focusing his energy on healing the burns. He was healing faster than the others, because most of the blisters were gone, and he looked sunburned rather than scorched.

"He ran to the field with the cars," Yrian answered, whipping off his belt and using it to bind Deus's hands behind his back.

Baltic looked astounded for a moment before his expression shifted to consideration. "Something has changed, then. Archer? Hunter?"

"No clue," Hunter replied, moaning softly when he tried to sit up. "He definitely went into it the last time Archer and I saw him."

"He should not have been able to go there," Archer said with a shake of his head when Thaisa pulled out a bottle of water and offered it to him. "He has allied himself with dark power."

"And in general, beings of dark power are forbidden entrance to the Beyond," I said slowly, more to myself than anyone else. "Although the point is moot, I guess, if he's not running there to hide from you guys."

"The fact that he hasn't makes it clear what happened," Yrian said, now dragging other dragons over to plop them in a sitting position up against one of the trailers, while the vampires did the same for the dragons that had succumbed. "Becket was correct. Xavier is working for Kashi."

Silence fell over the group, even the surviving dragons now silent, although their expressions showed a wariness that I felt needed watching. Aisling, with a final *tut* at Drake's missing teeth, moved over to cast what I assumed were binding wards on the prisoners.

"It may be that Xavier is working with him, rather than for him," Drake said slowly, his gaze going around to the other wyverns, all of whom nodded. "It makes sense that he would wish to use Bael rather than vice versa."

Yrian made a face. "It doesn't matter what his wishes are. The minute he came into Kashi's domain, he became a puppet, whether or not he realized it."

"You think Bael gave Xavier his talisman?" Baltic asked Yrian.

"I think it is the only way to explain Xavier being able to use the Beyond," Yrian answered.

"I should have realized that," Baltic said, his lips twisting. "I assumed he hadn't really gotten into it, since it would have been impossible any other way. I will not underestimate him again."

"Who?" I asked, confused by the pronoun use. "Bael or Xavier?"

"Both," Baltic said with a grimness that I felt in my gut.

"What's a talisman?" I asked Yrian, then immediately modified the question. "That is, what does it mean in this instance?"

"All Firstborn receive a talisman from the First Dragon marking them as his children," he said, walking over to where Hunter sat on the top of the picnic table, his face still covered in blisters and blackish-red skin. "It would be enough to allow Xavier to use the Beyond. Why are you not healing as fast as the others?"

"We weren't born balanced," Hunter said, flinching backward when Yrian reached for him. "Archer was all dragon, while I got the fun side of dark power, demonic traits, and a good three hundred years of self-loathing. I'm still getting used to having the full complement of dragon abilities."

"Stop moving, or I won't be able to help you," Yrian said with a hint of steel in his voice. With his hands on Hunter's shoulders, he leaned forward, his face filled with concentration.

Gabriel lurched to his feet and came over to stand next to us, obviously curious. "You are a healer, too?"

"No. But these wounds were caused by my fire, and I can ease their effect."

Hunter took a deep breath, his eyes wide with surprise for a few seconds before he sat up straight, moving his shoulders when Yrian released him. The redness and blisters faded immediately, leaving him looking normal. "That is so much better. Not that I knew I could be burned by anyone's dragon fire, but still, thank you for the healing boost."

"Speaking of Yrian's fire, why did it not affect clothing, but only the flesh beneath it?" Ysolde asked, nodding when her son murmured something about Pixie and him patrolling the area just in case any stray dragons remained.

"I'm willing to bet it's something to do with his mom and the way furies work," I said after giving Yrian a few moments to reply. He didn't. Instead, he started searching the ground where the battle had taken place. "What are you looking for?"

"My phone device. It fell out of my pocket when those green dragons jumped me," he answered.

"They weren't members of my sept," Drake said, acid all but dripping off the words. "They were ouroboros, members of the Chaos Tribe who left the green dragons centuries ago."

"What on earth happened?" Allie appeared at a trot, stopping at the sight of the decimated area, the bodies of dead dragons, and the group of four who'd survived and were now stuck to the ground by Aisling's wards. "We just disposed of the last demon when we saw what looked like a fireball explode. Oh no. Are they—"

"Do not look, Allegra," Christian said, immediately moving to stand between her and the deceased dragons. "I take it the dragon we saw carjacking some mortals was the one you mentioned as causing problems?"

"Carjacking?" I asked at the same time Ysolde said, "Wow, Xavier must really be hurting if he had to steal a car to get away from you guys."

"You'd think he'd have planned better," Aisling said.

"I think there's a little wine left back in the library," Allie said, gesturing toward the castle. "Looks like you guys could use it. Our people can finish up here, if that works for you."

I suspect in normal circumstances the dragons would object to being treated as if they were so frail, but obviously, Yrian's blast did more than scorch off a few layers of epidermis. They were a bit shaken, but whether it was due to Yrian or Xavier, I didn't know.

"You coming?" I asked him as the others headed off.

"I just purchased this phone device," he said, still searching.

Exhaustion hit me then, leaving me feeling as if I were underwater, struggling to move my limbs. All I wanted to do at that moment was crawl into bed and sleep for a few days. "I'd offer you mine, but it's filled with pug memes. You do that side, and I'll look over here."

It took us another seven minutes, but at last Yrian found it halfway under one of the big trailers. Another ten minutes, and we arrived at the library, which was full of dragons and vamps, the former guzzling the last of the wine.

"We saved Yrian a glass," Thaisa said, offering it when we arrived. "Not that he was burned, but still. I figured he might like it."

Yrian took the glass and offered it to me. I smiled, took one sip, gasped at the fire that burned down my throat to my belly, and handed it back. "That really is potent stuff."

"Given that the place is evidently crawling with demons and bad quasi-dragons, we are happy to have you all stay here," Allie said. "We have plenty of room, so please don't feel like you'll be putting us to any trouble."

The others who weren't a part of the original visit murmured their appreciation, and Allie left to arrange for the rooms to be made ready.

"We will leave you in peace, since I suspect you have much to discuss," Christian said as he and his team left the library.

Yrian surprised me by standing and making him an elegant bow. "I extend my thanks for your security team guarding Becket. My youngest brother has made money available to me. I will be happy to give some of it to you for her care."

I caught a glimpse of surprise in Christian's eyes before he made an almost equally nice bow to Yrian. "Your gesture is not necessary. As my Beloved is wont to say, it is not a bad thing for Dark Ones to extend our concerns to other beings in the Otherworld, and we are happy to aid the dragonkin as best we can."

"Now, that's what I call polite," Aisling said softly when the door closed behind Christian. "He seemed so rigid at first, but I think Allie's right and he's just a big ole teddy bear underneath. Not unlike some wyverns I could mention."

Naturally, all the men bristled at the implication that they were softies, but just as naturally, the women ignored their fussing.

"What we need to do before we retire for the night is discuss what our next step will be," Drake said, frowning at nothing in particular. "I can't help but feel the fact Xavier ran away rather than remaining with his attack force is regrettable."

A silence fell over the room, one that I suddenly realized was pointed in our direction. "If you are hinting that Yrian should have taken Xavier down, I would like to remind you that a whole herd of evil dragons were attacking you guys, and Yrian was a little busy keeping you all alive!"

"Because what are a few layers of skin between friends?" Hunter said sotto voce to Jim.

"Dude doesn't seem to have the best grasp on his fire," Jim agreed. "You're lucky you didn't go up in smoke."

I tweaked the glamour I was creating, hidden by the table I sat at, and, instead of throwing it on Hunter, tossed it onto Jim. It squawked, its appearance now that of a chicken.

"What—" Aisling stared at Jim the chicken as it blinked its beady little eyes at me; then she shot a furious glance my way. "OK, I admit Jim's comment wasn't necessary, but a chicken, Becket? Really?"

I shrugged. "Blaming Yrian for your troubles isn't fair, and I hate unfairness, bullies, and Nazis. Not necessarily in that order."

"Please change it back," Aisling said, breathing a bit heavily.

"It'll wear off in a few minutes," I said, ignoring her thinned lips and glare.

"The fact remains that Yrian agreed to help us with Xavier, but when he showed up, nothing was done to stop him," Hunter objected in a flurry of confusing pronouns, watching as Jim began to peck around on the carpet, obviously scooping up crumbs from the snacks Allie had set out for the postfire recovery. "The First Dragon made it clear that we can't stop him on our own, but when we have Yrian with us, Xavier still escaped."

"Are you going to take that?" I asked Yrian in a near whisper. Oddly enough, he didn't look as outraged as I felt; instead, he watched the others with the same sort of inscrutable expression his brother wore. "It's not your fault that Xavier got away."

"No, it is not," he agreed, but said nothing more. I expected him to lecture his family for assuming he would be the great hero to swoop in and save their respective asses, but he didn't. He just sat there, relaxed, but somewhat distant. I had the feeling he was thinking hard, but whether it was about the scene we'd just experienced or something else was beyond me.

"You assured us you would help take down Xavier," Archer said slowly, his expression troubled. "Not that we expect you to do it on your own—Hunter and I are the best ones to strike a harsh blow against him, but we can't do it alone. We need you for that, and yet, as Hunter pointed out, when we were all there, he escaped."

"You did not tell me Xavier possessed a shard of the dragon heart," Yrian said, leaning back in his chair.

A second silence fell while the dragons all looked at one another.

"Does that matter?" Drake asked after almost a minute of no one speaking.

"It does when he has it on his person," Yrian said, his gaze shifting to his brother. "Did you know he had a shard?"

"Yes." Baltic frowned. "But like Drake, I don't see why that matters. It's not as if it could be damaged even if you were to outright kill Xavier."

"You might not be able to destroy a shard, but I can," Yrian said, then rose, holding a hand out for me. "Becket is tired and needs to sleep. I will guard her so that the Dark Ones may rest."

"Wait, what?" Aisling said at the same minute Ysolde asked, "You can break the shards?"

"Yes."

I got to my feet, but slowly, wondering at this man who had appeared abruptly in my life earlier this morning and now felt like I'd known him a lifetime. "Am I the only one who doesn't understand the significance of a shard?"

"The dragon heart was created by the First Dragon. It is made up of four shards, one granted to each of the original four septs," Gabriel said with obvious hesitance. His eyes were shadowed as they watched Yrian. "It is the most valuable relic of dragonkin. I had never heard that it could be destroyed, however. Re-formed and then sharded again, yes. But destroyed?" He shook his head, clearly confused.

"Is it possible for you to … I don't know, banish or remove Xavier from the mortal plane without hurting the heart shard?" I asked Yrian.

"Not if he has it on his body, which he does. I felt its presence as soon as he attacked. If I had destroyed him as I did his followers, it would have meant the end of the dragonkin."

"Are you saying that if a shard is destroyed, we all die?" Aisling asked, leaning into Drake just as Jim's glamour dissolved into nothing. I'd set it to last only five minutes, feeling that was just punishment for speaking unfairly of Yrian.

"Die? No." Yrian took my hand again, and I was distracted by the sensation of his fingers around mine. My libido kicked into high gear despite the situation. I told it to chill until such time as I decided whether I wanted to get involved with Yrian on a romantic level. "But it is the heart of the kin, and without it, we will decline. No new dragons will be born."

"Holy shit," Thaisa said, looking at her dragon. "We haven't even talked about kids yet. What if we can't ever have them? Who will take over the tribe when you want to retire?"

"I know Drake has our shards tucked away safely in his lair, but I sure as shooting hope Gabriel and May are doing the same, because man alive! I didn't know we had *that* hanging over our heads!" Aisling said, her expression stark.

"The shards have survived since the creation of the dragon race," Drake reassured her at the same time Gabriel murmured that their shard was safe. I couldn't help but notice the similarly stricken expressions on all the other women's faces. "There have been wars and attacks, and they have not been destroyed. Until now, I wasn't aware that was a possibility."

Everyone looked at Yrian.

"Hey!" I said, taking offense on his behalf, since he didn't seem to want to do the job. "You can just stop looking at Yrian like he's a villain. He's here to help you guys … and me … and is not Mr. Destruction. I'd think you'd be a bit more grateful that he realized what was going on and didn't damn you all to declining."

Yrian gave me an odd look. "What are you doing?" he asked.

"Defending you to your family," I told him, my ire spiking despite my exhaustion.

"Why?" he asked, tipping his head a little to the side, an act that made my stomach go wobbly with want and need and a plethora of other emotions I decided I didn't want to deal with at that moment.

"I told you—I don't like bullies."

"We're not bullies," Ysolde said, but her expression was troubled. "We just want Xavier dealt with, especially if he's now targeting the green dragons."

"You'd think with a roomful of wyverns, they'd suss out what's going on, huh?" Jim asked Yrian, giving me a side-eye as it approached him.

"What do you mean?" Gabriel asked, now frowning at Jim.

"Jim!" Aisling said almost at the same time, clearly outraged at her demon dog. "I shouldn't have to do this, but may I remind you that you are on Team Green Dragons, and that insulting everyone here is not likely to get you vacation time in Greece when Amelie and Cecile go there next month?"

"I second Gabriel's question," Ysolde said, her fingers twitching. "Would you mind explaining your accusation, Jim?"

"That depends," Jim answered, watching her closely. "Are you going to bananate me if I don't? Because those crumbs I found when Becklestein chickened me—which I gotta admit was more fun than I thought it would be—ain't gonna hold me over until breffy."

Aisling took a deep, deep breath, and said through gritted teeth, "Answer the question, Jim. Yes, that is an order, and furthermore, you will continue to answer any questions that anyone else puts to you in the next ten minutes."

"Why only ten minutes?" Jim asked, also doing a head tip. It wasn't nearly as effective as the one Yrian did.

"That's the length of time you have to convince me not to banish you to the Akasha for the next month," she said in a tone that would have had me toeing the line immediately.

Evidently Jim thought better of continuing down its path of mischief, because it plopped down next to Yrian and said, "You want to tell them, big guy, or should I?"

"Jim!" Aisling said with an edge to her voice that could have cut cement.

"Demon lords," Jim said with a roll of its eyes at Yrian. "Can't live with 'em, can't live with 'em. I'm talking about just why Xavier is after Drake's shards. None of you other than the Big Y seem to be asking why Xavier wants the shards so much."

The dragons all exchanged glances, then turned en masse to Yrian.

Just as they did so, I could see enlightenment striking Baltic.

"Ah," he said, his gaze on Yrian. "You think he wishes to re-form the dragon heart?"

"Why would he do that?" Gabriel asked, his brows pulled together as he obviously tried to follow that line of reasoning. "How could he benefit from re-forming and re-sharding the heart?"

"*He* couldn't," Yrian said, starting for the door, but I didn't move, wanting to hear what the dragons said about their big, bad enemy.

"Then who—" Drake started to ask, but stopped, a horrified expression crawling over his face.

"Bael," Baltic said, his eyes still on Yrian. "You think Bael wants it to get out of the Duat?"

The other dragons didn't exactly gasp in horror, but I got the feeling they were doing so mentally.

Yrian's expression turned sour. "I think he's using Xavier to gather up the things he needs to escape, yes. But that would do him little good if he arrived in the mortal world without any power."

"Which he'd have if Xavier attacked the septs in order to steal or force the delivery of the dragon shard like he did Bastian. With that in his hands, he could effectively destroy us all with it," Drake said, putting his arm around Aisling when she pressed tighter against him.

"Oh my god, he could be targeting the children," Aisling said, worry and distress evident in her eyes. "Maybe we should fly home tonight rather than tomorrow."

"The children are safe," Drake said in a smooth tone, but it was a bit crackly on the edges. "There are twelve guards on top of the electronic security. No one can as much as step on the grounds without us knowing."

Despite his words, I noticed his gaze met Baltic's for a few seconds, and I realized that Ysolde and Baltic had sent their young son to stay with Aisling and Drake's kids.

"While I agree it's entirely possible he would target weaker members of your septs in order to force you into compliance, the rest of what you describe doesn't sound like Xavier," Archer protested. "He's no one's lackey. Taking the shards fits in with his motive of destroying us."

"This has the stink of Kashi all over it," Yrian insisted. "It's likely that Xavier has no idea he is playing into Kashi's hands, but that doesn't negate the point. This is why I have wanted to attend to Kashi before your sire. Xavier may be a threat, but it is not as dangerous as that hatched by Kashi. Stop resisting me, Becket. You are tired, and need sleep."

I slid a glance up at him. "You really are an annoying man sometimes."

"Yes, but that doesn't change the fact that you need sleep. Come." He tugged at my hand again, and I decided the dragons would probably prefer to discuss things without me, so I let him lead me out of the library.

"You know, I am a big girl, and I can put myself to bed just fine all on my lonesome, in case you wanted to stay with your family and work out the next move."

"I don't need to discuss it with them. I know what we need to do next."

"We?" I asked as we mounted the stairs. In the distance, I could hear the sound of a TV and children singing along to it.

Yrian opened the door to my room. "Yes. I will need your assistance in the Duat."

ELEVEN
YRIAN

Becket looked like she might explode. Yrian, who had entered her room first to make sure there were no threats—not that he expected any, since the Dark One Christian now had an adequate amount of protection set into place—glanced back at her as she stood just inside the room.

Her face expressed an interesting series of emotions: confusion, surprise, disbelief, ending up on thoughtfulness. Yrian was intrigued by that, fine-tuning his estimation of her. That she continued to rise in his appreciation was a moot point—his role was to protect her, nothing more. The fact his body had distinctly other ideas was not important. "You want me to go to the Egyptian underworld with you? I assume to confront your evil brother?"

"I need to see what plans he has put into place there," Yrian told her, checking the windows. "And I won't be able to do that without a powerful glamour. I wish to shower. Do you mind if I do so now? The room appears to be secure."

"No, go ahead. I need to call my bandmates anyway and find out when we're on tomorrow."

He locked the bedroom door, then entered the attached bathroom, quickly completing his ablutions. When he emerged eight minutes later, Becket was sitting on the end of the massive bed, typing on her phone device. "Good news for your Duat plan—which I'm still a bit confused about, to be honest—we're the last of the three finalists, so we won't have to hang around all day waiting for the results."

She looked up at him as she spoke, and for a moment, he was overwhelmed with two needs: the first was to protect her against all the evils of the world, and the second to bury himself in her heat.

"I must ascertain how much power Kashi has amassed, and the only way I can do that is to go into the Duat and see for myself," he told her, mindful of his first need. "I will not allow him to harm you, if you are concerned about your safety."

She waved away that idea, patting the bed in an obvious invitation. He wondered for a moment if she was interested in bedsport despite refusing earlier, and regretted getting into the clean clothing that Allie had provided him.

"Oddly enough, I'm not worried. So long as you're around, that is. You can clearly take care of the worst of Bael's minions, even the wrath demons, and you said he can't do much while he's in the Duat." She scooted a little to the right when he sat down on her left. "I'm just not sure what you think I can do in the underworld. It's likely that they have a prohibition about the sort of magic I use to create glamours."

"You won't be able to create a glamour once you are there, no," Yrian told her, wanting to touch her, but reminded himself she needed to be wooed. He wondered what form wooing took amongst modern beings. All he could think of was what he had used to sway Amice. He quelled the bitterness at the memory of that betrayal, saying instead, "Do you like tales? I'm not very good at them, but if it would amuse you for me to tell you one, I will try."

"I kind of figured I wouldn't be able to make them there, which is the only reason I'm not running screaming from you right now. It leads me to believe that I'm more valuable to him—and thus Candy and Andy—out here in the mortal realm. … What? Tales? What sort of tales? You mean stories? Like books? I'm a big fan of audiobooks. I like to listen to them while I'm cleaning and taking my neighbor's dog for a walk."

"I enjoy audiobooks, as well," he said, brightening at yet another sign of compatibility. He had been too hasty earlier in deciding he didn't need another mate. Becket was not Amice, after all. Just because one mate betrayed him and the dragonkin so viciously didn't mean this one would do the same. Not with her obvious appreciation of dancing-cat videos. "I listened to many on my first phone device. I particularly enjoy a woman named Christie. I learned much about the mortal world from her tales."

"I'm a huge classic-age-of-mystery fan, too!" Becket said, her face expressing her pleasure. "And I love Agatha Christie, as well, although I don't know how helpful she would be to learning about life as it is today. Maybe we can swap favorite authors later. I'm pretty tired right now, though."

"Very well. You sleep. I will watch over you." He moved to the chair opposite the big bed, refusing to allow himself disappointment at the lack of bedsport.

Wooing took time.

She glanced at the chair, then at him, then back to the bed. "Oh, hell. I'm too exhausted for this. Get in bed, Yrian. There's no reason for you to sit up all night being uncomfortable when you could rest, as well. I'm going to take a shower."

She was gone into the bathroom before he could protest that he couldn't watch over her safety if he was asleep, but after reflecting on the security measures Christian had assured him were in place, he decided that if Becket wished to bedsport, then who was he to refuse?

He was in bed, naked, his rod as hard as marble at the thought of her delectable curves, and his mind full of a number of lascivious things, when she returned wearing a long T-shirt that reached almost to her knees.

"So, I was thinking about it, and I'm OK going into the Duat with you, but I think we ought to take some protection against Bael realizing I'm me," she said as she climbed into the bed, her eyes filled with contemplation. He rolled over onto his side, propping his head on his hand while she spoke, her gaze focused apparently on her feet. "I was thinking of who I could resemble, glamour-wise. I mean, I could just create a random appearance, but sometimes, it's better to pick an identity the person knows. That way, half the work is done, because they already know the person I'm being. The key is to not get someone too close to the other person, which could lead to exposure. Oh man, that got really grammatically confusing. Did I just make things more convoluted?"

She looked over at him when she finished, her eyes widening as she did so.

"Whom did you have in mind?" he asked, wanting to pounce on her, but telling himself that he was no longer a volatile youngling dragon. He was now sophisticated. Learned. Urbane, even, he thought as he eyed Becket's shapeless T-shirt. And sophisticated, learned, and urbane males did not jump their bedsporting partners without first receiving an indication that such actions were welcome.

"Er ..." She gave a little cough. "You appear to be naked from the waist up."

"Yes. Also, from the waist down. Although the act of removing clothing can be enjoyable, in general, I find it a hindrance in bedsport. What sorts of things do you like? Amice always insisted that bedsport wasn't enjoyable for females, but one of my brothers told me that his mate did not find anything lacking in that regard. I did not have complaints by the females I bedded before Amice, but perhaps there is something special you would like me to do?"

She blinked at him a couple of times. "Er ... I'm not going to say I'm surprised by you wanting to get down and funky, because to be honest, it sounds really good right about now, especially with you lying there being Chesty McChesterton, but I didn't actually invite you to join me in bed to have sex."

He pursed his lips, and waited.

Her gaze crawled over his chest and arms, ensuring that his rod was now harder than marble.

"Fine. I admit that I invited you to join me hoping that you'd get bossy on me, and we could have sex without me admitting that I want to jump a man I met this morning, and that's wrong. I just …" She made an abortive gesture. "I guess I feel a bit shy about doing this, because we don't know each other well."

"I knew Amice for seven years before she agreed to be my mate," he said, wondering what was harder than marble. Steel? "That did not help, although I recognize you are not she. Also, my rod has now attained steel level, so if you desire me to pleasure you, I will happily do so."

"Steel level?" she asked, obviously fighting a smile. She glanced at the bulge beneath the duvet. "Er … would you mind if I looked?"

"You are welcome to look and touch whatever you like," he said, mindful of a book his youngest brother's mate had given him about modern-day females. "Will you grant me the same?"

She paused in midreach for the duvet, apparently thinking about that for a half minute.

"Yes, I will," she said, nodding decisively before bursting into laughter. "Holy cats, Yrian. We sound like two attorneys negotiating a contract or something equally unsexy. Yes, yes, I'd like you to touch me, but only after I get to touch you first."

He flung the duvet off himself and lay on his back, gesturing toward his rod. "Have at it."

She laughed even harder, but knelt next to him, one hand on his thigh as she wiped tears with the other. "One of the things I like the most about you is your sense of humor. It's subtle, what the British call dry, but it tickles my fancy."

"I wish to make a risqué comment about tickling more than your fancy, but I can't think when you are so close to my rod."

"Yeah? Then I bet this is going to make you go gaga," she said, and leaned over his groin. He stopped her before she could do more than take his rod in her hand, although admittedly, it took him a few moments to uncross his eyes at her touch.

"I wish to bed you, but not *this* you," he said, hoping she wouldn't be offended, but knowing that if he wanted a future with her—and he was starting to understand that was going to be a necessity rather than an option—then he wanted to do it right.

She hesitated, her fingers wrapped around the base of his rod, glancing down at herself. "Oh. The glamour?"

He nodded. "I prefer you in your natural form."

The glamour dropped, and her face, which had been a warm brown, paled into the freckled countenance that went so well with her hair. "My previous sexual partners always preferred me to keep a glamour on. One pointed out that I was stereotypically redheaded, with fish-belly-white skin, way too many freckles, and ugly pubes, so before you say you prefer me like this, I think you'd better see the whole package."

"I don't need to. I don't care about what you look like. I just want to see the real you," he said, wondering what a pube was. "Also, I don't know where you store your pube, but I doubt it is ugly. Everything about you is delightful. Enticing. Tempting."

She gave a little laugh. "I would like to say that just earned you a blow job, but I don't believe in transactional sex, so instead I will simply thank you for the compliment, and add that 'pubes' means pubic hair. I prune, so mine isn't too unsightly, but still. Shall I continue on my exploration?"

"Please," he said again, fighting to keep the hand nearest her leg from sliding up it.

He wanted to give her the time to get comfortable with his human form, since it was evident by the fact that she stared at his chest for a good three minutes she would need time to get used to him.

"Right. Let's take our time, shall we?" she said, sliding his legs apart as she knelt between his feet. "There's so much delicious Yrian to explore, it would be a shame to rush. Your feet are nice. Not weird, or too hairy, or even too wimpy. I don't like men with wimpy calves and feet, but yours are well formed."

He looked down at his feet. "They are feet. They do what I want them to do."

"Yes, but there's a difference between nice and creepy. Your knees are cute. I like them, too, but holy crap, Yrian, your thighs! They're all hard lines, with great vast sweeping planes of taut flesh. And the muscles! I just want to stroke the long lines of your muscles. Truly, they are the thighs of a god!"

"Demigod," he corrected, taking a quick look at his thighs. They looked as they ever did. "I'm glad you like them, although Amice never commented on them. She said she found me pleasing to the eye, but never had she remarked about my body except for the times I returned from battle infested with lice and fleas. Then she had a great deal to say, but most of it was a demand to take myself to the bathhouse before I sullied the solar or bedchamber."

Becket had stopped stroking her hands up his legs as he spoke, a curious expression frozen on her face. "OK, putting a pin in the topic of your ex for later discussion … are you saying that *you* are a demigod? I know your dad is, but I thought you were just his kid."

"He is a demigod, yes, as is my mother."

Her jaw sagged a little for a few seconds. "So … you're a god, too? An actual god? Like your dad?"

"No, he is the First Dragon. He created the race of dragonkin. I aided him with the kin once I was past the chaos stage that came from my mother's bloodline. Do I get to touch you now?"

She put her hands on his knees as she sat back on her heels, obviously struggling with something related to his birth. He didn't understand why she was so confused, but wanted her comfortable with who he was. "It's still my turn. But … you can do the same things your father can do, like zap in and out of places?"

"No, I do not have his power or his abilities. We are different people, Becket," he said. "I am as I am. He is the First Dragon. Tenite is a fire fury. Neither gave their specific abilities to Kashi and me, although Tenite kept Kashi at her side because he favors her, whereas I am more like the First Dragon."

"I know that you're not him, but it's just … you're a freakin' god, Yrian! You have to admit that's pretty amazing." Her eyes positively sparkled at him.

He loved her eyes, loved the clear topaz blue of them, but most of all, he loved the direct manner in which she met his gaze.

He never did well with people who toadied around him, which was why he enjoyed the company of both his youngest brother and his mate. Ysolde was not in the least bit impressed by him, a fact that greatly amused him.

"You carry traits from your siren mother," he said, wanting her to be comfortable with his true self. "That does not make you her."

"True. I do have a bit more wallop to my singing voice because of Mom, but I don't have many other siren abilities." She looked thoughtful. "My dad was a mage, although I only saw him a few times before he managed to blow himself up with too much arcany. It's why I make sure I discharge myself when I create a bunch of glamours. OK. Point taken. We are not our parents. I think, since I need sleep in order to perform tomorrow, and I really want sexy time before that, we'll move past our respective families and focus on ourselves."

"What part of you would you like me to start with first?" he asked, wanting to peel off her shirt.

"I'm not done taking my turn with you. But, yes, let's focus. OK. Thighs of a god, check."

"Demigod."

She gave his rod a pat. "Your penis is nice, too. Not the sort of massive that means I would walk funny after we indulge ourselves, but a goodly size and shape. And I like that you aren't overly hirsute. A little body hair is pleasant. Enjoyable, even. But too much … no."

"No," he agreed, wondering what on earth she was talking about.

He had hair just as did other dragons in human form, but since she clearly felt better being able to catalog his body, he'd let her do so without complaint.

"Your chest and belly are truly godlike, so whether that's a hereditary thing, or just you working out a lot while you were locked up, I don't know, and frankly, I don't care, because I've never met someone who had an actual six-pack. You can rest assured that your chest makes me feel five degrees hotter than I am."

He gave in to the temptation he could no longer fight, and stroked his hand up her bare leg until it reached the material of her shirt.

She froze, her eyes growing huge. "Oh."

"Oh?" he asked, his hand on her warm, delicious hip. He fought every urge inside him demanding he claim his mate right then, wrestling with need, lust, and something warm and glowing that he suspected would bring him both pain and pleasure.

He had loved once before, and been betrayed.

"Oh, as in … I don't know. I can't think. Your hands are like fire. It makes me want to … want to …" Her voice was tight, which almost pushed him over the edge of control.

"What do you want?" he asked in a voice that was rough as granite.

"You," she said on a whisper as she leaned down to kiss him. Her mouth was as sweet as he remembered, but infinitely hotter, and he knew he wasn't going to be able to keep from claiming her as every iota of his being demanded.

"I must … if you don't want this, you must tell me now," he said, fighting to keep his desires leashed.

"I want it. I want you, Yrian. I don't know why it is that I've fallen for you so fast, but I have, and you're so … I mean, yes, please, I want this."

He didn't bother speaking—he simply sat up, pulled her T-shirt off, and had her on her back before a second passed. "Now, I shall catalog your parts," he said, allowing his gaze to feast upon her enticing self. "Your legs are beautiful. Your hips are sublime. Your belly makes me harder than I've ever been. And your breasts—"

"Are kind of small, I know. I'm sorry about that. I did get that from my mom, sadly," she said, her hands moving to cover up the mounds that made his mouth water.

"They are not small. They are perfectly formed, and just the right size for me to caress with hands and mouth," he said, suiting action to word, moving between her legs so he could lave her breasts first with fire, then with his tongue.

She arched back, her legs moving restlessly around him, her hands caressing his arms and shoulders as he gave himself up to the joy of her breasts. "Fire?"

He released the nipple he had been caressing with his tongue, and glanced down, worried for a moment that his fire had slipped his control, but beneath her were the linens of the bed. "Sometimes it gets away from me, but not in this case."

"No, I meant I want more of your fire," she said, biting him gently on the shoulder.

He glanced around frantically, desperate to make love to her, to claim her as his mate, to give her the pleasure she so clearly deserved. If she wanted his fire, then she'd have it.

He slid off the bed, cherishing the little moan of displeasure she gave when he released her breasts, but before she could protest, he hoisted her off the bed and strode to the bathroom, yanking one of the plush towels to spread on the floor with his foot before he laid her carefully onto it.

"Um … " she said, looking around.

"The bed is not fireproofed. This room is done in ceramic tile," he told her, then eyed the pair of underwear that hid her woman's secrets from him. "I wish to remove your underwear, but the book that Ysolde demanded I read said that consent is necessary. Do you—"

"Oh, hell yes," she said, wiggling out of her underwear. "Now, give me your fire, you badass dragon demigod!"

"I like that you say exactly what you think," he told her, kneeling between her knees. He lifted one leg, and started kissing at her ankle, working his way up to her lovely, rounded thighs, his mouth trailing fire.

"Oh, goddess, I never thought a man's mouth on my leg could push me right to the brink of an orgasm, but … yes, yes, rub your stubble on my thighs!"

She shivered and tried to pull him down over her, but he gave her a stern look. "I am taking my turn."

Her laughter rolled above his head as he bent to his work, stopping just short of her women's area. He eyed it for a moment before saying, "I see nothing wrong with your pube. Would you like me to breathe fire on it?"

"Yes!" she almost shouted, pulling his head down to the parts in question, her legs moving alongside him.

He chuckled into her just before he breathed fire, his rod hardening to the point where he thought it might never slumber again. She bucked and writhed as he continued up her body, bathing her in fire that simmered along her skin before sinking into it.

He wanted to tell her how beautiful she was, how much pleasure she gave him just by being herself, and how much he wanted to claim her, but words dried up on his tongue when she wrapped her legs around him and dragged her nails up his back.

"Tell me if I do something you don't like," he managed to get out before he lifted her hips, and, with gritted teeth against spilling his seed before she found her pleasure, plunged into her, taking her cry of ecstacy into his mouth. She lunged upward beneath him, their bodies out of rhythm for a few moments before the world seemed to shift into place, and he knew that what they were doing was right.

She was right. She was his mate, his second chance, and he swore that he would not fail her like he'd failed Amice.

And when her moans of pleasure turned to gasps of ecstasy, her inner muscles rippling on him, he had just enough presence of mind to pull back, flip her over onto her belly, and stroke hard into her, finding his release as he breathed fire on her upper arm.

"That … I just … and then you … holy magical demigod dragon, Yrian. That was incredible."

His body felt as limp as sodden wool, but he managed to roll off her, the cold of the floor tile a pleasant sensation against his back. He struggled to catch his breath even as he automatically tamped out the various patches of fire that burned merrily on the floor tiles.

"Not that I'm trying to inflate your ego, or anything like that, but really, Yrian!" Becket moved to the side before draping her upper parts across his chest, another sense of rightness filling him. "It was fabulous until you flipped me over, and then you were hitting spots that I swear I didn't know I had. I've never been multi-orgasmic, but I'll be damned if you didn't push me there. Hoo!"

He had a moment of pride that he could bring such pleasure, but honesty prompted him to admit, "Your hips and thighs and breasts and all the rest of you made me lose control. You fill my mind. I will devote myself to your well-being."

"Aww," she said, stroking a hand down his chest. "That's so sweet. I like you, too. A lot."

He waited, hoping she would say the words of fealty that would complete their bond.

She propped herself up on one arm and leaned down to kiss him, her breath feathering his lips, ensuring the fire in him remained simmering. "I want you to be happy, Yrian. It's why I'm going to help you with your rat bastard brother, and to take down that annoying Xavier dude who is threatening your family. I hope you know that you're not alone in this. I'm with you one hundred percent."

Relief filled him at her oath. Now she was his, and no other could take her away from him.

"I could not do it without you," he said with absolute honesty. He knew now why the First Dragon had encouraged him to leave his griefscape. Somehow, the First Dragon knew that Becket was waiting in the mortal world, clearly in need of Yrian as much as he was of her.

"In fact, I think—ow. Damn, did your fire burn me? I have a mark!" She sat upright, pulling her arm around to look at the small tan symbol he'd placed on her bicep. "It looks like a stylized flame."

"It is my mark," he answered, suitably recovered that he could get to his feet, holding out a hand for her before taking her back to bed. "The First Dragon placed it on me when I was a youngling. All members of my sept bore it."

She slid into bed, watching as he lifted his arm to reveal the mark on the underside of his bicep. "Oh, is that what that is? I thought it was some kind of pretty birthmark." She leaned over when he got in beside her, studying it before looking at her own arm. "So, it's a brand? It doesn't really hurt, more like it's a bit pinchy."

"It is a sept mark, not a brand. I'm sorry that it hurt, but the pain should fade in a few minutes." He wondered if he had the strength to remain awake for the remainder of the night, then decided that he would trust to Christian's security measures.

"I mean, it's pretty and all, but I wish you'd asked me before you—" Becket stopped prodding at the sept mark and looked up, her eyes filled with suspicion. "Your sept mark? Like … I'm a member of the sept?"

"You are my mate," he said, wondering that she didn't feel the rightness of them being together. It had to be the modern woman's need for wooing, he told himself, and moved making her feel suitably courted up his list of things to do, right behind destroying Kashi and eliminating Xavier from the dragonkin's sphere of existence. "We swore an oath to each other. It is only fitting you should bear the mark of a wyvern's mate. We will find the descendants of my chil-dren, and I will introduce you to them. The shadow sept is no more, but we will form another."

"I have many things to say to you," Becket said after two minutes of silence where she loomed over him, staring deep into his eyes, one hand absently stroking his chest. "Many, many things, and fair warning, not all of them are kind. In fact, many involve ranting, and quite possibly a pointed comment or two about men who think they can take deci-sions away from women, but right now, I'm a boneless blob of satiated artificer, and I have to get sleep or I'll sound like a frog tomorrow. So consider yourself on probation until I can figure out what I want. Good night, Yrian. Thank you for the mind-blowingly fabulous sex. We'll talk more about this tattoo or whatever it is, and you deciding I'm your mate, and all the rest of it."

"Yes," he agreed, tucking her in next to him when she lay down, a sense of fulfillment that had long eluded him now wrapping around them like the softest of silks.

He closed his eyes, breathing deeply of the scent of her hair, and, for the first time in more than two thousand years, relaxed into sleep without pain, worry, or guilt.

All would be right. He had Becket now.

And he would destroy the Egyptian underworld itself before he allowed Kashi to harm her.

TWELVE
BECKET

"Oh good, you're here. Drake and I are taking off in about ten minutes, and I wanted to wish you and your band good luck with the performance. I hope you won't be upset that we can't stay—Drake is in a swivet about being away from the children, despite the fact that a small army of dragons is guarding them." Aisling stopped me when I made my way downstairs in search of some much-needed food.

"I don't mind at all. I completely understand that you're worried about your kids, although from what I've seen of your abilities and Drake's presence, I have full confidence that not even Candy and Andy would be able to get near them," I answered, wondering where Yrian had gotten to. His side of the bed had been cold to the touch when I woke up, letting me know that not only was he quiet—since I'm not a terribly sound sleeper—but also he was thoughtful enough to let me sleep rather than waking me up to indulge in fiery lovemaking.

My libido mourned his consideration, but since I had to perform today, I appreciated the extra sleep.

"Knowing that Bael is most likely behind Xavier—even if he's just doing so to stir up trouble—has everyone worried." She studied me for a moment. "I'd feel bad about leaving you without our protection, but I am pretty sure that

Yrian will keep you safe from both. Regardless, I'm sure we'll see you soon, once you're back from the Egyptian underworld. It's a very cool place."

"You've been there?" I asked, moving past her to pour myself a big cup of coffee from a carafe on a sideboard loaded with food.

"Once, yes. When the wyvern of the red sept was created. That's kind of a long story, so I'll save it for one of our mates' meetings. We have a union, so to speak—it's really just a way for the mates to all stay in touch and manage the dragons when they get outrageous. And speaking of outrageous dragons, Ysolde and Baltic already left, but they hope you and your band win. I wish we could stay to watch you sing, but …" She gave me a rueful smile.

"Family is more important," I said, nodding, watching when Jim the demon dog approached, hauling a sparkly blue-and-purple unicorn backpack. I thought I should say something regarding her assumption that I was Yrian's mate, but my own feelings were too confused on the subject, so I decided to deal with it later, when my life wasn't so chaotic. "I'm not in the least bit offended by you having to leave."

"Heya, Becky," Jim greeted me; then its nose tipped up as it took a couple of deep breaths. "Noms!" it said, and dropped its bag before heading straight for the sideboard.

"No!" Aisling said, quickly moving in front of it. "You've already eaten, not to mention stealing Drake's croissant when he was thanking Christian. You absolutely don't need—"

"Um …" Allie appeared in the doorway just as I helped myself to a plate of scrambled eggs and potatoes, a small bowl of fruit, and yogurt. She glanced to the left, toward the entrance of the castle. "There are some people here to see you."

"People?" Aisling asked, her brow wrinkling. "More dragons? The others left already. What sept are they?"

"When I say you, I actually mean Jim," Allie said, shuffling to the side when a man and a woman appeared in the doorway. The man was tall and imposing, with dark hair and eyes. The woman had equally dark hair and eyes, and a no-nonsense gaze that seemed to strip me down to my soul.

"Heya, Desi. Heya, Parisi," Jim said, moving over to snuffle the newcomers. "I don't suppose you remember me, yet?"

I was confused by its question until Allie, who had slid around them into the room to stand next to me, whispered, "Those are Jim's parents. Its dad created Abaddon, while its mom was a Sovereign at the Court of Divine Blood. She was in the Beyond so long that it pretty much wiped her memory, including who Jim is."

I goggled at the pair of people, my brain having trouble coping with the fact that the creators of what mortals thought of as hell and heaven were evidently not only a couple but standing right there in front of me.

"Do you know where Yrian is?" I asked Allie in a whisper, suddenly feeling like he needed to be here.

"With Christian and Drake, but I've just told Christian to get everyone here pronto," she answered.

"Of course I remember you," Parisi answered, her voice so lyrical I wondered if she had a siren mother, too. "You are the demon Effrijim, who Desi insists is our child." She patted it on the head. "He likes dogs, so it is understandable he wishes you were our son."

To my surprise, the man named Desi gave her a long look. "Smell him," he said, gesturing toward Jim.

"What?" the demon asked, its eyes round as it backed up a step. "I just had a bath four days ago. Ash took me to a doggy spa before we came here, because she said she couldn't take me to a real castle smelling like I rolled in something stinky, which I did, but still, it was rude of her to come right out and say I stunk."

Aisling made a choking sound.

"Smell him," Desi said again, his gaze on Parisi.

"Why?" she asked.

"Because scent remains in the memory long past other senses," he said, then knelt next to Jim and buried his face in the demon's furry neck. "Yes. He smells the same as when he was a babe. Come, my love. Let us see if your memories can't be stirred."

"This is silly," Parisi said, but, after giving Jim another pat on the head, leaned down to sniff delicately at its neck. "A dog, even one that is a demon, smells like a do—oh." She pulled back, looking at Desi with confusion.

"Yes," he said, nodding. "Try again."

Parisi frowned, but this time, she knelt in front of Jim, its head in her hands as she studied its face.

"I feel like I should ask Jim to shift into human form, but since it would be naked—and no one needs to see that—plus it's weird to sniff a person, I think it's better if it stays in its current form," Aisling told Allie and me in a hushed tone.

Jim stood perfectly still when Parisi took a deep breath, her nose next to Jim's shoulder.

Silence filled the room for a few moments before Desi asked, "Does it bring forth memories of our babe?"

"I don't know," Parisi said, her expression troubled as she absently stroked Jim's head. "It reminds me of ..."

"Baby me?" Jim asked, hope evident in its voice.

"I'm not sure. The memories are confused, and slip away before I can get ahold of them," she said, taking Desi's hand to rise.

"Maybe you need a few more sniffs?" Jim asked.

Parisi's gaze was on Desi. He evidently felt distress in her, because he ruffled the fur on Jim's head and said, "It was a first step. It will take time to awaken all her memories, but we will not push for more now. However, I believe the time has come for you to join us, Effrijim. Your place is at our side."

"Uh ..." Aisling was clearly startled, but at that moment, the sound of hurried footsteps heralded the arrival of Yrian, Drake, and Christian.

I met Yrian's gaze for a few seconds before he focused on the two newcomers. Desi turned to face them, his right hand making a movement that I realized was muscle memory reaching for a sword.

Yrian and Desi considered each other for five seconds before Yrian inclined his head. "Desislav."

"Yrian Shadowsworn," Desi answered, making the same head bow. "You are here? I thought you long dead."

"I was," he said simply, then raised his eyebrows at Parisi before making a full bow to her. "Sovereign. I did not realize you had survived. The First Dragon will be most interested to hear news of you."

She smiled, and suddenly, I felt lit from within with happiness. Next to me, Yrian took a deep breath, as if he, too, felt the impact of her smile. "I remember you! You are the son of that fury, the one who wrought so much trouble within the Bitu."

"Bitu?" Aisling asked, automatically reaching down to pet Jim when it sat next to her and leaned on her leg.

"It is an old word," Desi answered. "It is what immortals called the L'au-dela before it was so named. I was told there was a gathering of wyverns present. We have come to demand the return of the blood moon. If you refuse, we will be forced to war against you in order to regain it. Understand, Aisling Grey, we do not do this lightly. We know you have taken care of our son, and it is for that reason that we wish to treat with you first, rather than simply striking."

Drake and Yrian both stepped forward at Desi's last couple of sentences, their body language reading the same defensive mood.

Christian, evidently not liking guests to be accosted in his home, also took a menacing step forward.

"What's going on?" I asked Aisling. "What is a blood moon?"

"A relic," Yrian answered before she could. He held out his hand for me, but rather than pulling me to his side, as I expected, he more or less pushed me behind him. I stared at the back of his neck for a few seconds before pinching his arm and moving to his side.

"I relinquished it to the princes of Abaddon in order to guarantee the safety of my son," Desi said, his gaze flicking impersonally over me. I felt like I was covered in Yrian's fingerprints, and that everyone knew we'd had wildly fabulous sex the night before. "It was taken by Bael. We have learned that the dragon sire banished him to the underworld governed by Osiris. Thus, the dragonkin are responsible for its loss. It must be returned."

Yrian stiffened at the name of his brother, his fingers tightening around mine momentarily until I gave his a squeeze to let me know the grip was almost painful.

"You assume much that is incorrect," Drake said stiffly. "Bael has not been a member of the kin since the First Dragon stripped him of that right, so your supposition that we are responsible for him or his actions is false."

"He has your relic?" Yrian asked Desi, his voice tightly controlled, but I could feel the fire within him. I didn't even wonder at that oddity; it was something else I set aside to think about later.

"I thought we decided that Bael used the blood moon to make the Tools," Aisling said, now pressed closely to Drake, Jim at her side. I wondered about that. Why would the demon choose to be with what was technically its boss rather than with its very powerful parents?

"What tools?" Desi asked Aisling, frowning at her in a manner that had her taking a step back, while Drake took one forward, with Jim glancing worriedly between its parents and the green dragons.

"The Tools of Bael were three powerful items created by an alchemist mage several centuries ago." Drake's voice turned the same sort of gravelly that beset Yrian when he spoke of his evil brother.

"Drake actually had all three for a while, but Bael manipulated them away from us," Aisling said, covertly drawing wards on Drake's back, on her own, and, after turning to the side to block Jim, on it, as well. "So if he used your relic to make them, it's long since been destroyed."

"It can't be destroyed any more than your dragon heart can," Desi said, his eyes narrowed on Yrian. "Its power can be re-formed, however. Why are you here?"

I wanted to tell Desi a thing or two about manners, but reminded myself that I was a newcomer to the dragon world, and Yrian probably wouldn't appreciate me lipping off for no reason other than being annoyed at yet another bossy demigod.

"Kashi." It was only one word, but the emotion Yrian put into it had Desi's eyebrows rising.

"You seek to destroy him?" Desi asked.

"Kashi? I remember him, too, although Desi always called him Bael."

"He took that name when he embraced the dark power," Yrian said, his voice low and rough.

"And he murdered your Life Mother, did he not?" Parisi asked him.

"Bael killed Iceni? The First Dragon's mate?" Aisling looked astonished, her gaze slipping to Yrian for a few seconds. "I always wondered why the First Dragon stripped Bael of his dragonness, but now I can see why he did. Holy *merde!*"

"With the aid of our mother, yes," Yrian answered before considering Desi. "You think Kashi has the blood moon with him?"

"He would be foolish to leave it," Desi answered.

The two men stared at each for about ten seconds before Yrian nodded. "You wish for the return of your relic. What will you give the dragonkin for it?"

"Oh, for the love of Pete …" Aisling had to bite off her objection at a sidelong look from her dragon. She leaned to me and whispered, "If you haven't noticed by now, dragons love to bargain."

"Peace," Desi said. "If you fail to return it to us, then we will have no choice but to reclaim it however we can."

"I mean … you said when we rescued you, you were grateful for the dragons and the others. You can't attack if you owe Ash and Drake and everyone else a debt," Jim pointed out. "It's just not cool, and honestly, I don't know how I'm going to hold up my head the next time I'm in Abaddon, and everyone knows that my own dad didn't honor his word."

Desi's lips thinned for a moment as he glared at Jim, but at a touch on his arm from Parisi, he sighed heavily, and said, "You are correct. We do owe a debt for your care, as well as aiding in my release, but I must have my blood moon back, or we will never be able to destroy the Court of Divine Blood."

"My love," Parisi said slowly, her expression thoughtful as she looked at Jim. "If we are unable to punish the Court for their actions until you have the blood moon—and Jim's family is agreeable to returning it should they manage to destroy Bael—then perhaps we could turn our attentions elsewhere."

"If Kashi still has your relic, we will discuss the terms of its return to you," Yrian told Desi, but the latter was distracted by Jim's mom.

"Of what do you speak? What could be as worthy of our time as the punishment of the Court for leaving me in the Thirteenth Hour, and you in the Beyond?"

Parisi smiled, but this time, I felt a chill grip me. "Did you not say that Abaddon was in disarray? Who better to put it to rights than the man who created it?"

Jim sucked in its breath at the same time everyone present froze. "Oh, man, that's not gonna be good."

"You wish for us to rule Abaddon?" Desi asked, his frown smoothing out until he almost looked happy. "The idea has much merit. It is obviously being mismanaged, and needs for us to take command of it, but this time, I will not give control of it over to others."

"Who better to ensure the downfall of the Court than us?" Parisi asked, leaning forward to press a kiss to his cheek. "With your demon dog at our side, they will have no defense against us."

"Aisling?" Jim's voice rose as it pressed itself into her leg.

"No one is taking you away from us," she said, and, to my amazement, moved forward to stand next to Drake. "I get that you guys are pissed at people in the Court, but we've had the discussion about Jim remaining with us before. It may be your child, and we're happy for it to have a relationship with you, but there will be no talk of it being at your side unless that's what it wants."

"I'm all over visiting you guys in Abaddon, because I'd give a lot of money to see what the premiere prince is going to say when you roll into town, but yeah, as Aisling says, I'm happy with her and Drake and the spawn," Jim said.

Desi and Parisi exchanged looks.

"We did allow him to remain with the dragons last year," Desi told her.

"I hate for you to miss your dog, but if you are agreeable to him visiting us in Abaddon, then I don't see that it would be harmful," she answered.

"Very well." He eyed all of us. "We will renew the terms of our agreement for our son to reside in peace in the care of the green dragons, but only so long as you bring the blood moon to us."

Drake started to protest, but Yrian gave a sharp nod. "I agree to your terms. In return for your relic, you will agree to not harm the dragonkin."

"You have a knife?" Desi asked.

Yrian plucked one from the sideboard, and before I could ask him what he was going to do, he slashed his palm and handed the knife to Desi, who repeated the action. Then the two men clasped hands, clearly making a blood bond.

"That was intense," I whispered to Yrian when Desi and Parisi, with a few hugs and words of farewell to Jim, headed out, escorted by Christian and Allie. No doubt the vampires wanted to make sure the obviously volatile pair were fully out of their hair. "Is your hand OK?"

"Of course." He showed me his palm before pulling out his phone. "You must rehearse shortly, yes?"

I glanced at the clock. "Shit! Yes, and I need to eat or I won't have the oomph later for the glamours."

"I'm so confused," Aisling complained as Drake hustled her out. "Do you think Jim's parents are going to involve us in their war against the Court? Because we have enough on our plate as is. It's like we keep going from the frying pan to the fire. … Good luck, Becket! Text us the results of the contest!"

"The Dark Ones will guard you while I'm gone," Yrian told me as I sat at the table and, as swiftly as I could without making a pig of myself, consumed my breakfast.

"OK, but where are you going? Are you looking for Candy and Andy?" I asked, feeling itchy, a sensation I put down to them being near. I could almost feel them amongst the crowds, hunting for me.

"No." He had his phone in hand as he walked out the door. "I must see the First Dragon."

I won't say I didn't have about a million questions for him, some of which included why he needed to talk to his dad, how we were going to get to the Duat, and how he expected me to help him there if I couldn't create glamours, but instead of sending him copious texts, I thanked Allie and headed down to the festival grounds.

"Do you have all of your glamours made?" Skye paced past me an hour later. We'd had a quick rehearsal and were back in one of the tents turned over to us. Since the competition was winding down, many of the bands had already left, but it was the weekend, and the crowds seemed to have grown exponentially. I couldn't help watching the streams of people as they milled around, and despite my contingent of vampire guards, my stomach felt tight and heavy.

"Yup, although maybe I should make a few extras. Does that person in the pink kerchief look like a demon to you?" I squinted against the sun, shading my eyes to watch a woman who I thought looked a bit suspicious.

"She looks fine to me, but I have only seen the one demon, and he looked normal, too," Billie answered as she strolled over to where I peered around the edge of the tent at passersby heading for the main stage, which was being set up for the first band's final set. "You are so jumpy, Becket. You should meditate."

"I've never been able to do that," I said absently, my attention shifting to one of the vampires, who was patrolling the area behind the stage where we were resting. "But I do think I'll make a few more glamours."

"Just don't get yourself electric," Skye warned as I retreated to the back of the tent, where I could sit in peace and focus on crafting, not only a few more visual effects for our set, but also a couple of glamours for Yrian and me.

"I'll discharge, don't worry. I don't want to electrocute myself when we're onstage," I answered, and spent a productive half hour crafting glamours, getting up to vigorously dance off the buildup of magic, and then returning to watch the crowd.

"Revolution is done, and I have to say, whoever is making their glamours really came up with some nice effects—they had white doves flying from the stage, a line of waving French flags, and even a shadow crowd marching off the stage and into the audience," Skye said when she and Billie returned from watching our competition.

"Shadow crowd?" I asked, looking up from where I was creating a detailed glamour for Yrian. "I don't think I've heard of that."

"They were transparent, like spirits," Billie said, plopping down next to me, her face flushed with both time in the sun and excitement. "It was straight out of *Les Mis*, you understand. The shadow people marched down off the stage, and everyone danced with them."

"People interacted with these spirits?" I asked, wishing I'd gone with them to see the band. I had a feeling something wasn't at all right.

"Yes! There weren't enough of them for the entire audience, but everyone at the front was dancing with them," she answered, casting me a curious glance. "Can we do that?"

"No," I said, thinking hard. "To be honest, I don't think that's a glamour. Even my best illusion glamour can't make something that is an image be corporeal. It's why we don't get burned by the firework glamours being cast so close to us. Shadow crowd … I think I'm going to mention that to Yrian."

Just as I pulled out my phone, Deni trotted up with one of the competition officials, a thin man with blue hair. She spoke so rapidly in French that I only caught half a dozen words.

"Our time has been moved?" I asked the official, since Deni and Billie ran into the tent to start changing into their outfits.

"Yes, yes, the Furry Kittens of Unbridled Doom have had a catastrophic argument, and three of the five members have already left," he answered, running a hand through his choppy hair. "I tried to reason with them. I told them they were just twenty minutes away from performing, but the ladies, eh. They did not wish to stay when Daoud and Carlton insisted they bring in a Swede to join them in bed, so they left. They said that since they are currently in second place, they are guaranteed at worst the third-place prize. I tried to tell them that was only if they performed, but they would not listen, and drove off in Daoud's van."

"Ouch," I said, feeling conflicted. I sympathized with the female band members, but at the same time, I was hoping that Yrian would be back in time to see us perform. Immediately, my inner narrator pointed out how telling that thought was. I ignored her, as usual.

The official took a deep breath, glancing over his shoulder toward the main stage. "Carlton said they would perform without the women, and asked if they could take your spot. I said no, but you know how he is."

"Bitchy," Skye said, going into the tent, obviously to change, as well.

"Very much so, yes," the official said, and spread his hands wide in supplication. "He insisted, and since you were all here, I told him they would take your spot. You have ten minutes."

He hustled off before I could protest. Given that the ladies were clearly not bothered by our change in time, I kept my disappointment to myself, and simply texted Yrian that our set was moved up, just in case he finished with his father early.

The crowd was pretty amped up by the time we stepped onto the stage, and once again, I doubted if I needed to deploy the special-effect glamours, but cognizant that the other bands were using them, as well, I lined ours up, and set them off as we progressed through our four-song set. We had fireworks that sparkled despite it being the middle of the day, and showers of light resembling glitter that drifted down onto the crowd, only to fade to nothing before actually touching them.

For our final song, a thousand butterflies made of light flitted around the audience. I'd worked hard on those butterflies for the last week, and was proud to see that they not only landed on people but remained with wings gently fanning for a good three minutes before they disappeared into nothing.

"We have to win. We were so good!" Deni crowed when we made our way back to our tent after taking three bows. "The butterflies were the best I'd ever seen, Becket! And I love the silver shower of sparkles that trailed after me on my song. You didn't tell me you'd made that!"

"I figured we needed a little extra oomph for the finale," I said, sipping at an icy bottle of water. One of Christian's vampires, a tall black woman named Hannah, poked her head into the tent and told me to not wander, because they'd caught sight of a couple of lesser demons. I nodded to her, and added, "But I agree we were on fire—so to speak—and everyone did phenomenally."

"There's no way we can't win," Billie said in voice thick with satisfaction. "Especially since the Doom Kittens can't possibly be as good without their singers."

"Mm-hmm." I checked my phone, but there was no response from Yrian.

I stayed in the tent for the next hour, aware that the last band was performing, but not needing to see them. "I feel guilty that I'm more focused on the demons lurking out there than the actual contest," I confided to Hannah, who had remained on guard outside the tent. "The band has worked so hard for this, but …" I stopped, not wanting to admit just how selfish were my thoughts.

"You're more concerned about your safety," she finished for me, nodding. "I don't see anything wrong with putting self-preservation at the top of your concerns."

Ten minutes after the Kittens finished their set—complete with two rather confused-looking replacement singers who warbled their way through the band's songs—we were summoned to the stage for the awards.

The final three bands were lined up across the stage in small clumps. As the tallest member of my group, I stood behind the other three ladies, the emcee to my left, while beyond him were the others. The audience was loud and clearly had imbibed the local beer, since many of them were dancing and singing despite no music being played.

"We so have this," Billie whispered to me over her shoulder, her eyes dancing with anticipation.

After a good two minutes of the emcee praising all the festival workers, administration, and executives, he finally heeded the crowd's chanting to name the winners.

"Third place," the emcee almost yelled into the microphone, the roar of the excited audience nigh on deafening. "With one hundred ninety-seven points, the Furry Kittens of Unbridled Doom!"

"Shit!" their drummer snarled, then stormed off the stage, while the other members—including the two ladies roped into singing—accepted a glass trophy with much more grace.

It was at that moment that I noticed a man standing to the side of the stage. When I turned my head to look more closely, he immediately turned around and was swallowed up by the mass of people pressed up against the stage.

It was the same person wearing a poorly made glamour.

"Demon," I said under my breath, and glanced to the rear of the stage where my vampire guard had left me, hoping to see one or more of the guards, but the back area was filled with festival workers, volunteers, and the technical crews hired to deal with all the equipment.

"Second place!" the emcee screamed into the mic.

My bandmates clutched one another's hands, Billie shooting me an excited grin over her shoulder.

"This is it!" she said.

A nasty, smoky smell hit my nose. I glanced to the side again, expecting to see the demon, but the herd of people bopping up and down and yelling enthusiastically appeared to be all mortal.

"I should say there are only three points separating second place and the winner of the Battle of the Bands!" the emcee said, causing another eruption of cheering from the audience.

"In second place with two hundred forty-two points, Unstoppable Beings!"

My bandmates, despite no doubt being disappointed we didn't win, cheered, hugged, and blew kisses to the crowd, Skye accepting our glass trophy and check.

"Which means our winners tonight are Revolution!"

Just as I was turning to congratulate the winners, a shape loomed up behind me, and Candy's sibilant voice hissed in my ear, "This time, you won't escape," before stabbing something sharp and painful into the back of my neck.

I half turned, catching the sight of a syringe in Candy's hand before blackness seemed to flop over me like a wool rug, dragging me downward with it until I sank into a pool of ebony, the sounds of the celebration around me fading away into nothing.

THIRTEEN
YRIAN

Yrian returned to the grounds of the festival just in time to see Becket perform her last song, but he wasn't present for more than a minute before he sensed demons nearby. Immediately, he searched the crowds looking for either the demons or the vampires that Christian had promised would be patrolling the area. He found Christian and two of his guards behind one of the food trucks that was in the process of packing up, the ground stained with four sooty spots.

"Four demons?" Yrian asked the Dark One, anger rising that Kashi dared to continue to send his minions after Becket.

"Yes, and another seven that we dispatched earlier," Christian said grimly. He studied Yrian for a moment, then said, "I won't deny it has been enjoyable to remove demons from their forms, but in the future, I'd appreciate it if your mate did not perform here again."

"There's no sign of the wrath demons?" he asked, rubbing the back of his neck. He felt prickly, and oddly unsettled, not to mention annoyed that he had missed Becket singing. He made a mental note to ask her to sing for him later, once he had her in a place of safety.

A roar went up from the crowd, and both men turned to look at the stage. That's when Yrian saw the wrath demon named Andy striding past the food truck, heading straight for where Becket stood with her bandmates, awaiting the awards.

Christian must have spotted the demon at the same time, because he suddenly shoved a sword at Yrian and started forward, but Yrian simply leaped onto a nearby picnic table and flung himself onto Andy's back, taking the demon with enough surprise that he got in a good swing with the sword before he was sent flying backward.

Andy snarled an oath and, without looking at the left arm that was now mostly severed, lunged at Yrian.

Christian whacked the demon across the back of the head with a morning star, but at that moment, Andy pulled out a black bit of crystal that suddenly elongated into a wrath sword.

It gave off a faint shimmer of black smoke, a warning that it was imbued with curses and banes, all the better to destroy its victims. "Stand back, or you'll both die!"

Yrian smiled, relishing the chance to destroy one of Kashi's minions. "You have a thing to learn if you think to challenge us, demon."

"Like I care about dragons and Dark Ones? You are the ones who do not know whom you face. I bear the devastation of Bael! None survive when I so choose."

Yrian didn't wait; he attacked while the demon was still gloating, his sword flashing in the light of the setting sun, while Christian wielded his morning star.

In the end, the fight lasted longer than Yrian expected.

"I will admit that this one surprised me," he said six minutes later, panting, his fire raging inside him to the point where the grass around him was merrily burning until he managed to tamp it down. "I didn't think the demon could stand against us for so long."

Christian, who had a wicked slash across his chest that was bleeding sluggishly, grimaced as the decapitated corpse of the wrath demon dissolved into an evil-smelling, oily black smoke that drifted away on the breeze. "I agree. I had not thought wrath demons would be so hard to destroy, but I see I was wrong."

"It was more than a mere wrath demon," Yrian said, wiping the blade of his borrowed sword on a bit of cardboard box before returning it to Christian. "Clearly, it carried some sort of favor from Kashi. Do you see the second one?"

"No, but I swear I can feel its presence." Christian was about to continue when his phone rang. Yrian started toward the stage, hoping to watch Becket win, since he'd been denied enjoyment of her performance, but turned when Christian shouted his name.

"What?"

Christian bolted toward the stage. "The other one has her!"

Yrian didn't bother to ask for clarification—his blood felt as if it curdled in his veins as he raced past Christian, his mind filled with horror, a terrified chant taking up his mind. *Let it be a mistake … let it be a mistake …*

It wasn't a mistake. By the time he made it to the back of the stage where three of Becket's guard stood clustered together, the sensation caused by the demon's presence had faded away to nothing … as had Becket.

"Where?" he all but snarled at the Dark Ones, who turned to face him with angry expressions.

"I don't know. The demon tore open space and hauled her through it," the woman named Annaliese answered, her gaze shifting beyond him when Christian arrived on his heels. "We had no sign one was here. One moment, everything was fine, and the next, a demon injected something into her neck and hauled her through the rip before we could take two steps. I don't know if it was the wrath demon who was here earlier, but I suspect it was. I'm sorry, Yrian. It's our fault she was taken. We should have been on the stage with her, but the festival people insisted we remain back here."

Yrian wanted to rage. He wanted to scream, to fight, to destroy those beings who thought they could take Becket away from him, and he wanted badly to blame the Dark

Ones for not guarding Becket with more care, but he was an honest man, and he admitted it wasn't their fault.

"I do not hold you to blame," he said, running a hand through his hair as he thought furiously. "These are not normal wrath demons. This one would have destroyed you had you stood in its way. What I want to know is where it has taken her. If it tore the fabric of space, it has limitations as to the destination."

"Abaddon?" Christian suggested, having had a few quiet words with his guards.

Yrian thought about that, then shook his head and retraced his steps behind the main stage. "I see no benefit to Kashi to have her taken there. I can only think that he wants her in the Duat, but for what purpose, I don't yet see. She can't work magic for him there."

"Perhaps she has something he wants. Some relic or valuable artifact?" Christian asked, falling into place beside him as they strode up the path to the castle. Yrian still wanted to rage against the injustice of having found a woman who would fill his life as he had so yearned, only to have her snatched from him, but he had given in to his rage before, and all that had resulted was death and destruction to everyone he held dear.

He would not make that mistake again.

"No," he said after a few minutes' consideration, all the while wrestling with his fire, which continued to roar inside him, demanding to be let loose. "But the reverse might be true."

Christian's eyebrows rose. "You believe Bael has something he wishes to give her?"

"Yes." His discussion with the First Dragon had been enlightening. "He will most likely give her an object of such power that, using it, she would be able to craft a glamour allowing him to escape the Duat."

"You mean—"

"The blood moon," Yrian said with a grimness that gave him a perverse sense of satisfaction. Of course Kashi would do the one thing that would make his life infinitely more horrible. It was ever thus.

"I will contact other Dark Ones," Christian told him a short time later, while Yrian collected the few things he'd purchased, as well as Becket's possessions, and accepted the offered use of Christian's plane to fly to Prague. From there he would suffer untold torments by using a portal to Cairo. "If Becket is seen, I will get word to you."

Yrian offered his hand, as he had learned was the proper way males thanked other males, gravely shaking it. "My youngest brother's mate informed me that you have your own troublesome ancestor to deal with. I cannot speak for Becket, but I will do what I can to assist you with him."

Christian gave him a little bow. "The thane in question has gone to ground, but when he is found, we will be grateful for any help."

They parted with the sense of a debt owed on Yrian's part, but he set that aside to focus on what was most important: getting to Becket before she entered the sphere of Kashi's influence.

To his surprise, Ysolde was waiting inside the Prague portal shop when he arrived there an hour later.

"Baltic thought you might need a little help getting through the portaling experience, since you won't have Becket to put you to rights." She smiled as she spoke and held up a bottle of dragon's blood, and Yrian felt a moment of pleasure knowing that his youngest brother had chosen his mate well. "He would have come himself, but he got dramatic about how awful portaling is for a Firstborn, with lots of far too detailed descriptions of the sort of torture he'd rather endure over taking a portal, so in the end, we decided I'd pop over and help you get to Cairo."

"The portals do not bother you? Baltic said you were part dragon," he answered, handing over to the attendant the small bit of plastic that acted in place of coin.

"I'm all dragon, but most of it is repressed or something weird like that, because I died and was resurrected, and the

First Dragon needed me to save Baltic so he didn't alienate the weyr," she said, waving away the subject when the portaling attendant gave him back his plastic and murmured something about the portal being set to Cairo. "So the answer is no, they don't bother me in the least. OK, shoes off. Baltic finds it best if he hugs himself when he steps into the portal. Oh, and you are wearing undies, yes? Gabriel always loses his pants, and sometimes that effect hits the other wyverns, as well."

Yrian bent a stern gaze on her that just made her giggle, but she stepped through the portal, saying, "See you on the other side!"

The next twenty minutes were not ones Yrian wished to relive, but at last, after three paper cups of dragon's blood, he was up on his feet and able to walk without lurching and holding on to whatever piece of furniture was within grasping distance.

Ysolde sent him off with the remainder of the wine and her good wishes. "Let us know if you need help in the Duat. Baltic may grumble about taking a portal, but I think he's worried about Bael."

"He should be," was all Yrian answered after thanking her for her assistance.

He arrived at the riverboat named *Wepwawet* just as the gangway was being retracted, the boat obviously about to start its journey from Cairo through the Duat, and thence to the destination with Maat, who would weigh the passengers' souls upon arrival. He'd learned all this from the First Dragon, and although at first the ferryman Kherty didn't want to allow him on board, all it took was Yrian unleashing his fire on the upper deck to make the ferryman change his mind.

"You will pay for the refinishing of the deck," Captain Kherty said, his mustache bristling with indignation as he looked around at the scorched planks. "In addition to the cost of your cabin."

"That is immaterial. What matters is my mate, Becket. Where is she? Is she on board? Have you seen her?"

"Becket?" Kherty frowned, his prodigious eyebrows pulled together in a way Yrian found oddly menacing. His fire rose in reaction to it, but he beat it back, feeling he'd made his point already. "I do not recognize that name. Akbar!"

A minion ran up, still holding a fire extinguisher, his eyes wary when he glanced toward Yrian. "Yes, Captain?"

"Do we have a passenger named Becket on board?"

The minion consulted his tablet device. Yrian couldn't help but wonder what sorts of cat videos they might have in the Duat, but instantly dismissed that thought as unimportant. First, he must find Becket, following which he would destroy Bael, and only then would he and Becket see what sorts of videos were available. "I don't have anyone listed by that name, sir."

"There you are," Kherty said, and added, "There is already a champion on board for the trials, but he will no doubt welcome your assistance."

"There is also a wrath demon on board," Yrian said, stopping the ferryman before he could leave. "Its name is Furcand. It kidnapped my mate and brought her here."

"A demon?" Kherty looked at him as if doubting his sanity. He'd seen that look far too often over the last two years. "How could a demon get into the Duat?"

Yrian spat out one word. "Kashi."

"I do not know this name, either," he replied, taking a step away, obviously losing interest in the conversation.

"He is known now as Bael, and has imbued his power into Furcand," Yrian said, his fingers twitching with the need to find Becket.

Kherty was silent for a few seconds, then said, "That name is known to me, unfortunately. Very well. I don't see how a demon could reach the *Wepwawet* without my crew or me being aware of its presence, but we will conduct a search of the ship. I will alert you if we find the demon."

Yrian watched as the ferryman and his minion strolled off, his mind turning over the possibilities. There was only one way into the Duat, and that was on the *Wepwawet*. Which meant if Kashi was having Becket brought to him, she had to be on board.

"If she's here, I will find her," he said to no one, and after dropping their luggage at the cabin the ferryman had grudgingly placed at his disposal, he began to search.

The passengers were less than thrilled at his demands to inspect their cabins, but only one gave him any real trouble.

"You can't come in here!" the man snapped, his glare prodigious. "This is my cabin. I paid for it!"

"My mate has been kidnapped—" Yrian started to explain, but when the man slammed the door shut in his face, he decided to take matters into his own hands.

So to speak.

He shifted into dragon form, kicked the door off one of its hinges, and stomped into the cabin, the door hanging crookedly behind him.

The man squawked, but after Yrian checked the bathroom for signs of Becket, he marched out, shifting back into human form as the man shouted obscenities after him.

"There's a problem with his door," Yrian told a crewman who came running at the noise, then blithely continued his search.

It wasn't until he reached the hold that the increasing sense of worry that gripped him was suddenly eased.

He could feel her presence. It was an awareness that was foreign to him, but he accepted it just as he accepted the fact that Becket had found her way into his benighted heart.

"Becket?" he said loudly, squinting through the dim light at all the trunks, crates, and luggage, and even a motorcycle, that crowded the hold.

The air in it was stifling, stale, and musty, and he had a sudden surge of panic as he thought of Becket being confined there.

A muffled thumping caught his ears, and it was only a matter of a few seconds before he located her in a massive leather and wood trunk. He all but ripped the lid off it, relief driving away the fear as he gazed down on a red-faced, sweating, furious Becket.

"You are my mate," he told her, lifting her out from where she'd been crammed into the trunk, his hands on her waist as she tried to stand but crumpled when her legs failed. He removed the gag that had been tied across her face, his fingers gentle on the red marks left on the corners of her mouth.

"What a—oh my god, the pins and needles have started, ow, ow, ow!—what a bizarre thing to announce while rescuing me," she said, clutching his arms as he helped her over to sit on a packing crate.

"You were unclear on the subject before," he told her, struggling to leash his fire, lust, and need to reassure himself that she was not harmed. "But by now, it should be clear to you that we are meant to be mated. I felt it was important you know that fact, hence why I mentioned it."

She gave a hiccuping sort of laugh as she slid a glance upward at where he stood, one protective hand on her back. "How very thoughtful of you to keep me informed. No, thank you, I don't need you to carry me. If I take your arm, I think I can walk out all the pins and needles. How did you find me? Where are we? Are we in the Duat? And did you catch Candy?"

Slowly, he helped her exit the hold and climb the two flights of stairs to the cabin deck.

"Technically, yes, we have started the journey to the Duat. We destroyed the demon named Andromalius, but could not find the one who took you. No, this way. The ferryman has given us a cabin."

"What about Candy?" she asked as they made their way to the bow of the ship.

"We have not caught that demon, no. You are certain it was that one, and not another? Christian dispatched many demons during your performance, and his guard didn't get a good look at the one who took you," he said, a new worry moving to the top of his mental list.

"Yes, it was Candy who drugged me." Becket rubbed the side of her neck. "I woke up about an hour ago. I thought I was in a coffin at first, but then realized I wouldn't be folded up like a fortune cookie. Thank god you found me. I really need to pee, and thought I might have to just give in and go if you didn't find me."

"You were that confident I would come after you?" he asked, pleased that she had such faith in him.

"Of course. You're an honorable man, Yrian. You promised to guard me, so I knew that you'd come after me, and since there was really nowhere else that Candy would take me, I was pretty sure you'd look here for me," she said as they entered the room. "Oooh, this is nice! We have views on both sides. I take it you haven't searched for Candy on the ship?"

"Not for that specific demon, but I will," he answered, releasing her so she could use the toilet.

"Whew! So much better," she said, emerging from the room a few minutes later to accept the glass of sparkling water he poured for her. "Oh, that's perfect; I'm more than a little parched. Right, now what?"

"Now I must claim you, since we have been parted," he said, removing his clothing before peeling back the blankets from the bed.

"You wha—ooh!" Her eyes widened at the sight of him, her gaze crawling over his chest, arms, belly, and, finally, rod. "Man alive, Yrian! You are drop-dead gorgeous. Your legs—"

"No," he told her, deciding that the time spent in the overly hot hold had scrambled her wits a bit, and accordingly assisted by stripping her of the now-dusty clothing. He had her naked and onto the bed in a few seconds, his hands instantly taking possession of her delectable breasts. "There is no time for the cataloging of the parts of me that you enjoy looking at. Now is the time for claiming, following which I will allow you to admire my chest and rod, after which I will take my turn admiring your parts. Particularly your breasts and hips."

She laughed, her hands warm on his arms as he bent to breathe fire on her chest. "You're the only man I know who can look so stubborn at the same time you clearly want to indulge in some really steamy sexy time."

"You are my mate," he said.

"Yeah, that's still up for debate, despite that tattoo-mark thing you put on me," she said, then sucked in her breath when he rubbed his cheeks against the undersides of her breasts. She had admitted the night before that the sensation of his stubble on her breasts and thighs nearly made her come unglued, and although he wasn't quite sure of what an ungluing consisted of, her reaction indicated it was a goal he needed to achieve. "Regardless, I admit that lovemaking sounds pretty good to me. Only ..."

He knelt between her legs, lifting one to press hot kisses along her thigh, glancing up at her obvious hesitance. Before he could ask her what gave her pause, she made a face.

"I know you like to see the real me, but if I can't apply a glamour here—"

"Do not drop it," he said quickly, feeling the need to have her protected from curious eyes. "I prefer your natural form, yes, but your protection is more important." He eyed her woman's mound speculatively, wondering if she'd react to him blowing fire on her as she had done the night before.

"That's kind of what I was thinking—goddess above, Yrian! Your whiskers are ... oh, lordy. Are you sure we should be doing this?"

"You were taken from me. It is the way of dragons to claim mates who were parted." He ignored the demands of his rod. He would devote himself to making her wild with desire before he sated his own needs.

"I meant right now. Shouldn't we be looking for Candy so we can beat the crap out of it?" She sucked in her breath again when he slid a finger into her heated depths, remembering how much she enjoyed him tormenting her. "Never mind! We'll do this, then go find it. Only I get to have my turn with ... hrnn!"

He smiled with satisfaction at the way her hips bucked when he curled his finger inside her, the sight and taste of her driving him almost to the point of climax. He kissed a fiery trail upward, enjoying the soft, enticing curves, nibbling gently on her neck.

"I will see to your satisfaction and not spill my seed until then," he told her through gritted teeth, fighting the desperate need to just take her. "But it will be a near thing if you require much—"

"NOW!" she bellowed in his ear, temporarily deafening him, her legs wrapping around his waist as she tried to pull him into her.

"I am the wyvern. Wyverns do not like to be dominated," he told her, trying for a tone of stern—but benevolent—instruction, but she just growled at him, and bit him on the shoulder.

Hard.

That was all it took. He lifted her hips, praying she was ready for him, and thrust into her, the sensation of her heat almost pushing him over the edge. He hung on, moving with her, her moans of pleasure merging with his own until she gasped, her body tightening and rippling along his rod. He would have liked to continue to enjoy their lovemaking, but it was all too much for him.

"OK. First of all, I need to get into some sort of an exercise program, because I'm going to cork off from sheer, unadulterated pleasure if we continue this sort of thing," she said some minutes later. "And I very much hope we do, because man alive, Yrian! You're like the demigod of really good sex!"

Yrian lay on his back, desperately trying not to expire from the same sheer, unadulterated pleasure that Becket mentioned, his chest heaving as he tried to get air into his lungs. "If you find an exercise program, I will join you," he said once he could manage to make his brain work.

"Second—and you do not need to exercise. Look at you! You're ripped! Second, if we come through this whole thing with Candy and your asshat brother, then I agree that we could do worse than have a relationship. Hoo baby! I've never had an orgasm like that. It's like you're … you're …" She waved a hand, obviously unable to find a description she liked.

"Your mate," he said, wondering if he had the strength to roll onto his side so he could see her. And touch her. And kiss her, all over that deliciously tempting body. "It was very pleasing bedsport, although you deserve some of the credit."

She laughed again, his heart lightening at the sound.

"I'll take a little of it, but in truth, it was your really fine hip action that gets top honors for the day. Why are you giving me that look?"

"Amice never found bedsporting amusing," he said, managing to roll onto his side, pulling her closer to him so he could place a hand on her sublime belly, her flushed face and brilliant eyes warming him. "She endured it so that we could have children, but I always felt guilty in taking pleasure when she found none. I like that you are the opposite."

"Sex is supposed to be fun, so if you aren't enjoying it, then you're doing it wrong," she said, curling up against him, one leg sliding between his, her hand stroking a line down his chest. "And sometimes, yes, it's silly, and a bit ridiculous what with penises being all out there looking like they do, and then there's the squishy noises when you really get going. …" She trailed to a stop, her gaze dropping to her hand on his chest.

"Does it upset you if I talk about Amice?" he asked, suddenly worried that he had ruined the moment.

She was silent for a good minute before answering. "Not really, no, other than being sorry that your wife didn't enjoy you that way. You're really, really good at this, as I mentioned. Did she give you a complex?"

"Complex?" He didn't understand the word, searching for a context that made sense.

"Did she make you feel guilty for enjoying yourself when she didn't?"

"Yes," he said. "But she wanted children, and although I would have liked to wait until I had better control of my fire, I did as she desired." He pushed away the less-than-happy memories. "I prefer to remember the times when we weren't in strife, such as when our daughters were born."

Becket was silent, and he felt a moment of guilt that his need to explain to her why she was his mate had disconcerted her, but then she said, "I'm here anytime you want to talk about your past, Amice, your kids, and your other family included. And I'd say I'm sorry that Amice couldn't enjoy you the way I do, but that feels a bit weird. Have you found your descendants, by any chance? I'd love to meet your daughters' families. Why don't you tell me about them while I see if my heart rate is going to slow down to a reasonable level, or if we'll have to call a medic for a defibrillator."

He spent the next twenty minutes telling her about his daughters, briefly touching upon, but not dwelling over, the deaths of the three who did not survive him. When he was finished, he traced an intricate pattern on her hip and asked, "You do not have children?"

"No. I didn't think it would be fair to a child to have a mother who was always in hiding, running from people who want to use her, or just being away from home for long stretches of time." She stretched, grimaced, and sat up. "I'm going to take a bath. I'm still a bit dusty despite having a quick wash earlier, and I feel like I'm covered in Yrian."

"My what?" he asked, confused.

She grinned as she rose, and he took the moment to admire her plump ass. It was a joy to behold, that ass, and made him think he might possibly be able to indulge in more bed-sporting in the immediate future.

"Just you." She paused at the bathroom door, giving him a look that went straight to his belly and groin. "If only I had someone to help wash my back ..."

He was in the bathroom before the door swung shut.

And he was right—her ass, and all the rest of her, stirred his passion to the point where they had a very satisfactory lovemaking session in the tub, albeit one that resulted in Yrian asking the steward for extra towels to mop up all the water that had been splashed around the bathroom.

FOURTEEN
BECKET

"So, you're on a cruise?" Billie's voice was full of mingled disbelief and amusement. "With Yrian?"

"Yes, but it's not like that. The demon who kidnapped me dumped me on a ship that makes its way through the Egyptian underworld. You can't leave until you pass muster with a goddess named Maat, who basically checks to make sure you're a good person. If you are, you can go wherever you like, including back to the regular world. If not, you're stuck here." I paused in my explanation and eyed Yrian, who lay spread-eagle on the bed, sound asleep.

Even asleep, he made my heart race and my libido kick into high gear.

"At least you won't have to worry about being trapped there. You're one of the nicest people I know," Billie said, giggling a little. "And your boyfriend is so thirsty."

I puzzled over that for a few seconds, then realized what she'd been trying to say. "I certainly am thirsty for him. Did Skye divide up the winnings?"

"Yes, and she put yours in your account. She also said that since we don't have any gigs for six weeks, that we should use that time to write a few more songs. When will you be back from your cruise that isn't a cruise?"

"Yrian says it takes four days to get through to the end with Maat, so I imagine that we'll hang around for a few days trying to find—and deal with—his evil brother. I'll text or call when we're back, all right?"

Billie agreed to pass on my plans to the others, and after another fifteen minutes of excited chat about what the others were going to do with their winnings, the few weeks off, the next event, and even how she had gone out on a couple of dates with one of the women from the Revolution band that won the contest, we hung up and I stared down at my hands, lost in thought.

"You frown. You are not happy? Has your bandmate said something to upset you? Would you like to see a pug-dancing video?"

I turned my head to find Yrian watching me, still spread out on the bed, his delectable self calling to me. I was up and moving over to him before I realized it, curling up next to him. "Did I wake you? I'm sorry if I did so, but you said I wouldn't disturb you if I stayed in the cabin. And thank you for the offer of dancing pugs, but I don't think I need one right now."

"You did not wake me." He didn't embrace me as I expected him to, and for a few seconds I wondered if he was pissed that I had (despite him refuting the fact) woken him up, but that thought melted almost immediately under the molten look of his eyes. "Do you regret offering to assist with Kashi?"

"Who, me? No, of course not." I stopped cuddling into his side and sat up, my leg pressed against his because I could not stop touching him when he was close. "It's part of the deal. I help you, you help me, and everyone is happy, right?"

He just looked at me with those glorious eyes, and it struck me at that moment how comfortable I was with him. It was more than a little amazing I'd known him for a few days, and yet, I was seriously considering the idea of being his mate, of committing my life to his. It was both a frightening thought that I could be dependent on someone, and a joy that filled me with so much happiness I wanted to sing all the time.

"I will always help you, Becket," he said slowly, something on the edge of his voice that had little butterflies of excitement fluttering in my stomach. "There is no barter, no deal. You are my mate, and I can do no other but protect and cherish you until the end of my days. If you fear I will not protect you, and will retreat to my griefscape again—"

"No," I interrupted, seeing a flash of pain in his eyes. I put my hand on his chest and leaned down to feather kisses along his delectable lips. "I have zero doubts you will protect me from Candy and Andy—I guess it's just Candy now—and the issue of me being responsible for my own safety aside, I am not worried in the least that you will abandon me. Yrian, stop looking like that. I know you carry a lot of guilt about what happened to Amice, and your daughters, and all your family, but truly, it wasn't your fault. Your brother killed them. Not you."

He rolled onto his back, and I felt his withdrawal. "If I hadn't gone to aid my sister, Kashi would not have had the opportunity to corrupt Amice and destroy the sept."

"Did you ever ask yourself why your sister needed such urgent help right at that time?" I asked, lying down next to him, my arm on his belly as I snuggled into his side. "You said she was under attack by some demonic beings, right?"

"Yes, but if you think it was Kashi's doing, he was not yet a demon lord. That didn't happen until later, when the First Dragon stripped him of kinhood in response for killing my sept and Iceni." Pain twisted his lips for a few seconds until I placed a finger on them, following with another flurry of kisses. He smiled, his hands coming up around me, caressing my butt with one, while the other tangled in my hair.

"I think I'm falling in love with you," I said after a few breathless minutes when I let him take charge of the kiss. I froze the second the words left my mouth, having intended on keeping that thought to myself, but my inner narrator had other ideas.

He looked smugly satisfied.

I nipped his lower lip. "And this is the point where you tell me how you feel about me, so I'm not lying here in abject embarrassment that I like you more than you like me, and yes, I do realize how juvenile that sounds, but all of a sudden, I get the feeling that all this mate talk had nothing to do with your emotions and was just a chemical thing between us. Oh goddess, it is, isn't it? You're not saying anything! Shit! Shit, shit, shit!"

He laughed, he actually laughed at me.

I thought hard about punching him on the arm, but given the muscles therein, I went for a nipple instead, pinching it gently.

"Oh, you think it's funny, do you, Mr. Dragon Demigod? Well, let's just see how fancy-schmancy you are when you're mono-nippled!" I said, glaring at the man who had so quickly filled my heart and soul.

He looked down at where I was still clutching his nipple, and carefully unclenched my fingers. "What I find funny is the idea of you believing we are here, now, because of chemicals. I don't even know what chemicals you are talking about, although I did learn much about the periodic table during one of my imprisonments in the mortal jails. When we have taken care of Kashi and Xavier, I would like to set up a chemical laboratory in our home. Do you enjoy such things?"

I allowed him to kiss my fingers before answering, "As it happens, I have a great love of learning. It doesn't matter what—I just like to learn, so, yes, I'd enjoy a lab to play in. Where is your home?"

"What home?" he asked, looking genuinely confused.

"The one where you want to put a lab."

"Ah." He gave me a long look. "That is up to you to decide. We could live in the mortal world, but I believe that a residence in the Beyond would provide more safety for you, much like Charity. The First Dragon said the mortal world was harassing her, too, and he brought her to his home."

"He lives in the Beyond?" I asked, startled by that for some reason. I knew a lot of denizens of the Otherworld hung out there, but never heard of demigods residing in it.

"No, he lives in a plane of his own making, but it touches the Beyond. I could ask him for help in creating something similar for us—"

"I'd rather you didn't," I said, noting the reluctance in his voice. "I don't need a whole Yrianscape. The Beyond would be nice, but I also like seeing the mortal world. I like traveling, and singing with the band, and I have a few friends who I'd miss if we stayed out of the mortal plane."

"Then we will have homes in both worlds," he said easily, just as if that settled the matter. "And we will have a chemical laboratory where we can experiment, and you will have pugs to make you laugh, and we will purchase them little dance outfits, and will film them so we may share the joy with others. When you wish, or when the kin needs us, we will return to the mortal plane."

"If I get pugs, then you get to have cats," I told him, warmed to the tips of my toes by the fact that he wanted me happy. "And you can be our muscle when the band performs."

"Muscle?" he asked, pinching my butt. I sat up again, suddenly feeling warm. I thought of having my way with him, but the memory of the pool on the upper deck called to me.

"Bodyguard," I answered, heading for the door. "Come on, let's go to the ship's shop and buy swimsuits. I want to frolic in the pool, and watch water drip down your magnificent chest." He hesitated, and I paused at the door. "What? You don't want to let me ogle you? Is it Candy? You said you searched the whole ship and it wasn't here."

"Yes, and that is something I can't explain, but I do not sense a demonic presence nearby, so I assume it has had assistance in leaving the ship."

"Then why aren't you allowing me to fit you into the skimpiest of swimsuits?" I asked as he slowly got to his feet.

He grimaced. "Water is the green dragon element."

"OK," I said, about to ask more when a possible explanation rolled through my brain. "Do you know how to swim?"

"No," he admitted, his lips thinned.

"That's OK, it's nothing to be stressed about," I told him, taking his hand and pulling his reluctant self out of the cabin. "I spent two years at the local YMCA teaching kids under the age of ten how to swim, so I should be able to handle one badass dragon demigod."

His protests fell on deaf ears, although I was mindful of not forcing him to try swimming if he was really opposed to it.

The shop had a small variety of summer wear available, including shorts, a few swimsuits, and a crap ton of costumes for the costume party held on the last night of the cruise. Since I couldn't create glamours in Duat, we purchased a steampunky Mad Hatter's outfit complete with top hat for me, while Yrian was wholly smitten by a Beetlejuice outfit, saying he loved the wig and striped suit. Between the shirts and his costume, it turned out that his sartorial aesthetic was a bit more eccentric than I expected.

Three days passed more peacefully than I might have guessed when I'd been abducted. We swam—Yrian turned out to be quite good at an Australian crawl—ate far too much, and had steamy, sweaty nights in which we both gave up the worries of the world and just enjoyed finding out what things gave us the most pleasure.

And I fell deeper and deeper in love with the complicated, sometimes contradictory man who I realized simply wanted to protect those who needed it.

We met Yusuuf, an Egyptian man whom Osiris had sent into the mortal world, and who was subsequently returning to Duat and was the designated champion expected to conquer various challenges that were part of the voyage. We missed the first one due to Yrian being so sexy I couldn't resist him when he emerged from the shower one morning, but he was present with Yusuuf when facing some fire challenge.

At the end of the four days, we arrived at one of the small, dusty villages where a couple of sleek cars from the 1930s were waiting.

"According to the gossip that you missed because you were fighting with your nascent YouTube channel—and really, you should probably wait until we get a home and cats to film before you worry about what sort of graphic suits the channel best—Osiris and Maat will come on board. Maat will make sure we're good people; then we're free to get off the ship and find your evil brother," I told Yrian as we finished packing our things.

"Osiris will not be here. The First Dragon said he was in the mortal world, trying to find the sons of Horus," Yrian told me, shoving a pair of salmon-colored shorts into a newly purchased suitcase before setting our luggage outside our door. He'd not only discovered the joy of shorts, but fallen madly in love with Hawaiian shirts, the more colorful the better. He bought six of them, and was beyond delighted with his choices.

"We had nothing at all like this when I was last alive," he told me at the time, holding up a pink-and-lime shirt decorated with flamingos, flowering cactus, and margarita glasses, admiration making his eyes glow.

"I bet you didn't," I had murmured, and kept my giggles to the mental variety.

He'd worn shorts and colorful shirts all four days, and since the former showed off his legs, while the latter made him happy, I had no complaints, although I much preferred his minuscule swimsuit that turned heads when we indulged in pool time.

The fact that he didn't give a damn about any of the women (and some of the men) admiring him in the skimpy suit gave me infinite joy.

"Horus?" I dug through my memory of long ago when I was in college. "Isn't he Osiris's son?"

"Yes. Ah, it is Isis who is presiding over the event," Yrian said as we reached the upper deck. Several people had emerged from the cars and were making their way up the gangway.

"Isis?" I asked, peering around him at the newcomers. "*The* Isis? The actual one?"

"You have no problem with Maat passing judgment on us, but balk at Isis overseeing the proceeding?" he asked, his gaze serious as he considered me.

"I'm weird that way," I said, turning when the group marched up the stairs to where everyone was gathered. Leading the way, a woman in a white leather bustier, with glossy black hair that hung down to her butt, strode across the deck, ignoring the murmurs of excitement from the passengers, and heading straight to where the captain held out a tall flute filled with champagne.

"Ah, Kherty, how well you know me," the woman said, tipping her head back and pouring the entire glass of champagne down her throat. "Perfect temperature, as usual. Now, where are we? Maat, are you ready? I have a seaweed facial in an hour, and I will not keep Anton waiting for anyone, not even pilgrims, so let's get a move on the proceedings."

"That's Isis, I assume," I said quietly to Yrian as a shortish, curly-haired woman smiled at everyone waiting, and moved over to where a table had been set up by a couple of men in ancient Egyptian linen kilts. She had a white feather stuck in her hair, and lovely brown eyes that beamed with a joy so potent, it seemed to light up an already bright day.

As I spoke, Isis turned to gesture toward the passengers, but she froze when she saw Yrian.

My soul stopped feeling the happy effects of Maat and suddenly felt dank and lumpy.

"Nephew!" Isis said, coming forward to stand in front of Yrian.

He bowed, one of the big, respectful bows. "Isis, it is a pleasure to see you again. This is my mate, Becket."

"Mate? I thought she died? Never mind, I haven't the time." Isis spun around and gave Maat a pointed look. "Anton is waiting. Let's get the line going."

"Nephew?" I said in an exaggerated whisper as I clutched Yrian's arm. "Isis is your aunt?"

"Yes," he said, watching Maat with interest as the passengers submitted themselves to her examination.

"Your *aunt*, Yrian?" I poked him in the side until he glanced down at me, a question in his eyes. "She's a god. Not a demigod, an actual god. An Egyptian god. *Your aunt.*"

"She is," he said, a little frown pulling down his chocolate-brown eyebrows. "Why do you have trouble with that? She is the sister of the First Dragon, as Osiris is his brother."

My nails dug into his arm until I realized what I was doing. I forced my fingers to relax, rubbing the crescent marks on his skin as I said, "OK. I'm going to need a moment to process this. Holy carp on rye."

"You make too much of the First Dragon's siblings," Yrian told me sternly, then approached Maat when she gestured toward him.

He held out his hand as ordered, and watched as she dropped a feather on his palm. It bobbled up and down a few times, making Maat laugh as she took it back.

"You may pass, much to my feather's delight," she told him, her smile once again warming everyone. He bowed, and held out his hand for me.

"This is Becket, my mate. Your feather will like her, too," he told Maat.

She gave me a quick once-over, then laid the feather on my palm. It didn't hop up and down with joy, like it did for Yrian, but it rested there quietly.

"Indeed, she is welcome to pass, as well," Maat told me, and to my utter surprise, she winked.

"Are we done? I have just enough time to get back to Anton. Oh, nephew. There was something I was supposed to tell you if I saw you. ..." Isis approached, expensive perfume wafting about her as she stopped in front of Yrian and tapped one perfectly manicured nail on her lower lip. "Ah! I have it! Osiris wanted me to warn you that Maat's sister has been buddying up with that troublesome brother of yours."

"Asfet?" Maat asked, as she stuck the feather back in her hair. Her expression turned somber as she watched Yrian. "She has returned to the Duat?"

"Evidently," Isis said with a careless gesture. "It matters not to me. Osiris handles that sort of thing. Guards! We leave."

The three shirtless men in ancient kilts immediately fell into line behind her as she departed, the captain in tow.

Maat looked troubled. Yrian looked furious. I just felt lost. "I get that anyone hanging around Bael is not good, but is there a reason why we have to be warned about it?"

"She is the other half of me," Maat answered, but I had a feeling she was not really paying attention. "I am order; she is chaos." Her gaze slid from looking at nothing to Yrian, her expression shifting to sympathy.

"Would she have the power to bring people into the Duat without using the ferry?" Yrian asked, his fire so high I worried it might spill out onto the deck.

"Yes," Maat said, her gaze dropping to her hands. "She is a deity, as am I. We do not need the *Wepwawet* in order to travel in the Duat. I must contact Osiris. He has dealt with Asfet in the past. He must return from the mortal world."

"I doubt if he would, not while the sons of Horus are running amok," Yrian told her, then held out a hand for me, giving Maat a little bow. "We thank you for your help."

"Be careful," she warned as we turned to leave the boat. "Asfet has always embraced that which will cause the most trouble, and if she is working with Bael ..."

"So, now we have a new bad guy to worry about?" I asked as we trotted down the gangway. A couple of dusty taxis were waiting for the passengers, along with stacks of luggage. Most of the people had left, but there were a few remaining who took pictures, chatted excitedly, and consulted maps as to where they wished to go next. "Like we don't have enough with Bael and Xavier?"

"Asfet is the least of my concerns—" His phone started playing an operatic song I recognized as "The Cat Duet." "It is my youngest brother. Yes?"

He put his phone on speaker just in time for me to hear Baltic explaining that although Deus escaped while being transported to Drake's country house, he had spilled a few secrets about Xavier.

"He admitted that Xavier seeks to become a new demon lord." Baltic's voice sounded tinny and thin, which I put down to the Internet connection in the Duat. Most underworlds had less than sterling reception with the mortal plane. "He did not say that Xavier sought help from Bael for that purpose, but I can't think of any other reason for consorting with him. It also explains why he is trying to gain the shards."

"It is as we thought," Yrian agreed. "Kashi would have little use for someone unless they provided the potential for his release, and I can think of nothing he would want more than the dragon heart itself."

"Deus refused to answer when asked where the blue shard was now," Baltic added, an obvious warning in his voice. "The others—particularly Archer and Hunter—don't believe Xavier would hand it over to Bael, but I am not convinced."

"Speculation about what Xavier might do is useless. It's clear he's already given the shard to Kashi," Yrian said, watching as the last batch of tourists left. One taxi remained, and I gestured to the driver that we would be a few minutes. She loaded up our luggage, pulled out a handheld game console, and proceeded to lean against the taxi playing a game.

"You think Xavier has been to the Duat since we last saw him?" Baltic asked. "The ferry leaves once a week. You were on the sailing that he must have joined, since we saw him four days ago."

"He was not on the ferry, nor was the demon who kidnapped Becket. I believe now he bypassed the trip altogether," Yrian answered, his voice flinty and full of pointy bits. "Becket and I were just warned that Maat's sister, Asfet, has been working with Kashi. Since the wrath demon who kidnapped Becket disappeared off the ferry, we must conclude the same about Xavier, assuming he was bringing the shard to Kashi."

I rubbed my arms against the goose bumps that formed despite the heat of the afternoon.

"The other shards are no doubt the target of Xavier and his tribe," Yrian continued when Baltic swore in French. "This circumstance is why I created the weyr. The kin must pull together to defend the shards. Summon the tribes friendly to you. Guard those septs with shards."

I said nothing as Yrian hung up, wanting to hug him, kiss him silly, and find the nearest fireproof bed so I could make him forget all the woes hanging over his head. Instead, I asked, "What next?"

"We find Kashi, and I destroy him," Yrian answered.

"Just like it's that simple?" I asked as he held open the taxi door for me.

"It won't be simple at all, but it must be done," he answered, then told the driver to take him to the home of Kashi.

"Who—" she started to ask.

"He's also known as Bael," I said with a quick glance at Yrian. He was looking out of the window, his expression stark, little tension lines forming around his mouth.

"Oh, him." She made a face. "Are you sure you wish to go there? Most people avoid that section of the fields."

"Fields?" I asked, putting my hand on Yrian's and giving it a supportive squeeze.

"Yes, since Bael did not pass Maat's test, he has to remain in the Duat, and all who reside here must work. Lord Osiris made it a rule many years ago. He said he was tired of freeloaders. Bael was assigned to labor in one of the fields." She grinned at us in the rearview mirror. "I chose to drive tourists and pilgrims. It's so much better than slaving away in wheat and barley fields."

"Oh, you're here because you ... er ..." I stopped, mentally swearing at my foot-in-mouth gaffe.

"Yup. I was a thief before I died. A really good thief, mind you, which angered many a pharaoh, so when one finally caught me, I was put to death. Maat didn't like the deaths that followed my thefts, and held me to blame for them, when it was really just the pharaohs having meltdowns, but it is what it is. I'm Neferu, by the way."

I introduced Yrian and myself, and with a feeling that the more information we had, the better we'd be able to tackle Bael, I asked, "Do you know Asfet, by any chance?"

"Nope. I try to stay clear of the troublemakers, if you know what I mean. You guys aren't going to stay here?"

"Not staying, no," I answered, my gaze on Yrian. He continued to look annoyed.

"Here's my card." Neferu stopped for a small herd of goats attended by two young girls in sparkly princess costumes as they crossed the road, twisting in her seat to pass me a business card. "Call me if you need a ride. I'm happy to take you wherever you need to go in the Duat."

I ignored the anachronism of modernity in the Egyptian underworld, and accepted it, murmuring my thanks.

"What's wrong? Why do you look so pissed?" I whispered to Yrian as we drove along dirt roads, heading roughly south. On the left, distant fields of varying shades of gold indicated fields of wheat and rye, while on the right, the vegetation petered out to nothing, with large sandy outcroppings of rock casting shadows on villages made up of dusty, flat-topped clay domiciles.

In direct contrast to what appeared to be Egypt from a few millennia ago, a handful of cars, golf carts, and motor scooters dotted the homes. I was heartened to see that the dogs and cats roaming around all looked well fed and healthy, as did the goats that occasionally popped up out of nowhere and bleated at us as we passed.

"I'm thinking about Asfet and how I will destroy Kashi if she has lent him her power," he answered, his eyes glittering brightly, but with a light that left me almost shivering with cold.

"I didn't know gods could lend their power. Is she that dangerous that she could make a difference with Bael?" I asked, my gut turning at the idea of so many problems lining up, just to deal with one heinous brother.

"Power can be lent, yes. The mark the First Dragon placed upon your brow to help you make my glamour was an example of that." He put his hand on mine when I started absently stroking his thigh. He shot a fast look at Neferu before saying quietly, "If you continue to torment me that way, I will have no choice but to take you right here in the car."

"I am so not into exhibitionism," I whispered back, but retrieved my hand. "Besides, I was trying to comfort you in a time of stress, not turn you on."

He cocked one eyebrow at me.

"All right," I admitted, glaring at the eyebrow. "I may have enjoyed stroking your leg a little too much, but that's a good thing!"

"It is right and proper you should want to arouse me, and although I would normally acquiesce to your demands, you are not safe until I destroy Kashi," he said in what I was coming to think of as his instructing tone. He said it with so much gravitas that it just made me want to laugh. I didn't, of course. I wouldn't hurt his feelings for the world, so instead I schooled my expression into one of regret, and kept my hands to myself. "As for Asfet … I don't believe she would be so foolish as to give power, even temporarily, to Kashi. It is on him we must remain focused."

We spent a little while discussing what he would say when we found Bael.

Most of his initial suggestions were profane at best, but after he worked that out of his system—and had a break wherein we watched three cat videos in order to calm him down—he settled on a basic plan.

"He should not recognize you as an artificer, since your glamour is strong enough to avoid detection," he said, pulling me up against his side. "Regardless, I will not allow Kashi to harm you."

"I'm not worried in the least about that," I lied. I *was* worried, but not about Yrian's ability to keep me safe. It was more the unexpected that had me anxious. What if Asfet threw in her lot with Bael? What if Xavier had fetched other items of power for him, not just the dragon shard? What if Bael lost his shit at his older brother coming around to squash him into a powerless puddle of goo? There were so many worries swirling around in my head, mixing up with all the emotions that rose whenever Yrian was near me.

"He has a mage sword, one made of light that was given to my youngest brother," he said meditatively, his fingers now absently stroking mine. "I wish to retrieve it."

"For Baltic?" I asked, a bit confused why dragons would want a mage sword. "He can't use it, can he?"

"All Firstborn have some degree of affinity with arcany," he said, looking out of the window again. Neferu had slowed down due to the kids playing soccer in the street as we approached the outskirts of another small village, deftly avoiding hitting the kids, or the dogs that ran around with them. On our left, the land opened up into a vast, flat plain with the glint of water shimmering beyond it. "STOP!"

Neferu slammed on the brakes, exclaiming at the same time as I clutched the arm Yrian had shoved in front of me. "Huh?"

"What's wrong?" I asked Yrian. Instead of answering, he leaped out of the car and ran back along the road about fifty feet, heading for a cluster of three clay buildings.

Neferu turned around to look back. "What bee got up his butt?"

"No idea, but just in case it's one of the several baddies who are evidently lining up in wait for us, I'd better check." I hopped out after Yrian, the kids in the street chasing after us. Yrian paused at a small sign that I had missed while perusing the fields, then hurried around to the rear of the building.

"Oh lord," I said as I trotted up to the sign. I sighed, ignored the children as they clamored around me, asking in English who we were, if Yrian was a dragon, because he looked like a dragon, and one of them—Hama—loved dragons, although the ones she liked were proper dragons, not a dragon who looked like a man. "Yes, he's a dragon, and no, he doesn't have wings if that was what you were going to ask next, and I suspect it was. Right. Let me go stop what is potentially a disaster in the making."

I escaped the kids and ran around the building, slowing down when I hit a stone patio set with a couple of benches and a fenced pen about three square feet. A tall lady stood next to Yrian, her hands gesturing as she spoke.

"—they are twelve weeks old now, and although the one with the black spot on the side is reserved for the head priestess, the orange one is available."

Yrian turned to me as I approached, a small bundle of orange clasped to his chest.

"Yes, you can have a kitten," I said, the objection I'd had on my lips since I'd seen the KITTENS FOR SALE sign out front dying at the look of delight in his eyes. "And yes, I realize I don't have the right to give you permission to have a pet, but in case you were going to ask if I minded, I don't. Although I really think you should have cats in pairs, so they have company."

"We will get another later when we have a home," he said, offering the kitten to me. It looked sleepy and somewhat annoyed at having been woken, but offered a rusty purr when I gave it a quick snuggle. He turned back to the woman, gesturing toward the orange purr machine. "Will you guard our kitten for us for a short while? We are going into battle, and it would not be safe for her to be around while we rid the world of my brother."

"Him, and I'll keep him for a few days so long as you put down a deposit, but if you don't come back for him by Friday, I'll look for another home," the woman warned, her gaze turning stubborn.

Yrian had taken the kitten from me prefatory to handing it over to the woman, but reeled back like she had struck him. "You will not give away our kitten. I have funds put at my disposal by my youngest brother. What amount do you want?"

Payment settled, five minutes later I managed to pry Yrian away from the orange kitten, its sibling who was promised to the local priestess, the mama cat, and even a baby lizard that he rescued from the mama, and herded him back to the taxi with promises of lots of critter playtime once we had finished our task.

"That's it, the second from the end," Neferu said about a half hour later. We were on the edges of a medium-sized village, one with a few shops, as well as dwellings. There were no people roaming around the village itself, but to our left where the fields spread out like a vast, golden blanket, a good two dozen or so people worked the land.

"I don't get why they don't use a proper tractor when they have cars," I said eyeing a man and his ox as they plowed the nearest edge of the field. "It seems like this way would be so much slower and harder."

"That's the whole point, though, isn't it?" Neferu said, one arm out of the window as she contemplated the pastoral scene. "Osiris expects those who are unable to pass on to work as a form of penance, so he doesn't want things made too easy. Anyway, I'm off. Give me a call if you need a ride to the nearest portal, OK?"

"Will do," I said, hurrying to catch up to Yrian when he stalked across the dusty dirt road toward a set of four small clay buildings.

I wanted to hold his hand, if for no other reason than comfort, but to be honest, I wasn't any too happy with the idea of standing in front of Bael. I let Yrian move in front of me when he approached the wooden door of the third house. A symbol was scratched into the wall, but what it meant, I had no idea. It gave Yrian a moment of pause, however.

"Do not speak to Kashi. He lies," was all he said before flinging open the door without so much as a knock.

"Yeah, this is so anticlimactic," I said a half minute later, after Yrian had marched through the house. It had only one bedroom, a minuscule bathroom with a toilet and sink, and the main room that housed a long table, two chairs, and a wall full of bladed weapons. It was empty of all former demon lords. "Mind you, I'm not complaining, but I know you were all keyed up to—"

I stopped when Yrian held up a hand, his head cocked slightly to the side. I wondered what he was listening to, since I didn't hear anything, but just as I was going to ask what was wrong, a woman's voice carried in on a breeze from the river.

"—can't believe you have not yet done away with that annoying dragon. Why you insist it's better to keep him alive is beyond me. You got what you wanted from him! We don't need any loose cannons—"

The door opened to reveal a woman. She stood taller than me, was of a substantial build, and had black eyes and long chestnut hair.

Yrian took a step back, his expression as frozen as the woman's.

At least, for a few seconds, then all hell seemed to break loose.

The woman screeched something in a language that felt really old; then she spun on her heel and ran off toward the road.

"Was that Asfet—" I started to ask, but Yrian was gone, racing after her.

By the time I made it outside, the muffled cough of a motor scooter could be heard, accompanied by a cloud of reddish-brown dust from the road, the obscured image of a woman bent low over the handlebars visible as she sped off. She pulled something black out of the robes she wore, and for a moment I thought it was a Taser, but since she kept fleeing, I figured it must be a cell phone.

When I reached Yrian's side, he swore in three different languages for a good minute and a half.

"Why did Asfet run from us? We haven't met her, have we?" I asked, coughing and waving away the swirl of dust.

"Why did she look so surprised to see us? I think she had a phone. Do you suppose she was calling Bael to warn him we're here?"

"That wasn't Asfet," Yrian said, whirling around to search for something. "It was Tenite."

"Who—wait, isn't that your mom's name?" I asked, a chill gripping my bones.

"We need a form of transport," Yrian said, marching to the road, looking up and down it. The houses here didn't have anything more than a couple of beat-up bicycles, but just as I was about to pin him back with a dozen questions, a tinny horn sounded as a golf cart bounced its way around the edge of a building, moving slowly through a flock of ducks and chickens.

"That will do—" Yrian stopped speaking, but a sudden rush of his fire had me gasping with the intensity of it.

The golf cart bounced to a stop on the road on another cloud of dust, the driver barely visible through it, but I caught a glimpse of an extremely old-looking man with a bald head, clad in nothing but a loincloth, holding a cell phone that he clicked off as he stopped in a swirl of even more dust. But it was the man who emerged from the cart through the brownish-red haze that had me taking several steps back before I realized it.

"Is that—" The words were barely audible, since my breath seemed to be caught in my throat.

"Kashi." Yrian all but spat the name out, as if it fouled his mouth.

The driver slid out of the golf cart and, with a back bent by extreme age, shuffled the way he had come, then disappeared around the house without a backward glance.

As the dust dissipated, I could see Bael clearly. He didn't look even remotely like Yrian, but I had a feeling I wasn't seeing his true form. This one was of a tall, elegant man with dark blond hair swept back, clad in a black pinstripe suit that was extremely out of place in the rural setting of Duat. "Yrian Shadowsworn. I had heard a rumor that the First Dragon dragged you kicking and screaming out of your pity party. I am disappointed to find it true."

His gaze raked Yrian, but as I could feel the latter drawing in power to himself, I kept my attention on him. I couldn't help him by creating a glamour in the Duat, but I sure as hell could cast any of the premade ones I'd brought with me. I angled myself so that I could dig through the small cross-body bag I'd donned before leaving the *Wepwawet*, and felt through the glamours searching for the insensibility one that would hopefully stun Bael for a few seconds so Yrian could deal with him.

"You have become too much of a threat to the dragonkin to tolerate your continued existence," Yrian told him, his voice so icy goose bumps rose on my arms. "Either you cease your actions, or you will be destroyed."

Bael looked bored. "You think to command me? I am the premiere prince of Abaddon, dragon. I give commands, not take them." His gaze shifted to me, and I had to stop myself from hiding behind Yrian. "You have a mate? After swearing you would never replace your first? Perhaps you welcomed her death so that you might consort with this mortal."

Bael gestured toward me as he spoke, and for a moment, I sagged in relief against Yrian's back. He hadn't seen through my glamour.

"My mate is of no concern to you," Yrian snarled, and I think he would have attacked his brother except Bael seemed to expect that.

"You can't kill me, you know," he said in a voice that I'm sure he thought was pleasant. It wasn't. I swore it took years off even my immortal life. He lifted a hand and gestured toward the clay houses. "Like me, your powers were limited the minute you stepped foot in the Duat."

"I don't need powers to throttle the life from your body," Yrian said in a low, deceptively soft tone that sent another round of goose bumps down my arms.

Bael laughed, he actually laughed. It was a horrible thing to witness. "If only it was that simple. Alas, unless you have something along the lines of this, there is no threat you can make that I would take seriously." As he spoke, he pulled out of an inner pocket a small bluish crystal.

Yrian's fire roared at the sight of what I figured must be the mage sword, and before I could think of the wisdom of the situation, I flung the insensibility glamour over Yrian's shoulder, smack-dab into the face of Bael.

"What did—" Yrian half turned toward me, but evidently realized what I'd done, because before I could warn him we had about five seconds at most, he snatched the crystal from Bael's hand. It elongated into a long, glowing blue-and-white sword.

I spun around just as he raised it, not wanting to see someone decapitated, not even the most heinous of all demon lords, but the red cloud a dozen yards away and moving fast had me shouting a warning.

"Your mom is coming back, and she's got someone with her!" I shouted, digging through my bag for a hardcore compliance will glamour.

Bael snapped out of insensibility at that moment and, with a snarled obscenity, lunged at Yrian.

"Mate!" Yrian yelled, twisting to try to protect me at the same time he slashed at Bael.

"Right here, and about to let fly with another glamour—" Just as Tenite on her motor scooter—and the dark-haired Xavier behind her—came to a fishtail stop, I threw the compliance glamour on her, feeling she was the more dangerous of the two.

"I should have killed you myself when I had your brother take care of that whiny mate of yours," Tenite snarled to Yrian as she flung the scooter away in order to stalk toward us. Evidently, my glamour wasn't strong enough to overcome her demigodhood. She wore black and bloodred robes that looked like they were straight out of a video game, her hair twisted into several braid loops that poked out all over her head. A sensation of rage poured out of her as she headed straight for Yrian, along with Xavier.

I didn't like Yrian's odds at all. The man might be a demigod, but so was Tenite, and Bael was no slacker. I felt in my bag for another glamour, hoping that if I stacked a few on Tenite, they might have an effect, but before I could do so, Yrian spun and slashed off her right arm, kicking out immediately with enough force to send her and Xavier staggering backward. Before they had stopped moving, the sword flashed in the air, and Bael's head went flying off to the side, bouncing twice in the furrowed field, finally coming to a stop next to a flat rock.

Tenite screamed, a sound so filled with rage I doubled over in pain, my hands on my ears. Yrian staggered back at the sound, but lifted the sword again as he faced Xavier and his mother.

I swear I saw a moment of utter stupefaction in Xavier's eyes before they went blank, but Tenite evidently read her fate in Yrian's face as he moved, the sword high over his head.

"You are even stupider than I thought you were, but you will not ruin our plans. We have put too much into them to be destroyed by a dragon." She almost spat the words as she snatched up her severed arm and flung herself into the golf cart, slamming her foot on the accelerator, clearly intent on running us over.

It wouldn't kill us, but it could do enough damage to maim or hurt us, so when Yrian jerked me out of the way of his murderous mom, I didn't protest. I did, however, try unsuccessfully to throw a sleep glamour on her.

She was gone on a cloud of dust, Xavier leaping into the back as she sped past him, the inevitable dust cloud rising around us, obscuring our view for a few seconds.

When we could see again, I turned back to find Yrian kneeling at Bael's headless body, going through pockets and inside clothing, no doubt searching for the blood moon.

"Is it there?" I asked, my adrenaline finally starting to subside.

"Desi's relic? No." Yrian's lips tightened as he gave the body a second, equally fruitless search. "This makes no sense.

He has to have it. It is too valuable for him to leave it in his house."

"Let's go look again," I said, feeling twitchy from both the fight and an odd buildup of magic.

We searched first Bael's house, then the other three, but found nothing. I examined the area around the buildings, finally returning to where Yrian now stood over Bael's lifeless body, his head propped up next to his feet.

"I didn't find anything out back, I'm afraid. How are you going to keep him from coming back?" I asked.

He glanced at me, obviously confused.

"This is the underworld. You can't truly die here," I pointed out. "One of the ladies on the boat said that if you die, you simply return here, whole again."

"Ah," he said, looking back at the body. To my complete surprise—and horror—he lifted the sword and sliced off Bael's arm. "There is one way. If the body is chopped to bits and spread around the Duat, it will not be able to re-form. Go back into Kashi's house, Becket."

I weighed my options, decided I really didn't want to see a dismemberment, and hurried into the empty house, my arms wrapped around myself as I danced out my twitchiness, mulling over the events of the last half hour.

We might have taken care of the biggest of the threats, but Xavier had escaped, and evidently now Yrian's mom was going to be another problem.

"It's like we can't win," I said to my shoes as I sat on a hard wooden chair, ignoring the sounds of a body being hacked to bits by a magical sword. My inner narrator pointed out that Yrian had fulfilled his goal. Bael was dead, so there was no reason to be glum.

"My brain is warring with the rest of me," I told Yrian a few minutes later, when he appeared in the open doorway.

"Over the death of Kashi?" he asked, brushing a bit of black blood off his hand.

"No. Yes. It might be related. I'm happy you did what you wanted to do, and yet ..." I stopped and tried to pinpoint the sick feeing in my belly. "I guess I'm a bit down that we have more work to do."

"Xavier, you mean?" He didn't nod as I expected, just looked down at the hand holding the blade. Despite having been used to lop off bits of Bael, it wasn't in the least bit stained black by demon blood. "There is good reason for your feeling such. Come. We must leave before Tenite finds Asfet."

"You think your mom's going to attack us?" I asked, following him outside. To my relief, he'd bundled the pieces of his brother into several bags used to hold grain. I averted my gaze from the black stains growing along the bags, instead watching as he doled out money to a handful of workers he'd evidently gathered, giving them instructions to spread Bael's remains around the Duat.

"Yrian?" I asked when he pulled the motor scooter up from where Tenite had thrown it, dusting it off before swinging a leg over the seat.

"We must leave now," he repeated, his legs braced on either side of the scooter, obviously waiting for me.

"Do you know how to ride that?" I asked, pointing at the machine.

"Yes. Before I was imprisoned, a mortal donated his motorcycle to me."

"Donated?" I asked, slowly approaching.

He gave a one-shouldered shrug. "He decided it was better to give it to me than be set on fire."

"I had a feeling it was something like that. I have at least twenty questions for you to answer, the first of which is where we're going. The second is what we're going to do with your mom and Xavier." I climbed on behind him, wrapping my arms around his waist, my head tucked in behind his, relishing the scent and feel and heat of him despite the worry still fussing in my stomach.

"Xavier is not an issue," Yrian shouted as we sped off down the road. I pulled out a silk scarf I'd bought from the *Wepwawet's* shop, and, without blinding him, managed to get it wrapped around his nose and mouth before tucking my head behind his again.

"I know you're angsty that your mom was being an as-shat and took Xavier with her, but I don't see why you're beating yourself up over the situation. You did what you wanted to do—you killed Bael, and assuming spreading him hither and yon does the job, then he'll stay dead."

"That wasn't Kashi."

The wind was whipping past us at such a rate that I wasn't sure I heard him. I tipped my head so I was speaking close to his ear. "It wasn't? Who was it? It was definitely someone with demonic power, Yrian. He bled black blood, but even without that proof, I could feel the dark power in him."

"It was Xavier. Kashi must have switched bodies with him." Yrian's fire poured out of him, leaving a blazing trail on the dirt road behind us. "And now, thanks to Tenite and Asfet, he is about to return to the mortal world."

I swore into his neck, my stomach giving up all hope of ever feeling normal again.

FIFTEEN
YRIAN

"I have failed, dragon sire." Yrian bowed his head, braced for the disappointment he would see in the First Dragon's eyes. He wanted to rail against it, to explain that it wasn't his fault that Tenite had been in the Duat helping Kashi, but none of that would matter. He had gone to the Duat to remove Kashi as a threat to the dragonkin, and he had failed to do so.

The First Dragon would not be happy.

Becket moved closer to him, her fingers twining around his in an obvious show of support. A warm rush of emotion filled him at the gesture.

The First Dragon stood in the garden surrounding his home, silent, with crossed arms, the late afternoon sun casting a golden aura around him that heightened the lack of expression on his face.

"It wasn't really your fault, though," Becket said, her voice forceful and full of sharp edges. Yrian was simultaneously surprised by the fact that she was defending him to the First Dragon, and warmed even more by the emotion that continued to drive away dark patches on his soul. "He looked like Bael. He spoke like Bael. He had black demon blood, and that fancy blue sword. How were you to know it wasn't Bael? Also, the fact that your mom was there stirring things up didn't help."

That seemed to provoke the First Dragon into an actual reaction. He considered first Becket, then Yrian. "Tenite was in the Duat?"

"Yes. She was working with Kashi to manipulate Xavier and, I assume, others. Maat mentioned Asfet aiding Kashi, as well."

A look of speculation crossed the First Dragon's face as he unbent, no doubt because his mate emerged from the house and made her way to his side, sliding her hand into the crook of his elbow. "Asfet. She is the other half of Maat. I will speak to Osiris about her. As for the other ..."

"No!" Becket tossed a glamour onto the First Dragon, taking everyone there by surprise.

"Hey!" Charity said, indignation rolling off her as she moved in front of the First Dragon, taking his face in her hands while she studied him. "Are you OK? What did she do to you?"

To Yrian's amazement, the First Dragon actually smiled, his eyes warming to gold as he gently moved Charity back to his side, going so far as to place an arm around her. Yrian had never in all the thousands of years of his life seen the First Dragon do such a thing with Iceni. He had always assumed his father felt such displays of affection beneath him, and yet, here he was, pulling Charity against his side.

"Dammit!" Becket snarled under her breath, another glamour in her hands, one she clearly intended on using on the First Dragon. "Demigods are just so very—"

Both the First Dragon and Yrian looked at her with lifted eyebrows.

She growled, actually growled in frustration as she stuffed the glamour back in her bag.

"It wasn't anything to get your knickers in a twist about, Charity. It was just a clarity glamour, one that I hoped would make the First Dragon see that Yrian did not fail. He did what he was asked to do. It wasn't his fault that Bael had

Xavier so wrapped around his little finger that he would convince him to swap forms."

"I don't care what it was. Don't do it again," Charity answered, her brows pulled together.

"Mate," Yrian said to Becket, bending what he hoped was a stern eye on her. He was secretly so delighted that she stood up for him, he couldn't truly be annoyed with her. "I appreciate you wish to avert some of the First Dragon's wrath due to fall upon me, but you need not attempt to sway him with glamours. For one, it won't work on him unless he allows it, and for another, it will put him further out of humor, and I would rather receive his punishment now so I might continue my search for Kashi."

The corners of the First Dragon's mouth twitched, but his face was as impassive as ever as he continued to watch Yrian for another two minutes before he said in a slow, measured manner, "You state you have failed, and yet, you eliminated one of the risks to the kin. The one called Xavier was a pawn in Bael's hands, which made him all that much more dangerous. That threat is no more."

"But I did not kill Kashi," Yrian insisted, suddenly irritated. Was this his father's punishment—to keep him standing there, feeling every ounce of the weight of his failure, when all he wanted was to get Becket to the nearest bed, where he could reassure himself that her heart was truly his?

"Did you really believe you could do so?" The First Dragon gave a little shake of his head. "Has time in your griefscape made you forget that your powers were limited in the Duat, just as they are in every other underworld?"

"I did not forget," Yrian said, his jaw setting despite his trying to appear humble before his sire. "On the contrary, I had little choice but to attempt to honor your request. It is in that I failed. I was too weak to overcome the forces Kashi had rallied to his side."

The First Dragon continued to consider him for another few minutes before he did the last thing Yrian expected— he put a hand on his shoulder, saying, "You, Yrian Shadowsworn, are stronger than you think, but you are not capable of overcoming the restrictions set for underworlds. You did not fail."

"I had hoped to keep Kashi away from the mortal world because he was weaker in the Duat," Yrian said, fighting briefly with his fire. It threatened to explode out of him, but he wrestled it back under control at the same time the First Dragon gave his shoulder a squeeze before dropping his hand. "Now I must defeat him where others could be harmed. That is the weight of the failure I bear."

Once again, the First Dragon took him by surprise. Instead of agreeing, or even heaping more scorn and chastisement upon his head, his father asked, "Why did you create the weyr?"

"The weyr?" Yrian frowned, momentarily distracted when Becket rubbed her thumb across his fingers, obviously trying to provide support in the face of the upcoming punishment. The First Dragon knew full well why he had felt driven to form the weyr. Was this yet some other form of torment, a way to drive home just how much he'd failed the septs? "To bring the kin together."

"Why?" the First Dragon asked again.

Becket opened her mouth as if she was going to speak, shot Yrian a fast look, then closed it again, and scooted closer to him.

"The weyr has strength where smaller groups do not," he answered, confused what his father wanted him to admit. He'd already stated he'd failed, and his willingness to bear the First Dragon's punishment.

"This is so," the First Dragon answered, blinking his eyes in a manner that had Yrian remembering a long-dead Persian king's favorite pet tiger.

Yrian was at a loss for a few seconds until Becket said softly, "Bael isn't wholly your problem, Yrian. I think your dad is saying that you should let the other dragons help you."

The First Dragon gave her a brief nod before turning back to him. "Baltic was intended to bring balance to the weyr. He has finally seen fit to do so. But even with that, the weyr cannot destroy Bael by itself any more than you can do so alone."

"Kashi will not hesitate to destroy as many dragons as he can," Yrian said, feeling the full weight of his responsibility. "I hesitate to involve the others in the fight lest he obliterate them just as he did my sept and your mate."

Silence fell over them, even the birdsong stilling for a half minute. "You created the septs. You drew them into the weyr," the First Dragon told him. "Do you believe both are so insignificant that together you can't face this threat? Look to your past, wyvern, for it is there you will find the answers you seek. There … and in Paris," the First Dragon said, then, without another word, and with his arm still around Charity, returned to the house.

"I know he's your dad and a god and all—OK, yes, demigod—but there are times when I want to do something to him. Something … I don't know. Not truly cruel, but maybe just a little mean. Maybe pinch him hard on the arm," Becket said, glaring at the glass doors to the house. "What did he mean, look to your past? What answers are you looking for? And why Paris? What does he know that we don't? Why is he so very … gah!"

Yrian was struck by a thought, one that clearly the First Dragon had intended for him to realize some time ago.

The answer lay with the kin.

"Look to my past," he said meditatively. "He was talking about Kashi destroying my sept."

Becket, who was busily creating a glamour that Yrian suspected would do something objectionable to the First Dragon, continued to mutter to herself but stopped at his words, glancing up at him. "You're not to blame for that—"

"I am, but …" He thought about what the First Dragon had said. "But I see now that I failed because I tried to protect my sept from Kashi, rather than relying on them to help defeat him." He turned a stark face to Becket. "It's my fault he is here now, posing such a threat to the weyr. If I had taken care of him in the past, he wouldn't have survived to threaten the dragonkin now."

"No!"

He jerked back at her bellow, taken aback by the fact that not only was she suddenly furious; she had manifested his fire around them both in a blazing ring.

"Just no, Yrian!" Becket grabbed his shirt in both her hands, shaking the material as her eyes blazed a brilliant blue at him. "Stop martyring yourself! I know times were hard back in the day, what with you trying to come to grips with your fire, and making the dragons behave so they could join the weyr you created for them, but you are not responsible for the actions of anyone else, including your dick of a brother. Do you see your dad blaming himself for Bael? No, you do not, and do you know why?"

Yrian opened his mouth to protest, but Becket's ire was truly up and aimed directly at him.

"He knows he's not responsible for Bael any more than you are. I mean, he's Bael's father, so really, if there is any blame to be spread, he should get the bulk of it, but I don't hold with that idea. I believe people are responsible for their own fates, and that includes Bael. Yrian—" Her expression went from furious to something soft and filled with understanding and warmth. She leaned forward and feathered a few kisses along his lips. "You did what you could to save everyone in the past. Bael and your mom were just too much for you to handle on your own. So yes, look to the other dragons for help, but don't do it with the mindset that you're to blame for the situation with Bael in the first place."

"I wish to kiss you," he told Becket, his heart lighter than it had felt since his last child was born.

"Goody," she answered, rubbing her hips against him in a way that instantly had him hard.

"I can't do it here," he told her, gently removing her from his person.

"What? Why—oh, your dad? You think he'd get his knickers in a twist if he saw us smooching?"

She was clearly about to laugh, leaving him mildly scandalized.

"He is the First Dragon," Yrian told her with much sternness, which she summarily ignored. "This is his domain. It would be disrespectful to indulge ourselves here. Since you desire bedsport, we will leave and find the closest bed. I do not wish you to be frustrated."

She did laugh then, and took the hand he offered as he escorted her across the garden. "Thank you for such consideration. I'm not going to say no to lovemaking, but it probably can wait until after we talk to the other dragons and warn them about Bael's trickery, and new threat. I assume we're going to Paris?"

"Yes," he said, sobering at the thought of the battle ahead of him. No, not just him ... the kin.

A sense of comfort settled onto his shoulders, leaving him feeling strangely euphoric. He needn't fight alone anymore. Now he had Becket and the dragonkin. How could he fail with that help?

"Yes, we should wait, or yes, we should find the nearest bed in Paris?" she asked. "Or yes, your dad was right, and now you realize that you're not going it alone?"

He smiled, a sudden memory coming to mind as he led her out of the garden, returning to the mortal world. "You are not alone in finding the First Dragon to be sometimes irritating. Once, when my eldest daughter was born, Iceni was admiring her and demanded the First Dragon pay respects to his first grandchild. He took one look at her, and prophesized that chaos would trail her footsteps. Iceni was most vocal in her dismay that he would say such a thing about an innocent babe. I believe she did pinch him on the arm. He was not pleased."

"And was your daughter chaotic?" Becket asked as he consulted his phone device, adjusting his exit from the First Dragon's life space into the mortal world.

"Very much so. Everything was a drama of the most magnificent proportion to her. She was exhausting, but she was also the smartest of all my children." They emerged onto a tree-lined residential street in what was clearly an expensive arrondissement in Paris. A large three-story house in shades of cream and pale green stood next to them.

Becket looked around with obvious surprise when he turned her toward the door and proceeded up the three marble steps to the entry. "Is this your brother's house?"

"No, he said he does not have a home in Paris. This belongs to the green wyvern. We have much to do if we wish to stop Kashi from destroying all. We must rally the dragons."

"Now, that's what I like to hear. Wait—I get to help, right? Because I'm feeling particularly creative when it comes to making up some glamours for your dill weed of a brother," she said, her voice round with satisfaction.

He wanted to tell her it wouldn't be safe to be around Kashi now that he was in the mortal world, but mindful of his new insight, he simply said, "I couldn't do it without you."

The smile she gave him chased out the last of the shadows on his soul. "You remember when I said I thought I was falling in love with you?"

He paused in the act of ringing the bell, fear gripping him with steely claws. "You are no longer so?" emerged from his mouth before he realized how pathetic it sounded.

She kissed him again, a fleeting kiss, to be true, but it was enough that it warmed his heart. "Just the opposite. I love you, Yrian. I love the fact that you think it's your job to protect everyone—although if you could do it without the martyrdom, that would be great—and how contradictory you are, and the fact that you love cats so much that just watching videos of them doing silly things brings you endless delight. I love seeing how much you enjoy the modern world. And I love seeing how much you care about your family. I just …" She sighed, her eyes misty with passion and tears. "I just love you."

"You are my mate," he said, feeling as if he could conquer the world when she looked at him like that. "It is right and proper that you love—ow!"

"You big oaf!" she said, laughing at the same time she pinched his wrist. "This is the exact moment when you are supposed to tell me you love me, too. And don't deny you do, because your eyes downright glow when you look at me, and that has to mean you love me." Her voice faded away on the last couple of words, doubt flashing across her face.

"Wyverns," he told her, still wanting to shout from the tallest part of Drake's house the fact that he had a mate who loved him, "swear an oath to protect and honor their respective mates. I have done so for you."

Her eyes narrowed on him at the same time her fingers started dancing in the air, drawing a glamour. "There had better be a second part to that statement, buster."

"Yrian," he corrected, then gave in to his inner joy and scooped her up against his chest, breathing in deeply of her scent, relishing the feeling of her pressed so tightly to him. His heart was overflowing with emotions that he hadn't felt in so long, he wasn't sure they were real. Becket had driven away all those doubts, however. "If I told you that you matter more to me than all the dancing cats in the world, would that suffice as a declaration of my emotions?"

"Not in the least," she answered, relaxing despite her objection. "Tell me what you want, Yrian."

"Other than Kashi's destruction?" He smiled to himself when she growled again, slapping both her hands onto his chest. He pulled her up so he could plunder her mouth as it deserved to be plundered, stripping the breath from her lungs, saying when he had to stop lest he pass out, "You have my heart and soul, Becket. You are the mate I never thought to have, one who is brave, and clever, and enjoys dancing cats and bedsport. Not at the same time, though," he qualified.

She burst into laughter at his declaration. "Definitely not at the same time. Are you going to say it?"

He had his hands on her hips, those delicious hips whose curves made him want to bury himself in her. "You are so sure that I reciprocate your feelings?" he teased.

"No," she admitted, her smile fading a little.

That was all it took. He couldn't stand for her to doubt the depths his emotions ran. "You fill my mind," he murmured as he kissed the line of her lips, moving over to the spot near her ear that she'd told him drove her wild. "You are the air and sun and moon and everything. If you were not here to fill my life with happiness, I would retreat to the griefscape, there to stay until I took my last breath."

"That is the sweetest thing anyone has said to me," she answered, sliding her hands up his chest.

The door opened behind her as he gave in to her tugs on his shoulders and kissed her with all the love that shone so brightly inside him.

"Whoa, gettin' it on right there on the front step," a male voice said from behind Becket. Jim the demon gave them both an amused glance before a female green dragon holding a backpack hurried out after it. "Can you hold off doing anything really spicy until I get back from my visit to Cecile?"

"Jim!" The female dragon gave Yrian a little bow before sidling past them. "You should not speak so. It is disrespectful, and Aisling told you to mind your manners."

"Yeah, yeah, but Eerie and Beckatude love me, right? Right?"

Yrian ignored the demon, escorting Becket into the house, his pleasure in being the focus of her love fading as he realized he had much work to do before he could enjoy a peaceful life with her.

It was time. He would gather the kin to him, and together, they would stop Kashi before he did any more harm.

There was simply no other option.

SIXTEEN
BECKET

"I'm ashamed of myself," I told Aisling two hours later. She, Ysolde, May, and I were out in the small garden at the back of her house, absently watching as four children ran around screaming while shooting one another with fancy water pistols. "Ouch. I hope Anduin is all right," I added to Ysolde when her son did a face-plant after leaping off a kid's plastic play castle.

"Eh," Ysolde said, glancing at the boy. He was up and chasing after the older kids without so much as a pause. "He's tougher than he looks. He gets that from me."

Anduin yelled something quite rude in Russian.

Ysolde pursed her lips. "And *that* he gets from his father. Anduin! You know better than to use that word!"

May laughed, then quickly stifled it with a glance toward me. "Sorry. I know this is a solemn moment and all."

"It may be solemn for you," I said, alternating between on the one hand wanting to march back into the room where the wyverns were present to give them all another piece of my mind and, on the other, wishing to apologize again to Aisling for defending Yrian with such vehemence the men threw me out of the *sárkány*. "I'm mortified that I let my temper get the better of me in front of everyone. But really, your wyverns were being unreasonably mean to Yrian, and I'm not going to stand that from anyone. Not even his brother."

"I don't think Baltic was being mean so much as just pointing out the obvious problem," Ysolde said, but patted me on the arm to show support. "I agree that Hunter and Archer went a bit over the line saying Yrian cheated them out of the right to kill their father, but I can understand that emotion."

"It didn't give them the right to be so snappish at him," I said, taking a chair when Aisling gestured toward a patio table. "Telling him he did it on purpose because he has main-character syndrome … that's just bullshit. Yes, Yrian came out of his griefscape to help you guys, but to accuse him of wanting to be the hero of the day is ridiculous. He's gone through hell trying to cope with Bael, and honestly, it's not like any of the other dragons are helping him. They just tell him to do the job, and then don't lift a finger to help."

Silence fell and my shoulders sagged at the sound of my words, guilt piercing me like shards of glass.

"Well, now," Aisling said, blinking a few times as she gazed at me.

"I'm sorry," I said, lifting a hand in apology. "That came out a lot harsher than it sounded in my head. Obviously, I'm not blaming you. It's just so frustrating when everyone piles their expectations on Yrian and doesn't realize that he's just one man."

"A demigod, evidently," May said, since I'd let that slip earlier during my verbal explosion at the wyverns. She slid Ysolde a look. "Does that mean Baltic is one, too?"

"Goddess, no!" she answered, looking mildly horrified. "It's no doubt because his mom was a dragon, while all the other Firstborn had two demigod parents. And frankly, I'm happier that way. I can only imagine how annoying the First Dragon would be if Baltic had the same sort of abilities as Yrian."

"You don't like him very much, do you?" I asked, suddenly distracted.

"Me?" Her eyes widened. "I like Yrian quite a bit. He's intense, but in a good way, if you know what I mean."

"No, I meant the First Dragon. He's basically your father-in-law, right?"

"Oh, him." Ysolde gave an abbreviated eye roll, followed by a little laugh. "I'm actually fond of him, not that I don't think he can be an interfering boob sometimes, but I know he loves Baltic, and to me, that's the most important thing. I mean, obviously he loves all the dragons, but Baltic being Baltic, I appreciate the fact that his father cherishes him so much."

The ladies murmured their agreement while I thought about that.

"So, does the fact that you glamoured Hunter and Archer into toads when they got shouty about Yrian mean you've accepted him as your mate?" May asked. "I realize that it's prying, but I'm acting secretary for our Mates Union, so I need to know if I should add you in to our group chats and private Zoom sessions."

"Also, we are nosy and want to know," Aisling added, shouting a warning to her children to stay in the section of the yard in front of us. She was clearly still concerned about the safety of the green dragons even though Xavier was no more. "Not that you're obligated to tell us, but we do like to keep track of all the mates."

I touched my hair. The *sárkány* was the first time I appeared in public without a glamour, knowing Yrian preferred my true appearance, a fact that spread a lovely warm glow inside me. "Yes, I've accepted the fact that I'm bound to a man who is obsessed with cat videos, and who also just happens to be six or seven thousand years old, which let me tell you, is a bit of a mind ... er ... rush." I censored myself when Aisling's youngest ran up complaining that the others weren't letting her shoot Anduin.

"Wow, he's really that old? That's like ... caveman times, isn't it?" May asked, watching as Ava ran back with a fresh water pistol.

"Stone Age," I answered. "He says he remembers when the mortals saw people he called proto-mages wielding metal weapons, which they then copied. I believe that was the start of the Bronze Age."

"Proto-mages?" Aisling asked at the same time Ysolde said, "Someday, you should sit Yrian down and have him dictate the story of his life. I bet it was fascinating."

"I plan on doing just that—" I started to say, but paused when Aisling's phone sang out a chorus from a popular Romanian song I recognized from some twenty years before.

"I think I'd better take this. It's Dr. Kostich," she said, getting up and moving a few yards from the table.

"Have you met him yet?" Ysolde asked, not waiting for me to answer. "I used to be his apprentice, so I feel I have the right to say he is the biggest pain in the butt ever."

"What?" Aisling almost shrieked the word, spinning around to look at the French doors leading into her house. "Right now? How many … yes, but it's not our fault. … Well, that's true, but … fuck!"

The last word was spoken after she'd clicked off the call, her eyes scanning the yard. "Who wants cookies?" she bellowed across the sound of the kids playing.

All four of them turned with hopeful faces and cheers, leaping up from where they were rolling around on the grass..

"Cookies and ice cream in the playroom," she said, her eyes filled with warning as she herded the kids into the house, pausing to stick her head into the kitchen, no doubt to have her housekeeper send up the treats.

"What's going on?" I asked when she raced down a back set of stairs after getting the kids upstairs to their play area.

"Grace is with them," she told Ysolde before grabbing my wrist and hurrying toward the big room where the *sárkány* was taking place. Grace, I knew, was her nanny. "Houston, we've got a problem."

"What?" both May and Ysolde asked, but she just shook her head, releasing me to dramatically throw open a pair of pocket doors.

Hunter was stalking around the room, clearly expounding on some point, but he paused in midstep when we burst into the room.

Drake rose at once, his eyes locked on Aisling.

"The kids are upstairs," she told him, and something about the timbre of her voice sent goose bumps down my arms. "But I think they should go to the château. Ysolde, Anduin is welcome to join them, if you don't want to send him home."

Drake half turned away, making a fast phone call, while the other dragons all demanded to know what was going on.

"I don't know," Ysolde told Baltic, who'd moved over to stand next to her, a question in his eyes. "It's something to do with Dr. Kostich, so it's bound to be highly annoying."

"Tell us what has happened," Drake said, finished with his call.

Aisling took a deep breath, her gaze slipping from me to Yrian before it turned to her husband. "Dr. Kostich just called me to demand we do something about the mass of demons that have descended upon Suffrage House."

Drake said nothing, just waited, but his eyes were narrow green slivers.

Her mouth tightened for a few seconds before adding, "He said that Bael was there, too, along with a woman he claims shouldn't be in the mortal world."

I'd moved over to lean into Yrian, but froze at her words, my gaze on him. Instantly, his fire roared to life, spreading out from his feet until I tamped it out by doing a little dance on it.

"Tenite," he said, his eyes blazing a brilliant gold. "What is this Suffrage House?"

All the wyverns were on their phones now, obviously notifying people and hopefully rounding up help.

"It's the Otherworld's headquarters," May said, looking worried. "Dr. Kostich is based there, although why Bael would want into the building is beyond me ... oh." She exchanged a meaningful look with Gabriel.

"I think you're right, little bird," he said, nodding, then told Yrian, "There is a vault in the basement, one where artifacts are stored. Drake's broken into it before, as has May … but there is nothing of great value held there. Just minor relics, lesser grimoires, etc."

"What would your brother want with minor relics?" I asked Yrian, one hand on his arm.

His lips twisted. "He wouldn't bother with something insignificant. There must be something more to draw him."

"Gabriel is correct. The truly valuable relics—such as the light sword that Kostich took from Baltic—are kept elsewhere. I can think of nothing held at Suffrage House that would interest a demon lord," Drake said, looking thoughtful. "Unless something was added of late."

Yrian stilled for a few seconds, then released a long breath. "He put it there. That's why I didn't feel its presence in the Duat. He hid it at this Suffrage vault."

"Hid what?" I asked, then sucked in my own breath at the memory of our time with Allie and Christian. "The blood moon?"

"We leave now," Yrian said, taking my hand as he headed for the door.

"Others are on their way," Gabriel protested, following. "There aren't many silver dragons in Europe, but those that are will be in Paris as soon as possible."

"There are several of my sept nearby. They are en route now," Drake said with a frown. "It would be folly to make an attempt on Bael without support."

"The folly would be allowing him to regain the blood moon," Yrian said without stopping, going straight for the front door. "With it, he can do untold damage. We are a sufficient number to stop him now, before it comes to that."

All the wyverns followed, although they didn't look happy … everyone but Hunter and Archer, who I knew were itching for payback. A few other men came running from another section of the house, guards appointed to the various wyverns, Aisling had told me when Yrian arrived earlier.

"Thaisa has asked if she should take a portal here, but I told her to stay with her grandmother," Archer told Hunter as they gathered up the two swords that they'd left in the hall.

"No sense in putting her in danger," Hunter agreed.

To a man, the wyverns all considered the mates.

"Don't even," Ysolde told Baltic, sailing out of the open door with a dark-haired man named Pavel on her heels.

"I'm sorry to ruin Jim's visit with Amelie and Cecile, but this is more important," Aisling said to no one in particular. "Effrijim, I summon thee."

The demon dog appeared with a squeaky toy in its mouth. It immediately dropped it, saying, "Sheesh, Ash! You gotta warn me when you're going to do that. I was putting on a squeaky puppet show for Cecile. Heya, everyone. What's going on? Why do the dragon hunters have their swords? Aw, man, you're going to fight someone, aren't you?"

There was a bit of a kerfuffle when everyone burst out onto the sidewalk, what with cars having to be fetched. Yrian was beyond impatient, pacing in front of the door while Drake's car was being brought around.

"This delay is intolerable," Yrian said to me as he stalked past before turning around and retracing his steps.

"I know how much you want to find Bael, but you're setting the sidewalk on fire, and I don't think the mortals who live next to Drake are going to understand," I said, stomping on the fiery footprints that trailed him. "And before you think about running off to tackle him alone, remember that you said you needed the weyr for this."

He made a sour expression that quickly faded away, his eyes searching my face. "Do you have a glamour?"

"Several. For whom did you want one?" I asked.

"Yourself. I don't want Kashi to know who you are. Can you look like you did in the Duat?"

"Sure," I said, my hands already weaving bits of magic into the appearance. "But I doubt if I'm going to be his focus, not with you and the other dragons rolling up."

"He would mark your appearance, and seek you out to destroy me, just as he did Amice." He checked himself, saying, "Rather, as he and Tenite did, since she was evidently part of his plot."

He must have told the wyverns that after I'd been banished from their meeting, because no one appeared surprised by his statement.

The ride to the large sandstone building sitting on the edge of one of Paris's small parks was relatively short, although fraught with some argument when Drake, again, pointed out that several green dragons were on their way, and the handful that were in Paris had already set off for Suffrage House.

"What sort of protection does the vault have?" Yrian asked Drake.

"A very strong series of electronic locks that will take some time to work through. In addition to that, there are a variety of magics woven into the material."

"Banes," Aisling said. "The wards are easy enough to break, but the banes, songs, and prohibitions are going to take some time—and a whole lot of demons—to break."

"Kashi will have demons at hand," Yrian said grimly.

"Which is one reason why it is important to have as many members of my sept as can be rallied quickly," Drake pointed out, clearly annoyed.

"We do not have time to wait for others," Yrian insisted, his body tense and poised for action. "If Kashi regains Desislav's relic, it will make him much harder to destroy. The kin who are present are enough."

"I wish I had your confidence," Aisling said softly. She sat across from us, pressed into Drake, Jim lying at her feet.

The demon, I noticed, was oddly silent. Before I could ask what that was about, we pulled up to the headquarters of the L'au-dela.

The second we stepped out of the car, Aisling sucked in her breath. "Demons," she said, rubbing her arms, immediately drawing wards on all of us. The other cars pulled in behind us, with the assorted wyverns, mates, guards, and four of Drake's sept members adding to the company.

Suffrage House looked perfectly normal from the outside, but I could feel that something was wrong. It was as if the air was thicker, somehow tainted.

There was a brief discussion of who would do what— May slipped into the Beyond to reconnoiter, with Gabriel parking his body in Drake's car so he could follow her in an incorporeal state—while the guards and Drake's green dragons would surround the building and dispatch any demonic beings who attempted to escape. The wyverns assigned themselves to tackling Bael, while the mates were instructed to remain in positions of safety.

"You know us," Ysolde told the men when they appeared to close ranks in order to boss us around. "Do you really think we're going to just stand back and do nothing?"

Baltic's martyred expression was mirrored by Drake, but Yrian, I was pleased to see, looked thoughtful.

"Do you have more of those frog glamours?" he asked.

Archer and Hunter both glared at me.

I refused to look at them. I was still annoyed at how they had blamed Yrian for doing exactly what they'd asked him to do. "No, but I can whip up a few other transformation glamours. They won't last long, but it should give you up to a minute to disable or destroy the demon. You're sure I can't glamour Bael?"

"Not in the mortal world. He has too much power here," he answered, then, taking me by the hand, marched up the stone stairs to the entrance.

Behind us, Aisling was still arguing with Drake about helping with the takedown, but in the end, we all piled into the building.

Straight into chaos. Literally.

"Asfet!" Yrian snarled, catching sight of a woman who looked almost identical to Maat, although she was surrounded by little tendrils of dark power that moved around her like she was a Gorgon.

She screamed, and a dozen or so demons poured down a staircase and into the foyer.

"Give me your sword," Yrian said when Baltic hefted a massive two-handed sword that he'd had stashed in his car.

Baltic frowned, but the second Yrian pulled the light-sword crystal from an inner pocket, his eyes lit up. "You took the mage sword from Bael?"

"From Xavier pretending to be Kashi, yes. No doubt he gave it to Xavier for safekeeping. You appear to have an affinity to it, and will wield it better than me."

"And you just earned a friend for life," Ysolde murmured, smiling when Baltic accepted the crystal in trade for the sword, his expression almost joyous.

They had just enough time to prepare before the demons hit the marble floor, Yrian going straight for Asfet, while the others tackled the demons.

I stood back next to Aisling, who was casting wards on everyone, both protective and prohibitive depending on the target, while Jim darted in and out, leaping on demons in an attempt to send them into the path of the wyverns. All were equipped with bladed weapons, although the swords belonging to Archer and Hunter were spelled and runed, making them glow with power.

More demons appeared, throwing themselves down the stairs to tackle the semicircle of dragons.

"I just hope Dr. Kostich—dammit! That was my best arcane ball! I really have to figure out how to fix my magic so it doesn't keep turning into tropical fruit—I hope he's doing something other than calling people and demanding they take care of his problems," Ysolde said as she continued to fling small balls of blue-white arcany at the demons.

May popped up suddenly next to me, making me squawk and half turn to throw the glamour I was weaving. "Sorry," she said, giving me a little pat on the arm just as Gabriel burst into the foyer, a very pointy mace in his hand. "Didn't mean to startle you. No one is in the vault that we could tell, but Bael is downstairs, working on the vault lock."

"Yrian!" Gabriel bellowed as he swung the mace, taking down two demons that had headed straight for May. "He's downstairs with the fury."

May pulled out two daggers from somewhere within her leather vest, immediately disappearing as she obviously went into the Beyond.

Yrian stopped fighting his way toward Asfet, who was cowering behind a pillar with a shield of demons in front of her, and yelled, "Dragon hunters! Keep them up here, and capture Asfet. Baltic and I will deal with Bael."

"Not without me, you're not," I said, running after him when he dashed toward a sign that pointed to the lower level.

"And me!" Ysolde waited for Baltic to finish destroying the form of a particularly large demon before following us.

I had expected the basement of such an important building to be full of high-tech security devices, and I wasn't disappointed. The hallway stretched the entire length of the building, various doors opening off the corridor, each bearing not only electronic locks but what looked like retinal scanners. But there was one set of double doors halfway down, and it was there a knot of demons stood next to two people. Around them, littering the floor, were crumpled bodies of demons that periodically poofed into a nasty black smoke, leaving nothing behind but a stain on the floor.

"Why is he killing his own demons?" I asked Ysolde.

"That's the only way to break the banes and prohibitions," she answered, tossing arcany at the demons.

Yrian handed me his phone as he started forward. I was touched, knowing just how much he treasured it. That he trusted me to keep it safe had me weepy-eyed, and I stopped him for a moment, pulling him around to face me. "Just so you know, I love you more than I can possibly describe. You are the most wonderful man—dragon—and I'm so proud of you I could burst. But if you let your brother kill you, I swear to everything and everyone that I will hunt you down in whatever afterlife you find yourself in, and I will have many things to say to you. *Many. Things.*"

He didn't smile, but his lips twitched twice before he gave me a swift, hard kiss. "Stay back, mate. Do not listen to him. Do not go near him. Do not attempt to glamour him."

"And *you* stay safe. Yrian." I stopped him as he turned away, obviously champing at the bit to confront his brother.

He cocked an eyebrow at me.

I let him see the confidence in my eyes. "You can do this. You have your family around you. You have the strength to do this."

He nodded, then, with Baltic, charged down the hallway, slaughtering demons left and right.

"I think a few spells are in order," Ysolde said, cracking her knuckles. She began to intone softly, her hands making wide gestures, while I gathered up the slug glamours I'd woven while upstairs, and began to fling them like Frisbees. A few landed, instantly turning the demons into slugs, which Yrian and Baltic stomped on before the glamours faded, effectively destroying the demons' forms.

"Kashi!" Yrian roared, outright roared, when Bael turned to face us. His form was that of a smallish, black-haired man, but I wasn't fooled. Even as far away as I was, I could feel the dark power rolling off him.

It wasn't Bael who responded, however.

"What is *he* doing here? By the gods! He should be trapped in the Duat! Didn't Asfet say he was trapped? Why is he here?" Tenite stood behind Bael, working on the vault doors with a couple of plastic devices, no doubt attempting to break the code.

Bael snarled something in Latin that stung like a whip, causing Yrian and Baltic to both leap at him, their swords singing in the air. Bael took one look at the light sword and shoved his hands forward, a black miasma made up of his power slamming into the men, and sending them flying a good twenty feet back behind us.

I threw two identical slug glamours on him, half hoping their combined force would take him out, even if just for a few seconds, but with no luck.

Ysolde started flinging arcane balls at Tenite, who screeched, spread her hands wide, and lowered her head.

"Mate!" Baltic yelled, a panicked note in his voice that had her checking for a second, before spinning on her heel and racing back toward him.

At the sight of Tenite clearly getting ready to blast us with her fire, Yrian snarled, "Get out of here. Get everyone out of the building."

"Bael—" Baltic started to protest.

Yrian's fire burst out of him, but he directed most of it forward, into a cone that hit both Bael and Tenite.

"GO!" he bellowed, raising his sword again as Bael and Tenite staggered backward five steps, both of them hit—but not harmed—by Yrian's fire. I assumed that because Bael was also the son of Tenite, he was immune to its potent nature, whereas the others were not.

Baltic didn't waste time arguing. He threw Ysolde up the stairs, leaping up after her.

I didn't particularly like the odds of Yrian taking on Bael and Tenite by himself, but I knew he would protect the dragonkin with his life.

"And I'll be damned if it ends like that," I swore, falling in behind Yrian as he passed me. My hands instinctively reached for the magic inherent in the building, somewhat hindered by all the dark power released by the demons as Bael destroyed them in his attempt to break the magic protecting the vault.

And just at the moment that Tenite released her fire, Bael's form rippled in the air, a blue crystal held in his hand. For a moment, I thought it was the light sword, but I realized that it had to be the shard of the dragon heart that everyone was so fussed over.

Yrian's fire burst forth from him a second time as he screamed an oath in an ancient-sounding language.

"Did you think you could best me?" Bael snarled, fire from both Tenite and Yrian erupting around us, filling the hall from floor to ceiling, the pain of it leaving me wrapping my arms around myself, gasping for air. "You are too like your sire."

The sword swung down in a fiery arc just as Tenite screamed, flinging her hands wide, letting off what I figured was equivalent to a massive firebomb.

At that moment, there was a sensation of the dark power surrounding us being drawn into Bael, and then he slammed the shard forward to the vault door.

Silence reigned for a fraction of a second; then the air around us exploded, and I felt myself flying backward into a wall that suddenly wasn't there.

"Becket!" Yrian yelled, running to me, pulling me out of the burning rubble.

"I'm fine, just winded. Get your brother," I said, clambering to my feet.

He whirled around, stalking through the surrounding inferno to the spot where Bael had stood. He was gone, but the door to the vault was blown off its hinges, fire filling the space inside. I could see Tenite's shape there, as well, obviously searching for the blood moon.

Yrian whirled around to me. "Gather the energy!"

"What energy?" I asked, stumbling forward, ignoring the pain of the fire. I didn't think it could kill me, since I was Yrian's official mate, but it still hurt like the dickens.

"He broke the shard. Gather the energy into a glamour so it can be re-formed," he said before diving into the fiery vault.

I tried to focus, but the pain, as well as all the dark power still present, made it difficult, but as I closed my eyes and allowed myself to be open to the possibilities, I automatically began gathering up the magic released by the breaking of the shard, weaving it into a glamour that I prayed would hold it safe until Yrian could do what he needed with it.

I slowed with each passing second, feeling my flesh start to burn. "I guess ... ow ... I'm not as immune ... shit, that tendril is just out of reach ... as I thought. Oh goddess. Not more."

Another wave of fire poured out of the vault, Yrian being knocked backward past me. Just as I forced my blistering legs to move forward a few more steps to catch up the last bit of shard magic, Tenite appeared, laughing maniacally.

"You never learn, do you?" was all she said before she literally exploded into a massive ball of fire, hate, and vengeance.

The walls cracked and rumbled, and I knew the whole building was about to come down upon us.

Yrian wrapped his body around me, his breath harsh in my ear as he lurched forward, half dragging, half carrying me to the stairs.

I honestly don't know how he got us out of there in time. I clutched the precious glamour to myself, my skin peeling, my lips cracked, as I hoarsely cried out when I tried to get my legs to function. Just as the pain was too much, black blotches starting to fill my vision, air hit us, blessedly cooler air.

Noises were all around us, voices that I recognized, and some I didn't. Everyone was talking at once, shouting, demanding to know what happened, and why they felt as if pieces of their souls were destroyed.

Yrian staggered to a stop, and hands took me from him, holding me up while the voices continued. I managed to peel my swollen eyelids open, staring in horror at Yrian. He was scorched black, his flesh cracked and peeling, his mother's fire clearly too much even for him.

"Where's Bael?" Baltic asked, his arm around Ysolde. "Was that the shard we felt?"

"Yes. Kashi destroyed it to open the vault. Becket ... Becket ..." He toppled over without another word.

I struggled to free myself, tucking the glamour into my shirt as I knelt next to him. Around us sirens pierced my eardrums, but I had no mind for the destroyed, burning building in front of us.

It was the man who lay before me blackened and burned that held my full attention.

"You are the most amazing man," I told him, taking his face in my hands just as Charity had done his father. I kissed one spot on the side of his mouth that was less burned than the rest, tears splashing onto both my hands and his face.

He moaned softly, his arms moving.

"He's alive," Gabriel said as he knelt next to me, reaching out when May handed him a couple of tubes of what appeared to be ointment. "But you are badly burned."

"I'm fine," I said, flinching back when he reached for me. "Take care of Yrian. He took the full brunt of his mom's anger, not to mention a face full of magic dragon shard exploding."

Gabriel quickly examined Yrian, then gave me a little nod. "He'll survive this, although he may have some scars."

"As if I cared about that. Just make him better. I am not going to fall in love with the big galoot only to live without him." My voice broke on the last few words, and I gave in to the misery of the moment, curling up next to Yrian while sobbing with relief, anger, fear, and so many other emotions I couldn't begin to pick them apart.

It took almost an hour before the dragons got Yrian to Drake's house. Gabriel didn't feel he should be moved until Yrian's natural healing abilities started to function, but after much weeping on my part, hand-wringing by Aisling, Ysolde, and May, and some soft, wet snuffles by Jim that I interpreted as being an attempt to offer comfort, Yrian came around.

"Don't try to talk, not yet," Gabriel warned him.

Yrian made a horrible noise in his chest, one hand moving.

"Becket is here. She is burned, but she's been your mate long enough to start her regenerative powers. Just lay still and try not to move. We have an ambulance for you." Gabriel moved aside when I dragged myself the few feet to Yrian's head.

"Everything's fine," I told him when his eyelids fluttered. I leaned down to kiss the unhurt spot. He didn't look one iota better to me, but Gabriel had assured me that Yrian's healing process had started, along with that offered by the silver dragon medicine. "You are the bravest person I know, and all the dragons will sing your praises for many, many generations."

"Does that mean he destroyed Bael?" Aisling asked, then made an apologetic gesture. "Sorry, I know now is not the time to recap what went on down there, other than evidently Yrian's mom blowing up the place, but we don't know where Bael is. Is he still down there, trapped in the rubble? Did he go up in flames, too? Did Yrian kill him?"

I kissed Yrian's face three more times, quieting him when his voice rumbled deep in his chest. "It's all right, my love. You rest and heal. I'll tell them."

"Let's get him off the street," Drake suggested, and I glanced up, realizing that the dragons had formed a circle around us, obviously keeping the mortals away. "We're beginning to draw attention from the police. Kostich and his people have kept them back from us, but he can't do that much longer."

By the time Yrian was loaded into the ambulance, I was sobbing, ignoring my own pain, knowing how much being moved would hurt him, but after twenty minutes that I will try very hard to forget, he was laid onto a bed in Aisling's house, Gabriel still in attendance.

Tipene, one of Gabriel's guards who was also a healer, urged me to a chair so he could attend to my burns, but I refused unless I could sit on the edge of the bed.

Tenite's fire, like Yrian's, affected only my flesh, so at least I didn't have to pick bits of melted fabric from my charred skin.

I peeled off my clothing, sitting in my underwear while Tipene applied a cold ointment to my arms, legs, and face. When he came to my upper chest, he paused.

"I don't think you are copping a grope, if that's what you're worried about," I told him, the burned part of my chest feeling so tight I thought my flesh might split.

"No, it's … you have something coming out of your … erm …" Tipene gestured toward my boobs.

I looked down, and caught sight of the glamour stuffed into my bra. "Oh, that. It's the blue shard energy."

"It's not just the shard," came a croaking whisper from the bed. Yrian was awake again, his head turned slightly so he could see me. I was delighted to see that his skin was healing, patches of the burned bits fading into his normal dark tan color.

"It isn't?" I looked down at it, noticing that indeed the glamour had faint black filaments woven into it.

"Kashi allowed himself to be destroyed by the shard's explosion," Yrian said, his voice cracked and rough.

"Why would he do that?" May asked, holding out a bottle of water for me. I took it, grateful for its icy goodness as it slid down my scorched throat.

Yrian didn't answer, but I felt him relax.

"Because he thought Tenite would return to gather his essence and place it in a new body," Baltic said slowly, his eyes on his brother. "But Becket got to him first."

I stared in horror at the glamour, wanting badly to fling it away from me. "Holy shit. Can I just throw it away? That would ruin the dragon-shard thing, though, right?"

"Do not, under any circumstance, use the glamour," Drake said, his nostrils flaring. "You'd imbue whoever received it with not only the power of the shard but Bael, himself."

"Holy shit," I repeated, looking around for something to put it in.

"*Kincsem.*" Drake turned to Aisling. "Do you still have the prototype of the vessel for our shard?"

"Yup. One sec." Aisling hurried out of the room.

"We were making a new set for our shards, and Aisling commissioned a trial one. Ah, yes, I believe your glamour will be safe in this." He took the long, oval silver object that reminded me of an oversized test tube with fancy metal scrollwork all over it.

Carefully, I folded the glamour so that it slid into the opened case, breathing out a sigh of relief when Drake—just as carefully—screwed tight the lid.

I held out my hand for it, and for a few seconds, he looked at my hand.

"Sweetie, I think most everyone here would have a thing to say if you held three shards," Aisling told him, patting his arm.

Reluctantly, he gave it to me. "It would be safe with us."

"Of course it would," Aisling said in a soothing tone. "But considering how much Becket and Yrian went through, I think it's probably better with them."

"Not us," Yrian croaked again, his voice a smidgen stronger. His color was better, and some of the flesh that had been burned off was beginning to regenerate. He was a gruesome sight, but he was mine, and I was profoundly grateful that I wouldn't have to spend my life alone.

"Who, then?" I asked him.

He closed his eyes, his hand moving until his fingers found mine. Gently, ever so gently, I curled my fingers around his. "Thirteenth Hour."

"Oh, what a good idea. It should be safe there, so long as no one goes to all the trouble we went to when we got Desi sprung," Ysolde said.

The others murmured agreements, and eventually, after a few more questions about what exactly had happened— which I answered, since Yrian was clearly focusing all his energy into healing—they left us alone.

"You didn't die," Yrian told me when I scooted over on the bed, sitting at his knees so I could hold his hand.

"No. Neither did you, although your mom gave it her best shot. Did you think she got me?"

"You are strong," he said, shaking his head slightly. "I knew you would not succumb, either to Kashi or Tenite."

I leaned forward to kiss his mostly healed lips. "I am not Amice. I am your mate, the woman who loves you more than you can possibly imagine, and I will never leave you.

There are far too many cat videos left to watch, after all, not to mention an orange kitten to pick up from that expensive cattery you found once we left the Duat."

He almost smiled, winced, and instead squeezed my hand. "Gabriel gave me a drug to sleep, saying it was best for repairing the damage. You will sleep, too?"

"Right here next to you," I said, slowly curling up next to him, careful not to touch his still-healing skin. "Rest, and when you wake up, I'll tell you how handsome you are, and how much I like your chest and thighs, and if you are very good, I'll let you do the same to me."

He did smile that time, his hand resting on my leg as he let the drugs whisk him off to sleep.

I lay next to him, my heart so full of love and joy, I was able to push away the worries that lurked at the edge of my awareness.

The situation with the blood moon, Tenite, and Asfet would have to be addressed at some point, but for now, I was content. The dragons were saved from Xavier, Yrian had redeemed what I knew he thought of as his past failure by protecting his family, and most of all, he'd bested his evil brother.

I fell asleep planning a trip to the local pet store to stock up on supplies for Yrian's kitten.

EPILOGUE ONE
BECKET

"It's a shame the men can't have their fun 'beat the ever-living tar out of each other' time, because Archer is always so much calmer after he recovers, but I gather a decision was made to forgo it so that Yrian wouldn't be tempted to join in." Thaisa popped a chocolate-covered strawberry into her mouth after speaking, bliss spreading across her face.

"It's hard to say no to a demigod, even one as nice as Yrian," Aisling said, nodding as she perused the offerings. "OK, pairing tortellini with salami, cheese, and roasted peppers on a skewer is sheer brilliance. It's like an antipasto plate on a stick!"

"Yum," Jim said, its nose in the air as Aisling selected a few bits of cheese crostini for its plate. "Love me some salami!"

"Salami is on your naughty list," Ysolde said as she helped herself to some of the fruit skewers, including one of the melon and prosciutto offerings I had just consumed with very unladylike haste. "Aisling, the esquites are fine for Jim to eat, since they're just corn fritters, but that lime dip has garlic, so be warned."

"Esquites!" Jim said, doing an excited dance as Aisling added watermelon and corn fritters to its plate. "I've said it before—Soldy does the best noms."

"Most of this is from Pavel, who just started the fancy cooking course we gave him last Christmas, so he's very inventive with appetizers right now," Ysolde pointed out as the other women, now with loaded plates, murmured agreement with Jim.

I settled down with a big serving of street-corn nachos, and managed to wrest my mind from the food to say to Aisling, "It may be hard for you to say no to Yrian, but I assure you, I don't have any such problem, and I told him yesterday that there was no way in hell—"

"Abaddon," Jim interrupted somewhat indistinctly around a bit of cheese.

"—that he is going to fight anyone until he's completely healed up," I finished with a little glare at the demon.

"And speaking of you and Yrian, as membership lead, it's my pleasure to officially welcome you to the Mates Union," Aisling said, sipping some of the ice-cold champagne that Ysolde had passed around.

A smattering of polite applause rippled around the table, hindered mostly by the food everyone was consuming.

"As is traditional when a new mate joins, we have a few questions," May said, peering at a strawberry feta dip before spooning some onto her plate.

"What kind of questions?" I asked, suddenly wary.

"What sexy time with a demigod is like," Jim said with a rusty heh-heh-heh chuckle. "Do they do it better than others? Is there a magical O thing happening? Does it involve fire?"

"Right, that is the limit. I warned you earlier that you were being rude when you made comments about the likelihood of Yrian being insane because his mom clearly has issues, and you know better than to say something so out of line. You may spend a little time in the Akasha to go over your bad behaviors," Aisling said, standing up in order to banish Jim. It had just enough time to snatch up its plate before it was sent away. "I'm so sorry, Becket. Jim isn't normally this obnoxious. Please ignore its rudeness."

"Am I late? Dammit! I am!" Charity emerged onto the patio where we were all seated, her smile twisting a little when she glanced at her watch. "I thought telling Stewart that it started half an hour early would get me here on time, but I was wrong."

"Actually, you're right on time. We started early, because Pavel is working on appetizers in his Cordon Bleu course right now, but there is plenty of food, so dive in," Ysolde said, pouring Charity a glass of champagne.

"Oh, good, then my plan worked after all. Goodness, it all looks so delicious. My compliments to Pavel. Is that strawberry and feta with balsamic vinegar? I recently introduced the First Dragon to balsamic vinegar, and he's become very fond of it." Charity loaded her plate, and sat down with a smile shared amongst us all.

"And how is the First Dragon?" Phyllida, whom I had met earlier when she arrived with her dragon, Bastian, seemed fairly shy, but there was something about her that kept catching my notice. I realized after a few attempts to study her without being obnoxious that she had an interdict bound upon her. I wondered what that was about, but didn't feel comfortable enough to ask.

"Well. He left this morning to help find his grandnephews, the Sons of Horus. And if it sounds like I capitalized those last words, it's because I did. Horus is the son of the First Dragon's brother Osiris, and his sons are troublemakers from way back who left their afterlife and are now in the mortal world. The First Dragon said they hadn't done anything wrong yet, but he emphasized the word *yet*, and we all know what that means."

"He's usually right about that sort of thing," Ysolde said, nodding.

"I can't stand this," Aisling said suddenly, getting up and pulling out her phone.

"What's wrong?" May asked her.

"I feel guilty about sending Jim to the Akasha for lipping off. It normally isn't quite that obnoxious, and it just struck me that it's probably acting out because it's worried about Desi and Parisi. I think I'll ask Amelie if she can take it for a couple of days, so it can chill and relax without worrying about what's going on with family." She moved off to make a phone call.

"There's so much happening of late," Phyllida said quietly, popping a bit of melon in her mouth. "What with fiery furies out after Yrian's blood, and Deus escaping and going to ground so that even Bastian and the blue dragons can't find him, and Jim's parents and all. It's terribly exciting, but I'm really not used to such an adventurous life."

"And then there's Yrian's kitten," I said, glancing at my phone to check the time. I'd made an appointment for Yrian and me to visit a shelter that afternoon, in order to look for a companion for his kitten.

"Yrian has a kitten?" Phyllida asked, her eyes wide. "I've never heard of a wyvern liking cats. I mean, Bastian loves all animals, and I'd like us to get a couple of dogs once our home in Oregon is finished, but it just seems kind of odd that someone as powerful as Yrian would fall for a kitten."

"I have zero doubt that the kitten will wrap him around its little finger. Or rather, claw. He loves cats," I explained. "He said watching cat videos kept him sane while he was imprisoned. When we saw one for sale in the Duat, he couldn't resist. It's at a very expensive cattery in London for the few days we're staying here, because Pavel's mate, Holland, is allergic."

"Right, Jim situation sorted. I gave Amelie temporary powers over it, and she was going to summon it right away because she's taking Cecile out for a day trip down the Seine, and she said Jim will enjoy that. What did I miss while I was giving in to demon lord angst?" Aisling asked as she sat.

"Yrian loves cats. Phyllida wants a couple of dogs once her house is built. This lemon pepper hummus is to die for," May summarized, dipping a piece of naan into the hummus. "Also, Deus is still missing, and I don't know what's up with Yrian's mom."

"No one knows, other than she's definitely not in the Duat anymore," I answered, a pang of worry souring the content feeling that had settled on me once we'd arrived at Ysolde's house. "Also, I'm hoping that Yrian will want us to live in England. We haven't talked about where we want to end up finding a home, but I've always been an Anglophile."

"Are you American?" Phyllida asked. "You sound like you are."

"Technically, I was born in Peru, hence my surname, but we lived in Northern California for most of my childhood," I answered. "My mom and I were both addicted to British TV shows, though."

"Being in England would make you handy for mates' meetings, although the really big ones we do what the men do, and have a Zoom call. The more social ones, like this, are in person only," Aisling commented, glancing at her phone when it pinged. "Oh, good, Amelie already has Jim, and says it's flaked out on the floor next to Cecile, happily bitching about its life."

"Who is Cecile?" I couldn't help but ask.

"An elderly Welsh corgi," May answered. "Aisling and Jim are working on a way to make her immortal, because Jim says it won't be able to go on if it loses one more person it loves."

"That's so sweet," I said, blinking back a few tears.

"It is, and Amelie is go with the immortal-corgi idea, since obviously we would take her in if anything happened to Amelie, but it's still a pain in the bitch to get someone to work with us on the immortality spell." Aisling gave me a wan smile. "If you know of a magister who is open to that, please let me know."

"Magister? A mage, you mean?" I asked.

"No, magisters are different. They're kind of specialized mages," Ysolde answered. "They are pretty rare, since their field of study takes centuries to master, but that's why people go to them for the really big spells. Dr. Kostich studied under a magister for a couple of hundred years before he shifted over to work on his archimagedom. Who needs more Bolly?"

I looked at Charity, who, when she noticed, cocked an eyebrow at me.

"I'm willing to bet the First Dragon has the ability to make a dog immortal," I told her.

"I'm sure he does, but whether or not he would is another question," she parried, then to my surprise smiled broadly. "And I'm equally sure that any other demigod probably has that in his wheelhouse, as well."

"Oooh," Aisling said, her gaze on me. "That's an idea. Would you mind asking Yrian? Or I can, if you didn't want to get involved."

"I don't know that he has that sort of power," I said slowly, musing on the idea. "I can't see him refusing if he did. I'll ask him later."

"We'd be infinitely grateful if you could," Aisling said, looking hopeful. "Jim is in despair as each year passes and Cecile gets more and more frail. We really need her immortalized now, before she gets more infirm."

"I'll see what I can do," I promised.

"I'm surprised we don't have Pixie in our midst, not that she's a mate, but still, this is an informal gathering," May commented.

"That would have something to do with yesterday, which Brom and Pixie spent not talking to each other. There was some sort of a disagreement, with the result that Pixie holed up in her room and refused to come out, and Brom stormed around being so dramatic, Baltic sent him off to work on his archery with one of Drake's men. This morning heralded the return of Pixie to public spaces, since Karma told her to make herself helpful, and we had her underfoot all morning until I remembered that she likes cooking, too, so she spent a much more fruitful time helping Pavel in the kitchen. I believe the hummus was her own recipe."

"Please pass along my admiration for the hummus," I said, plopping more of it on my plate.

"What about your band?" Thaisa asked as we all continued to munch. "That is, what will you do now that you and Yrian are together?"

"Oh, I angsted over that while Yrian was recovering, but as soon as he was able to focus on something other than healing all his wounds, he pointed out that there was no reason I couldn't still sing with them, so long as he was around to protect me. As it happens, it's kind of a moot point. One of my bandmates is dating a woman from the band who won the contest, and she texted me last night asking if I minded if Arwen—the girlfriend—joined the band. After a discussion, we decided that Arwen would take over my spot for most of the gigs, and when I wasn't helping Yrian deal with his crazy mom and that Deus guy, I could pop in and perform with them. They said so long as I give them glamours, they'd all be fine with that arrangement." I smiled, remembering how happy the ladies were that we'd worked everything out.

"In green dragon news, I caught Drake castle shopping online." Aisling pursed her lips for a few seconds before laughing with us when we all gave in to mirth. "He claims it will be handy to have should someone else try to attack the sept, but we all know the real reason he wants a freakin' medieval castle."

"Jealousy," May said, nodding.

Thaisa giggled, then said, "If we're giving mate updates, here's mine: Archer says he and Hunter are going to the Duat so they can dance on Xavier's remains, but really, I think they just want to make sure that his body parts are secure in a way that makes certain he won't ever be resurrected."

"I don't blame them at all," Ysolde said, making a face at the empty bottle of champagne. "We all hope he stays dead. The light dragons are doing our thing—right now, that includes hosting Yrian and Becket, which I think is a perfect way for Baltic and Yrian to bond."

"They seem to be an awful lot alike," Phyllida said, pushing away her plate as she leaned back in the chair. "Both are kind of intense and watchful, if you know what I mean. Lordisa, I am so full, I'll have to be on the treadmill for a whole week to work off this lunch."

"Same, girl, same," Aisling said. "And I agree that Baltic and Yrian are similar in that regard, although Yrian seems a bit … er …"

"Quirkier, I believe, is the word you're searching for," I told Aisling with a raised eyebrow.

Charity laughed as Aisling gave a little eye roll. "It is, in fact, exactly the word. He is quirky, but that's part of his charm."

"It is," I agreed, and also leaned back, filled with good food, friendly and supportive company, and the knowledge that the love of my life was indoors having some male-bonding time.

I remembered the nightmare that was my life before Yrian, and sent a wave of happiness out into the universe in thanks.

EPILOGUE TWO
YRIAN

It took two days before Yrian was able to attend the *sárkány* held at his youngest brother's house in England.

"I believe we should get started, especially since the mates are holding their union meeting, and we all know how inventive they are when they get together." Gabriel was taking the lead for the meeting, his eyes dancing with amusement despite the seriousness of the last few days. "Hunter, fair warning—they feel that since they found Charity for the First Dragon, they are the ultimate in matchmakers, and have been making noises about finding mates for all the unattached tribe masters friendly to the weyr."

Three dragons—Hunter of the Shadow Tribe, Feo of the Fire Tribe, and Anniki of the Moon Tribe—all flashed identical looks of horror.

"Since Yrian is back amongst the living, perhaps he will bring everyone up to date with what happened in the Duat and inside the Suffrage House vault," Drake suggested.

Yrian considered the dragons around the long table. Outside, on a patio that overlooked a small lake, he could hear the females laughing as they held their own gathering. He wasn't quite sure what they did at their meetings, but Becket assured him she was happy to spend time with the mates. He was equally pleased that she had so embraced the dragonkin. He smiled to himself at the surprise he had waiting for her in the bedroom his youngest brother had given over to them while they were searching for a home.

"I told you that Xavier was killed. I severed his remains into twelve pieces, each of which was buried as far apart as was possible, so that he cannot be resurrected."

Bastian, the blue wyvern, gave a relieved smile. Hunter swore. Archer looked both annoyed, and relieved.

Yrian, no stranger to the idea of fratricide, told the twins, "It was not my intention to usurp your right to destroy your father. He was in the guise of Kashi, and it wasn't until I saw Tenite's lack of emotion in response to his death that I realized the truth."

"It's just frustrating as hell," Hunter said, glowering. "Here we go through hundreds of years figuring out how to take him down, only to be finally given the means to do so—"

"When my mate broke the curse," Archer interjected.

Hunter waved that away. "And for what? So our revenge is snatched away? It's as if all our work was for nothing."

"On the contrary," Yrian said, annoyed that he had to explain the obvious, while also pinched with guilt that he had—inadvertently—snatched from the twins the revenge due them. "Xavier, with Kashi's help, was far more powerful than he would have been on his own. You two stood between him and the havoc he would have wrought had he not been in fear of you."

"He didn't fear us," Hunter said, disgust dripping from each word. "As he stated many times."

"And yet, he did not attack once he knew you had regained your balance," Yrian said, his attention caught again by laughter from the patio.

"Yrian has a point," Drake agreed. "If Xavier was as powerful as we now know him to have been, then he must have had a healthy respect for you both. Otherwise, he would have simply cut you down before attacking the rest of the dragonkin."

"In fact, I think it's fair to say that you two were responsible for keeping him at bay," Gabriel added.

The other wyverns nodded their agreement.

The twins exchanged glances, and Hunter finally allowed, "I suppose that's true. That doesn't eliminate the fact that we went through everything, including Thaisa almost killing us both when she broke the curse, for effectively nothing."

"If you believe that is the only repercussion from Archer's mate breaking the curse binding you, you should reevaluate the happenings in the Otherworld," Yrian said, his lips thinning at the dragon.

"What do you mean?" Drake asked, his eyes narrowed.

By way of answer, Yrian turned to Gabriel. "You said your mother is a shaman. Do you not feel a disruption affecting the kin?"

Baltic leaned back in his chair with a flash of insight in his eyes.

Gabriel was silent for a handful of seconds before he said slowly, "My mother says the songline touching the dragonkin has been changed somehow. Altered. She could not pinpoint the source, but the answer to your question is yes. I have felt … something."

"Do you know what this threat is?" Bastian asked, his fingers flexing as if he wished for a sword at hand.

Yrian knew just how he felt. "No," he admitted. He glanced at his youngest brother.

"I don't know anything specific," Baltic said with an abrupt shake of his head. "But I am uneasy, and I don't like the fact that Bael and Xavier have been removed as a threat, and yet the feeling remains."

"And speaking of that …" Gabriel gave a little nod to Yrian. "The honor is yours."

Yrian rose, met the gaze of each of the wyverns and tribe masters present, and pulled out the crystal container chased in silver. He held it up for all to see before presenting it to Bastian.

"The weyr wishes me to offer this to you, as it contains, in part, the remains of your sept's shard."

"Former sept," Bastian said with a somewhat tepid smile.

Yrian continued. "With it in your possession, the weyr is prepared to accept the blue dragons back. You will have to send it to the Thirteenth Hour after you rejoin, but the shard is acknowledged to belong to the blue dragons."

Bastian, who had reluctantly taken the crystal, studied it for a few minutes before casting a glance at one of his guards, a woman with piercing blue eyes and hair the color of a raven's wing. "It would be our greatest joy to rejoin our kin, but much though we appreciate the gesture, I believe we can do more good if we continue as the Song Tribe. We have yet to deal with Deus, and the Chaos and Blood Tribes, even if Xavier is no more. So, we thank you, but we will be content to remain as a tribe who works outside the weyr to aid it."

Bastian gave the crystal case back to Yrian.

Silence fell over the room, allowing everyone to hear clearly the females laughing. Yrian caught the ripple of Becket's laughter, and something inside him lightened and made him feel almost giddy with joy. One part of his mind was both shocked and mildly disturbed that he could feel giddy about anything, but the other part, the sane part, reminded him that he'd sworn to Becket that he would cherish her to the end of their days, and by the sun and moon above, he would hold to that. He would delight in her laughter, and if it made him giddy, then so be it.

"Your shard lies within," he said, holding the crystal up again. "Broken, and now tainted with the essence of Kashi, but one day, it will be restored. At that time, I will have the ability to modify the weyr so that tribes might be counted as its members."

To say pandemonium broke out at that point was an understatement. The wyverns—all but his youngest brother—demanded to know what he meant.

"You said you couldn't change the weyr when we asked you earlier," Archer pointed out.

"That was before I knew the blood moon was no longer being held by Desislav," he answered, feeling enough time had been spent with his kin.

He rose, tucking the crystal into his pocket. He wished to make sure his surprise for Becket was set properly, since the mates' meeting was sure to end soon.

"Are you saying that if you had the blood moon, you could change the weyr?" Gabriel asked, looking a bit stunned about the eyes.

"With the help of the dragonkin, yes," he answered. "As well as separate the blue shard from Kashi. Becket and I will travel to the Thirteenth Hour this evening. The Sovereign will meet us there. We will place the shard and Kashi's essence into her keeping. You are all so agreed?"

Everyone stated their approval of this plan. Yrian escaped even as more questions were thrown his way.

Becket emerged from a bathroom, her lovely eyes crinkling with happiness at seeing him. He couldn't think of a specific deity upon whom he could heap thanks that she had come into his life, but just as soon as he could, he'd offer up many prayers of gratitude, and several offerings of the brightly colored cat toys he'd seen in a shop.

"Done with your *sárkány*?" she asked, her hair gleaming almost copper in the sunshine. "We're almost finished, as well, mostly because Aisling got annoyed with Jim lipping off to everyone, and banished it to the Akasha for a bit, before feeling guilty and sending it to a friend's house."

"Then we can retire to our room, so that I might pleasure you with energetic bedsport," he said, one hand on her back as he climbed the stairs.

"Are you cleared to do that?" she asked, a shadow of concern on her face. "Gabriel said you might have some residual soreness on your front side, since it took the brunt of your mom's fire. Maybe we should wait another day or so—"

"It has been two days and I will wait no longer." He hesitated. "Is it that you no longer desire me? Do the scars on my chest and arms repulse you?"

"Are you kidding?" She slid him a look so warm he felt it to the tips of his toes. "It's been all I could do to keep my hands off you for these two days that Gabriel said you needed to heal fully. And your scars don't bother me. They're a reminder of just why you are the Firstborn."

"Because my mother is a fury?" he asked, opening the door to their room.

She stopped just inside, turning to him with a seductive smile that had him hard in mere seconds. "Because you are the bravest of all your dragon family. I will admit to being glad your lovely back tat wasn't touched—what the hell?"

A noise from the attached bathroom had her spinning around. Yrian strode into the small room, picked up a plastic crate, and returned to Becket, placing it at her feet. "This is a pug. The former owner died. She had named him Galahad, but the people at the shelter said you are free to rename him."

Becket stared open-mouthed at him for a few seconds, then whooped and knelt when he set down the crate, opening it so that she might see his gift to her.

"Goddess above, Yrian! A pug? Oh my lord, you are the cutest thing ever!"

He watched with much pleasure as she sat on the ground, accepting kisses and many licks by the small, very round dog. "Ysolde has arranged for us to use a fenced off section of the garden as his latrine, although it would appear he has used his domicile for that purpose, as well."

She stood with the squirming, licking pug in her arms, her eyes glittering with tears, but with an expression that once again made him feel as if he could accomplish any task she asked of him. "You are the sweetest, most thoughtful, sexiest dragon who ever lived. Thank you for Galahad. And thank you for leaving your griefscape so you could save me from Bael."

"You saved me, as well," he told her, relishing the kisses she pressed to his lips after setting down the dog when he protested being caught between them. "If it wasn't for you, I would even now be confined to the Thirteenth Hour. Would you prefer to find a home in the Beyond first, or in the mortal world?"

She hesitated, watching the dog as it wrestled with her shoelaces. "It makes sense to go to the Beyond. Candy is still out and about, although if Bael is no more, it's probably searching for another demon lord to serve. And of course, there are the myriad other people who'd like nothing better than to make me do their bidding. It would definitely be safer there."

He watched her, waiting, having a pretty good idea of what she would decide.

"But you've just reacquainted yourself with your family, and I know they are going to need help with that Deus character. Also, I think we should try to find your descendants, so you can catch up with them. And then there's your mom." She gave him a long look. "Do you think she's done with us?"

"Not by any means," he answered.

"Then we'd better stay out here for a bit, in the mortal world, where you can continue to be the hero all the dragonkin—including your dad—know you to be, and once things settle down, we can look for a safer home."

"I will not allow anyone to harm you," he promised, pulling her against his chest, his soul singing at the way her body fit against his, confirming the belief she was made for him.

His heart quietly tucked away the good memories of his time with Amice, finally able to set his past to peace.

Now he had Becket, an orange kitten, and a rotund pug who snored. With them, a new life opened up before him filled with endless nights of bedsport, the company of a woman who made him want to get down on his knees in gratitude, and more dancing-cat videos than he could count.

LATTSA

To the members of the Otherworld: Henceforth, Abaddon is under new control, and will be closed temporarily due to restructuring. The seven princes have been removed. Desislav the Destroyer and Sovereign Parisi have taken charge. All questions and concerns may be addressed to me, Lattsa, daughter of Haka, and head of the Jabmead Sisterhood.

To the Court of Divine Blood: prepare for your destruction.

* * *

CALL ME, MAYBE?

My lovely one! I hope you enjoyed reading THE DRAGON WITH A GIRL TATTOO, which I handcrafted from the finest artisanal words just for you. If you are new to my dragon books, and want to see more about Jim, Aisling, Drake, and all the other denizens of the Otherworld, feel free to dive into <u>YOU SLAY ME</u>, the first book in the dragon series.

Want more? <u>Join my newsletter</u> for news, exclusive reader bonuses like sneak peaks, extra scenes, and bonus epilogues. It's free and fun. And full of weirdness. Admittedly, lots of weirdness…

ABOUT KATIE

Bird skeleton washer.
Doll's house salesperson to royalty.
King Tut tour guide.

Katie MacAlister has not just worked odd jobs, she's lived an even odder life. Luckily, she's always had a book with her to take her away from the weirdness.

Two years after she started writing novels, Katie sold her first romance, *Noble Intentions*. More than seventy books later, her novels have been translated into numerous languages, been recorded as audiobooks, received several awards, and have been regulars on the *New York Times*, *USA Today*, *Wall Street Journal*, and *Publishers Weekly* bestseller lists. Katie is a widow who lives in the Pacific Northwest with two dogs, and can often be found lurking around online.

You are welcome to join Katie's official discussion group on Facebook, as well as connect on Instagram and Discord. For more information, visit: katiemacalister.com

www.ingramcontent.com/pod-product-compliance
Lightning Source LLC
Chambersburg PA
CBHW061224310726
48971CB00007B/1938